Her perfect assistant. . . .

The tall, dark-haired man walked into the room wearing a windowpane suit in charcoal with a chalk line in the subtlest lavender, and a lavender shirt. She'd dreamed of meeting a man who could wear a windowpane pattern with élan. When she tore her eyes from his clothes, she noticed that he had a strikingly attractive angular face, an elegant hawkish nose, and deep blue eyes.

"Good afternoon, I'm Derek Cathcart," he said with an English accent.

"I'm Nancy Carrington-Chambers."

As they shook hands, she saw that his nails were clean and buffed. He smelled subtly of something woodsy and masculine. He wore his straight, espresso-dark hair and sideburns long, but beautifully cut—too beautifully for a straight man.

Her heart leapt with hope. "Please have a seat, Derek," she said, indicating the chair opposite hers.

He sat down and crossed one long leg over the other at the knee. He glanced around the room and then he caught sight of the arrangement of blue carnations and Mylar balloons that she'd set on a side table.

Nancy was suddenly terrified that he'd be snatched away by some vulgar arriviste who'd parade him around like a prize poodle. Still, she had to be sure that he was the real deal.

Nancy asked, "How do you like the ca_____tions and balloons?"

He squared his shoulders and gaz____ ____ Carrington-Chambers, I do not wish ____ ____ look like a dog's dinner."

"You don't offend me in the least, ____ offer you the position."

Nancy's Theory of
Style

Grace Coopersmith

G

Gallery Books

New York   London   Toronto   Sydney

G

Gallery Books
A Division of Simon & Schuster, Inc.
1230 Avenue of the Americas
New York, NY 10020

Lyrics for "Escape (The Piña Colada Song)" used with kind permission of Rupert Holmes.

First Gallery Books trade paperback edition June 2010

GALLERY BOOKS and colophon are registered trademarks of Simon & Schuster, Inc.

For information about special discounts for bulk purchases, please contact Simon & Schuster Special Sales at 1-866-506-1949 or business@simonandschuster.com

The Simon & Schuster Speakers Bureau can bring authors to your live event. For more information or to book an event contact the Simon & Schuster Speakers Bureau at 1-866-248-3049 or visit our website at www.simonspeakers.com.

Manufactured in the United States of America

10   9   8   7   6   5   4   3   2   1

Library of Congress Cataloging-in-Publication Data is available.

ISBN 978-1-4165-9886-2
ISBN 978-1-4391-1575-6 (ebook)

With love to Peggy, who is always fabulous

Delight in Disorder

A sweet disorder in the dress
Kindles in clothes a wantonness.
A lawn about the shoulders thrown
Into a fine distractiön;
An erring lace, which here and there
Enthralls the crimson stomacher;
A cuff neglectful, and thereby
Ribbons to flow confusedly;
A winning wave, deserving note,
In the tempestuous petticoat;
A careless shoestring, in whose tie
I see a wild civility;
Do more bewitch me than when art
Is too precise in every part.

—Robert Herrick, 1648

one

god is in the details

*N*ancy Edith Carrington-Chambers was mistress of all she surveyed: specifically, the lively groundbreaking party on the expansive lot where her dream house would be built. Each time a guest called her name, she felt such elation that she thought it was a portent of something magical. Perhaps with every "Nancy!" an angel got its wings.

These attractive and successful people wanted her attention because she'd done everything right.

Nancy had been born into the right family, studied at the right schools, befriended the right people, dressed in the right clothes. She'd read the right books (in hardback editions), seen the right movies, had subscriptions to the right arts programs, traveled to the right countries, and joined the right clubs.

Most people lived messy, disorganized lives, driven by foolish impulse, but Nancy tried not to feel disdainful. Foresight, like having perfect pitch, was a gift.

There was never any question that Nancy would marry the right man, especially since she had the qualities that successful men valued in a girl: a slim figure, naturally blond hair, a degree from a prestigious university, a happy disposition, and a talent for making others believe that she was listening to them. Successful men would have pursued her even if she didn't have a substantial trust fund.

Nancy had been a freshman when she met Todd Booth Chambers. She'd been sitting on a bench under a palm tree at a midquarter kegger when she noticed the brawny, laughing junior. One of her friends saw her looking and said, "Todd Chambers. Kind of cute if you like them hulky."

Immediately after learning that Todd was captain of varsity crew and that his parents were Lewis and Claire Chambers of Lake Oswego, Nancy had known instinctively that he was the right man for her. She'd begun planning their future together even as he engaged in a beer-soaked pileup with his frat brothers. Nancy admired manliness in men.

But that was then. Dousing guests with German lager and wrestling with them on the lawn wouldn't do here and now, especially since there was no lawn on the lot that had been scraped raw from a hillside. Ancient California live oaks had been ripped out (thanks to a wink and a nod from Todd's friend on the city planning commission), leaving a pristine canvas for construction, if not for a party.

Nancy had had the contractor haul in a truckload of sand

for a beachy effect. She'd rented banana trees and ordered huge urns filled with vibrant tropical flowers. White muslin screens hid the construction equipment from view and white umbrellas shaded seating areas.

Todd had suggested hiring a videographer, but she'd vetoed that idea on the grounds that people behaved unnaturally when they were being taped or filmed.

Nancy wished she had thought of a way to incorporate mirrors into the decor. She would have enjoyed watching herself going from friend to friend, laughing in the charming way that she'd practiced, and touching their shoulders with her graceful left hand, so that everyone could admire the trio of emerald-cut diamonds on her engagement ring and her platinum wedding band.

A mirror would have reflected Nancy's honey-gold honeymoon tan, her golden honey loose curls, her blue eyes shining with health, and how lithe and carefree she looked in a simple aqua and white print frock.

It would have shown Todd, impressive in the blue pinstriped shirt she'd picked out for him. It was unfortunate that he'd fallen asleep on the private beach in Tahiti, where they'd honeymooned. The skin on his snub nose was raw from her attempt to exfoliate away his sunburn.

"Nancy, Nancy," her friend and bridesmaid Lizette called. Lizette's bleached blond hair was growing out, revealing a thick stripe of her natural dark brown hair color along her side part. "This is so pretty. You look so pretty."

"So do you," Nancy said.

"I look like a badger," Lizette said with a laugh. "I can't believe you convinced me to color my hair for your wedding."

"You looked beautiful. All the bridesmaids were stunning."

"Thanks to you. Your parties are always amazing."

Nancy smiled, accepting the truthfulness of the compliment. She'd quit her job and spent a year organizing every aspect of the wedding and reception. "I'm starting an event planning company, Froth, as soon as the house is finished."

"Froth, what an excellent name. It will be perfect, like everything you do, like the house will be," Lizette said with a roll of her eyes.

"I wanted Maya Lin to design the house, but she's only doing public spaces. It took me a while to recover from that blow, but once I talked to Henrik about vernacular architecture, it was kismet."

"Henrik?"

"He's Danish. It's part of my international plan. I yearn for a French chef, a Thai masseuse, and an English assistant, quietly homosexual, preferably. I'd like a Scottish housekeeper who's terrifyingly grim, very Mrs. Danvers of *Rebecca,* and obsessed with me and my exquisite undergarments."

"Why wouldn't she be? How was Tahiti?"

"So stunning that I was beside myself, like a doppelganger. We had a bungalow over the water and could see the fish through a window in the floor. The water was crystalline and something . . . Blue is inadequate to describe the color. It was the color of happiness. Bluepiness," Nancy said. "I'm going to have our pool painted the exact shade. It will be a beach-entry pool, so every time we wade into the graduated slope, we'll remember our honeymoon."

"That's what I mean. You always know the right details." Lizette waved her hand to indicate the waiters, in white wifebeaters, sarongs, and sandals, carrying platters of Tahitian-inspired food and flutes of the same Taittinger that had been served at Nancy and Todd's wedding. "I can figure out a five-year sales projection for our zinfandel, but I can't organize anything more elaborate than burgers and the family's secret potato salad. The secret is bacon drippings and sweet pickles."

"Sales projections and parties both require precision," Nancy said, although her own experience as a financial analyst almost made her give up the will to live. "Why don't you have a weekend soiree at the winery? I'll help you." Nancy immediately began imagining romantic strings of lights on the pergola, a singer crooning Italian love ballads, and a Sunday brunch.

"You would, really? I would be eternally grateful. I'll even forgive you for destroying my hair."

"Then it's a deal!"

"Nanny!" called a familiar but completely unexpected voice.

On the off chance that Nancy had been having an aural hallucination, she ignored the voice, but it trilled "Nanny!" again, like a canary in a coal mine. That is, if the canary was personally responsible for sucking the oxygen out of the mine.

Nancy reluctantly abandoned the hope that she was experiencing mental problems and turned to see her beautiful cousin Roberta gliding toward her, because Roberta was one of those women who moved so smoothly you glanced down to make sure she wasn't levitating.

Roberta, known as Birdie, was arm in arm with one of her grimy male companions. She swung a small glossy shopping bag in her free hand. Birdie had a child, but you wouldn't know it from her delicate shape, encased in a boatneck jacquard sheath dress.

Smiling at Lizette, Nancy said, "Let's talk tomorrow about your party," and went to meet her cousin.

"Birdie," Nancy said, and was going to give her cousin a kiss, but Birdie turned to intercept a drink from the smiling waiter who'd suddenly appeared.

Birdie's black hair was cut short so that it accentuated the clear, green eyes that photographers loved because of the way they caught the light. Her appearance of fragility, which men mistook for *actual* fragility, always made Nancy feel like a clumsy twelve-year-old with a self-inflicted haircut and nails bitten to the quick.

"Thank you," Birdie said throatily to the waiter. Birdie wasn't a snob about men, as was evident by her current escort. Turning to him, she said, "Leo, go entertain yourself."

The hollow-eyed skeleton trembled even though he was wearing a peacoat. He muttered an assent before heading for the nearest tray of canapés.

Birdie handed Nancy the shopping bag and said, "I picked it up at La Maison Guerlain because it reminded me of you. Not the way you are now, but the way you should be, Nanny Girl, when you grow up."

Nancy glanced in the bag and saw an elegantly wrapped box. "Thank you, but as a grown-up and a married woman, I wish you wouldn't use that nickname."

Birdie laughed, a seductive ripple of sound. "You've only been married a month, Nanny. I wanted to lay bets on how long it will last. Mother said that was rude, but really, Nanny, you'll be gnawing your arm off to get out of this trap. Todd Chambers, he's as dull, lumbering, and braying as a walrus."

"Birdie, I know how much you enjoy getting a reaction, but I'm afraid I'm too busy to accommodate your special needs today. Everyone adores Todd." Nancy saw Birdie's friend stuffing coconut prawns and mango skewers into his coat pockets. "Where did you dig Leo up? Literally, since he has a formaldehyde-in-the-veins aspic."

"Suspended in gelatin?" Birdie said with a smile. "You're so funny, Nanny. Leo's very special. He's a musical genius. His father's a fire-and-brimstone type from the Central Valley, so the boy's irrevocably damaged." Birdie said it as if it was an accomplishment. Then she looked around at the crowd. "Are these your friends?"

"You would have met them had you come to the wedding."

"I promise to come to your next wedding."

"One is enough for me, thank you, because it was an utter dream. It's *so* happy-making to see you again. I had no idea you were around."

"I tried to visit my parents, but you know how that goes," Birdie said. Her parents had a beautiful place in Santa Barbara, and Nancy loved to visit them. "The lifelong parent-child relationship is unnatural in the animal world. I don't know how you put up with yours."

"I adore my parents, Birdie. They are delightful people."

Birdie raised her neatly arched eyebrows. "Anyway, my mother mentioned that you were having a get-together with the 'lively young people,' her words, and I brought Leo because I thought it might be amusing."

Birdie gazed upon the flat lot and the new development of enormous houses on low hills, which would soon turn brown and dry with summer heat. "Such a dismal landscape."

"It takes a little vision to see what it will be," Nancy said, trusting that Todd had been right when he said the area would be the Marin of the South Bay Area. "Villagio Toscana is an *extrêmement* desirable community." Nancy hoped that Birdie wouldn't answer in French, since Nancy had missed her year abroad to stay close to Todd.

"Sweetie, there's nothing Tuscan about this place. You know I don't care about these things, but is it the right time to build? Your father was going on about how he told you to buy in an established neighborhood."

Nancy had asked Todd the same question. "Location is more important than the market, Birdie; the timing is right to buy this choice lot and hire the contractor we want. We're going to be very happy here."

"Oh, that naive American dream that a house can bring happiness and fulfillment."

Nancy smiled pleasantly. "Birdie, I know you don't mean it, so I try not to take your little jabs personally."

"Always exhibiting such self-control, Nanny, always the good little girl."

"Speaking of which . . ." Nancy was about to ask where Birdie's daughter was when Birdie tilted her neat head on her elegant neck, as if she'd heard a distant martini shaker.

"Well, I've got to dash. Leo's got a gig in Santa Cruz. Why don't you come with us? It's never too late to begin to live an authentic life."

Nancy laughed and said, "Run from bliss to chaos? Thank you, but no."

"Consider it an open offer. Ciao, Nanny."

"Bye, bye, Birdie." Nancy watched to make sure that Birdie actually took Leo with her and saw them get into a dusty new burgundy Cadillac sedan that was missing license plates.

Nancy could relax now that Birdie had left. She turned

to look at her laughing, happy friends and caught Todd's eye across the lot. He smiled and raised his glass to her. She blew a kiss to him.

Everyone was having fun, except for one gangly young man half hidden behind the vermillion and emerald fronds of a potted banana tree. Nancy took two flutes of champagne from a passing waiter and went to the man.

Her pal, GP, which stood for Geek Prince, gave her a grateful smile. His long face, Eurasian features, and bleached hair would have worked on someone with confidence. He twitched his shoulders in his beautiful sooty black suit.

"GP, how *are* you?" Nancy asked, and handed him the drink.

"Hey, Nancy," he said as he stepped in to give her a kiss, and then changed his mind and patted her back awkwardly. "Thanks for inviting me."

"I'm ecstatic that you came," she said, happy that Todd had let her invite the classmate who'd lived down the hall from Nancy frosh year. She'd been charmed by his awkward sincerity and his attention to her invaluable observations about life.

She slipped her arm through his and said, "Who dressed you?"

"I have a personal shopper. Is it wrong? It's Armani. I heard you mention Armani once."

"You always listen so well. The suit is exquisite, but it's not who you are. We should always live an authentic life," she said, paraphrasing Birdie, even though Nancy believed most people should run screaming from their authentic selves.

"It's not comfortable," he admitted with another twitch.

"It's not comfortable because you keep fidgeting. I know it seems counterintuitive, but I really think you should embrace your inner nerd to be chic," she said. "I'll go shopping with you and give you a reverse makeover. It'll be noodles of fun, a lasagna of laughs. How's business school?"

"Even worse than summer camp. I hate it."

"Everyone does. Except Todd, because he's so competitive. Why don't you drop out and get a PhD, so I can call you Doc?"

"In what? All I ever liked was history, but I don't want to be a prof. I want to do something that makes a positive contribution, something that improves lives. Like the way you've hired all these people to work on this party."

"GP, I shall give your career path some pondering. Now come and mingle. I know I've taught you how."

He smiled. "Like a hundred times. All I have to do is ask questions and people will think I'm fascinating."

"You're my best student," she said, and pulled him over to Lizette's husband, Bill.

"Bill, you remember GP, don't you? He's wild about vineyard history." Then, addressing GP, she said, "Bill's doing all sorts of mad experiments in ebology at his family's Paleolithic vineyard."

"It's enology and our vineyard only goes back to the 1870s," Bill said, and to GP he added, "Nancy always looks bored when I talk about grape genomics and flavor chemistry."

"I categorically deny that! I'm passionately interested in the minutiae of your whatever. However, I must go check in with the caterer about canapés."

As Nancy walked away she heard GP say, "Grape genomics? How's that applicable to winemaking?"

She smiled and thought of how much good she was doing just by being in the world. She spotted Todd, who was cornered by Junie Burns, and hurried to rescue him.

"Junie!" Nancy reached out to the tall woman with unruly russet hair. As they exchanged air kisses, Nancy noticed harsh aldehyde notes in Junie's perfume and saw the unevenness of her thick liquid eyeliner on her melty chocolate brown eyes.

"How have you been?" Nancy said. Over Junie's shoulder, Nancy saw Todd mouth a "Thank God" and move off.

"Good! Well, you know," Junie said in her whispery voice. The sleeveless blouse she wore now was too tight in the shoulders and the armholes gaped, showing a slice of beige bra. "Busy with work and I just got named president of the Alumni Singles."

"Maybe you'll meet someone!"

Junie's head shook as loosely as a bobblehead doll. Then she looked around and noticed that Todd was gone. "The guys I meet always want feminine girls, and I'm, well . . ."

"You're fabulous, Junie! I'd kill to be as tall as you. I'd wear four-inch heels and stalk into rooms like an irate dominatrix. Let's spend a day together soon, okay? We'll go shopping and to the salon." Nancy wanted others to see how attractive Junie could be.

"I'd love that," Junie whispered.

Nancy heard shouted hellos and looked to see a tall, sandy-haired man walking into the party. "Excuse me, Junie. I've got to say hello to someone."

Junie followed Nancy's glance and blushed, so Nancy said quietly, "When we get together I'm going to give you some flirting tips, too. Won't that be fun!"

She made her way over the sand to the good-looking man

in the jeans, white shirt, and lightweight blazer. "Why, Bailey, Todd said you couldn't make it."

Bailey Carson Whiteside III was well over six feet and he bent to give her a kiss on the cheek. "I rescheduled a few things so I could see you. This is for you. It's heavy." He handed her a large silver gift bag with a red ribbon tying the handles together.

She took the bag and said, "Bricks for the house?"

"Books on Mies van der Rohe, Alvar Aalto, and Jean Prouvé. I thought you might like reading them while you work on the house."

"You're always so thoughtful, Bailey!" His hazel eyes looked right at her in a way that made her feel shy. "You shouldn't have."

"Less is more, except where books are concerned," he said. "I envy you building a house."

"Why not buy one of the lots here?" Nancy said. "Wouldn't it be fun to be neighbors?"

"It would be great, but I'm going to study the housing market a little longer before making any decisions. Where's Todd? I want to tell him about a great opportunity with a sports medicine group."

"He's somewhere nearby." Nancy looked around but didn't see Todd. She dropped her voice. "No doubt he's hiding from Junie and her monologues about city zoning law."

She wished they could have talked more, but she was pulled away by her other guests. After the party, Nancy and Todd drove back to San Francisco and the condo that he'd bought as a bachelor. On the ride up the elevator, Nancy noticed a chip on the baseboard, and as they walked down the corridor she saw the unevenness of the paint on the walls. Someone

(Todd) had spilled coffee on the carpeting months before and a shadow of the stain remained.

So many little things, but they had the cumulative effect of making the world a tackier place.

The interior of their condo was taupe, black, and gray, the default masculine color scheme. Whenever Nancy suggested changing it, Todd countered that they were moving soon. It was true, too, that she could always escape to the charming apartment she still kept in a family-owned property.

While Todd showered, Nancy sat cross-legged on the bed with her new design books, but mostly she was reveling in the success of the party.

When Todd came out with a towel wrapped around his waist, he saw the books and said, "Don't get any more expensive ideas. Every change to the plans jacks up the cost."

The skin on his broad shoulders was peeling and Nancy chided herself for not rubbing sunscreen on him when they'd been on their honeymoon. But every time she'd tried, he'd misinterpreted it as foreplay.

She put the books on her bedside table and said, "It shouldn't be an issue of money, honey bunny. It's about quality. I want our house to be beautiful next year and ten years from now and a century from now."

He lay on the bed next to her. His eyes were an unfortunate shade of acid-wash denim blue, with lashes as pale as straw.

"Old classics get rebuilt and improved over the years," he said. "We can always take our equity and move up."

"I thought we agreed that we were going to stay there." She wished they lived in a time when she could give her house a name. Peregrine House, the Meadowlands, Carrington House.

"All I'm saying is we have a budget, and we've got to stick to it. I'm not going to shortchange my business for a house." He and some biz school buddies had started a venture capital firm and were still seeking investors and exploring start-ups. "You said you were *thrillified* with the plans."

"But I could be *more* thrillified. I just want it to be right." Nancy was thinking about a guest bath now, and how perfect it would be to have a Japanese soaking tub with views across the hills. She knew that she couldn't compromise, shouldn't compromise, and said, "If I think we need improvements to the original plans, I'm willing to cover the additional costs, because excellence cannot be reduced to a parakeet."

She saw his confused look and said, "A parakeet is also called a budgerigar, or a budgie, thus budget."

"I'm not verbal enough to keep up with your word associations," Todd said as he put his arm around her waist. "I'm more physical. You live with me, which proves you can live with imperfection. Your father is not going to let you sink any more into construction."

She laughed. "Everyone knows I *can't* live with imperfection. I'll sell off the stock I got as a wedding present, and that way he can't stop me." She wove her fingers through Todd's dry hair and made a mental note to buy a different conditioner for him.

"Overimproving a property is never advisable."

"Either you believe the development's property values will increase, or you don't. Tell me now."

"Yes, yes, it's prime, but that isn't the issue. Your ideas about what's necessary are way beyond what anyone else cares about or notices. What you spent on the wedding . . ."

"The wedding was incredible. Everyone said so," she said. "It's my money. I want to do it for us and the family we'll have."

Todd stared at her and finally said, "I'd argue, but I know how you are when you've set your mind. But make all your decisions prior to construction. Remember that many calculations lead to victory, and few calculations lead to defeat."

"Is that from *The Art of War* again? You can't apply Sun Tzu's rules about military strategy to modern life, Todd."

"Yeah, you can," he said. "For example, I should have taken evasive maneuvers to avoid Junie Rug-Burns Butt."

"I wish you wouldn't call her that dreadful nickname."

"I'm not the one who came up with it," Todd said blandly. "GP's another loser, but he's setting up a meeting for me with his family's people."

"GP is adorable and bursting with potential. I'm his career counselor and I'm giving him a reverse makeover."

"Whatever that is. You just like him because he takes every crazy thing you say seriously," Todd said. "You know how his family got their money?"

"Everyone knows. High tech."

"That's the story they tell. But his mom's family had a crappy little deli in Cupertino," Todd said with a smirk. "She traded sandwiches for stock with start-ups, and turned a few hundred bucks' worth of greasy cold cuts into a fortune."

"Smart woman. Todd, he may be new money, but in a century his family will be oldish money. It doesn't hurt to build a relationship now. Speaking of old money, I was thrillified that Bailey came. You should convince him to buy a Villagio Toscana lot. All our friends should buy lots and then we could have incredible block parties."

"You and parties," he said, tumbling her back on the bed. "I love you, Mrs. Todd Carrington-Chambers."

"I love you, too, and I'm going to love our house." As Todd's big red hands grabbed the thin straps of her silk charmeuse cami, Nancy tried to imagine what their children would be like, but her imagination couldn't extend that far. She hoped they would be exactly like her; she had been a delightful child.

two

the devil is in the details

*N*ancy Carrington-Chambers looked at the diamond and sapphire watch that encircled her slim wrist. It had been her grandmother's, and Nancy was so angry that she only briefly admired the graceful rectangular design. Todd was now an hour late for the dinner that she'd so laboriously directed the housekeeper to prepare.

The ice in the cocktail shaker had long ago melted. She drank down another watery martini. Gin on an empty stomach left her feeling both light-headed and dramatic. She checked her watch again before going to the enormous kitchen.

After an extensive search, Nancy found red diagonally striped oven mitts and wondered where they had come from.

They were disagreeably holidayish. She took the platter with grass-fed organic beef roast out of one of the warming drawers and walked outside.

The lawn was overgrown, and weeds had sprung up since their yard maintenance company had gone bankrupt. The neighbors' trio of slobbering Chesapeake Bay retrievers immediately began barking and lunging against the tall redwood fence, as they did every time she came outside.

Nancy hefted the hunk of meat over the fence and heard a gnashing of teeth and gruesome chewing that sounded like Cerberus devouring unfortunate souls, thereby confirming her own hellish existence.

As she turned back to the house, she saw the vulgar rectangular, electric blue pool, each corner of which was marked with a tall plinth bearing a shoddy reproduction of a Greek statue.

It was all so different from the plans she'd approved.

The architect's design had been exquisite, so Nancy had felt comfortable taking her mother to Sedona for an extended spa retreat and then to Heidelberg for a long visit with her oldest sister. Nancy had explored the streets of the Altstadt, photographing the Baroque architecture and thinking of how her own house would be admired in the decades to come.

She'd returned home to find that Todd and the contractor had radically altered the house plans. Todd knew people in the county permit office who would sign off on anything he asked them to, and the construction was already too far along for her to have them tear it down and start over.

Construction had continued for over a year, and during that time and in the two years since then, Nancy and Todd had argued every single day. In addition to her initial contribution to the construction, she'd cashed out her wedding stock for high-end improvements, and then tried to borrow against her trust fund's future earnings.

Now she was glad that her father, who managed her trust, had vetoed her request, since no amount of window dressing could disguise this wreck.

Nancy went back into the house and threw the candy-cane oven mitts in the garbage compactor. She walked down the long hallway with its too shiny polished black granite floor, humiliated that her money had paid for this ugliness. *I am walking on my money*, she thought.

She went into her bedroom suite and locked the massive double doors. She might as well spend the evening going over the plans for her next Froth event. Todd could sleep in one of the guest rooms.

Her gaze went to the thing that she hated most: a granite-topped wet bar of monstrous proportions. Its permanence mocked her.

Nancy used the remote to open the panels that inexpertly hid a fifty-two-inch television and turned the channel to one of the PBS stations. She found the inflectionless voices reassuring, a sign that somewhere in the world there was civility.

As she took off her new little black cocktail dress, she heard heartbreaking music and turned to the television. On the screen, a thin man was hunched over an organ. His eyes were closed and he lurched in time to the music. She wondered where she'd seen him before.

Then a date flashed on the screen and the announcer said, "Leo Emmanuel McElroy, one of the most promising new artists of progressive classical, passed away today at twenty-eight after an extended illness."

Nancy stood motionless, recalling her cousin Birdie and Leo at her party on that sunny May afternoon three years ago. She had mocked the way he looked and hadn't noticed that he was sick. How many other things had she misjudged as she'd chattered to her friends about her dream house, her dream honeymoon and wedding, and her dream marriage?

And, although Nancy hadn't known him, Leo's death changed everything for her, like a click of the optometrist's lenses that brings everything into sharp focus.

She didn't have to stay here. She was Nancy Carrington-Chambers and she had options, the most significant of them being the apartment she still kept in San Francisco.

Nancy went into her dressing room and gathered her luggage and cases. She placed all her intimates in silk pouches and shoes in their own zipped bags, and she folded her essential garments compactly.

The house was so big that she didn't know Todd was back until he rattled the bedroom doorknob. "Nancy? Honey?"

"Go away."

"What have I done now?"

She zipped up a carry-on filled with her skin care products and went to the door. "I cooked dinner for you! You said you'd be home. This is our ten-year anniversary!"

"What are you talking about? Our *third* anniversary isn't for two months."

"The anniversary of when we met. You should remember!"

After a moment he said, "You expect me to remember the date of a kegger? Give me a fucking break, man."

"That is no way to speak to your wife. Go away, Todd Chamberpot. You are banished from my bed."

A minute later he came in through the door that led from the hall to his dressing room and bathroom. He was wearing pants with pleats that made his hips look wide, especially since he'd taken off his tie and shoved it in his pocket, one end dangling flaccidly out.

Nancy tried to remember when she'd found Todd's features aristocratic. Now she thought he looked as overbred as a shih tzu. She could endure his ruddy complexion, dry, maize yellow hair, and pale eyes. But she loathed the way his nose turned up at an angle that exposed his nostrils. Could she really live as a character in an Edgar Allan Poe horror story, going mad as she watched Todd's nose hair grow long, thick, and gray?

"What are you doing?" Todd asked.

"I'm leaving." Nancy began placing her favorite pieces of jewelry in a leather travel box.

"What's your problem, Nance? Okay, I'm late. I'm sorry." He smiled and said, "Come on, baby," and tried to put one of his tree-trunk arms around her.

She twisted away. "You treat each incident as if it's isolated, but I see them in historical context. Every day it's something—work, your pals, a meeting, the gym. You're never here, and I'm entombed in this ghastly mausoleum."

"Not this again. I hope your father's right and you'll calm down when you get pregnant. After all, your clock is ticking away."

"I'm only twenty-eight!" She thought with revulsion of grubby, stubby-fingered Toddlings. "That's all you want me for anyway, spawn incubation and to entertain your gauche business associates."

"This is why I can't stand talking to you. You twist everything I say. You're always waiting for me to fuck up, to say the wrong thing. Sometimes I think . . ." He shook his head. "Sometimes I think you're trying to find an excuse to leave me, Nancy. Like there's someone else. Is that what this is about?"

The accusation hung between them and then she turned back to her packing. "Don't be insulting. You're the one who dragged me to this hellhole, and I'm sick of it."

"Not as sick as I am of your constant bitching and whining."

Nancy felt at a distance, as if she was watching old hacks perform a tired domestic drama. The wife made accusations that the husband was a jackass, had bad taste, and didn't spend time with her. The husband responded that she was a bitch, spoiled, and a control freak.

Still, being professionals, they found the energy to improvise. Nancy recalled Birdie's comment and told Todd he was as boring and braying as a walrus, and Todd said that she was sexually unavailable, a term he'd probably read in *Maxim*.

She never raised her voice, though, because a lady didn't shout and scream even when her husband acted badly. If she took pleasure in the way her coolness infuriated him, that was just a perk.

Act Two of their argument featured halfhearted, blaming-the-victim apologies. He claimed that he had to work so much in order to provide her with the lifestyle she demanded. She said that she was sorry if he was offended when she called him an uncouth barbarian, which she wouldn't have said if it wasn't true.

She was willing to go straight into the next act, when Todd changed the script with a bit of melodrama and stormed out of the house.

Nancy waited for Todd to return. But the intermission stretched on, and the lights on his approaching car didn't flicker in the window, signaling the recommencement of the performance.

Needing reassurance, Nancy called Junie Burns, because

Junie stayed up late and because she could confide in the still-single friend without losing status.

Junie answered after several rings in her breathy voice. "Hello?"

"Junie, I'm sorry to call so late, but I knew you'd be up and . . . Oh, everything's a disaster."

"Are you all right?"

"Things with Todd are awful. He's an abominable human being."

"You don't mean that."

"Yes, I do." Nancy launched into a long litany of Todd's faults, something she'd done before when talking to her sympathetic friend. "I'm sorry. I'm ranting."

"Oh, Nance, isn't there any bright side?"

"I honestly don't know. I look at Todd and all I can think is that I don't want to be with him. I get so furious that I don't even want him to touch me."

"But he built you that beautiful house and he works so hard for you. Is there another reason maybe? Or another *someone*?"

No matter how often Nancy had lectured Junie about the ugliness of the house and Todd's bad behavior, her friend just didn't get it. "The house is reason enough," Nancy said.

"Nancy, is it that bad? Divorce bad?"

"I really don't know, Junie. I'm just glad that I listened to my father about a prenup. People told me it wasn't romantic, but what's less romantic than being forced to stay with someone because he'll take half your wealth otherwise?"

"So your money is well protected?"

"Absolutely. The only way Todd could break the prenup and ask for community property is if I misbehave, and, Junie, you know I am an exemplar of moral gooditude."

"Everyone has secrets. Even I've done things you wouldn't believe," Junie whispered.

Nancy stopped Junie from confessing some tedious sin, like not flossing daily, by saying, "Thanks for listening, Junie."

The third act of the Carrington-Chambers playlet began shortly after sunrise, as an exhausted Nancy wheeled the first of her cases along the shiny shiny hallway into the kitchen.

Todd came in through the door that led to the garage. He looked as if he hadn't slept all night and smelled sourly like sweat and beer.

"You're really leaving," he said.

"I just need a break. I'll be at my apartment."

He bit his lower lip in the time-honored way of important men who've overplayed their hands and been caught out. "I'm sorry, Nancy. You're right. I screwed up with the house. I screwed up by not paying enough attention to you, not taking your business seriously."

She felt a pang as she looked at him. Why couldn't she care for him the way she once had? "I'm sorry. I know that I'm . . . particular." She stopped herself before she said *It's not you, it's me*, because it really was his crassness and negligence.

"About the house . . ." Todd shook his head. "We've got to stay here until the market improves. Otherwise we'll take a huge-ass hit. I told you not to invest so much in one asset."

"You told me so? You were the one who assured me that this development was a sure thing," she said. "Anyway, I don't care if this stupid house sits empty. I can't stand living here."

"Oh, really? Because I'm not throwing away *my* share of this property when we can wait and it will recover eventually. Besides, there's no way your father's going to let you buy another house if you abandon this one, and you know that."

"It's bad enough that my father is more concerned with my holdings than with my happiness," Nancy said. "Why do you have to be that way, too? I can't even get my business going because he says it's a waste of time." She began crying out of sheer frustration.

"Baby, he's trying to protect you," Todd said.

"I'm an adult. Either I should be in control of my life and my money, or I don't even want it." She began sobbing, and she let Todd put his meaty arms around her while she blubbered sloppily into his stinky shirt.

"I'll do anything for you, Nance, whatever it takes to make you happy."

She managed to choke out something that sounded enough like "Really?" for him to understand.

"Really. I'll even pay for an assistant for you. You're always saying you want an assistant."

Nancy looked into her husband's bleached denim eyes and said, "You'd really do that for me? For Froth? Even if I take a break?"

"If you need some time off, I can accept that," he said. "When we've had time to regroup, we'll figure out how we can make this work. You want that, too, right?"

"Yes," she said, and she was already thinking about having an assistant, a small bespectacled person who carried a notepad and said, "I'll get right on that!"

"A break is what we need," she said. "If I could focus on my business for a few months and really get it off the ground, maybe I wouldn't get so fixated on this house and . . . and other things."

"We're smart people. We can figure this out," Todd said with a smile. "I'll contact the staffing agency we use and line up candidates. I'll take care of it all."

She decided to believe him because a wife should try to believe her husband even when he's wearing ugly pleated pants and smells a little.

Todd carried Nancy's bags from the bedroom to the cavernous garage. When she had conducted a final check to see that she had everything she needed, she went to join him. She automatically stepped toward her silver Lexus, but she didn't see her bags or her husband. "Todd?"

"Here," he said, and walked into view from behind his Range Rover.

She looked at her car and said, "Where's my stuff?"

"In the Mini. I'm going to need the Lexus because the Rover has to go in for repairs. The transmission's fucking up."

"You take the Mini!" She walked around the Rover to stare at the dented and dirty white and black Mini Cooper. Todd and his buddies had each ordered one on the Internet one night after watching *The Italian Job*. They spent a few months racing them around tracks and desert roads before forgetting about them.

Todd said, "I can't use it because we go to meetings as a team. It's a great city car. It hauls ass on the hills and it fits in any parking space."

"I'm not taking your filthy dash-and-crash."

Todd frowned and said, "I thought you were going to try not to be so picky."

"I thought you were going to try to be supportive."

"I'm paying for your assistant, aren't I? Can't you compromise for once?"

"Whatever, Todd," she said, remembering what Junie had said about Todd's devotion. "I want my car back as soon as your behemoth is fixed."

As she was about to get into the little car, stuffed with her things, Todd said, "I'm going to miss you. You're sure there's not . . . you're not seeing someone else?"

"I told you already. There's no one else. I should be worried about leaving you alone for long. Some slutty girl will set her sights on you," she joked. Nancy saw Todd anew for a second, in a strobe-light flash, as a big, blond, successful manly man, and she realized she was taking a risk leaving him.

"I don't like slutty girls. I like you." He gave her a dry-lipped peck, his standard kiss when there wouldn't be a payoff of sex, and she got in the car.

"Pull out front and I'll hose the car off," Todd said.

So on April Fool's Day, after two years of entombment, Nancy backed the Mini out of her prison and swung into the long paved drive. While Todd hosed off the car's crust of grime, Nancy glared at the house, all 8,270 square feet of gangrenous stucco, disproportionately narrow columns, slapdash masonry, and slipshod workmanship.

Nancy drove out of Villagio Toscana, past the sad mix of ostentatious houses, abandoned construction, and empty lots. Along a sandstone wall bordering a foreclosed house, huge cats sunned themselves, the biggest cats Nancy had ever seen, with beautiful spotted fur. She was already down the street when she realized they were bobcats reclaiming their habitat.

She headed north, toward San Francisco, She had tried all her life to do everything right, yet mediocrity had descended upon her like the grit that settled on everything at the revolting house.

She'd lost forever all those evenings waiting for Todd to come home from work, his office, business meetings, and male bonding. She'd tried to fill her time with small parties she put together, but she'd begun to avoid seeing her friends, because she thought her smiles must have seemed as false to them as Fendi knockoffs at the flea market.

There was a curve on the freeway when the San Francisco skyline suddenly appeared before her, a sight that had exhilarated her ever since she was a child. As the temperature dropped into a civilized coolness, Nancy relaxed.

She drove to the classical gray apartment building in Pacific Heights that the Carringtons had owned since the 1930s. She loved the building's garland and rosette moldings in pure white and the vistas of Alta Plaza Park on one side and the bay, glimmering pewter and green, on the other. Lavenders and white alyssum filled the mossy stone planters out front.

After parking in the street-level garage, Nancy began unloading her suitcases. She usually took the stairs to her fourth-floor apartment, but today she had too much to carry. She made several trips in the small elevator, balancing her bags on the narrow mahogany bench.

She was carrying the last of her bags to the elevator when she ran into Miss Elizabeth "Binky" Winkles. The elderly spinster came into the lobby, looking like a sack of flour wearing a blue knit suit, a pillbox hat, and white gloves and carrying a red patent leather handbag. She saw Nancy and said, "Look who's here."

"Good afternoon, Miss Winkles. How lovely you look today!"

The woman shuffled in, her ankles swollen above the low black pumps. Nancy couldn't believe she was still walking the hills in heels.

"Hold the elevator, Girl Carrington!" The woman used the term for Nancy and all her female cousins.

Nancy took a suitcase out of the elevator. "You can go ahead and I'll take it up later."

"Nonsense. You're a puny thing. There's enough room for both of us."

Nancy stood taller. She wasn't as tall as the older woman, but she was by no means puny. Then she reluctantly got in the claustrophobic elevator, pulling the suitcase after her, and wondering why Miss Winkles smelled so deliciously like a patisserie, until Nancy spotted the white cardboard box in her shopping bag.

Nancy politely observed, "Very nice weather."

"It's the same as yesterday and will be the same tomorrow. What are you doing with all this luggage? Running away from that husband of yours?"

Nancy continued to smile. A lady was respectful to her elders. "I'll be staying here while I establish my event planning business, Froth. Todd is being unbelievably patient with this brief respite! We have a modern relationship."

Miss Winkles snorted. "Nothing new hidden in the fog, Girl Carrington. One of my sisters, I don't recall if it was Dody or Ferny, dated a Chambers, some relation to your fellow. He played the ponies and had a weakness for *light opera*."

According to Miss Winkles, the last of the famous Winkles Triplets to remain in San Francisco, she and her sisters had dated everyone and knew all their unsavory habits, be it mass murder or a fondness for Gilbert and Sullivan.

"There's nothing wrong with that," Nancy said, nonetheless thinking about Todd's appearance in the chorus of *H.M.S Pinafore* during campus follies. The elevator bell dinged softly for the fourth floor. "It's always wonderful seeing you!"

Nancy pulled her suitcase out of the elevator, leaving Miss

Winkles to go up to her four-bedroom penthouse apartment with 360-degree views and a terrace. The Winkles Triplets had taken the flat in their heyday, when they'd been sought after for every advertisement and public function.

Sometimes Nancy fantasized about cutting the elevator line. She'd hear Miss Winkles's muffled shriek of terror and the building would shudder as the elevator crashed down on the garage level. There would be a somber citywide day of mourning for the icon, and after a respectful week or so, Nancy would take rightful possession of the top floor.

The penthouse was even big enough for a married couple, she thought, before realizing that it wasn't big enough for Todd. He liked owning a swimming pool, home gym, movie room, and game room, so Miss Winkles was safe for one more day.

three

creating ambience and mood

As soon as Nancy walked into her one-bedroom apartment, she felt a wave of melancholy. She'd painted the walls sea green with ivory trim, like the sea and sand of her honeymoon. When she'd married, she'd replaced her pink velvet furniture with Louis XVI reproductions in mahogany, which weren't nearly as amusing, but much more appropriate for Mrs. Todd Carrington-Chambers.

Nancy opened the sash windows to air out the rooms and unpacked and put everything away, because she couldn't function without perfect order. "Order brings harmony, and harmony brings happiness," she said aloud, and then jotted the sentence in a black-and-white pasteboard composition book.

The notebook, which was titled "Theory of Style," was filled with her opinions about style and beauty. Most of what she wrote had been said before by someone bitchier and wittier, but the individual comments weren't as important as the process. Nancy was waiting for some great truth to reveal itself to her like the concept of gravity to Sir Isaac Newton—in a single blinding epiphany.

She placed the notebook back on her writing table, beside the silver dish of Froth business cards. As she ran her finger over a letterpress card, white with sea green type, she noticed that her Louis Ghost Armchair was a little dusty, so she went to the laundry room, one of the luxuries of this city apartment, and took out the vacuum cleaner, duster, and polishing rags. In thirty minutes, the rooms were up to her standards.

Nancy was hungry, so she went to her small kitchen and opened the Big Chill retro buttercup yellow refrigerator. She surveyed the neatly arranged bottles of water and picked out the one in the top left-hand corner. She then shifted the remaining bottles so that they were evenly spaced.

She wasn't puny. She was elegantly slender. Water was refreshing and it didn't stain or get stuck between your teeth.

Then Nancy walked down the hill to Fillmore Street to see if there was anything new and interesting in the chic shops since her last visit. A trio of chattering young mothers with massive double strollers hogged the sidewalk, making it impossible for Nancy to window-shop.

"Hey!" one woman said rudely, jerking her stroller sideways when Nancy accidentally bumped into it.

Nancy glanced down at the woman's blobular offspring in terrifying tiny velour warm-ups. "Hey is for horses," she said, and kept walking.

It was really remarkable how everything essential could be found in one neighborhood, Nancy thought as she entered a favorite boutique. Fresh-faced clerks with shiny hair and solemn expressions refolded the already neatly folded garments.

Sometimes Nancy felt as if she had more in common with these shopgirls, who understood that texture and construction were more important than color, than she'd ever have with Todd.

She bought a short blossom pink dress with a side seam folded like paper—it would be perfect for Lizette's wine country weekend. Nancy had helped to make the semiannual event a highlight for their crowd, so she was expected to look fantastic. It would be odd going by herself, but Todd hadn't liked the weekend of wine tasting and amazing meals anyway. He preferred being at home with his king-size bed and ESPN on the Jumbotron.

Nancy went to other shops, buying lotions, magazines, and flowers. She was thrilled to find a set of etched pink tumblers in the collectibles section of a charity shop, and she picked up a copy of Simon Doonan's *Eccentric Glamour* for a friend.

Then she went to the wine shop to order a delivery.

The man at the counter took her address and said, "That's Château Winkles. How's Miss Binky?"

"She's as fascinating as ever."

The man grinned and said, "When I was a kid, I was always excited to see the Winkles Triplets. I'm throwing in a bottle of cream sherry for her. Older ladies like their sherry."

"You're too kind." Nancy glanced at the total on the receipt and thought she would have to be more careful.

She carried her purchases back to the apartment building, and by the time she walked up to the fourth floor, she was exhausted. She put everything neatly away before she drank another bottle of water and went to her laptop to sign up for delivery service of Blue Bottle coffee beans.

She looked out the window toward the park at the gauze of fog blowing in. She was so deep in her thoughts about the importance of good neutrals that the ringing of the house phone startled her. The house phone was reserved for family calls.

It was Todd's dull little secretary, who said that three candidates had been identified for the assistant position and that she'd set up interviews.

Nancy took down the names and appointment times and thanked her. Todd was trying. He always tried.

Her personal phone rang. She glanced at the screen, answered, and said, "Hi, Junie."

"Nancy, I wanted to call earlier, but I was stuck in meetings," Junie wisped. "How are you doing?"

"I'm at my apartment and everything is fine. Todd and I agreed that I should stay here and focus on Froth."

"Oh, Nancy, you seemed so angry last night . . ."

"That's how relationships are. They go through ups and downs. This is one of the difficult times." Nancy regretted having talked so honestly about her problems. "But, Junie, the important thing is that Todd and I deeply heart each other and we're committed to the success of our marriage. So please don't take the things I said seriously." She forced a little laugh and said, "No one takes anything I say seriously anyway."

"I have to go, but promise you'll call me later if you need to talk."

"Why don't we get together for lunch? Or dinner? My schedule's open."

"I'd love that, but work's so intense right now. I barely have time to breathe," Junie said, but Nancy could hear her dramatic little intakes of air. "I am sneaking out of the office for an appointment with your hairstylist tomorrow."

"You will adore her. She's the Leonardo diCaprio of hair design."

"Do you mean Leonardo da Vinci?"

Nancy sighed. Junie was as linguistically limited as Todd. "No, diCaprio, all windblown, I-am-the-king-of-the-worldish."

Nancy ran water for a bath, thinking that her conversation with Junie had gone extremely well. She'd set the right tone for this separation, making it sound friendly and professional, like a sophisticated bicoastal marriage without the annoying luggage searches.

Nancy slid into the steamy water, looked at the immaculate white marble tiled room and the snowy white towels aligned on the gleaming chrome towel bars. Would she, could she, ever convince Todd that perfection was both achievable and desirable? she wondered as she sank deeper into the tub.

Nancy ordered a writing table and chair (cabriole legs and a simple leaf motif) and now all she needed was someone who complemented her decor as perfectly as the Gino Sarfatti steel tube and chromium chandelier complemented her furniture. She was pleasantly surprised when a new laptop and phone were delivered.

Nancy called Todd that evening to thank him, but he didn't answer, so she left a message. Now he could stay at the office as late as he liked and hang out with his buddies to his heart's content.

Nancy contacted her closest friends, those in her bridal party, to announce that she was back in the city and had a window of opportunity for spa days, lunches, shows, and shopping. They seemed happy to hear from her, but explained that they were so incredibly busy. They left her with vague promises that they would call soon.

Well, Nancy had important things to do, too, including orchestrating the party for her social godmother, Gigi Barton. Gigi, heiress to the Barton tissue paper fortune, had hosted Nancy and Todd's wedding. Gigi hadn't seemed to like Todd, but she did like parties, and now Nancy had to make sure that every detail was flawless.

The event was only a week away, and Nancy quickly became so engrossed in her planning that she went for fifteen minutes at a time without thinking about her marriage.

She also reviewed her finances. She had enough cash in her personal account to live comfortably for about three months, the time she planned to stay here. By the end of that time, she'd be earning income from Froth and wouldn't need to withdraw money from the accounts she shared with Todd.

On Monday morning, after Nancy had had her first low-fat cappuccino of the day, she dressed in a vintage ink blue Valentino silk suit with an ivory collar, bow closures, and a knee-length skirt. She wore it with new black suede pumps.

She had positioned her own writing table so that the indirect light from the bay window was most flattering to her golden and rose coloring. She'd even practiced smiling in a way intended to be friendly but authoritative.

The first person who came for an interview was chewing gum and wearing such hellish hippie shoes that Nancy didn't want her to befoul the hand-knotted rug on her hardwood floor.

The second person bragged that she'd held her own

wedding at a theme park. She described the event as "magical." Nancy rushed through the interview, trying not to shudder visibly.

She was feeling disheartened when it was time to interview the third applicant.

The tall, dark-haired man walked into the room wearing a windowpane suit in charcoal with a chalk line in the subtlest lavender, and a lavender shirt. She'd dreamed of meeting a man who could wear a windowpane pattern with élan. When she tore her eyes from his clothes, she noticed that he had a strikingly attractive angular face, an elegant hawkish nose, and deep blue eyes.

"Good afternoon, I'm Derek Cathcart," he said with an English accent.

"I'm Nancy Carrington-Chambers."

As they shook hands, she saw that his nails were clean and buffed. He smelled subtly of something woodsy and masculine. He wore his straight, espresso-dark hair and sideburns long, but beautifully cut—too beautifully for a straight man.

Her heart leapt with hope. "Please have a seat, Derek," she said, indicating the chair opposite hers.

He sat down and crossed one long leg over the other at the knee. He glanced around the room and then he caught sight of the arrangement of blue carnations and Mylar balloons that she'd set on a side table.

Nancy said, "Your suit . . . how it suits you."

"Thank you," he said simply.

"Please tell me a little about yourself and your experience as an assistant."

"I've been in service for over ten years. I was the assistant to a gentleman, managing staff, arranging travel, and attending to his scheduling, including those matters that required the utmost discretion."

Nancy thought his pronunciation of scheduling, "Shehjooling," made it sound more sophisticated. His voice was as mellifluous as a character's on a British historical drama, the kind where everyone is always running to the haberdashery for new ribbons to trim a bonnet.

"While I cannot disclose my former employer's identity . . ."

"Is he a royal?" Nancy asked.

Derek smiled slightly and then said, "Mr. Chambers has spoken with the gentleman and received a letter of recommendation."

"It's a pity that Mr. Chambers has remained at our home in the hinterlands, because he could certainly do with a man of your skills," Nancy said. "This is a three-month assignment and your primary responsibility will be helping me plan parties, receptions, and weddings. I need someone who is detail oriented and able to get along with a variety of people."

"I strive to treat all with respect, from the humblest chambermaid or stable boy to the most honored and titled members of society."

Her heart, already aloft, danced like a kite in a spring breeze. "I may also need someone to assist me with a writing project."

"This would be no hardship, madame, as I am an experienced scrivener."

She knew she should ask more questions and check his other references, but she was suddenly terrified that he'd be snatched away by some vulgar arriviste who'd parade him around like a prize poodle. Still, she had to be sure that he was the real deal.

Nancy asked, "How do you like the carnations and balloons?"

He squared his shoulders and gazed into her eyes. "Mrs. Carrington-Chambers, I do not wish to offend you, but they look like a dog's dinner."

"You don't offend me in the least, Derek. In fact, I'd like to offer you the position. If you'd like the job, when can you start? Do we have to submit a request?"

"Mr. Chambers authorized the employment agency to handle the paperwork, and I can start immediately," he said, thereby fulfilling her girlhood dream of having a gay English assistant.

Nancy spent the rest of the afternoon in an ecstasy of efficiency. She showed Derek how to operate the espresso maker and he caught on immediately. He seemed impressed by the contents of her refrigerator.

"Such an astonishing array of beverages," he said while observing the neat rows of bottled waters, the glass bottle of organic low-fat milk, and the lemons and limes in her fridge.

"Thank you. You can have as much water as you like, and I've got it in still and sparkling from several different countries. I only buy the ones in attractive bottles because that improves the whole water-drinking experience, don't you think?"

"Unquestionably."

"I'm doing clear bottles this month, but sometimes I like green bottles, and the frosted-glass ones are fab. You'll have to stock them for me."

"Your palate must be extremely refined to distinguish between so many varieties."

"Yes, but it's not just about taste. It's about purpose. For example, I think it's really important to drink Russian water when recovering from a vodka hangover. I believe in committing to a theme."

"Exceedingly admirable," he said.

"I love placing the round little bottles by those with elongated shapes. I know everyone raves about metal canisters being more ecological, but I find that metal tastes metallic."

Nancy showed Derek her intricate system for party planning. She was impressed when he caught on quickly to her spreadsheets.

"See, when everything balances at the end of the column, it gets highlighted in hyacinth, because the color is like a special treat. My father always says that if you take care of your pennies, your dollars will take care of themselves. Or, as you would say, if you take care of your pences, your pounds will take care of themselves."

"Thank you for the translation, Mrs. Carrington-Chambers. You make me feel so welcome in your country."

And though he looked solemn, she thought she detected some humor in his voice, so she smiled and said, "Enough hard work for now. I've got a stack of all the latest bridal magazines and I want you to go through them page by page and give me your overall impressions on critical trends for lace and veils."

Derek had a look on his face that Nancy could only describe as abject gratitude. "Certainly, madame."

"I've got to work on the final details for a birth—a party I'm organizing for Gigi Barton. It's not a *birthday* party, because Gigi claims she doesn't age. Have you heard of her?"

"Is she from the Bartons of Dalek Park in Scaro?"

Nancy wondered if she should have heard of Dalek Park. "She's one of the tissue-paper Bartons. 'It's not worth sneezing at if it's not Barton's tissue!' Of course, their real fortune was made in toilet paper. This will be a giant, grown-up slumber party. It's this Saturday night and I hope you're available to help."

"Certainly, madame."

She put a stack of wedding magazines in front of Derek and said, "Derek, I think it would be great if you did a collage of wedding trends, don't you? I like to be able to *see* things. But don't restrict yourself to just veils. If you see something else that looks fabulous, include it!" She gave him a poster board, scissors, and a glue stick and set him to work.

He took a different approach than Nancy would have, cutting out pictures in semicircles and laying them edge to edge. But when he was done, he'd created a mosaic of whites, ivories, creams, and blush colors.

Nancy propped the board up on the bookshelves and inspected it. "You have incredible instincts, Derek. One suggestion, though. Don't be quite so safe. After all, good taste is not style."

"I shall bear that in mind, madame."

As soon as Derek left, Nancy admired the collage again and felt a thrill. It had been a test to make sure she could trust his sense of aesthetics, and he'd passed superbly. She even sensed that he'd been holding back on his own artistic style.

Nancy called her freshman roommate, Milagro, and asked her to dinner, saying, "I have news for you, but you must promise not to get gloaty."

"That is so unfair, because I rarely get to gloat over you. However, I promise. Tell me now."

"Patience is the virtue of the artist formerly known as the artist formerly known as Prince."

"I thought it was promptness."

"Be on time, then."

four

matching the outfit to the occasion

*N*ancy thought it was exciting to be friends with someone completely outside her set, because she could say things she never would say to her sorority sisters. Milagro was from some godforsaken suburb called *El* or *La* or *San* something and had intriguingly appalling opinions, including a pathological hatred of Todd.

They met at a Japanese restaurant and jazz club in the Fillmore. Milagro, a stunning, curvaceous Latina, was wearing a snug black cotton sweater, a leopard-print miniskirt, and black boots.

"Milagro, hon, *que sera sera!*" Nancy said, and the friends exchanged kisses. "I am so loving the cat woman vibe."

"*Que sera* yourself, Nancita," Milagro said as they followed the hostess to their table. "Are you coming to the show with me after dinner?"

"You know that jazz puts me into a parabolic trooper."

"I suspect that it's the sake shooters that put you in a catatonic stupor," Milagro said.

Nancy reached into her bag and took out the book she'd bought for her friend. "This is for you, although I don't know if I should be encouraging you."

"*Eccentric Glamour*! Thank you, Nancy. I shall study it like the Dead Sea Scrolls for spiritual guidance."

While they ordered, Nancy looked around the restaurant. She loved sushi because it was as delicious as it was attractive, but even more she liked the simple elegance of the restaurant. There were pale birch tables and bleached floors. She could see exactly what the chefs were doing, so there was no chance of anyone spitting into her food if she complained.

The waiter left and Nancy said, "The minor news is, and remember, no gloating, that I'm taking a break from Le Todd."

Milagro's dark brown eyes widened and then she slipped her hand briefly over Nancy's. "I won't gloat, but it would be nice if you never go back to him."

"Everyone hearts Todd but you, and your dislike is based on politics, my loony lefty pal."

"Not entirely! He repels me in myriad ways."

Nancy held up her hand, palm outward. "Do not go into specifics. I heart Todd, and Todd hearts me."

"You've been defensive about your relationship with him since frosh year, and I don't know if you actually heart him, or merely say that."

"Neither do I," Nancy admitted. "My antipathy for the

house is so overwhelming that I can't tell how I feel about Todd anymore. I'm hoping the time apart will give me a little clarity."

"I hope so, too, Nancy Fancy-pants," Milagro said. "How is Miss Winkles?"

"As iridescent as ever," Nancy said, and shared a smile with her friend. "Now for my news. You will never guess what I have!"

"A venereal disease? The Holy Grail?"

"Eww to the first, but the Holy Grail would look fab on my mantel," she said. "I have a gay English assistant named Derek!"

"You unspeakable bitch! I yearn for a gay English assistant—but named Trevor, or maybe Clive. Is he fabulous?"

"You think anyone in possession of a penis is fabulous, and *yes*, he's completely fabulous. He was wearing a shirt the same color as the wisteria on my aunt Frilly's arbor. He calls me Mrs. Carrington-Chambers in a way that makes me feel very Madame de Pompadour."

"Your head has sometimes resembled a giant puffball, but I thought it was impolite to say anything."

"Jeanne-Antoinette Poisson was the king's mistress and the greatest fashionista of her time, including her hair, you hysterical dance."

"Historical dunce?"

"Heretically dense. I wish there were more kings around these days."

"There is a surfeit of queens, and it sounds as if you've got one of your own. How are you going to pay his salary? I thought your money was controlled by your father-slash-trustee, who is fab, but notably deficient of frivolousness."

"Alas, the frivolous gene is recessive. Todd is gifting the assistant to me!"

"Toad?" Milagro said. "Why would he do that?"

"He's trying to support Froth. You always think the worst of him and that's why I'm always defensive about him with you." Nancy sighed. "Do you think I've overreacted to that house?"

"How would I know, since I've never been invited there? He cut down ancient oaks and went behind your back on the construction."

"I can't invite you because you and Todd and the mutual hatred thing. Back to my story about hiring my fabulous new assistant," Nancy said. She placed her palms together and gazed toward the ceiling. "It was like a magical fairy tale."

"Please stop looking as if you're having a vision of the Virgen de Guadalupe because it's seriously freaking me out."

Nancy stuck her tongue out at Milagro and said, "Derek noticed an awful flower arrangement. It was as if he was trying to sleep on one hundred Shifman mattresses, but couldn't because he was so exquisitely sensitive to the vulgarity of blue carnations."

"I couldn't sleep in a room with blue carnations and I'm not exquisitely sensitive. Is Derek diminutive with little rimless glasses? That would be divine."

"Sadly, no. He's tall and lanky, which are generally fatal flaws in an assistant, but he is, as the French would say, *beau-laid,* ugly beautiful, because he's still fabulous despite the non-spectacle quality. His eyes are stunning. He has black lashes that make them intensely azure, like, um . . ."

"Like azures?"

"I was thinking of something less semiprecious. But sapphires are the wrong shade."

"Peculiar that Toad would fulfill one of your fantasies, i.e., said gay English assistant, when he's always been fixated on his own crude wishes, i.e., offering you implants when you have always been madly in love with your perky pair."

"They are marvelously perky, but Todd actually thought I would *want* implants. He's only aware of obvious trends and knows I like to be fashionable," Nancy said.

"Nonetheless, I took umbrage on their behalf," Milagro said. "Does Derek have a sense of humor?"

"He may. He thanked me for translating American English into British English, and I'm hoping he was being dryly or wryly sarcastic, but it's too early to tell."

"Continue to hope. I always thought you should be with someone who got your humor and realized that when you seem to be joking, you're serious, and when you seem to be serious, you're joking."

"You're speaking of yourself, not me. Derek can help me with my 'Theory of Style.'"

"How's that going?"

"Sometimes I worry that I'm like that deluded prune in that novel you like, Middle Earth."

"*Middlemarch*. You mean Casaubon, who spends his life writing the 'Key to All Mythologies,' which is discovered to be errant nitwittery only after his death."

"You know how I adore errant nitwittery," Nancy said, "but only when it's intentional. That's one of the problems with reading fiction; it preys upon impressionable minds and implies that life has subtext, when life is wont to ramble plotlessly along."

"I've been letting that idea percolate lately," Milagro said. "What if life isn't actually utterly aimless?"

"If it wasn't, wouldn't we eventually see a pattern, like a pointillist painting? We would. We'd see connections and structure and themes would resonate," Nancy said. "What are you wearing to Gigi's not-a-birthday party? And are you bringing one of your lovers?"

"A G-string and pasties, but I still haven't mastered twirling them in different directions. I already told you I'm not going. Gigi's friends have too much attitude. They look down their surgically altered noses at me."

"They look down on *all* nobodies. There's no need to take it personally. What can you expect when you insist on continuing to do garden work for Gigi?"

"I need to augment my writing nonincome and my only other talent is forgery."

Nancy was about to say something fun and bitchy, but just then a tall man stopped at their table. "Hi, Nancy," he said, and then to Milagro, "Hey."

Nancy looked up and said, "Bailey!"

Bailey Whiteside looked excitingly tall in a periwinkle blue button-down shirt and slim-cut slacks. His sandy hair was brushed straight back like an old matinee idol's.

"It's been ages!" Nancy said. "Would you like to join us?"

"Thanks, but I'm on my way out to meet some friends," Bailey said in his gravelly voice. "Todd told me you're staying at Château Winkles."

"For now. Bailey, this is my friend Milagro."

Milagro gave a phony smile and said, "Oh, we've met, Nancy, at your wedding."

"That's right," Bailey said with a nod, but he kept looking at Nancy. "Do you want to meet up after dinner?"

"Sorry, but I'm busy working on Gigi Barton's party. You never responded to your invitation."

"Didn't I?" He grinned. "Maybe I'll see you there. Bye."

He sauntered off and conversation grew quieter as he passed by and people saw him give a one-armed hug to a former mayor who was also walking to the exit.

Milagro said, "Bailey Whiteside is a major douche, although I believe that's required of political strategists. He's met me several times, and he always acts as if he doesn't know who I am."

"Bailey wouldn't ignore your bodacious charms if you'd had the sense to be born with a trust fund. Whenever we went on vacations together, he was always so nice to me."

"I'm sure he was. He was giving you the hairy eyeball."

"That's a vivid and unfortunate expression," Nancy said. "I've always wondered what would have happened if I'd met Bailey before I met Todd."

"Because a Whiteside is even more inbred and entitled than a Chambers, right?" Milagro said. "Nancy, I will concede that Bailey's kind of hot in a sleazy prep school way, but I wish you would consider dating someone for himself, and not because your parents would approve."

"If you had a good relationship with *your* parents, you might understand," Nancy said. "Are you going to eat that *uni*?"

Milagro pushed the plate toward Nancy. "You have it. You look like one of those lollipop chicks with the giant head and the stick body. Why have you starved yourself?"

Nancy used her chopsticks to pick up the piece of sushi. "I look fabulous and I haven't starved myself. I hate the food Todd likes, slabs of dead animal and tubers with cream sauces."

Milagro raised her sake cup. "Welcome back to civilization, Nancy."

* * *

48

Back at her apartment, Nancy went over the numbers for Gigi's party. Froth wouldn't make a profit on this event, because Nancy was spending her entire budget on a grand show that would promote her business.

She realized that she was biting at her thumbnail and chipping her sea green enamel. She filed the tip and touched it up instead of ignoring it, because that's how tackiness started: one day you neglect a chipped nail and the next you're wearing a stained sweatsuit with your hair in a scrunchie. If it ever came to that, Nancy would just lie down in a field and let the vultures peck out her clumpily mascaraed eyes.

It was almost eleven when her cell phone rang. She looked at the ID and was relieved when she saw it wasn't Todd calling. "Hi, Lizette!"

"Hi, Nancy. How *are* you?"

"Good. How are you? When are you coming to the city next? I'm just scheduling things."

"I can't make it anytime soon." Lizette paused ominously. "Nancy, I just wanted to tell you personally that . . . you know that spring *thing*?"

"Your weekend party at the vineyard? Don't worry. I haven't forgotten it."

"Well, Todd's coming this year," Lizette began, "you know how he and Bill have the bromance going—and we knew it would be totally awkward for you to come, too."

It took a second for Lizette's words to sink in. "Lizzie, I'm only away from the house so I can really launch Froth. It was a business decision that Todd and I made together."

"I'm sorry, and I *hate* being in the middle of this," Lizette said. "I would have fought Bill on this, honestly, Nance, except that he heard something and he won't even listen to me."

Nancy kept her voice calm. "What did he hear?"

There was an intake of air at the other end of the line before Lizette's words rushed out. "Bill heard that you left Todd for someone else. It wasn't Todd who told him so, and I promised not to tell, and I don't believe it for a minute. I know you'd never . . . you wouldn't, would you? I mean, *of course* you wouldn't."

Nancy wanted to hurl the phone against the wall and scream.

But the more you reacted to a rumor, the more people believed it. She hadn't endured Todd's blathering on about *The Art of War* for nothing: all warfare is based on deception.

"That's so funny!" Nancy said. "Because I had dinner with my friend Milagro tonight and she told me that she heard that I left Todd to be with you! She congratulated us on being so lesbilicious, and I didn't have the heart to disillusion her. I hope you don't mind that I said I was the girl and you wore the, um, lederhosen."

"Nancy, you can't let her tell people that!"

"Oh, Milagro doesn't know anyone. Although she *is* friends with Gigi Barton, but Gigi only gossips to her inner circle, or whomever she's partying with."

"But it's completely untrue."

"Technically, but rumors are so much more fun than my dreary business strategy."

"Sometimes the truth is better than a rumor, Nancy, even a fun one," Lizette said uneasily. "If anyone asks me, I'll tell them you're launching Froth."

"Oh, Lizzie, how unfun you'll make me seem. Have a wonderful party and I'm sure no one will remember last year's incident with Bill. Bye!" Nancy hung up before Lizette could ask about the fabricated incident.

Nancy couldn't believe her so-called friends were dragging her good names in the mud this way. Protesting gossip was the surest way to convince people it was true, but diverting gossip couldn't hurt, so she left a message for Milagro saying, "Milicious, be a sweetie and tell a few friends that Lizette and I are having a lesbionic liaison. Embellish as necessary."

Feeling better, Nancy went to the bedroom, which was painted ivory with blue-gray trim. All of the bed linens were white. Even though she'd changed her froofy pink decor, the color kept sneaking in. Now it appeared in a vase of peonies and on throw pillows.

She opened the doors to the walk-in closet and pulled the chain for the old-fashioned hanging bulb. She spritzed Jo Malone lime, basil, and mandarin room spray and then breathed slowly and deeply, admiring the rows of accessories, organized from small to large. Immaculate clothes hung on black velvet, no-slip hangers.

She rearranged her shoes, placing the lively spring collection at eye level. She moved her winter shoes from the main shelves and stored them in boxes, each with an identifying photo on the front.

Then Nancy selected her clothes for the next day. She was feeling efficient and Coco Chanel-ish, so she chose charcoal men's-cut slacks, a white poplin shirt, a narrow black belted jacket, and spectator pumps.

Once in bed, Nancy realized that she was lying on "her side." She wiggled to the middle of the mattress. Then her head was stuck between the pillows, so she wiggled back to one side.

She thought about Todd's nighttime routine. He used to kick his clothes off wherever he felt like it, roaming around the house in boxers with cartoon characters or sports-team logos.

She'd despised the baggy boxers, but a few months ago he'd bought form-fitting stretch briefs that disturbed Nancy even more. They were just too *European*.

If a girl truly loved a man, wouldn't she automatically be enchanted by that garment which caressed his most intimate parts? She remembered fantasizing about Todd when she was in college. Nancy's recollection of her teenage fantasies of Todd were as amorphous as the fog that shifted by her windows.

Nancy tried to enjoy the thought of Bailey in his undies. She hoped they weren't tighty whiteys or banana hammocks, since he might have been led astray by a tasteless girlfriend.

Then her thoughts turned to Derek. She wondered what kind of underwear he wore. She was sure they were heavenly.

The next morning, Derek rang the downstairs buzzer exactly at 9:00 a.m. Nancy had told him he could dress more casually unless they had meetings, and he arrived in a gray pin-striped jacket in a fabric that she needed to touch to identify, a gray and white geometric print shirt, stiff Japanese denim jeans, and chisel-toed black lace-ups.

"Good day, Mrs. Carrington-Chambers," he said in plummy tones as he came in the door.

"Good morning, Derek." Nancy fought the urge to excuse herself and change into jeans so they would match. "Why don't we start the day with cappuccinos?"

"As you please, madame."

When the gorgeous assistant returned to the room with their cappuccinos, she took a sip of the rich, foamy drink with just the right dusting of cocoa powder. "This is perfect! You're an espresso artiste."

"Tosh," he said with a modest tilt of his head.

For the next hour, Nancy answered e-mails while Derek became familiar with her project files. At ten she sent him downstairs to get the mail from the apartment lobby.

He brought back a stack of letters, magazines, and advertisements.

Nancy's eyes instantly went to the ivory envelope tucked between a trunk-show flyer and an announcement about the symphony. She pulled it out and examined the spidery black handwriting on thick Crane's paper, then flipped it over to see the return address. After carefully slicing open the envelope, she read the card inside. "Oh, my!"

"Good news, I hope."

"It's from Mrs. Bentley Jamieson Friendly," she said. "She wants to talk to me about her fund-raising gala for the Barbary Coast Historical Museum."

"A charity for an institution in North Africa?"

"Not quite. San Francisco's Barbary Coast was named after it because the neighborhood was inhabited by the very wickedest and most depraved," Nancy said. "Mrs. Friendly's a direct descendant of Dancing Dog Jamieson, a bartender who drugged his customers and sold them to sea captains. Her husband's great-great-something was Dr. Painful Friendly, who made his patients sign over mining claims if they wanted teeth removed. Isn't that marvelous?"

"Indeed," he said.

"It's such a thrilling part of our culture, making us all feel like dangerous renegades, living as we do on the edge of the continent," Nancy said. "The gala is exactly what I've been looking for, a social event that is established and yet unloved, like an annual visit to your ob/gyn—you're required to go, and even though they say oh, you might feel a little pinch, it always hurts like hell."

"It is a social obligation?"

"It's as obligationy as they get, but we can make it into a social triumph, just like pelvic exams could be a success if the doctor's staff would also do bikini waxes, so the pain would have a payoff. Let's dig up the dirt on the museum society's past soirees."

Derek and Nancy fell into a comfortable rhythm, and after a few hours they had compiled a history, from the museum's first tea to the present.

"You're very good at research," Nancy said.

"As is Madame."

"Thank you. But none of this information is useful, except to prove that the fund-raiser's always been shockingly dull." Nancy smiled at her assistant and thought that going out with him would be the best way to show that she was unconcerned by spurious gossip. "Let's do lunch."

five

accentuating your strengths

They went to the garage and Derek asked, "Would you like me to drive, Mrs. Carrington-Chambers?"

"No, thank you. After all, you're used to driving on the wrong side of the road." She slipped off her shoes and slid on soft, rubber-soled, dusty rose driving shoes.

She spotted a convenient parking spot near a Hayes Valley restaurant that Todd frequented when he had meetings in town. As Nancy pulled into the space, Derek said, "Madame, I would be remiss if I didn't mention that the sign specifies that this curb is for lorry deliveries exclusively."

"I'm *delivering* us," Nancy said. "Besides, if you take the narrowest interpretation of every traffic sign, you'll never find a space because there is *no* parking in this city. Isn't it fun having me as your chauffeur?"

Since they didn't have reservations, they took seats at the bar. Nancy didn't mind because she liked the opportunity to display her pert backside on a stool and she could people-watch in the mirror above the bar.

The bartender brought a small bowl of crunchy Marcona almonds with their menus. Nancy pulled out the Ferragamo wallet that she'd taken from Todd, who had a drawer filled with executive gifts, and took out the laminated sustainable fish guide. "I suppose I'll have the Pacific halibut *again*."

"Madame is interested in sustainable fishing?"

"Don't talk crazy, but you have to pretend. It's like feigning interest when someone drones on about their children. Children are so unformed, like amoebas, and just as indistinguishable. They're, you know . . ."

"Cheeky, with their annoying questions," he said with sudden enthusiasm. "As self-absorbed as cats."

"Yes!" She smiled at Derek in the mirror. She thought they looked like a really fascinating couple, Nancy all blondy liveliness and him all dark and broody.

He said, "Most ladies are infatuated with children."

"Most *ladies* think that you can buy a product that acts as both a shampoo *and* a conditioner." She ran her hand over the sleeve of his jacket. "What is this?"

"I believe it's called chintz-glazed linen."

"It is to die for. What are you having?"

"A cheeseburger and chips," he said.

"This is America, Derek. We call them *pommes frites*," she said, but before she could see his reaction she spotted Junie approaching in the bar mirror.

Nancy swirled on her bar stool and jumped up. "Juniekins!" She held her arms out and hugged the tall redhead.

"Nancy! What a nice surprise!" Junie said in her soft voice, and gave Nancy an extra squeeze before stepping back.

Junie's previously uncontrollable hair was now a shiny mahogany color, cut in a chic bob. She was wearing a structured dark gray suit that disguised her pear shape. Her makeup was different, too, making her small eyes look bigger and drawing attention from her long nose.

"The hair, the suit, you!" Nancy said happily. "You look wonderful."

"I took your advice and hired that personal stylist you recommended," Junie said.

"She did wonders. Seriously, you look terrific." Nancy took a sniff and recognized the floral and green chypre scent of Eau du Soir. "You're wearing my scent."

"I liked it so much on you that I bought some for myself."

Nancy smiled, but now she would have to change perfumes.

Derek swiveled on his stool, and Junie stared at him while saying to Nancy, "I'm so sorry I haven't gotten back to you, but work has been nonstop." She smiled at Derek. "Hi."

Nancy said, "Junie, this is Derek Cathcart, my new assistant. Derek, Junie Burns."

Derek held out his hand and said, "Good afternoon, Miss Burns."

Nancy thought Junie's knees would give way. "Derek and I have been conducting historical research for upcoming Froth events," she said.

"How exciting! I wish I could talk, but I've got to get back to my meeting," Junie said, and tilted her head toward a table of businesspeople. "I'll see you at Lizette's weekend party and we'll catch up on everything."

"Oh, I wish I could make it, but I'm utterly booked up. I'm sure they've taken care of the hantavirus-infected mice problem. Call me!"

After Junie had left, Nancy said quietly, "Didn't she look striking? Thank God she finally has a decent haircut and clothes that don't have an unpleasant *eau du* clearance rack about them."

"A professional acquaintance?"

"Heavens, no. Junie does boring zoning work. She's a friend, but you don't know how I had to nag her to dress more attractively. One should dress for the job one wants, not the pitiable, lonely grad student one was."

"It is kind of you to care about your friend."

"Well, that's who I am, a caring person," Nancy said, and then smiled. "She was eyeing you like a crazy lady eyes a box of kittens. That's Junie—she habitually crushes on unattainables."

Derek knit his nicely groomed eyebrows together and said, "I don't catch your meaning, madame."

"Unattainables—worthwhile men who have a game plan for life. They expect a girl to bring more to the relationship than enthusiasm. They could get that from a dog, and even then they'd go to a reputable breeder to ensure quality. I've tried to steer Junie toward guys who would be grateful for her attention, but she's delusional."

After they had ordered, Nancy glanced around the restaurant and said, "I used to know *everyone* in the city before Todd, Mr. Chambers, put me in exile in the provinces. Now I'm a hapless rutabaga, uprooted and ignored."

"Should you ever need to talk, Mrs. Carrington-Chambers,

I should be pleased to listen. A former employer said that it eased his heart to share his personal concerns."

Nancy looked deep and searchingly into his eyes. "Derek?"

"Yes, Mrs. Carrington-Chambers?" he asked softly, keeping his gaze locked on hers.

"What color are your eyes?"

"They are blue, madame."

"No, *my* eyes are blue. Yours are something else."

A smile flickered on his face and he said, "A friend calls them midnight blue."

"I memorized all the colors in my crayon box, and Midnight Blue is not quite right. I'll think of it, though. Was this a *special* friend?"

"I believe so."

"I'm so glad you have someone, Derek." She sighed. "I thought Todd was special, too. Maybe he is special and I'm just—"

Their food came then. Derek was good enough to share his French fries with Nancy and even welcomed her suggestion that they eat them with ketchup, the American way.

She almost wanted to talk to him about Todd, because that was what gay friends were for, right? She wasn't sure about the rules, since Todd wasn't comfortable having gay men around. He wasn't comfortable with anyone who wasn't just like him.

When they returned to the car, there was a parking ticket on the windshield. Nancy plucked it off and handed it to Derek, saying, "There are more in the glove compartment. Send them to Mr. Chambers, please. He'll have his friends take care of them."

Once Derek and Nancy were back at her apartment, she

called Mrs. Jamieson Friendly. After the phone rang and rang, the woman herself answered and explained that she was in her sunroom with her orchids.

Nancy resisted the urge to tell Mrs. Friendly that orchids were so eighties, since she might think Nancy meant the 1880s. "Let's talk about your fund-raising event. It's such an important date on all of our calendars!"

Mrs. Friendly barked out a laugh. "Come on, sugar, we both know it's as dried up as my lady parts! That's what I want to talk to you about. How soon can you drop by the Saloon?"

Nancy said that she could be there within an hour and asked if she could bring her assistant.

"The more the merrier."

Mrs. Friendly's mansion was only a ten-minute walk from Château Winkles.

"Is this saloon a pub?" Derek asked.

"No, her home is called the Saloon in honor of Mrs. Friendly's bar-owner ancestor, Dancing Dog Jamieson. Although once you see it, you'll need a drink."

The Saloon was a swollen red brick furuncle among its more gracious neighbors. A border of flowering plants in confetti colors lined the semicircular driveway that curved around an appalling fountain: portly cherubs squirted water from their chubby privates and frolicked in eternal stony abandon.

As Nancy and Derek approached the mansion, she said, "Why doesn't Zac Posen design a tote bag–size rocket launcher? But before we could do any aesthetic improvements, Mrs. Friendly's supersecret security team would whisk us away and we'd never be seen again."

Derek glanced around the house and grounds. "I see no guards."

"No one ever has, but they see us. Daddy says they're all former KGB or Mossad. When Mrs. Friendly was a girl, someone tried to kidnap her and she's been under guard ever since."

The theme of the house was "more." More turrets, more mullioned windows, more marble friezes, more statuary. Five minutes after they rang the doorbell, the door was opened by a scrawny and blank-faced old man in a misbuttoned gold blazer, striped pajama pants, and slippers.

"We'll take four boxes of the Thin Mints and one of the Gauchos," he told Nancy. Then he stared at Derek and said, "Heard you drowned off the Great Barrier Reef after you were sent packing. Damned nuisance." The old man turned and shuffled off.

"The quaint and ancient retainer," Nancy said, staring at the open door.

"I fear that you've glimpsed my future, Mrs. Carrington-Chambers," Derek replied, and made her laugh.

She saw it for the first time then, the way that one corner of Derek's lips went up in something that might be called a smirk rather than a smile. It made her feel as if they were conspiratorial.

They followed the old man inside and gazed in amazement at all the *things* that covered the two-story entry hall. The walls were barely visible under stuffed animal heads, paintings, hat racks, and mirrors.

"I hope he's gone to announce us," Nancy said to Derek.

He was staring in wonder at the wall. She followed his glance and saw a mallard head mounted on a wood plaque beside a cubist painting of female nudes.

The painting gave her a sense of deep comfort. Beautiful,

true things had that effect on Nancy. "She's got an astonishing collection of art."

"Hellooo," called someone from another room. "Come on in."

They followed the voice down a hall to a long drawing room stuffed with heavy carved oak and maroon velvet furnishings. A wall of windows had a glorious view of the white-capped gray-green bay.

Above the redwood fireplace was a cartoon-bright pop-art triptych portrait of Mrs. Friendly. When Nancy tore her eyes from it she spotted a tiny plump woman in a St. John orange sweater and a peach knit skirt perched on a brocade armchair.

Mrs. Friendly had never been a beauty; it was her money and lively personality that had drawn admirers. She'd been dying her hair flame red so long that it had cycled in and out of fashion through the decades. Now a darker scarlet hairpiece was pinned like a hat atop her own wispy locks. She powdered her face with haphazard enthusiasm and huge, thick glasses were propped on her button of a nose.

Mrs. Friendly stood, and the weighted hem of her skirt fell fluidly to the wrinkled "suntan" stockings that showed just above her purple suede and lambskin boots. "Did Greene show you in? Did you see where he went?" Her cloudy blue eyes searched the room.

"He met us at the door," Nancy said. "I'm Nancy Carrington-Chambers, and this is my assistant, Derek Cathcart."

"I know who you are, missy, and I know your family, too, and your cousin Birdie, of course. Quite the adventuress, that one."

"She does like traveling," Nancy said with a polite smile, and she thought, *Please, please, let's not talk about Birdie.*

"Come close and let me take a look at you. Everything's a blur these days, but I still like to look."

Nancy went to Mrs. Friendly, who put her face close and peered at Nancy.

"You *seem* pretty, but I'll be able to tell better once I have my cataract surgery. You know, they do it outpatient now, and it takes only a day to recover."

"Science is astounding," Nancy said, and hoped that she would be able to have a robot maid soon.

"Take a load off. If we're lucky Greene will show up with something to eat or drink. He gets upset if I ask one of the girls," Mrs. Friendly said, and waved off a uniformed maid who'd come into the room.

They sat on the deep, creaky sofa. Creaks, except on floors and staircases, always seemed a little rude to Nancy. "We're fine."

"Gigi Barton is raving about the slumber party you're arranging for her. I wonder how old she is now. She's had so much work done you'd have to saw her across like a redwood and count the rings to know her age."

Nancy had checked the guest list yesterday and knew that Mrs. Friendly hadn't responded to her invitation. "I hope you'll be able to make it this Friday."

"Lord, no! I made the mistake of going to Gigi's second wedding. Mr. Friendly and I woke up three days later on a tiny island in Belize with the worst hangovers of our lives—and the deed to the island in his pocket. It turned out to be a good purchase, though, because he loved to nap in his hammock there."

As much as Nancy wanted to gossip, she knew she had to act like a real businesswoman. "How fun! Now let's talk about the annual gala."

Mrs. Friendly adjusted her red wig and said, "Do you know that unlike all the fancy fund-raisers, mine actually raises money?"

"I didn't know that. But the primary purpose of the other fund-raisers is to promote the organizations. The more impressive the party, the bigger annual donor base you'll develop."

"That's what I'm talking about. My event turns a profit, but it's only one day of the year. The rest of the time, our operating fund leaks like an old whore. I'm tired of writing the checks, so I want you to bring in the glamour-pusses and let them take over the society."

As Mrs. Friendly spoke, Derek reached into his inside pocket and brought out a small notepad and a silver pen. He looked so comfortable taking notes, as if he'd spent his life transcribing conversations.

Nancy said, "I think there are a few ways we can make the event more of a social *must*!"

"Honey, talk straight. I can take it."

Nancy couldn't help smiling. "Your fund-raiser is stuck in a scary time warp of egg-salad sandwiches and canned lobster bisque. It's tacky and depressing."

Mrs. Friendly laughed. "Don't I know it! When I first joined, I tried dolling it up, but the hags on the board wanted me to fetch their tea and keep my yap shut. I've been serving crappy canapés ever since. Teach people not to get snotty with Mrs. Goddamn Bentley Jamieson Friendly."

"But those hags are long gone."

"It got to be a tradition, and Greene liked the pinwheel sandwiches."

As if summoned, her quaint and ancient retainer shuffled into the room, pushing a drinks trolley atop which teetered a frosty glass pitcher and a clatter of unmatched tumblers. He stopped in front of his employer.

"What have you brought, Greene?" Mrs. Friendly asked.

"If you like piña coladas and getting caught in the rain . . ." he warbled. He poured a tumbler to the brim, stuck a pink straw in it, and carried it out of the room, singing, *"If you're not into yoga, if you have half a brain . . ."*

"He remembers song lyrics perfectly," Mrs. Friendly said with an admiring tone. "He listens to whatever Cook is listening to, and Cook is an old pothead. I hear an awful lot of Rupert Holmes and the Doobie Brothers. On good days, we might get Tony Bennett or the Eagles."

"Allow me," Derek said, and he stood and poured drinks for the women.

Mrs. Friendly looked up at him. "You're a nice stretch of a fellow. Let me get a good gander." Derek bent toward her and she gazed into his face. "You remind me of someone I knew once. Where are you from?"

"Derek is English," Nancy said.

"That's how it is—the older I get, the more I keep imagining that I'm seeing ghosts from the past. Pour a drink for yourself, young man."

Derek didn't decline or accept, but politely handed the women their drinks.

Nancy took a sip of coconutty-pineappley goodness. "Yummy. It's a drink *and* a dessert," she said. "Your event has got to be so incredible that people are clamoring to come even though we'll triple the cost of a table. The best tables, of course, will require a long-term museum sponsorship that we can work out."

"How do you plan to get people to fork over?"

"We'll give them something that's unique and thrilling."

"You have no idea, do you, little miss?" Mrs. Friendly said, and then laughed. "Well, you couldn't do any worse than me. Spend what you need to spend, but don't take me for a fool. I'm not about to give away the Koh-i-Noor diamond as a party favor."

Nancy smiled and said, "I'll draw up a proposal and get back to you in a week."

When she and Derek left the house, Nancy felt dizzy with happiness, or possibly that second piña colada. "Derek, with your help, I'll make this an event that everyone will be talking about."

When Derek left at five o'clock, Nancy was still on the phone with Sloane Seitz, reviewing plans for Gigi's slumber party. Sloane had been a popular grad student when Nancy was a sophomore, but she got married and left. Now Sloane was a single mother who patched together freelance jobs to make ends meet.

"Let me read back my notes," Sloane said. "I'll pick up the robes and the gifts, and make sure that the linens will be delivered. I'll meet the spa manager to review the schedule. I'm lucky the boys will be visiting friends so I can stay late at the party."

"Lovely, Sloane. Ciao!" She hung up before Sloane could recite another endless saga about her children.

Nancy pulled out one of the six photo albums from her wedding. Her cousin Sissy had designed the tulle and peau de soie dress that made Nancy look like a beautiful and kind fairy princess. The photographer hadn't done as good a job with the groom, though. Todd looked *blockier* in the pictures than she remembered.

She was considering having Lizette digitally removed from all her photos when the phone rang.

"Hello, Nanny," Hester Carrington said.

Nancy had given up objecting to the nickname that had caused endless confusion when the family had employed nannies.

"Hello, Mommy. How are you and Daddy?"

"Wonderful!" Hester said too cheerfully. "Todd told us you're at the Château, and we decided to come into town. We'd like to take you out for dinner tonight."

Nancy glanced at the time. It was 5:20 p.m. Her parents had timed this call to ambush her. "Dinner would be lovely!"

"Lovely! Daddy's already made reservations at the hotel for six." Hester and Julian Carrington, who were so right in so many other ways, ate at a geriatrically early hour.

"Lovely! I'll see you then. Love you!"

Nancy freshened her makeup, revived her curls, and put her shoes back on. Lint roller in hand, she inspected herself in the mirror and removed stray hairs and particles of lint.

Traffic was awful, forcing Nancy to blare her horn once, swerve dangerously around a cable car, and cut off an eco-freak in an electric car as she sped up Nob Hill. As wrong as Todd was on so many things, he was right about the Mini: it was zippy.

There was a line of cars waiting for the valet in the brick entry courtyard, so Nancy parked across the street in front of a fire hydrant. She hurried through the majestic glass portico of the old hotel.

Even though Mr. and Mrs. Carrington lived less than forty miles away, they stayed overnight when they visited San Francisco, booking a suite at the hotel where they'd met decades ago at a tea dance.

Nancy walked through the cream and gilt lobby and glanced at the clock above the reception desk. It was five fifty-five. She waited anxiously for the elevator to the restaurant on the top floor.

six

the fluid rules of today's fashion

*N*ancy's parents were waiting at the host's station. They looked exactly the way they should, like *nice* people, people you wouldn't mind sitting next to on a plane or at the theater. They looked like people who took interesting vacations, read serious books, and never argued in public.

Hester's narrow, sharp features had softened with age, and people always assumed that she had been pretty when she was young. Her hair was a tasteful ash blond and in heels she was as tall as her husband. She wore a simple cream knit jacket with black piping, black slacks, and a gold necklace and earrings.

Hester's only flamboyance was her handbags, and now she

carried a ruby-colored handbag in shiny patent leather with glittering gold hardware.

Nancy smiled at her father. Julian Carrington was a good-looking, trim man in a navy blazer, tattersall check shirt, and gabardine trousers. His blondish hair had gone silver years before. He made a point of looking at his steel chronograph, which was precise enough to mark a daughter's tardiness to a fraction of a second.

Then he smiled and greeted Nancy with a kiss. "Hello, dear. You were *almost* late."

"Sorry, Daddy! Traffic was a grizzly. Hi, Mommy." Nancy gave her mother a hug and a kiss, inhaling the floral scent of L'Air du Temps, which her mother had worn since she was a student.

Hester released her daughter and looked her up and down. "Your nail shade . . . very *dramatic*, isn't it?"

Julian signaled to the maitre d', who immediately led the trio to a table by a window looking out to the city and the Bay Bridge stretching out to Treasure Island.

Nancy made sure to keep her fingernails out of view, which wasn't easy when she was holding a menu. She didn't bother taking out her sustainable-fishing guide, which would have given her father something to criticize.

"How is Miss Winkles?" her mother asked.

"She's as effervescent as ever," Nancy said.

After they'd ordered, Julian said, "Nanny, your mother and I came here because we're extremely worried about you. You left Todd and didn't tell us."

"Todd tried to put the best face on the situation," Hester said. Her eyes lit up as the waiter brought her double martini.

Nancy kept her voice as calm as theirs. "It's just a sabbatical, to get my business going."

"Planning parties isn't a business," Julian said. "It's socializing. If you really want to go into business, you'll get your MBA like you should have in the first place. Or you can go to law school."

"You should finish graduate school before you have children," Hester said. "After you have babies, you can't do anything. Even with nanny."

"What did *I* have to do with it?" Nancy asked.

"I meant *the* nanny." Hester finished her drink and said, "It would be a terrible shame if you were the first in our family to divorce."

"Not to mention the problems you'd cause in my dealings with Todd and his family," Julian said. "We're going in on a biotech business park in New Zealand, you know."

Nancy's smile was tense. "Yes, you've told me. Todd's told me." Her father's private equity firm and Todd's family were investing in the development to benefit Todd and herself. "I just needed a break from that house. That's all."

Her parents exchanged looks and Julian said, "You could have saved everyone all this trouble by doing what I suggested, buying a good house in an established neighborhood, like Bailey Whiteside did. There's a young man with some common sense."

"The house would have been livable if Todd hadn't hijacked my plans. There's a wet bar and a huge television in my bedroom!"

"A first house should be built with resale in mind, and that wet bar and TV are desirable features for *most* homeowners." Julian frowned and said, "I hope that your Foam foolishness doesn't draw the wrong kind of attention to our family."

Hester said, "No attention is always better, Nanny."

"Froth, not foam," Nancy said quietly, and reminded herself that a lady did not make a scene in a public place. She sipped her water and when she felt calm enough she said, "Mrs. Bentley Jamieson Friendly doesn't think Froth is foolish. She invited me to the Saloon and hired me to coordinate the Barbary Coast Historical Museum's annual gala."

Her mother's eyes widened and then she looked for the waiter. When she caught his attention, she lifted her fingers slightly toward her empty glass. "Well!"

Julian looked as if he was going to say something, apparently reconsidered, and finally asked, "Did you see her security guards?"

"No, and I looked all around. She has the most extraordinarily hideous fountain in the Western world."

"Nanny, please," her mother said.

"A party is only a party," Julian said. "However, it isn't a bad connection."

The appetizers and Hester's second martini arrived. She took a long drink of the cocktail before saying, "But what about Todd? We thought you were all settled and now . . ." Her gray-blue eyes welled. "What ever will happen to you now?"

"Probably debtor's prison, scrubbing laundry, and begging for gruel. Speaking of things English, do you know that I have a new assistant?"

"Does he eat gruel?" Hester said, confused.

"No, he's English. His name is Derek and he's fabulous."

Julian hmmphed. "What does Todd think of you having a male assistant?"

"One, I said he was *fabulous*, and two, Todd's paying Derek's wages. Daddy, what funds do I have that can be freed up now?"

"Haven't you been reading your monthly reports? I've

managed to stave off the hemorrhaging for now, but you shouldn't touch a thing."

"Is that your opinion as my trustee or as my father?" Nancy said.

"Both. Since we are on the topic of money, I hope you will study your prenup before making any decisions about your marriage. When we went through it point by point with Todd, you seemed more interested in staring out the window."

Nancy recalled the interminable meeting and the interesting view of a fabulous neoclassic building designed by Timothy Pflueger. "If I was getting a divorce, I'd be happy that Todd waived his right to community property, since I've wasted all that money trying to make the house less horrifying, but the ugly is woven in, like bad polyester."

"Infidelity nullifies the contract, Nancy, and Todd would be entitled to half of what you have," Julian said quietly.

"Are you asking if I've cheated on Todd?" Nancy said, and cringed back into her seat at the thought of her father bringing up her sex life. "Daddy."

"Julian, Nanny, please don't discuss these things at dinner," Hester said as she gazed at her empty martini glass.

Julian pushed Hester's water glass closer to her and said to Nancy, "You don't want to end up like Birdie. You're not going to do any better than Todd Chambers."

"I worry about that little girl of Birdie's," Hester said. "When she visited, the child was dressed in a costume."

"Really? I was just thinking about Birdie," Nancy said. "I heard that a friend of hers died."

"No surprise there," Julian said. "She surrounds herself with people as irresponsible as she is. She has nothing to show for her life."

Hester was fiddling nervously with her wedding ring. "That's right, Nanny. It's very important to your father and me that you show some maturity. Marriage isn't always easy. Happiness takes hard work and compromise."

Nancy heard the quaver in her mother's voice and felt awful that she was upsetting her so. "How is Birdie?"

"The same. She showed up unannounced on Sunday morning with baguettes and a jar of beluga. She made that poor child a caviar sandwich for breakfast. What kind of life is that?"

"I would have *adored* caviar sandwiches as a child," Nancy said, and tried to remember if caviar was on her fish list.

"Yes, but you used to sneak and eat the cat food when you were little, Nanny," Hester said. "Birdie asked about you. I told her that you were spending a lot of time at the Château and she said you should '*live in the now.*' Well, with the child sitting right there, I couldn't tell her that that's how she got pregnant and why she doesn't have a place to call home."

"What about the Redondo Beach house her boyfriend gave her?" Nancy asked.

"His wife found out about it," her father said. "Take Birdie as a cautionary tale."

When Nancy said good night to her parents and returned to her car, she saw a ticket on her windshield.

She was still so angsty when she got home that she decided to reorganize her bathroom. In the small linen closet, she found the unopened gift, a bottle of eau de parfum, that Birdie had given to her at the groundbreaking party.

Nancy needed a new fragrance now that Junie had stolen her signature scent. She dabbed L'Heure Bleue on her wrists, rubbed them together, waited five minutes, and sniffed. The scent was like yearning and passion, and she wondered why she'd ever worn anything else.

Nancy felt better in the morning when Derek arrived, perfection in a slim-fitting dark gray suit, a blue pin-striped shirt, and a black tie with a subtle pattern.

"Good day, Mrs. Carrington-Chambers. Would you like a cappuccino?"

"I dream of your cappuccinos."

She followed him into the kitchen, where he moved with efficient grace. "Did you make espresso for your former employer?"

He tapped the coffee grounds and said, "Indeed. He was fond of his coffee, too. I think that a taste for fine beverages is natural to the aristocratic character." Derek smiled at Nancy, and she felt a blush rising.

When he'd finished frothing up the milk and she was sipping her drink, she said, "I've never had a personal assistant before, so if there's anything else in your range of duties that you think I'd like, please don't hesitate to name it."

He tilted his head attentively and that smirk began to appear. "Madame, are you proposing . . ."

Suddenly she realized the sorts of things that a dazzling gentleman's gentleman might have had to endure. "Oh, no, no! That's not what I meant at all. I would never—not that you're not attractive, because you're extremely handsome . . ."

"You are pleasant-looking as well, Mrs. Carrington-Chambers. Forgive my presumption."

"Yes, of course! Anyway, I know I'm not your type."

"Yet one may establish a cordial association," he said. "I was once employed by a lady of distinction, such as you, and we became so at ease with each other that we would often exchange embraces, or, as you call them, hugs. She said it was very reassuring and I found the platonic physicality jolly agreeable."

"Really?" Nancy's parents didn't hug their staff, but they had never employed anyone as elegant as Derek.

"Indeed. May I demonstrate?"

"That would be fine," she said, and set her cup on the counter.

Derek stepped close and put his arms around her. Nancy slipped her own around his waist. He felt so different than Todd, taller and more sinewy, and his grasp around her was firm without being stifling. He smelled just faintly of cologne that had notes of sandalwood and verbena.

"You smell delicious," she said. "What are you wearing?"

"Creed Green Irish Tweed. You smell lovely."

"It's called L'Heure Bleue. It means that marvelous time when the day has gone but the night hasn't come. That's the color of your eyes." She nestled closer and felt his chin drop to the top of her head. His lady employer was right; it *was* reassuring. If he wasn't gay and her assistant and if she wasn't married and . . . She stepped away and said, "That was very nice. But we better get to work."

While Derek updated her contacts database, Nancy went through the slumber party to-do list. She talked to the caterer, the furniture warehouse manager, the entertainment agent, the photographer, and the valet service.

There were the expected glitches, and she handled each confidently. After telling the staging director that half-down pillows were not acceptable, she looked up to see Derek watching her.

"I don't compromise on quality," she said, even though

she knew it wasn't true. She had compromised her whole marriage.

Derek didn't ask, but he had his head tipped in that way that invited Nancy to share her deepest, most fervent, most private thoughts.

Impulsively she opened the slim drawer in her writing table, took out a composition book, and handed it to him.

He took the composition book almost reverently. "Is this your personal journal?"

"It's my 'Theory of Style.' Style isn't just trendy clothing. Style is a way to approach life so that everything is in harmony, so that form and function hold hands and go skipping," she said. "It's not Kierkegaard, I know, and it's too bad he didn't read it because a makeover might have gotten him his honey and spared us his melancholia."

"Mrs. Carrington-Chambers, you are not what I anticipated."

"Neither are you. Derek, I wouldn't share this with any other man, but there's something about you that I instinctively trust."

He smiled but didn't respond.

No matter how thoroughly Nancy planned an event, the last hours were insanely busy with all the things that could be done only during the final hours. On Saturday morning, she got up at five and dressed in denim leggings and a T-shirt with a campy superhero graphic.

She transferred the necessary schedules, printouts, and personal things into a roomy turquoise tote and gathered everything else she'd need into woven hemp bags with the sea green Froth logo. She methodically cross-checked her packing list with the items in the bags.

Derek came at seven fifteen, wearing black jeans that made his legs look even longer, a white button-down shirt, and a striped tie with a gold bar pin.

"Good morning, Derek."

"Good day, madame. What an amusing T-shirt."

"I thought I'd need all my superpowers today."

"What is your kryptonite?"

"Uninvited guests," she said with a laugh. "Electrical failures, flat champagne, a rabid skunk in the spa pavilion. What is your kryptonite?"

"If I told you that I would be at your mercy," he said.

At eight fifteen, they arrived at the Barton mansion. Nancy loved the front steps of the Italian Renaissance Revival building and the spiraled Corinthian columns that supported the arched entrance. "Line and form," she said to Derek. "I'll tell you about the nightmare that is my house sometime."

"If it is your house, then it must be elegant."

"Why do you think I'm not living with my husband?" she said, and then tried to counter the bitterness with a smile. "But it's just temporary. It's easier for me to concentrate on Froth if I'm here."

Mrs. Yao, Gigi's longtime executive assistant, met them at the door. She was tall and bony, dressed in a knee-length blue skirt and a rose pink sweater over a cream blouse. "Good morning, Nancy. I can always trust you to be on time."

"Hi, Mrs. Yao. This is Derek Cathcart, my assistant."

"How do you do," he said.

Mrs. Yao gave Derek a pleasant look, but Nancy knew she was taking in everything about him.

Nancy said, "Mrs. Yao, everyone will be wearing night clothes at the party."

"I'm glad they're not going to be naked. Some things are impossible to *un*see," she replied as she led them into the entry hall.

"So in the spirit of the party, you might want to wear—"

"Get that thought out of your head, Nancy," Mrs. Yao said. "I wear what I want to wear."

"Mrs. Yao used to model," Nancy said.

"For only two years. That was enough." The older woman guided them to the grand hall, a vast room that ended with views out to the garden shrouded in morning fog. "It seems like just the other day that we had your wedding reception here."

Nancy had been thinking about that, too, remembering the room filled with her family, friends, and the people Todd invited for business connections. "It was a lovely reception."

"You were one of the most radiant brides I've ever seen. Besides Gigi, of course. She always works the aisle like a runway. The caterers are already unloading."

"Wonderful. The other vendors will be here at nine."

"The music room was cleared yesterday." The music room was a long room with framed murals of the nine muses. Their nymphy garments were very nightgowny, which made it ideal for a slumber party.

"Wonderful," Nancy said.

Mrs. Yao crossed the room, saying, "We've already set up the Palladium Room for you." She opened the door to a room with long tables, two house phones, and a credenza with refreshments.

"This is perfect," Nancy said.

"You know where everything is, but you can ring my office if you need anything."

"You're a gem, Mrs. Yao."

When the assistant left the room, Nancy said, "Isn't this place beautiful? Look at these floors—Vincenza marble. I'll give you a tour."

Nancy had just showed Derek the narrow room by the grand staircase, saying "This is the cloakroom," when she was interrupted by a shriek. They turned to see a six-foot-tall woman coming toward them.

Gigi Barton was wearing a garish paisley caftan with a scarf wrapped around her head like a turban. Her famous cheekbones were striking even without makeup. She blew a kiss to Nancy and went directly to Derek. Putting her arm through his, she said, "We used to call it the coke room. Those were wild days, but I haven't been completely tamed yet."

She was gazing at Derek with a flirty smile on her newly inflated lips. "Who are you, gorgeous?" she asked.

"Derek Cathcart, ma'am."

"Derek's my assistant, Gigi," Nancy said. "Derek, this is . . ."

"Just Gigi," she said.

"A pleasure," he said.

"That's what they all tell me. Where are you from, Derek?"

"England."

"Whereabouts in England?"

"The north when I was but a wee lad, but we had occasion to move frequently, and my employment has kept me traveling."

"Ah, your accent is . . . a little different, isn't it?"

"That's what they all tell me," he said playfully.

Gigi was gazing at him with an I-have-vast-resources-for-your-amusement look, but Nancy wasn't about to let this man-eater get her hooks in Derek. "Gigi, what are you doing up so early?"

She waved one of her too-tan hands. "Oh, please. I haven't been to bed yet, but I'll catch a few hours before tonight. Just came to say hello." Gigi finally turned to Nancy and said, "I know you'll do everything beautifully. I'm counting on you."

Although Gigi was smiling, Nancy knew that she was a woman who was used to having things done exactly the way she wanted them to be done.

Nancy said, "It will be everything you want and more."

"That's very reassuring. Now, if that new girl hasn't stolen my Ambien again, I'll go to bed. Honestly, I'd fire her, but she always gets the best ganja. Until tonight." Gigi wafted away, her caftan floating behind her.

"That's real style," Nancy observed.

"You didn't think the ensemble was a tad costumey?"

"For anyone else, yes. But on Gigi's tall frame, it works. Like Elsie de Wolfe, she wears what suits her. De Wolfe was tall, too." Nancy sighed. "If only I was taller."

"My mum always said that so long as your feet reach the ground, you are tall enough," Derek said. "She had a difficult time always keeping me in shoes."

It was the most personal thing he'd told her. "I've come to accept your excessive height."

"Your acceptance means the world to me, madame," he said with that smirk, and she felt a pleasant frisson of something.

But before she could analyze it, vans and delivery trucks began arriving.

seven

chic looks for any hour

Sloane arrived at 10:10 a.m. with two assistants who would stay through the first shift. She was a brown-haired, brown-eyed type who blended into the background, especially in pouchy mom jeans.

"Sorry I'm late!" Sloane said. "I took the boys to the park and they were having so much fun that it was hard to get away. Dobler learned how to use the monkey bars! It's fascinating watching children develop their large and small motor skills."

Nancy couldn't imagine how dreary Sloane's life must be if she thought a child swinging from a bar was exciting. She introduced Sloane to Derek and then reviewed their schedule.

After Sloane left to assemble the swag bags, Nancy said, "I

remember her when she just *sparkled*. It's hard to believe, but she could light up a room. That's what children do to their victims. They leave them as flat and dull as a chalkboard."

"That would mean that our own mothers were desparkled by us," Derek said.

"There are exceptions. I'm sure we *added* sparkle, Derek. You certainly add sparkle to my life. You're a human BeDazzler." She wanted to continue the conversation, but the staging crew had arrived.

The theme was Hollywood Regency, and everything had to look swank and glitzy. The crew rolled out white shag carpeting and hauled in king-size mattresses that were dressed with luxurious white and indigo linens. The white and near-black flowers came: parrot tulips, roses, frilled poppies, musky tuberoses and even tiny black pansies.

Ivory velvet love seats and black lacquer cocktail tables were arranged in conversation groups. Venetian mirrors were positioned to reflect the spectacular chandeliers. Black-and-white versions of night-themed movies flickered on screens: Fellini's *Nights of Cabiria*, Capra's *It Happened One Night*, Huston's *Night of the Iguana* . . .

Tents were erected outside with massage tables, soaking tubs, and stylist stations. An al fresco café was created on the patio and a net of tiny lights replicated stars, since the night was overcast.

By the time Nancy and Derek checked the bustling kitchen, Derek's cheeks were flushed with his exertions and the heat of the room. Nancy saw him looking at the colorful platters of food.

He said, "Not exclusively black-and-white, Mrs. Carrington-Chambers?"

"The food is like a hand-tinted detail in a black-and-white photo—the neutral background allows the color to pop," she said.

One of the cooks wiped his hands on a towel and came over to her. "Hey, I just wanted to say thanks for the gig." He looked around at the busy kitchen and said, "We're all glad to have the work, especially at a time like this."

"You're doing a wonderful job," Nancy said. "I hope Froth will be able to hire your company for future events."

When the cook went back to his tasks, Nancy turned back to Derek and said, "It's time for us to get changed. I have a surprise for you."

When they got to the music room, Nancy unzipped the garment bag that she'd brought from home. Inside were two pairs of silk men's pajamas in midnight blue and two pairs of matching women's pajamas. Their names were monogrammed in ivory on the pockets.

"It's our uniform for tonight," Nancy said, and handed Derek the men's pajamas. "We'll be matching. I have moccasins for you, too."

"How very thoughtful," he said, obviously touched by the gift.

Nancy thought of suggesting that they change here together, the way models do backstage, because she was curious about his underwear, but she didn't know if he'd interpret it in the highly professional way she intended. So she excused herself to one of the upstairs guest rooms and got ready in a scant forty-five minutes.

Of course, she had a little assistance from one of the spa stylists. He applied Nancy's makeup, including Shu Uemura false eyelashes. Then he fluffed, spritzed, and crunched Nancy's hair, applied a fixative to seal her makeup, and gave her shoulders a minimassage.

Nancy did a mirror check and was pleased to see how authoritative and professional she looked in her pj's, cream marabou slippers, headset, and clipboard.

She descended the majestic grand staircase and paused halfway to observe the wonders she had wrought. Everything that could sparkle sparkled. The musicians were warming up. The waiters, spa attendants, and other staff wore similar indigo pajamas, but in a cotton-rayon blend. Nancy reached the bottom of the staircase feeling like the captain of a ship.

"Nancy!" Sloane was rushing across the hall in her pajamas, which had an unfortunate bag-of-potatoes effect on her figure. Her face had a sheen and her hair had slipped loose from its ponytail.

"Sloane, how is everything on your end?"

After Sloane reported her activities, Nancy said, "Do you want to go upstairs and touch up your makeup and hair?"

Her friend shook her head. "Thanks, but I can't spare the time."

"It takes five seconds. Turn around." Nancy pulled off the band around Sloane's hair, gathered all the strands, banded the hair again, and then tucked the ponytail into itself, making the mess look intentional. "Much better," she said. "I've got my makeup kit in the Palladium Room."

"Nancy, no one cares what I look like," Sloane said.

Nancy felt a pang of sorrow that even her friend's soul had been so desparkled, but her duties kept her from pondering whether the desparkling was a permanent condition.

Nancy and her team stayed on their feet all night making sure that the guests ate, drank, danced, and passed out in absolute comfort.

Sloane and the first shift left at midnight. At three in the morning, by which time most of Gigi's friends had visited her spa and were wearing their thick white robes (monogrammed with "I Slept with Gigi"), Nancy realized that she was having problems coordinating her body movements.

"Nancy!"

Bailey Whiteside was standing in front of her, wearing a red onesie and a flannel nightcap. In one hand, he held a tumbler of amber liquid. He looked good even in these ridiculous pajamas. *Especially* in the soft, caressing fabric of his pajamas. *Don't look down*, she told herself.

"So you decided to show up," she said.

"I wanted to see you again." His hazel eyes gazed into hers. "I remember your wedding reception here. You were so beautiful."

She was so exhausted that the compliment made her sad. Her eyes began to well. "Thank you."

"I wanted to carry you off. I could never figure out how Todd got to you before me." Bailey tipped his drink toward her lips and she took a sip of the scotch.

Her brain was foggier than the sky outside. "You could have tried to steal me away before I got married," she said. "You always flirted, but you're a flirt."

"I always flirted with *you*, Nancy," he said, "because you're so pretty and fun. I wasn't going to do anything unless you gave me an indication that I had a chance. Do you remember that winter when we went to that funky old lodge in Donner?"

"You came alone," she said. "I got a cold and you stayed

and made me cocoa and you taught me how to play Texas Hold'Em."

"Hoping for my chance with you. I really wanted to play strip poker."

"And then I got married," she said.

"Then you got married," he said. "But now that you've left Todd, maybe . . ." He began running his free hand up and down her arm, sending shivers through her.

"I haven't left Todd. I am focusing on Froth. I'm doing it as we speak. Froth. It's a funny word, isn't it? Froth."

"When do you get off? Come sleep at my place and we'll go out to brunch."

"I can't. I'm married, and I have to stay here and be the captain of the ship. Do you know that Todd put a wet bar in the bedroom?"

"Maybe you can show me your bedroom sometime." Bailey handed her his drink and said, "Go ahead, finish it."

She hadn't had dinner, and she was thirsty. The scotch burned nicely on the way down. "Are you going to Lizette and Bill's wine country weekend?"

"No, they'd just try to set me up so I can be stuck married and bored like them. Not that all married women are boring." Bailey put his hands on her shoulders and kissed her lightly.

Nancy could taste the scotch on his lips. Bailey put his mouth to her ear and whispered, "Come home with me."

Someone cleared his throat and said, "Mrs. Carrington-Chambers."

She pulled away from Bailey and turned to see Derek standing close. "Hmmm? Bailey, this is my fabulous new assistant, Derek."

"Hey," Bailey said.

"Good evening, sir," Derek said. "Madame, if I could have a moment?"

"Of course." Nancy noticed that she was wavering on her feet. Derek came to her side and she swayed against him and said, "Good night, Bailey."

"I'll call you, Nancy," Bailey said, and left, his red posterior hazy in Nancy's exhaustion.

She looked at her lovely assistant and said, "Am I supposed to be doing something for the party?"

"You're completely knackered. We're going to have a kip. The guest rooms are occupied, so I've set up something for you." Derek put his arm around her waist and she leaned against him as he took her to the Palladium Room. "Is Mr. Whiteside a special friend of yours, madame?"

"Bailey Carson Whiteside the Third came to my wedding. It was a very, very beautiful wedding. I looked like a fairy princess." Propped against her assistant, she stared into his sympathetic eyes. "My parents and all our friends think that I'm a failure for leaving Todd. But the house, that horrible house. It's in a hideous development, Villagio Toscana. Todd put a wet bar in the bedroom and . . ."

"Yes?"

"His underwear is always wrong," she said before closing her eyes. She had a sensation of falling and then strong arms around her, supporting her, and she knew she was safe.

Four hours later, Nancy was pulled out of a warm, deep sleep by the click-click-click of footsteps on the polished stone floor. She opened her eyes and saw that she was lying in a nest of soft comforters and pillows. Mrs. Yao had come into the room.

"Good morning, Nancy. You wanted a wake-up call."

"Thank you. I'll just brush my teeth and see to breakfast."

Mrs. Yao looked amused and said "That's a good idea" as she left.

Nancy got up and saw Derek rolled up in a blanket on the floor on the other side of the room. He had excellent bed head and his morning shadow made him look a little dangerous.

She went to him, bent over, and shook him. "Wake up."

He threw an arm around her legs, pulling her down beside him. "Come back to bed, Mel," he said, and rolled on his back.

Nancy shouldn't have been surprised at what she saw, because Derek was a man and men had natural bodily reactions, what Todd called his "morning rudder," but Derek was her assistant and she jumped up and away.

Her sudden movement was enough to startle Derek fully awake.

"Well, um, well," Nancy said, feeling envious of Mel. That must be Derek's lover.

Her assistant soon understood the reason for her reaction. He calmly arranged the blanket to obscure the protrusion. "My apologies, madame. I mistook you for my *special* friend in the depth of my slumber."

Nancy wasn't going to be less sophisticated than he was. "Don't worry about it. Meet me in the kitchen when you've, um, collected yourself."

She grabbed her headset, slipped on her marabou slippers, and hurried through the main hall, cupping her hand to her mouth to check her breath, and then went to the kitchen. Two cooks were already grilling traditional breakfast foods, and a woman was unpacking big plastic bins of cereals and toppings.

"Good morning," Nancy said brightly to her. "You'll be setting up the cereal bar on the patio-slash-café."

"Morning," said the spiky-haired woman. "You're rocking the Goth look."

"Thank you." Nancy tried to surreptitiously catch her reflection in the wall of stainless steel refrigerators across the room. "I have something urgent to take care of and then I'll be back to supervise."

"What's to supervise? It's cereal," the manager said flatly. "Trix are for kids."

"Yes, of course." Nancy smiled and nodded at a cook flipping hash browns on the grill. She continued to smile at the few guests she passed on her way upstairs to the room that was reserved for the spa stylists.

She rushed to the mirror. Her hair was completely flattened on one side and stuck out on the other. Her smear-proof makeup wasn't. Dark circles ringed her eyes, and one of her false eyelashes had migrated onto her cheek.

Nancy tried to wash off the makeup, but the fixative wouldn't dissolve in soap and water. She used a washcloth to scrub it off, leaving red blotches. She tried to cover the ruddy marks with powder, which caked on her wet skin.

Nancy was about to start over when she heard Gigi's contralto calling, "Nancy!"

Nancy went into the hallway to see her hostess strolling gracefully in a long, gossamer-thin silk nightgown and wrap. "There you are. Now we can finally talk over a bowl of Cocoa Puffs. Do you know that I've never tasted them? Milagro called and told me that you had taken a female lover, but she kept laughing, so I didn't actually believe her."

"But Gigi," Nancy began, and raked her hair with her fingers.

"I'm going to nibble and then fall asleep on the massage table." Gigi hooked her arm through Nancy's and pulled her toward the hall. "You don't happen to have any Halcion on you, do you?"

"No, but Gigi—"

"I was completely surprised when you showed up with that yummy assistant. Mrs. Yao tells me that you both slept in the Music Room."

"We slept separately, and he's gay."

"So was my third husband, but we were both flexible. He was double-jointed, as a matter of fact. He pretended to be an Italian count, but he was actually a Croatian bank clerk," Gigi said as they turned to the grand staircase and began walking down the polished marble steps. "He was after my money, can you imagine? But he was a wonderfully amusing man and he had a spectacular . . ." Gigi spotted a friend and held her arms out wide. "Peter!"

Gigi's gesture set Nancy off balance, and the heel of her marabou slipper caught in the hem of her pajama pants, yanking them down and sending Nancy slipping on the dangerous steps.

She desperately reached out for the banister and grabbed it, righting herself just as a camera flashed.

Nancy used her last reserve of energy to drive home from the party, and she slept until the afternoon. She dreamt about a tall man. His lips nuzzled her neck and he slipped his hand between her thighs, sending the most incredible sensations through her—and then a car alarm on the street started blaring. She fought to stay in the dream, but it was too late. She was awake.

Still, Nancy felt better than she had in years. She felt hopeful. Everyone had loved the slumber party, only a few had witnessed her stumble on the stairs, and Bailey had flirted with her. The faceless man in her dream must have been Bailey. Her subconscious was giving her a sign.

Nancy's family and friends might have a different idea about her marriage if she started dating Bailey. *Nancy Carrington-Chambers-Whiteside*, she thought to herself. *Nancy Whiteside. Nancy Edith Carrington-Whiteside. Mrs. Carrington-Whiteside.*

Nancy liked that Bailey was ambitious. She would look like the ideal confidante/advisor as he made his acceptance speeches for increasingly important offices. She'd have to find out his political party.

She drove to her favorite grocery store. The small parking lot was full, so she parked in a bus zone, since she'd only be a few minutes.

She walked in cheerful preoccupation through the aisles of the lavish market, pushing her cart of imported water, low-fat milk, and limes. She was wearing a short smocked pink dress and glossy flats, and looked as if she belonged here with the chic and conscientious shoppers, buying attractively arranged, spotlighted organic produce.

Like the stylish men in front of her, for example.

The auburn-haired man with the marvelous blazer and dark-wash jeans said, "Grilled fish or chicken? Because I can do sautéed veggies with either," to his lanky, dark-haired boyfriend with the great butt.

The dark-haired man turned his head and Nancy said, "Derek!"

He hadn't shaved and was wearing black Dickies and a worn-out Clash T-shirt under a faded blue plaid flannel shirt. His hair was still bed-headed in a way that made her think about him this morning.

Derek took a moment and then said, "Mrs. Carrington-Chambers!"

The other man turned to look at her, holding a bunch of baby bok choy aloft.

Nancy noticed that his Lycra-blend V-neck T-shirt fit snugly across his trim torso. She shouldn't have been surprised to see Derek here, since it was so close to Polk Gulch with all its boy bars. She smiled at him and his friend. This must be Mel. Nancy said, "You'll think I'm stalking you, but I needed to stock up on the essentials."

Derek said, "I'd like to introduce my very *special* friend, Prescott Bottomsley. Prescott, this is Mrs. Carrington-Chambers."

"Just Nancy," she said. "How nice to meet you, Prescott!" She held out her hand, but wondered, *Who is Mel?*

"Nice to meet you," the man said, and shook hands with her. He had an American accent and was more pretty than handsome, with gentle features and a round chin.

Nancy said, "Derek, I didn't recognize you at first in those clothes."

"This costume? Prescott and I are going to a Rockers and Boytoys tea dance. I'm Joe Strummer and he's a rent boy." Derek slipped his arm through his friend's.

"So that's why you look so rough! But I would have dressed you up as Tommy Lee. You have that look."

Prescott smiled and said, "Yes, there is a resemblance. An angularity. And elsewhere, if you know what I mean."

Derek raised his eyebrows. Then he said to Nancy, "Your party was fantastic. Was Miss Barton pleased?"

"I think so. Tomorrow we'll do our postmortem and then we've got to start on Mrs. Friendly's party."

Derek looked vaguely confused and Prescott said to him, "A postmortem is what Americans call the after-party dissection and analysis."

"I hope you won't be squeamish, Derek," Nancy said.

The boyfriend was looking at Nancy's pleated turquoise suede bag with gold studs. "That's a fabulous bag."

"It's not really mine. I stole it from my mother's closet."

"That's a closet I wouldn't mind being in."

"I get her scarves, too. I heart your blazer."

"Ted Baker. You should see the lining."

"You must be a *high*-rent boy, then," Nancy said, and they both laughed. "Derek didn't tell me you had such marvelous taste."

"He didn't tell me you were *so* very scrumptious."

"I don't think he notices. I'm not his type."

Derek said, "I endeavor to keep my personal and professional lives separate out of respect for the both of you."

"Oh, no need," his companion said. "You can share all the details of our steamy relationship with the world."

"And, I don't mind you sharing our relationship, Derek," Nancy said. "We have nothing to hide." As she put her hand on his arm and squeezed, she flashed back to her dream. But it was Bailey in her dream. "Have fun at your party!"

When she returned to her car, a ticket was stuck under the windshield wiper. She tossed it on the passenger seat so that Derek could mail it to her husband.

eight

bags that don't overwhelm

On Monday morning, Gigi Barton called just after eight o'clock. "Nancy, marvelous job on the party! Some of my guests are still here and we kept a masseuse and a guitarist to entertain us."

"I'm überthrilled that you were happy with it, Gigi," Nancy said. "I'll send the invoices to Mrs. Yao, and I hope you'll tell your friends about Froth for their events."

"I'll definitely tell them and I'll mention your delicious assistant," Gigi said. "Is he available for any freelancing?"

"Unfortunately not, Gigi. I feel dreadful as it is, keeping Derek away from his hunky boyfriend so often."

"So you're sticking to *that* story, you greedy girl," Gigi said, and laughed. "Tell him I'm very interested anyway, in case he should become available, won't you?"

"Of course I'll tell him."

When Derek arrived, Nancy said, "Gigi called to tell us how much she adored our event. It was spectacular, wasn't it?"

"Indeed, madame. I hope that she found my services satisfactory."

"I'm sure she did," Nancy said. "Now we'll have to start planning the museum gala. Let's look at my wedding albums. Maybe they'll put us in a creative mood."

They sat side by side on the sofa, close enough so they could both look at the same album together.

"You were a fetching bride." He stared for a long time at a photo of Todd and said, "I pictured you with a different sort."

"How so?"

"Someone more . . . a little more *fabulous.*"

"If Todd had been a little more *fabulous,* we wouldn't be apart now. He couldn't understand how living in an odious house was making me miserable. He thought that huge meant *awesome.*"

"You sound angry."

She laughed. "Oh, we Carringtons never get angry. We don't yell or have scenes in public. We hold everything inside."

"Some people explode," he said as he put his hand on her knee. "Others implode. I'm glad you didn't have to suffer through any ugly scenes or . . . any brutality."

"No, nothing like that! Nothing but a feeling, like when you taste coffee that's been sitting all day on the burner. It's bitter and gray. You can force yourself to drink it or try to disguise the taste, but the more you do, the worse it seems. It's like that. Maybe I expect too much. That's what my parents tell me."

"Isn't there anyone else who can be your ideal demitasse, madame?"

"There may be someone." She shut the photo albums and said, "Right now, though, we have to decide on a brilliant theme for Mrs. Friendly's event. And brilliant in the American way, not the British way, because you Brits will call mashed peas brilliant."

"Mashed peas *are* brill, or as you would say, awesome. They don't roll around your plate." Derek went to his writing table and picked up the folder with their notes from the library.

"I don't say awesome," Nancy said, "Todd says it. He says things like 'This steak is *awesome*, dude.' He actually calls me dude sometimes. It makes me want to scream."

"But Carringtons don't scream," Derek said.

"Only if we were being chased by a pack of liberals. Back to a brilliant idea."

They were sorting through fashion magazines, marking pages that had promising ideas, when someone buzzed Nancy's apartment. Derek went to the intercom and came back saying, "It's a Mr. GP. Is Madame available?"

"GP? *Awesome*," she said. "Let him in."

Two minutes later, her gawky friend arrived at her front door. She threw her arms around him, saying, "Hey, stranger!"

"Hey, princess."

When he stepped back, Nancy saw that he was wearing geek chic, a retro striped polo, brown cords, and black Converse high-tops, and he carried a shiny silver bag.

She introduced GP to Derek and they went into the living room.

Derek said, "Shall I fetch tea, madame?"

"Thank you, Derek." She wished she had cookies to offer her guest.

Derek nodded and left the room.

GP handed the bag to Nancy and said, "This is for you. I would have come sooner, but I didn't know you were here."

She opened the bag, unfolded tissue, and pulled out a silk scarf in watercolor aquas. "It's beautiful, GP!"

He blushed and ducked his head. "You told me that scarves are always good gifts and they should match eyes or contrast with hair color, remember?"

"It's one of my most fervent fashion beliefs," she said, and wrapped the scarf around her neck. She hadn't seen GP after Todd had gotten his family's investment and cut her friend loose. "It's great to see you. You look fab."

"Yeah, nice of you to say that when you've got that Zoolander here."

"You shouldn't judge an apple using an orange as your standard."

"Who's the orange, him or me?" he said with a grin. "I was bummed to hear about you and Todd, Nance, but I hope things work out for you."

"It's a temporary relocation until we can resolve what to do about that hell house. I can't stand living there, but Todd actually likes it. What have you been doing?"

Derek returned carrying a tray with a teapot, cups, and saucers.

Nancy said, "I'll pour. Thank you, Derek."

"I'll attend to the party billing, madame."

While Derek worked, GP told Nancy about his activities. "So I took your advice and set up a foundation. We give grants for training and job placement, but I still have time on my hands. What are you doing?"

"Right now, Derek and I are trying to come up with a theme

for the Barbary Coast Historical Museum Society Annual Gala. Mrs. Jamieson Friendly wants me to give it a makeover, but what *hasn't* been done and what *could* be done in that dingy little museum space? There's not even room outside to set up tents."

"The BCHM is one of my favorite museums."

"You've always been a pistachio for history."

"You should have called me an almond, which is a California nut," GP said, and scratched his head. "I always thought that it would be cool to have a place down on the waterfront, honoring the Barbary Coast. You know, with wooden sidewalks and saloons, gambling houses and ladies of ill repute. Gangs of hooligans for sure. 'Hooligan' comes from the Barbary Coast."

"That sounds more like a theme park than a one-night party," Nancy said. "Designing and building the sets alone would take months, and we don't have that much time."

"When's the party?"

"It's always held on the last Saturday in May, so we have a measly seven weeks. The donors keep it on their calendar from year to year, which is lucky for us since otherwise it would be much too late for invitations."

"Seven weeks is enough time if you rent the sets and costumes from that summer Gold Rush festival near Sacramento. They keep them in storage the rest of the year."

Derek looked up from his work and said, "What if you moved the party from the museum to a larger venue in the original Barbary Coast neighborhood?"

"That's what I mean!" GP said. "You could make it authentic. There's an empty old warehouse on the Embarcadero that I drive by all the time. I always think it would be perfect for a tourist attraction. Maybe you could swing a short-term rental."

"It would be a huge project," Nancy said, but she was already thinking of a spectacular event.

"I can help," GP said. "You don't have to pay me or anything and I know how to make it historically accurate."

Nancy could envision the rough-hewn bars, the smell of spilled whiskey and salt water, and the charged atmosphere of the demimonde. "Okay, let's do it. You are now an official Froth associate, GP. Let's draw up a plan."

After an hour of discussion, GP left the apartment, excited about his assignment to find out rental, shipping, and assembly costs for the sets. Nancy and Derek were going to visit the empty warehouse.

When they went downstairs to the garage, she handed him the keys. "Remember to drive on the right side of the street."

"Certainly, madame."

"You're being formal with me again."

"It's the best policy when we're out. I would hate if anyone made false assumptions."

"How could anyone say anything bad about us, Derek? Our association is all innocence and light, isn't it?"

He opened the passenger door for her, just as Todd had done on their first dates. "As you say in your 'Theory of Style,' madame, appearances are everything. Let us give the appearance of propriety at all times."

She slid into the seat and looked up at him. "You read it, then. What did you think?"

He didn't answer until he'd gotten in the car. "Most entertaining and illuminating. I shall use your advice as a guide to life. I'm reconsidering the Windsor knot, and still attempting to calculate my ideal trouser style based on the algorithm you provided."

"You need someone else to take your measurements because

they must be precise. Although I think your trousers always complement your body divinely," Nancy said. "I want my style guide to be more useful than Sun Tzu's *The Art of War*, which shouldn't be difficult since most of us get dressed every single day, and only infrequently enter into battle."

"Some would say that clothes are armor."

"Sometimes they are. Bring back my notebook tomorrow, and we'll work on it in our free moments."

They took an indirect route because Derek refused to ignore no-left-turn signs, but they soon arrived at a run-down warehouse with a faded "For Lease" sign hanging sideways from a post. "That's it! That's it!"

He parked in the broken asphalt parking lot, and they walked toward the weathered building. Seagulls above cawed sharply, and the salty wind whipped Nancy's hair and made her bias-cut skirt swirl around her legs. She was all goose-bumpy, but it wasn't the chill—it was the feeling that this was *right*.

They circled around the building, which stretched from the street all the way back to a pier, but the dirty windows were too high for them to see through.

"Isn't this just perfect?" she said excitedly. "I need a better view." They were on the side of the building, away from the street. Across the parking lot was an old shack of a coffee joint, but Nancy didn't think anyone could see them. "Give me a step up. I'll just take a peek."

Derek squatted down gracefully so the knee of his black pin-striped trousers didn't touch the dirty ground, and held his hands together. Nancy slipped off her anthracite ballerina flat and put her foot in his hands. Derek lifted and she stretched upward, trying to reach the window.

She was experiencing all sorts of very interesting sensations from the intimate contact with her assistant and the thrill of discovering the warehouse. "Higher, Derek."

He raised his hands farther and she was so close to the window.

"Just a few more inches." She gripped a narrow ledge farther up on the wall and pulled herself up. This move caused her foot to slip out of Derek's hands. She hung from the ledge and tried to decide if holding on was worth cracking all her fingernails. It wasn't, she thought as she lost her purchase on the ledge.

Then she felt Derek's arms around her thighs, her skirt rumpling upward.

They fell at an angle, Nancy tumbling atop Derek, and her head bashing back against his chest with considerable force. He yelled, "Shit!" and she said, "Sorry!" and he said, "It's okay," and she said, "Are you okay?" And he said, "Are *you* okay?"

They were trying to get up. She hopped on the foot with the shoe, holding on to him for balance, and that just sent him backward again. She fell so that she was atop him, her face against his. He had a peculiar expression.

"Are you hurt?" she asked.

"Only my dignity and likely my suit."

"I'll pay for the cleaning," she said. She became aware of contrasting temperatures on her hindquarters. The breeze was cold on her upper thighs, but her bottom was wonderfully warm. Which made sense when she realized that Derek's large, firm hands were gripping the flesh on either side of her thong.

A wolf whistle and a hoot came from the direction of the coffee shack. "Sweet ass!"

Nancy leaped up, stepping on Derek's arm accidentally, and this time his expression clearly communicated pain. "Ow!"

"Sorry!" She pushed down her skirt, almost wishing that she'd followed her mother's advice that a lady's panties should fully cover her posterior. Her face was hot, and the men standing by the coffee shack were laughing.

She slid her foot into the ballet flat and stomped across the asphalt lot to the shack. Derek followed.

One man in a dirty cook's apron was grinning. "Fancy panties! Coffee's on the house for you, hon."

"I am not your hon, and what I could really use is a ladder."

"I'll do you one better. Wait a sec."

Another man, who was wearing a navy twill mechanic's jumpsuit, said, "Do I know you?"

"I certainly doubt it," Nancy said. "My car is serviced at the dealership, which offers appointments twenty-four hours a day."

"Not you, doll," the mechanic said, and looked at Derek. "Dick, right? You ever go to Malloy's? What are you doing all pimped out?"

Derek shook his head and said in a clipped tone, "I don't believe we've met, sir."

"Sir!" The mechanic laughed a little, and then he pointed a finger toward Derek and said, "I'm good with faces. I'll remember."

"Derek is my assistant," Nancy said defensively. "He's from England."

"Oooh, England!" said the mechanic, flapping his hands and eliciting laughs from his pals.

The cook came out of the shack swinging a large ring of keys. "I'll let you in. I keep an eye on the place so squatters don't move in. Or artists." He said the last word with a sneer as he led Nancy and Derek across to the warehouse.

"I appreciate it. I'm thinking of renting the place for an event."

"An *art* fair?" he asked suspiciously.

"No, a fund-raiser for the Barbary Coast Historical Museum."

"That place still around? I went there on a field trip in sixth grade. I used to want to be a pirate."

"Pirates had such fabulous clothes," Nancy said. "I'm Nancy. And you are?"

"Aldo," he said. "Here we go." He opened the heavy lock on the door and pulled the tall door open.

The trio walked into the enormous warehouse. Dust motes floated in the beams of light that streamed down from windows that reached to the impossibly high ceiling. The stained, cracked cement floor stretched out forever.

"It's bigger inside than it is outside," Derek said, and began to snap photos with his phone's camera.

"You watch *Doctor Who,* too?" Aldo said with a grin. "Back in the day, they used to assemble cars here, just rolled them down the assembly line and shipped them off."

"How can a place like this be empty?" Nancy asked. "Real estate is still valuable here."

They walked the length of the building, their footsteps echoing in the vast hollowness.

Aldo said, "It's a historical site so you know how that is. No one can tear it down or do any serious remodeling, so it just sits and rots."

"It's perfect." She looked at Derek and said, "What do you think?"

"Madame's taste is infallible," he said with a smile as he took a photo of her.

When Nancy and Derek returned to her apartment, she called the warehouse's management company to ask about renting the space. The man she spoke to said he'd run some numbers and get back to her, but he thought they could work something out.

Nancy was elated. "Derek, we should celebrate! We could go out and have champagne and dinner—on me."

"Thank you, but I'm already engaged."

"If it's Prescott, invite him, too."

Derek frowned momentarily and Nancy thought, it isn't Prescott. It's Mel. She felt bad because she'd liked Prescott, and he and Derek had seemed so compatible.

Derek said, "I can make a call . . ."

"No, don't! Another time. You go have fun. Oh, and here are the keys to the apartment. So you can come and go during the workday if I'm out."

"Thank you," he said. "Good evening, Mrs. Carrington-Chambers."

After he left, Nancy moved restlessly around the apartment. Maybe she should cut back on the caffeine. Someone knocked on her door and she thought Derek must have changed his mind and come back. She rushed to the door and opened it.

It wasn't Derek.

Her cousin Birdie stood there in a sable coat over a taupe dress and red heels. Throwing her arms around Nancy, she said "Nanny Girl!" and gave her a kiss on each cheek.

Birdie smelled of cigarettes, Shalimar, and cinnamon gum.

When Nancy stepped away from her, she said, "Birdie!"

"Binky Winkles was leaving downstairs as I arrived. I love that she still calls me Girl Carrington. You remember my angel, Eugenia." Birdie turned toward the hallway and said, "Eugenia, say hello to your auntie Nanny."

That's when Nancy saw the tiny creature standing back in the hallway. Her faded sepia brown hair was cut into a ragged pixie, and she was wearing a hideous *Little House on the Prairie* ruffled plaid pinafore and red galoshes.

"Hello," the child said almost inaudibly.

Birdie swept by Nancy, into the apartment, and looked through the doorway into the living room/workspace. "My sister said you'd done it up like Barbie's Dream House, but it looks beautiful. You've always had a way with arranging things."

Nancy and the child followed as Birdie went to the kitchen and opened the buttercup yellow refrigerator. "All you've got is water. I'm *famished!*"

"The vodka is in the freezer and the champagne is in the chiller. Would you like a drink?"

"Vodka neat with an olive," Birdie said. "Eugenia will have water. French or Swiss, whatever is most suitable for a child."

When Nancy brought out the drinks, Birdie and her daughter were in the living room. Birdie was perched on the edge of the sofa, one slim leg flung over the other, her foot pointing gracefully. The child sat on the sofa close to Birdie, dangling her feet.

Birdie took a sip and said, "Very nice," and then opened her red beaded clutch and took out a red and gold box of cigarettes and a gold lighter.

Nancy said, "You can't smoke in here, Birdie. The smell will get in all my things." She thought that Birdie shouldn't smoke near the child. Eugenia looked unhealthy, with a grayish hue to her translucent skin, dull hair, and dark bluish circles under expressionless eyes the color of fallen leaves.

Birdie shrugged an angular shoulder and put the cigarettes away. "You need some art on these walls. I'll send you something. The light is excellent for a large piece above the mantel," she said. "I saw your mother the other day. I think she's having a nervous breakdown."

"I had dinner with her recently and she was absolutely fine," Nancy said. "I heard the news about your friend Leo. I'm sorry."

Birdie looked down at her cocktail and said, "He was a remarkable man. Such a loss." She sighed and looked melancholy for a moment.

"How long are you here?"

"I haven't decided. I met the most incredible Greek man in Nairobi, Yannis. We had a spectacular time traveling through Kenya. You *must* go as soon as you possibly can. Words cannot describe the twilight on Lamu Island. I had to wear a headscarf, of course, but Yannis said that I looked as mysterious as a sphinx."

Nancy felt obligated to say something to the child holding the glass of water. "Did you see any elephants or giraffes?"

The girl regarded her solemnly and said, "I saw a cow."

Birdie laughed, a delicious, captivating laugh, and said, "Oh, I didn't take her with me! She stayed on a farm with friends near Woodstock. They're all very organic this and slow-movement that. They make their own clothes and gave her that charming little frock."

Eugenia was swinging her stubby legs. Nancy tried not to react, hoping that the grimy red rubber boots wouldn't mark the upholstery.

Birdie said, "So you left Todd. That type habitually cheats so don't blame yourself. I knew he must be excruciating in bed."

Nancy glanced at the child, but the girl was looking off into midspace. "Birdie! He didn't cheat and I left temporarily to, um, explore career possibilities."

"Very loyal of you to pretend, but sad, too. I once considered seducing Todd to save you. I'd have to get paralyzed with drugs and drink to endure it, though, and you know how Sissy would twist that," she said, speaking of her younger sister.

"Birdie!"

"You need to find a Greek man. They are divinely passionate and know the art of making love to a woman." Her green eyes narrowed dreamily. "Yannis likes to undress me so slowly that by the time—"

Nancy quickly said, "Birdie, are you going somewhere tonight? May I see your dress?"

Birdie stood and gracefully slipped off her fur coat. The dress was an exquisitely draped jersey in a dark taupe-gray that accentuated Birdie's dramatic coloring. "Halston, would you believe it?" The dress had a high neckline, and Birdie pirouetted to show a sexy low back. Her beauty was both classic and utterly modern.

"You always know how to wear clothes," Nancy said. "Clothes never wear you." She didn't want to, but she had to ask about the scarlet satin T-strap heels.

"Louboutin," Birdie said. "Although you once told me that only whores and children wear red shoes. It's so cold here after Africa. I had to wrest Grammie's fur from my mother's death grip. She warned me to keep away from eco-terrorists, which is ridiculous since they're so exciting, always willing to do something adventurous in the middle of the night."

"I have a cape," the child said.

Birdie looked at her daughter as if surprised to see her in

the room. "Yes, sweetie, you can show Auntie Nanny your cape later."

"Auntie Nanny" sounded awful and Nancy said, "I really wish—"

Birdie tossed back the rest of her drink and said, "I'm very proud of you for setting up a new life for yourself. I've always said that you have more sense than most of the family."

"Is that a compliment to me, or an insult to the family?"

"Both. I've got to run. I'm meeting Yannis and he's a beast if I'm late."

"It was lovely to see you, Birdie. You, too, Eugenia. Maybe we could have lunch and go shopping." She stared at the child and said, "Or we could go to Steinhart Aquarium . . ." Nancy hadn't been to the gift shop there in years.

"Maybe. Yannis wants me to go to Corfu to meet his family, but you know how I feel about families." Birdie stood, put on her coat, and walked to the front door. "Nanny, I've got a blazing headache coming on. Do you have any opiates?"

Nancy wasn't going to aid and abet Birdie, who was already oblivious enough of her child. "I have Advil."

"I guess that will have to do. Would you please crush four of them into a fine powder and dissolve them in a glass of water with ice and a twist of lemon?"

"Still or sparkling?"

"Half and half. Not too fizzy, and not too flat."

Nancy went to the bathroom, got the Advil from the medicine cabinet, and went to the kitchen. It took her a few minutes to pulverize the pills with the back of a spoon. Even after she stirred the crushed pills in the water for a long time, they didn't dissolve completely. She twisted a sliver of lemon peel into the glass and she took the drink to the hallway.

Birdie was gone.

Well, that was typical Birdie. Nancy carried the glass back to the kitchen and poured the water into the sink. When she raised her head, she saw the reflection of something moving in the window before her.

She jumped and turned.

Ghostly little Eugenia was standing in the doorway.

"I'm hungry," she said.

nine

dress plainly, accessorize extravagantly

"*W*hat are you doing here?" Nancy asked.

"Mama said stay. I'm hungry."

"Where's your mommy?"

"She went away."

Nancy took the child's puny hand and led her to the entry hall. She opened the door and looked out. No one was there. She returned to the living room and saw an exquisite caramel leather overnight bag and a pink Little Mermaid backpack by her writing table.

"Love your bags, but *no*," Nancy said.

"No food?"

"No, you can't stay. What's your mother's phone number?"

The child scrunched her face in thought.

"I'll get you some milk." Nancy went into the kitchen and poured milk into a mug. The drink looked boring and unappealing. She added a few tablespoons of Italian almond syrup, frothed it up with her espresso machine's foamer, and sprinkled the drink with Ghirardelli chocolate.

When she returned to the living room, the girl was sitting on the floor.

Nancy said, "You can't drink it here. You'll spill. Come sit at the table." She led the girl to the eighteenth-century French mahogany table, a birthday present from her mother. Placing the mug on a coaster, Nancy said, "Be careful. I'm going to make a phone call."

Nancy went to her bedroom, but left the door open so she could hear if Eugenia dropped the mug. She called her mother first. "Mom!"

"Hello, Nanny Goat. I heard your party went well."

"Yes, and I would love to tell you all about it, but Birdie just showed up with her little girl."

"At the party?"

"No, at my place today. She said she was going out to dinner and asked for a glass of water. When I came back, she'd left Eugenia here. Do you have Birdie's phone number, or know where she's staying?"

"No." After a few seconds, Hester said, "I don't see why you can't take care of her until Birdie comes back from dinner."

"She went 'out to dinner' with her new Greek lover and she left the girl and her luggage, including a to-die-for overnighter the color of melted toffee."

"You always need to carry so many things when you have children. I'm sure Birdie will be back soon."

"We *are* talking about Birdie. Birdie, who considers her profession to be an artist's muse, which is just another way of saying—"

"Nanny! There is no reason to be vulgar. Just call your aunt Frilly and ask for Birdie's phone number. You have such *issues* with children, as though you'd never been one. It's no wonder that your marriage . . ."

Nancy could hear the quiver in her mother's voice. "Mom, I'll talk to you later. Love you."

She quickly called her aunt Phillipa, aka Aunt Frilly, who lived in Santa Barbara. "Hello, Aunt Frilly."

"Hello, Nanny, how nice to hear from you! Birdie was just asking about you, and I told her you were at the Château."

"Actually, I'm calling about Birdie. Would you please give me her phone number?"

"As soon as I get it, I will. She said she needed a new phone because she dropped the last one in an ice bucket."

"Why am I not surprised? I really, really need to talk to her now. Where is she staying?"

"What has she done now?"

"She left Eugenia here and took off for dinner without saying anything! Do you think she's coming back after dinner?"

"Your guess is as good as mine. Aren't you *lucky* to have a chance to spend time with your niece!"

"Technically, she's my cousin's daughter."

"That's not a very nice attitude, Nanny. When I took you out with Sissy and people thought I was your mother, I was so proud. I never said that *technically* you weren't my daughter, because the love was there."

"It's not . . . Oh, all right, I'll watch my *niece* for a few hours."

"That's very sweet of you! Yes, you keep her and I'm sure

that Birdie will be back soon! You're a good girl, Nanny, no matter what everyone says. Bye!"

"But Aunt Frilly—" Nancy said to the dead line.

It was okay. She was Nancy Carrington-Chambers, a woman who could put together highly detailed plans to entertain the most demanding. Surely she could watch over a child for two hours.

Nancy went to the dining room and saw the empty mug beside the coaster. "Eugenia!" she called, and went to the living room. The little girl had opened the leather case and was pulling out the contents.

"Eugenia, you forgot to use the coaster. What are you doing?"

"I want my cape." The girl took out children's picture books, a plastic dinosaur, one tiny plastic sandal, and clothes garishly emblazoned with cartoon characters.

"You don't need a cape. We're going for a quick dinner. Put those things away neatly while I clean up the disaster you left on my table."

Nancy cleared off the mug, and then wiped and buffed the table with a soft cloth and lemon oil. She lowered her head so that her eyes were level with the tabletop to make sure that the luster was even. Satisfied, she got a lightweight black coat and went to check on the child.

Eugenia had done a pathetically inadequate job of repacking the bag. She had placed a red terry-cloth towel over her shoulders and a paper crown on her head. "Will you tie my cape?" she said, clutching at the ribbons that had been safety-pinned to two corners of the towel.

"That is certainly some ensemble, Eugenia. You don't need the cape. As Coco Chanel said, when you're about to leave the house, remove one accessory. In your case, I would say remove two, that crown and the cape. You can borrow one of my shawls. Any color you want!"

Nancy plucked the paper crown from the girl's head and tried to remember where she'd packed away her collection of pashminas, assuming that they would eventually come back into fashion. As she reached for the towel, she saw panic in the child's eyes.

"No, no, I need my cape!" Eugenia whined. Her lower lip pouted, and she twisted away protectively.

Nancy wasn't in the mood for a struggle, so she said, "Fine, wear your 'cape.'" She bent over and tied the ribbons together. "What are you supposed to be? A clown?"

"Clowns are scary."

"Wiser words were never spoken. There's nothing more terrifying than deliberately bad hair and outlandish shoes." Nancy stood and said, "Let's go."

When the girl just stood there, Nancy reluctantly reached for her hand. It was so small, warm, and moist, like a little animal paw. Nancy thought it was probably teeming with bacteria. She led the child down the stairs and out of the building.

It was still early evening and urbanites were out with their offspring, children dressed and groomed as if they were going off to photo shoots that involved SUVs and Labradors. Nancy preferred children in magazines to the tantrum-throwing, nose-picking, noisome three-dimensional versions.

Nancy thought of the least popular restaurants in the neighborhood. "Eugenia, do you like noodles or muffins?"

"I like donuts."

"Of course you do." Nancy walked on, trying to look as if she was not actually connected to the child whose hand she was holding. She took Eugenia to the chain coffee shop that was reviled by all but the most rusticated tourists.

Only a few items remained on the crumb-laden aluminum trays in the display cases. Out of nowhere, Nancy felt a sense of responsibility. "You can have an apple turnover. It has fruit, and children need fruit."

"I want that." Eugenia stabbed her finger against the glass case, pointing at a muffin studded with chocolate chips.

"Okay, but only because this is a special treat. Don't think that I approve of this sort of food."

"Yes?" asked the impatient clerk.

"Two chocolate chip muffins, one carton of milk, and what kinds of coffee do you have?"

"Caf or decaf."

"Caf, please," Nancy said, feeling the thrill of slumming.

The clerk put the muffins on beige Buffalo china saucers and poured coffee into a matching cup.

After Nancy paid, they sat at a wobbly Formica table and Nancy took two thin paper napkins from the metal dispenser. She opened the milk carton and put the straw in it for Eugenia.

"Isn't this lovely!" she said. "Put your napkin on your lap, Eugenia. How old are you?"

The girl lifted one hand, smeared with chocolate, and made a clawlike gesture.

"Three?" Nancy guessed. She took a sip of coffee and immediately regretted it. She put a paper napkin to her mouth and surreptitiously spit the alleged coffee into it.

Eugenia said, "I'm almost five."

Ah, the gesture was her attempt at "half." "Wipe your mouth, please. Where are you and your mother staying? At a hotel?"

"Mommy stays with Yannis. We stay at the airport."

"You came *from* the airport, but you don't *stay* there. Where do you sleep?"

The question puzzled the girl. "Grammie has a room for me with a big bed and pictures of fairies."

Nancy smiled. "That's where I sleep when I visit your grandmother. Those paintings of ballerinas are by a painter named Edgar Degas. I used to want to be a ballerina. Then I wanted to be a fairy princess."

"Like Tinkerbell?" The girl wiped at her mouth with her napkin, smearing chocolate over her face.

"Yes, like Tinkerbell and like Glinda, the good witch in *The Wizard of Oz.*"

"You look like Tinkerbell. I like living at Grammie's, but Grammie was crying and Yannis called her a bad name, so Mommy took me away and said I could stay with you."

Nancy thought the word "stay" was ominously inexact. And why hadn't Aunt Frilly told her about the argument?

The girl brightened and said, "Mommy said you have a pony."

"I do! His name is Willoughby and he lives at my parents' house." Willoughby was a handsome and untrustworthy miniature horse that Nancy had gotten in high school. "I have a cart for him and we ride around a little track and I wear a wide-brimmed straw bonnet and hold a pretty whip of silk ribbons."

"I saw a cow. Her name was Lulu and she had spots. Can I see your pony?"

"You can meet him the next time your mommy takes you to visit my mother and father. Willoughby lives in a little stable and has his own corral. He has a luxurious long black-and-white mane and tail." Nancy had wanted to build a small stable and paddock for the pony at her house, but Todd said no. Just because Willoughby had bitten him once or twice.

Eugenia said, "I want a pony."

"Really?" Nancy was about to offer her the pet when she realized how unlikely it was that Birdie would settle down anywhere long enough to raise an animal. "Maybe you'll get one someday." Nancy sorted through her berry-colored patchwork bag and took out a packet of verbena-scented towelettes. Reaching over, she wiped the girl's mouth and then her hands.

"That smells good," said Eugenia as Nancy wiped her own hands.

"Yes, it does. Little girls and big girls should smell nice. Boys can be stinky and dirty."

Eugenia's laugh startled Nancy. It was a pretty little laugh, a child's version of Birdie's.

"We better get back in case your mother wonders where we are."

"Mommy said to stay with you, Auntie Nanny."

"Yes, I know. But we have to be ready when she comes back."

"I have to go to the bathroom."

"Okay." Nancy saw a sign for the restrooms. "It's back there."

"You have to come with me."

"You are very high maintenance." Nancy walked the girl to the back of the building and the unisex bathroom. She issued several "ewws" as she used a paper towel to lower the seat and then placed two seat covers on the seat. "You should never sit directly on the seats," she advised. "Full of gross cooties."

Nancy looked away politely as the girl used the toilet. "Wash your hands with soap and hot water for as long as it takes you to count to thirty."

"I can count to ten."

"Count to ten three times, then," Nancy said, but Eugenia could not grasp simple mathematical concepts.

Nancy held the girl's hot little paw as they headed back toward Château Winkles. They were near a posh children's boutique when Nancy spotted Junie Burns coming out with a floppy-haired boy wearing a blazer and slacks. Junie was carrying several shopping bags and chatting with the boy.

If Junie saw her with this tiny fashion disaster, she would lose all respect for Nancy. Nancy hefted Eugenia up so that the girl's body hid her, and the red towel covered her face. She walked blindly ahead, and when Nancy thought they must be safe, Eugenia cried, "Watch out, Auntie Nanny!"

Nancy peeked from behind the towel just as she was about to collide with an elderly woman. "Oh, sorry!"

At the moment that Nancy's face was visible, Junie said, "Nancy!"

Nancy smiled and put the child down. "Oh, hi, Junie."

Junie was dressed in a tailored gray pin-striped pantsuit. She and the boy stared with open curiosity at Eugenia.

"Junie, this is my cousin's daughter, Eugenia. And your little friend . . ." She flashed a smile while looking at the prep school crest on his jacket.

"This is Fielding, my nephew," Junie said, her slight voice almost blown away by the evening breeze. "We were just shopping for his little sister. What have you been doing?"

"We ate donuts," Eugenia misinformed Junie. "Auntie Nanny spit out her coffee and she has a whip."

"Really?" Junie said as she bent closer to the child. "What a bright cape. Did Auntie Nanny make that for you?"

"No. Yannis took it from the hotel. He's Mama's new bed-friend and he has a beard and paints pichers of her fanny."

"Really!"

Fielding frowned and said, "My father says that stealing from a hotel is wrong."

"Your father sounds like a charming man," Nancy said to the nascent bore. "Junie, it's crazy that we haven't been able to get together."

"I know! I'm going back to the office after I take Fielding to his oboe lesson. But I'll call you as soon as I have a free moment. I'm so *concerned* about you, especially with that photo going around."

The friendly fire caught Nancy by surprise. "What photo?"

"The one from Gigi's party of you collapsing," she said. "Oh my God, I can't believe you haven't seen it! Lizette sent it to me because she was so worried. Bill saw it on some site about, um, the city's party girls."

Nancy could have asked what Bill was doing on a party-girl website, but Sun Tzu had advised that victory was more important than protracted battle. "Oh, *that* photo! My publicist said that I need to be edgier to promote Froth. I was skeptical. How fabulous that it's being circulated."

"So it was planted?"

"Please don't tell anyone," Nancy said with a smile. "It's really ludicrous to pretend to be naughty, but it gives a girl cachet. Like that rumor about me and Lizette."

"What rumor about you and Lizette?"

"Between us, that's only part of the image branding," Nancy said. "Although I do think she's pretty and if I was going to, well . . . So wonderful to see you!"

"Oh," Junie said, looking confused, while her puritanical ward shifted from foot to foot impatiently.

Nancy smiled. "My cousin will be coming by at any moment to pick up Eugenia, so we've got to dash. Ciao!" She took Eugenia's hand and hurried down the street. She had to find that photo and see if there was any way of figuring out who had taken it and how to get rid of it.

Halfway back, Eugenia said, "I'm tired."

"It's only a little ways more," Nancy said, but the child was lagging behind. "You shouldn't be tired. You're young. You should be bursting with energy."

"I didn't get my nap and last night Yannis and Mama kept yelling. My feet are sweaty."

"Horses sweat, men perspire, and ladies merely glow." Nancy felt as if she was towing the child, whose steps got slower and slower. "All right, I'll carry you, but only this time because it's a special occasion."

Nancy lifted the girl. She seemed very heavy for such a small person. The tiny, hot arms around Nancy's neck were choking her. Once they got to Château Winkles, Nancy said, "You have to walk up the stairs by yourself. Walking up stairs has all sorts of health and beauty benefits, which is why I always use stairs."

The child stared at the steps and gripped Nancy's neck tighter.

Nancy loudly exhaled and said, "Fine, we'll take the elevator, but only because it's a special occasion."

Once inside the apartment, she looked at the clock. Einstein was so right about the relativity of time. One hour with Eugenia had seemed like five.

Nancy set the girl down on the sofa, and Eugenia flopped over bonelessly. Nancy put her hands on her hips and waited until she'd caught her breath. "Your posture is abominable. Let's get these shoes off."

When Nancy pulled off the galoshes she saw that the plastic shoes had rubbed large angry blisters on Eugenia's bare feet. "You see, that's why you should always buy the best shoes you can. It isn't just looks—it's the comfort and fit you get from well-made . . ."

The girl curled up and closed her eyes.

Nancy untied the cape and then got a comforter and a pillow from the hall closet. By the time she put the pillow under the girl's head, Eugenia was asleep.

Nancy sat down at her computer and did a search for "Nancy Chambers party girl." She found the photo on a site called "Decline and Fall-Down of the Rich Bitches."

She felt sick when she saw the photo. She looked like a beat-up smack addict taking a tumble, with one pink butt cheek visible in the shot. The heading said, "How the mighty (stuck-up) have fallen! Nancy Carrington-Chambers in the dumps after being dumped by hawt hubby on the grounds of felony skankitude."

It was awful, awful, and Nancy didn't know what to do. She stared at the sea green wall, overtaken by panic. Then a noise startled her. It was Eugenia shifting in her sleep. Nancy thought that when Birdie returned, she'd probably shove the galoshes back on the child's feet and drag her out.

The sleeping girl barely flinched when Nancy used a sterilized needle to pierce the blisters. She drained them with cotton balls, dabbed antiseptic ointment on them, and then put Band-Aids over them. She tucked the comforter around the child.

Nancy's phone rang and she ran to it, hoping it was Birdie. Her friend Milagro said, "Nancy, that photo."

"Oh, God, has everyone seen it?"

"Gigi told me about it when I went over to redo her garden urns. She was totally lusting after your assistant, and she thought the photo was funny."

"Gigi is not stealing Derek away, and the photo is so *not* funny! I'm the object of pity and disdain. Pisdain."

"Lighten up, Nancy-pantyless. Who's going to believe that you're a hoochie-mama? You are the antithesis of hoochieness."

"You make me sound like a priss. I'm not a priss. I talk about sex all the time."

"Yes, you *talk* about sex, the same way that I talk about *Ulysses.* I always intend to get around to it."

"I ran into Junie Burns and she was shocked by it."

"I'm shocked she even read it."

"The photo, not *Ulysses.*"

"Junie Rug-Burns Butt, gawd. I never trust women who speak with wittle, teeny baby voices. It's inherently manipulative because it makes the listener work too hard, and Junie Rug-Burns Butt never has anything interesting to say."

"I never should have told you that nickname. You hate all my friends."

"Sloane's okay and GP's delightfully geeky. You know I like Gigi," Milagro said. "Considering the nudity on Rich Bitches, no one's going to pay much attention to a photo of a thong shot, even with a cute little-boy butt like yours."

"Thank you for caring and sharing," Nancy said.

"You're welcome. Night beckons, Nancikins, so I must go out and shake my groove thing."

* * *

Nancy hoped that Milagro was right and the photo wouldn't draw much attention.

While waiting for Birdie, Nancy watched *Roman Holiday* with one of her heroines, Audrey Hepburn, on the flat-screen that was hidden behind a mirror.

Usually Nancy was able to study Edith Head's costume design, but tonight she was distracted by the plot: a beautiful young princess escapes her repressive entourage and has an adventure in Rome with a gorgeous reporter who hides his identity from her. Eventually, the princess comes to her senses and returns to her royal life. Well, it was sort of sad, but a princess obviously couldn't stay with a commoner no matter how fabulous he was. Who wanted to be a dull "Mrs." when she could be a splendid "Your Majesty"?

Nancy tried to shake off her uneasiness by watching another Audrey movie, *Sabrina*. The story was preposterous, a chauffeur's daughter falls in with an heir, but the costumes were gorgeous, especially Givenchy's exquisite white gown with black floral embroidery.

When the movie was over, midnight had arrived, but Birdie had not. Nancy tried not to overreact. Birdie kept late hours. She would come tomorrow to get her daughter. Nancy felt odd leaving the girl on her own in the living room, so she changed into her monogrammed silk pajamas, curled up in the corner of the sofa, and pulled the comforter over herself.

Eugenia woke up once in the middle of the night and called out, "Mama?"

"No, it's your auntie Nanny. Go back to sleep."

The girl turned around and snuggled up to Nancy. It was a very uncomfortable way to spend the night.

ten

dress like a pirate for fun and profit

*N*ancy had finally fallen asleep when a noise disturbed her. She ignored it and kept her eyes shut.

"Good morning, Mrs. Carrington-Chambers. I rang at the front door, but there was no response."

Derek stood in front of her, the shoulder strap of a black leather messenger bag over his shoulder, with no indication that the situation was in any way different than any other morning. "Shall I return later?"

Seeing him there, so composed and handsome, reassured Nancy. "Is it nine already? I have to get up." She looked over and saw that Eugenia was gazing at Derek. Nancy said, "Derek, this is my cousin's— This is my niece, Eugenia. Eugenia, this is Derek."

"Hi," the child said.

"Good morning, Miss Eugenia."

"Derek is my assistant," Nancy said. "He's going to make coffee while we get dressed."

"I'm already dressed," the girl said. "Will you tie my cape?"

"You're going to change into clean clothes, brush your teeth, and wash your face and hands. We'll discuss the cape after you do that." Nancy looked at Derek. "Would you please make cappuccinos for us and steamed milk with honey for Eugenia?"

She took the girl's bags to the bedroom and as she went through the garments, Nancy imagined the oily polyester content coating her hands. She was deeply offended by the blatant product placement for animated movies and toys. Human beings should not be used as walking billboards.

Nancy picked out plain underwear and a lilac sweatshirt and pants as the least offensive of all outfits.

"Why don't you have any real shoes?" she asked Eugenia.

"They're at Grammie's. Mama said we can't go back."

Nancy would have to have a talk with Aunt Frilly. "Just wear your socks while you're inside," she said as Eugenia examined the Band-Aids on her feet.

It took Nancy an eternity to wrangle Eugenia's body into the clothes, help her brush her teeth, and scrub her face and hands with a washcloth. The girl's fine brownish hair was impossible to manage, but Nancy combed out most of the tangles.

Nancy grabbed a pair of jeans and a stretchy peach top and got ready as fast as was humanly possible when one included a three-step skin regime and four attempts to enliven curls.

When she went to the kitchen, Eugenia was sitting on a

stool and watching Derek. Her red towel had been tied around her thin neck. Nancy made eye contact with Derek and he smiled, but there was an apprehensive expression on his face that she'd never seen before.

"Where's my breakfast?" Eugenia asked.

"You've got it," Nancy said.

"Grammie says I should eat a real breakfast, not fish eggs."

"Fish eggs are full of protein," Nancy said. "No fat, low cholesterol. They're the perfect breakfast food." She had a jar of domestic caviar that she'd picked up at the Ferry Building. "Would you like some?"

The girl shook her head.

Derek said, "Many children eat porridge for breakfast. We brought back a bin of assorted cereals from Ms. Barton's event. It's in the pantry."

"Really?" Nancy opened the pantry door and spotted the clear plastic bin with boxes of Count Chocula, Froot Loops, and Cinnamon Toast Crunch.

Eugenia's dull brown eyes widened at the sugar-coated glory of it all. When she was happily crunching and slurping her breakfast, Nancy pulled Derek to the living room.

"My cousin Birdie left her here last night and I have no idea when she's coming back," she said. "Birdie is not conventional."

"That is rather a sticky wicket, madame."

"Don't I know it? Will you watch Eugenia while I make some phone calls to see if I can locate her mother?"

Derek looked as if he was fighting the urge to bolt out the front door. "Madame, this is not my area of expertise."

"How hard can it be? She doesn't seem to need much beyond food and sleep and the occasional trip to the bathroom.

That would be loo, for you. No, you don't have to do that. I'll be in my bedroom if you need help."

He nodded and straightened his shoulders. "It's only a child."

"Exactly. But we should probably say 'she,' not it."

"Of course. *She*," he practiced. "She won't stay here long?"

"Good Lord, no! What would I do with a child? No, this is absolutely a very brief interlude. Practically an intermission at the opera when you're glad you preordered your cocktail because it goes by so quickly."

Nancy went to the bedroom and closed the door. The first call she made was to her personal attorney, Renee, who was in a meeting. Nancy left a message on Renee's voice mail saying that she needed to know if a photo online was actionable. "Also, I'm living at my apartment for a few months to work on Froth, my business, and figure out things about my marriage."

Then she called both Aunt Frilly's home phone and cell phone. She left messages to call back immediately vis-à-vis young persons who had been left on her doorstep.

Nancy called her mother, who didn't answer either. She began to think there was a vast family conspiracy to ignore her. In desperation, she phoned Birdie's sister, her favorite cousin, Sissy, who was a clothing designer.

Sissy answered on the first ring. "Hi, honey," she said. "Wazzup?"

"Sissy, no one says that since the nineties. Your sister . . ."

"I have no sister."

"I'm loving that you've denounced her so biblically, but I don't have time to squibble. Birdie came over last night and left her offspring here. In my apartment. And luggage, too, including a really gorgeous overnight case, and no word when she will return."

"Is it a caramel leather Prada? Because she stole the one that my father gave to me as a Valentine's Day present. If I never see Birdie again, it will be too soon."

"Sissy, are you still whining about that boyfriend?"

"He was my *fiancé*, Nanny! And he wasn't the only one. She sexed up every guy who ever showed the slightest interest in me. She is a nasty, selfish, horrible slut."

"To be fair, she always looks fabulous," Nancy said. "She was wearing a beautifully draped Halston dress—"

"At any other time, I would love to talk about the dramatic doings at Halson. Don't be one of my sister's casualties. Birdie lures people in, uses them, and by the time she tosses them aside, they're blithering, bitter, and broken."

"Thank you for the alliteration. Now, will you come get Eugenia, or should I drop her off at your atelier, or do you want to meet somewhere else? The de Young has a new show and we can lunch at the café."

"D, none of the above. Don't get attached to that kid."

"Sissy, what kind of crack are you smoking? Eugenia's an amuse-bouche of badness. Her conversational skills are abysmal, she doesn't make up in charm what she unfortunately lacks in appearance, and she's got a disturbing fixation on cows. She wears towels out in public. Is she all *right*? If you know what I mean, because on your side of the family there's your aunt Gert . . ."

"Leave Aunt Gert out of it. You made the mistake of letting Birdie into your apartment, so you keep Eugenia."

"When did you become so heartless, Sissy? I'm sure your mother will be obliterated to know what you've said about your own flesh and blood. She's very devoted to the responsibilities of family."

"My mother? Who do you think told Birdie that you could take care of Eugenia?"

"But . . ."

"I can't talk about this anymore, Nanny. My sister is so toxic that I need to schedule extra appointments with my therapist and kinesiologist whenever she makes an appearance."

"But . . ."

"Consider it your way of compensating for use of *our* apartment at the Château," Sissy said resentfully, because she had tried to get the apartment when Nancy got married. "Oh, and that picture of you online is hilarious. I sent it to all my friends. Bye!"

Nancy went to the living room and found Eugenia lying on the floor looking through one of her picture books. Derek was reading a paperback. He looked up expectantly as she came in and said, "I brought back your notebook. It's on your writing table."

"Thank you, Derek," Nancy said. "Isn't everyone busy? See how fabulously we all get along? What are you reading, Derek?"

He closed the book and held the cover for her to see. "*The Barbary Coast* by Herbert Asbury. Mr. GP recommended it very highly and I purchased a copy last night. It's a fascinating history."

"No need for you to read it since GP already knows about it. I'm meeting with the warehouse leasing agent this afternoon, and I'll be drafting my budget, although it all depends on whether GP can get the sets and costumes," she said. "Eugenia, you study your books."

"Can we go to the park?" It was obvious the girl had no work ethic.

"Today is a workday and I have very important things to plan for a very big party—with pirates," Nancy said.

Derek looked puzzled and said, "There were no pirates . . ."

"The cook we met yesterday, Aldo, gave me the idea. We're using our artistic license to create a postmodern oceanic environment—with pirates!"

He raised one eyebrow and said, "It is a universal dream to dress like a pirate."

"It's so true. Write that in the 'Theory of Style,'" Nancy said. "We can discuss pirates in fashion, like Vivienne Westwood's seminal Pirate Collection."

"I like pirates," Eugenia said. "Let me do something."

Nancy hated to turn down help, even if it was child labor. "Can you write?"

"I know my numbers and ABCs almost."

"Do you know how to use scissors?"

"I have scissors with my markers!" the girl said excitedly.

"Excellent. Fetch your scissors."

As the girl ran to the bedroom, Nancy took her least favorite issues of magazines from a shelf. "I was going to donate these to a homeless women's shelter because it seems that they need style more than anyone else, but this is critical," she told Derek.

When Eugenia returned with a purple plastic pencil case, Nancy set her at the mercury glass–topped cocktail table with the magazines, a poster board, and a glue stick. "I need you to cut out pictures that are good for pirates. Piratey colors and piratey clothes. Like Captain Hook and Jack Sparrow. Can you do that?"

The girl nodded solemnly. "Is Captain Crunch a pirate?"

"Possibly. When you've got enough pictures, you can glue them into a collage. Do you know what a collage is?"

"Pichers glued together?"

"Pic-tures," Nancy corrected. "Yes, but in an interesting and creative way."

When Eugenia was thus occupied, Nancy called Derek into the hall and said, "Something has happened and I need a dispassionate opinion on whether I'm overreacting."

"Something concerning the child?"

"She's a temporary problem. This is far worse. Someone posted a hateful photo of me from Gigi's party and called me a slut!"

"Anyone who was at the party knows you behaved with the utmost propriety," he said soothingly. "I'm sure it can't be as bad as you say. Let's look at it together."

They went to Nancy's writing table and she showed him the ghastly photo. "You see? Why would someone do that to me?"

Derek tilted his head as if examining the photo from another angle would improve it. "Oh, madame," he said, and then turned his face away.

"Are you laughing?" she asked, just as he laughed aloud.

When he stopped he said, "I regret my inappropriate response, but"—he started laughing again and pointed to the laptop screen—"your expression!"

Nancy looked at the photo again and saw her widened eyes, ringed like a raccoon, her mouth open, her arm flailing, and her lopsided hair. "Okay, so it's a little funny, but why would someone post it?"

"Madame, everyone who lives an enviable life is subject to

envy. But you are almost fully clothed, unlike the other ladies on this site, who are, please excuse the term, slags."

"What should I do?"

His clear, dark eyes looked into hers and said, "Princess Di faced vicious scuttlebutt and carried on with grace. Ignore it."

Soon after, Nancy's attorney called and advised her to do the same thing.

So they'd all been working in very companionable silence for at least five minutes when Derek realized that Eugenia should also be cutting out pictures of water and boats, and Nancy thought they all needed another hot drink, and Derek asked if he could have a bowl of cereal.

Nancy found number-crunching very absorbing and before she knew it, it was almost noon. She looked up and saw that Eugenia was asleep on the sofa and there were paper scraps scattered on the table and on the floor. Eugenia had glued cutouts of the letter *E* on her sweatshirt.

"At least she knows one letter of the alphabet," Nancy said. "It's terrifying how utterly incompetent the young are."

"Do you have any notion when her mother will return?" Derek said quietly.

"She could show up at any minute." Nancy wondered if she had the same worried look in her eyes as Derek. "Or maybe not at all. I don't know. Why Birdie left Eugenia here is an igloo wrapped in a quibble inside a condominium."

"Mrs. Carrington-Chambers, perhaps you should engage a nanny in the interim. I will call a service and . . ."

Nancy looked at the sleeping girl and thought of how Birdie had shuttled her around and deposited her with strangers. "It's probably too early to declare defeat."

What would it be like if Nancy returned to Todd and had the grimy Toddlings he desired? She thought of their bad personal hygiene and selfish natures. Her eyes welled with the idea that the world would be so unfair.

Derek stood and went to her. "Mrs. Carrington-Chambers?"

She wiped at her eyes, careful not to smudge her mascara. "I'm sorry that I'm such a mess today. I understand if you want to leave. I'd be happy to give you a reference and I know you'll find another job faster than you can say cheerio. Cheerio, the greeting, not the cereal."

He stared at the diminutive creature snoring softly on the sofa. "I know nothing of them. They don't seem entirely human."

"No, and their proportions are wrong. Their torsos and arms are long and they have stubby legs. And they're very, very self-centered."

"One can hardly hear one's own thoughts for all their prattling."

"They're messy. Look how she's destroyed my apartment."

"One can't reason with them. They ask *why* incessantly."

"You can't go out and have fun if you've got to worry about them," Nancy said. "No wonder her mother dumps her off at every opportunity."

As soon as the words were out of her mouth, Nancy heard how heartless she must sound. "Not that there's anything wrong with children per se."

"Not at all," Derek quickly said. "I think that the problem may largely lie with overindulgent upbringing, such as with dogs that are coddled."

"You may have something there. If one had total control of a child's environment, a child might be reasonably civilized." She looked into Derek's eyes. "What do you want to do, Derek?"

He thought for agonizing seconds before speaking. "We mustn't act hastily. Her mother will surely return soon. That is most natural to a mother, isn't it?" he said. "Of course, I shall stay here to assist you in any way you need and we can reassess the situation as it changes."

Nancy was so happy that she threw her arms around him. "Thank you! Thank you!"

And then she felt his arms go around her. "There, there, Mrs. Carrington-Chambers. You can rely upon me."

She felt marvelous there in his arms, enjoying this idyllic platonic relationship between a young woman and a gay man, both possessing excellent taste and similar outlooks. She leaned closer into him, inhaling his wonderful, fresh scent.

He dropped his face close to hers and said, "Your hair is so soft."

She thought she felt his lips grazing her ear when her phone rang and they jumped apart. Eugenia sat up and rubbed her eyes with her fists.

Nancy answered without looking to see who was calling. "Birdie?"

"I'll be a birdie, if you want me to," said a familiar gravelly voice. "I've been called worse."

"Oh, Bailey! I thought you were my cousin."

"Ah, the infamous Birdie," he said. "I don't think I've ever met her. Was she at your wedding?"

"If you met her, you'd remember."

"I'm holding you to your promise to go out with me. Are you free Saturday? I thought we could have dinner and see a show, or go to a club. Whatever you like."

Nancy glanced at Eugenia, who was walking in a circle, waving her arms, and singing to herself. Something was *wrong* with that child. "I think I'll be available, but I may have a commitment. Can I give you a call tomorrow?"

"If I have to wait, I suppose I have to wait. Don't think I do it for anyone else, Nancy."

Nancy walked into the hallway with the phone. "If I go out with you, it's as your friend only."

"Are you sure it's not a date?"

"I'm positive."

"You're wounding me."

She laughed and said, "Talk to you soon."

"Bye, beautiful."

Nancy savored the moment, smiling to herself. Birdie would come back, and she would be free to go out with Bailey and people would see them and know that Nancy Carrington-Chambers absolutely *should* be invited to their wine country weekends.

When she returned to the living room, Derek said, "You look happy. Good news?"

"Bailey Whiteside wants to take me to dinner on Saturday. Do you remember him from Gigi's party?"

"The chap in red undergarments? Yes."

"When I go out with him, someone prominent, people will see that the tawdry gossip about me is meaningless." She cast a glance at Eugenia, who was staring at her. "I'm sure I'll be available by then."

"Miss Eugenia has expressed a desire for lunch."

"But she just ate this morning. Eugenia, are you hungry *again?*"

"I didn't get my snack. At the farm they always gave us pumkin bread and orange juice."

"*Pump*-kin. That sounds terrifying. Pumpkins should

only be eaten between October thirty-first and Thanksgiving. They're orange and orange is the color of insanity."

"Do you really think so?" Derek asked.

"Well, the alternate theory is that violet is the color of insanity, but violet is a very flattering color for my complexion." To the child, Nancy said, "Can't you just eat another bowl of cereal?"

Eugenia plucked at her shirt in a way that was both pathetic and annoying.

"Mrs. Carrington-Chambers, I could go to the market and fetch some provisions for lunch, if you like. I could join Eugenia in a nosh."

Nancy realized that he'd been skipping lunch while he worked for her. "And you've been living off coffee with me."

"Excellent coffee and an impressive array of water."

"I guess that isn't enough for a man of your build."

Derek shook his head. "Both men and children need sustenance. And, if you will permit me to say so, you might benefit from an occasional meal so you can keep up your busy schedule."

"Let's all go out for lunch then."

"And the park?" Eugenia asked hopefully.

"You have a very idle disposition," Nancy said. "Yes, we can go to the park, because it's a special occasion. You can't wear that cape. Why did you glue paper to your top?"

"I want to wear my cape."

A battle of wills ensued. Nancy tried to follow Sun Tzu's strategic advice, but the child's maneuvers were unpredictable and irrational. Finally, Nancy said to Derek, "You convince her."

Derek thought for a moment before reaching into his pocket and pulling out a coin. "See here, Miss Eugenia, I will give you a shiny penny if you leave the cape here. You may put it on when we return."

Eugenia stared at the penny and then said, "It's not very shiny."

Derek shrugged and said to Nancy, "She's very contrary."

"That's it? That's your attempt at convincing her? Don't you have any secret Mary Poppins techniques?"

"I shall try again," he said, and turned to the girl. "Miss Eugenia, if you do not take off that towel right now, there will be no pudding for you tonight."

To Nancy's amazement, the girl considered the threat.

"Chocolate pudding?"

"Yes, chocolate pudding. Chocolate of some sort," Nancy said, and Eugenia permitted her to untie the towel. "Let's change your top."

"No."

"You've made a mess of it."

"It's pretty," Eugenia said, patting the magazine cutouts.

Nancy did a quick assessment and realized that the company of one Derek would more than balance out the presence of one Eugenia. "Fine. Let's go to lunch."

"And the park," Eugenia reminded her.

Nancy put another pair of socks on the girl so the red boots wouldn't slip on her feet, and then they walked to the shops. They went to a corner bistro and were given a table by the window. Nancy sat beside Derek so they could talk, and Eugenia sat across the table. Nancy handed her a notebook and pen and said, "Draw dresses and shoes."

Then Nancy looked out the window. "It's astonishing how many fashion crimes you can spot before your order is taken." Nancy saw a young man walking by and she said, "The faux-hawk, so over. That's how Todd does his hair when he goes out with his buddies. I always thought I could teach style.

But Todd actually *thinks* he has good taste. You're lucky that Prescott is so chic."

Derek smirked. It was a captivating smirk. "I face the problem of keeping up with his impeccable standards, but I borrow liberally from his wardrobe."

"That's why you're so happy together," she said, although she wondered who Mel was. "It's important to have the same sense of aesthetics and values. I should think about that for my 'Theory of Style.'"

"Are you certain that Mr. Chambers cannot learn from your finer judgment?"

"No, he's terrified that someone will think he's gay, and I don't see why. You don't have any problem with it."

Derek stared at the menu. "I think I'll have the grass-fed bison burger and *pommes frites*."

She laughed. "I'm glad you're speaking American now. Let's talk about Mrs. Friendly's party. Do you think everyone should wear period costumes? My instinct is no, except for the actors."

"I have a cape," Eugenia said.

"What have you drawn?"

"A pirate ship." Eugenia showed Nancy and Derek her drawing, which consisted of primitive rectangles with triangular shapes.

"Hmm, a deconstructionist approach."

Derek moved to Eugenia's side of the table and took a Rapidograph from his pocket. "Here," he said, and drew a grid of boxes with the fine black ink. "Draw a picture in each square and we'll add the captions, that is, the story, later about the pirates."

"Okay," Eugenia said, and Derek returned to his seat beside Nancy.

She smiled at him and said, "I'd like to hire a boat. We'll have everyone walk out to the pier after a few hours in the warehouse and then we'll give them a ride around the bay and have fireworks."

"Would you like me to find a suitable vessel for hire, madame?"

"That would be fab. We can have the crew dressed as pirates, I think."

Here she was a professional woman discussing exciting business plans with her fabulous assistant. Looking out the window, Nancy recognized a member of the ballet board. The woman glanced into the restaurant and Nancy waved hello. The woman turned her face away and kept walking.

The rebuke was as keen as a slap. "Did you see that?" Nancy murmured.

Derek's hand slipped under the table and rested just above her knee. He gave a gentle squeeze. "The window there reflects the street. I'd noted it myself as we came in."

She shook her head and laughed. "I must be getting paranoid. I'm imagining that everyone is out to get me."

He pulled his hand from her knee and said somberly, "It does no harm to err on the side of caution, madame, to guard yourself against those who might not have your best interests at heart."

"Do you mean Bailey? If we go out, it will be completely platonic, like the relationship we have," she said, and touched Derek's long, elegant hand. "Did you get a good look at him at the slumber party? He's very good-looking, don't you think?"

"I suppose women might find him so. He's not my cup of tea."

"You don't go for straight men?"

"I couldn't be less interested in them."

After lunch, they went to a chocolate café and bought *fleur de sel* chocolate cookies.

"That's not pudding," Eugenia observed.

"Pudding means dessert," Derek said. "Even a boiled sweet can be pudding."

On the way back to Château Winkles, Nancy paused in front of the children's store where she'd met Junie. She'd thought her friend would be thrilled to have her nearby, but maybe they'd get together when Junie had more time. Now Nancy looked at Eugenia's shoddy boots. "We'll just buy you some shoes," she said. "And some clothes that are not made with petrochemical by-products."

Derek paused at the door to the store, so Nancy added, "Why don't we meet in half an hour? That should be enough time."

When he came back thirty minutes later, Nancy was just coming out of the store with a shopping bag. "She *is* nieceish and I *have* missed her birthdays. Eugenia, do you like your new clothes?"

Eugenia was stepping carefully in a new pair of red tennis shoes, staring at each foot. "I like my red shoes. Can we go to the park now?"

"You are a monomaniac. Say 'Thank you, Aunt Nancy.'"

"Thank you, Auntie Nanny."

"Your mother can thank me properly when she returns," Nancy said, thinking that Birdie would show up that evening. "Yes, we'll go to the park. Consider it your first annual outing with your favorite aunt."

Eugenia seemed happy to clamber up and down the steep steps and she also liked petting the neighborhood dogs, allowed to run amuck despite the numerous ALL DOGS MUST BE ON LEASH signs.

Nancy and Derek enjoyed the views of the bay. They didn't talk much, just sat there in the sun and the fresh breeze. Something fluttered on a nearby shrub and Nancy said, "Look, a butterfly! I love butterflies, don't you? I'm always astonished that something so beautiful can exist."

"Indeed, madame," he said, and they watched the colorful insect before it flew away on the breeze.

Nancy said, "I love this city."

"I enjoy it more each time I visit."

"I thought you lived here permanently. With Prescott."

"Our paths take us apart for months at a time, but I am here for the foreseeable future."

She exhaled in relief. "So you successfully live apart and then come together again? Perhaps that's the key to a healthy relationship. I never thought it would be so hard to live with a man. My parents think I should compromise more with Todd."

"When one is cohabiting, compromise is necessary, Mrs. Carrington-Chambers."

"I like it when you call me that. It's like Mrs. Thatcher, a voice of authority."

"Or Mrs. Peel," Derek said.

"Who's that?"

"A character in an old telly show called *The Avengers*. She wore a skintight black leather, now, what is the word for it, a one-piece outfit?"

Nancy smiled. "I know that catsuit! John Bates designed it. He also created the miniskirt, even though most people think it was Mary Quant, and bare midriffs, see-through panels, and PVC dresses. He was a visionary."

"Did you study fashion, madame?"

"I wanted to, but my father refused to pay for fashion design school. He wanted someone to follow in his footsteps, and I was his last hope. My oldest sister, Blaire, is married and doing art history postdoc work in Germany, and Ellie is a vet in Boston. I studied economics."

"You could have done it without your father's money and survived on Pot Noodles like many students."

"I thought about it, but I realized that I have a talent for *appreciating* design, not for creating it. My cousin Sissy has real talent and she's starting her own clothing line," Nancy said. "My talent is knowing when something is beautiful and true. It calls to me. I recognized it when I saw you."

"You enjoy offering extravagant compliments, madame. No man could be worthy of such praise."

"I'm serious. It was different with my husband, because he's not *fabulous*," she admitted. "But everything else was so right about us. We were so popular together." She looked out toward the water, remembering sailing parties, first nights at the symphony, ski weeks at his family's lodge, tailgaters, weekends surrounded by friends.

"How did you come to plan parties, madame?"

"I was a financial analyst, but I was miserable being in a hideous office every day. I swear, the 'corporate art' used to taunt me. I used my wedding as an excuse to quit and found out that I loved planning events," she said, thinking of how happy she was to walk out of that office tower for the last time.

Derek seemed to be actually listening, so she said, "Something magical happens when the ambience is right and people are celebrating. It's momentary and elusive, but as glorious as a butterfly. I want to think that helping create that shared joy is important."

She smiled and said, "Then I got stuck in the House of Horrors and here I am. The short and dull history of Nancy Edith Carrington-Chambers. We'd better go or I'll be late for my meeting about the warehouse."

She and Derek collected Eugenia, who was throwing a ball to a slobbery Labrador, and they walked back to the apartment. Nancy set the girl on the sofa to watch a cartoon about a smart-aleck cow and said to Derek, "I know you'll manage beautifully while I'm gone."

"You are more confident than I, Mrs. Carrington-Chambers," he said with a look toward Eugenia.

"She seems to like you. Why shouldn't she? You're irresistible," Nancy said with a smile. "My opinion on these things is inflatable."

"Does Madame mean infallible?"

"No, inflatable, likely to swell."

"Things that swell are inclined to explode," he said. His mouth edged up a bit at the corner and she had a mad desire to kiss him.

She bit her lip and then said, "I'll rely upon you to make sure nothing does." She really needed to go out with a heterosexual man because this was the dirtiest conversation she'd had in years.

eleven

accentuate the positive

Nancy's meeting with the leasing agent went well. They negotiated until they found a rental rate and conditions that suited them both, but he was firm about a high insurance limit.

"I always get special events coverage in excess of any possible damage," Nancy assured him. "Not that you need to worry. I stringently control every detail of my parties."

She drove back to the Château hoping that Birdie had reappeared. Nancy wanted to celebrate with Derek—celebrate the job, the warehouse, surviving a day with a child.

She found him sitting with a sketch pad beside Eugenia, embellishing her drawings and saying, "If he's a boy, why is he a cow? He should be a bull."

"He gots an under and cows got unders. Dinosaurs don't got unders."

Nancy felt sorry that Derek had had to endure this blather. "Thanks for watching her. Birdie didn't come by or call?"

He shook his head and stood. "No, but Mr. GP called to say he was able to lease the sets and costumes under the projected sum, and he'll send you the logistics tomorrow. Was your meeting satisfactory?"

"Yes! Now that it's settled we can move on to the invitations, caterers, staging, la-la-la. Did you find a pirate ship?"

"I did. The information is on your desk. I'll be off then. I shall see you tomorrow, Mrs. Carrington-Chambers, Miss Eugenia."

Nancy didn't want him to leave her alone with Eugenia, but she couldn't think of any reason to make him stay. "Okay, I'll see you tomorrow! Bye."

"Bye, Derek," Eugenia said.

"Cheers then," he said, leaving Nancy alone with the strange small person.

It was just after five and the evening stretched out before her. "Eugenia, what time do you go to bed?"

"I'm not sleepy."

"Eugenia, you need to learn to answer the question you are asked. Does your mother make you go to bed after dinner?"

Eugenia considered the question. "Grammie says girls shouldn't go to grown-up night parties."

"Your grandmother is right. What do you do in the evenings?"

"Mama and her bed-friends go out."

Nancy sighed and tried again: "What do *you* do?"

"I like to stay with Rochelle."

"Who is Rochelle?"

"She brings the towels."

"Your mother leaves you with a hotel maid?"

"Rochelle can blow smoke in circles and she has a tattoo of a unicorn and rainbow on her tummy."

Nancy winced. "Stay here and watch television and I'll be in the kitchen."

Nancy went to the kitchen to call Aunt Frilly. She dialed repeatedly and her aunt finally picked up on the sixth call.

"Oh, Nancy, what a nice surprise to hear from you."

"Hi, Aunt Frilly, I was beginning to think you were avoiding me."

"I wouldn't do such a thing. You're my favorite niece."

"Your granddaughter is still here. If *someone* doesn't come get her, I might have to leave her at the animal shelter down the street."

"What a dreadful thing to say, Nanny!"

"It's not as dreadful as 'Birdie, you can dump your daughter off at Nancy's.'"

"Nanny, when you got married and Sissy wanted that apartment, I told her not to put up a fuss because I knew you'd need to get away from Todd now and then."

"Would you please repeat that because my ears couldn't have possibly heard what I thought they heard?"

"We love Todd, but he's a big frat boy, and you need your girl time. Think of the fun you'll have playing with Eugenia until Birdie comes back!"

Nancy closed her eyes and took a long, slow breath. A lady did not scream at her nicest aunt. "Do you know where Birdie is?"

"She mentioned Corfu, but she was arguing with that awful bearded man, and I don't think she'll make it to the airport without ending that relationship. Foreign men are much more attractive on foreign soils than at home. I'll call you the minute I hear from her."

Nancy panicked. "I'll bring Eugenia to you, Aunt Frilly!"

"I'm sorry, Nanny," Aunt Frilly said in a more serious tone. "Your uncle Robert gave one of his edicts about Birdie. I'll get him to change his mind soon, but in the meantime please watch Eugenia."

"I have things to do. I have a business to run."

"Can't you do this one thing for me? Please? If you do, I'll take you to Fashion Week."

"Which one?"

"How about New York with Sissy! We'll go to the show-rooms and the museums."

Nancy loved joining Aunt Frilly and Sissy on their fashion pilgrimages. "If I do this, you've got to tell me the nanosecond you hear anything about Birdie, or if Uncle Robert changes his mind."

"I will, darling! Birdie's probably *somewhere* close. You know how she loves the West Coast."

So Nancy was stuck with babysitting Eugenia for the foresee-able future. She needed to hand-wash her delicates so she threw Eugenia in the tub with them and used a little bubble bath to clean everything. Eugenia seemed happy splashing in the water and provided enough agitation to clean Nancy's garments.

As she was shampooing Eugenia's hair, Nancy asked, "Who cut your hair?"

"I cutted it."

"Never cut your own hair, even if you've had a glass of wine and think it would be fun, okay?"

"Okay. Your hair is pretty, like corn."

Nancy assumed that she meant cornsilk, not corn. "It's not pretty by accident. It takes professional styling and constant upkeep. However, I have suffered from heartbreaking haircuts in the past, so I sympathize."

After the bath, Nancy gave Eugenia a bowl of cereal. She watched the child spooning Raisin Bran and decided to have a bowl herself.

Eugenia then wanted Nancy to read to her. Nancy read *The Cat in the Hat* to Eugenia and said, "The Cat is quite the style icon. The extravagant hat and bow tie, the dramatic wide stripes—not everyone could get away with that."

"Cats don't have unders."

"Astute and yet inane observation, Eugenia."

"You're funny!"

Nancy smiled. "Don't tell anyone. It's a secret. Let's look at better picture books."

She and Eugenia flipped through Marnie Fogg's *Boutique: A '60s Cultural Phenomenon*, because Nancy was still thinking about the minidress. "The designers started creating clothes for *real* girls, like girls in shops and girls who had moved to the big city and were trapped in dreary offices and girls dreaming about being in love when the world and their futures seemed so exciting, so full of possibilities."

Eugenia yawned, and Nancy realized how late it was. She didn't want to leave the girl on the sofa every night.

"Where will you sleep?" she said to herself.

"I like the liddle room."

"Lit*t*le. What little room?"

"The one with the preddy clothes."

"Pre*tt*y. You must learn to enunciate. My closet? You want to sleep in my closet?"

Eugenia yawned again.

"Please cover your mouth when you yawn. You can't touch anything. My closet is precisely ordered and I want it to stay that way."

Nancy folded a comforter and placed it and a pillow under the rack with her blouses and sweaters. "Do you want me to leave the light on?"

Eugenia nodded and crawled onto her makeshift bed.

Nancy covered her with a quilt and said, "Good night, Eugenia."

"Night, Auntie Nanny."

Nancy had a glass of Sancerre and cleaned the apartment. Then she applied online for insurance for the fund-raiser. She knew the standard conditions and exclusions—of course no one at her party would intentionally cause bodily harm or damage—so she felt comfortable submitting the policy application.

Froth business concluded, Nancy needed to attend to personal matters. She didn't want Bailey to lose interest, but knew she had to play her hand carefully with him. She called him and left a message saying, "Hello, Bailey. Nancy here. My schedule should be clear for Saturday. Looking forward to seeing you then."

Nancy peered into her closet to check on Eugenia. She noticed that the girl had the same heart-shaped face that made her mother look as if she'd stepped out of a Fitzgerald story. And, like Fitzgerald's women, Birdie was careless with others.

Nancy left the closet door open and went to bed.

As the days passed, Derek relaxed in Eugenia's company. He showed her how to draw simple shapes and seemed to enjoy their daily outings to lunch and to the park.

He carried a sketch pad in his black leather satchel and sometimes he'd pull it out and draw. One day he surprised Eugenia with a child-size soccer ball, which he called a football, and showed the girl and her aunt how to dribble it on the empty tennis court.

Nancy stopped waiting at the Château for her cousin, and they ventured out more often. She bought Eugenia two T-shirts with a pirate motif and had her hair trimmed at a salon that specialized in kids cuts.

Derek and Nancy congratulated themselves on their skill in caring for a child.

"What is the big deal?" Nancy said to Derek as they looked through photo books at a boutique on Fillmore.

Eugenia had found a pair of men's boots and was on the floor trying to put them on over her own shoes while pale, androgynous clerks walked over and around her.

Nancy opened another book and said, "People make such a big deal about raising children, when it's not much more trouble than watering a plant." She didn't have any plants in her apartment, but if she did, she was sure they'd be glorious.

"People make things more complicated than they are," Derek said. "Perhaps it makes them feel as if they are accomplishing something difficult."

"As usual, you are right," Nancy said as they moved to the sales counter. "Which of these sunglasses do you like best?" Nancy was pulling sunglasses off a display case.

"Try on this pair. I think the shape complements your face."

Nancy tried them on, sucked in her cheeks, and posed for Derek. "I like them. Well, you know, I always say, dress plainly and accessorize wildly. Write that down."

Derek pulled out his notepad and jotted it down.

Nancy bought the sunglasses and a deliciously hefty photography book by Patrick McMullan. While the sales clerk brushed the lint off her velvet sunglasses case, Nancy handed the book to Derek.

"This is a present for you!"

"Oh, Mrs. Carrington-Chambers, you shouldn't."

"It's nothing—and he's a marvelous photographer. His talent is in capturing the dream of an era, how people want to be perceived."

Derek opened the book and flipped through it. "This year's model, and there will always be a new model."

She leaned into him to look at the photographs. "It's all so fleeting. That's why quality is important. Quality endures."

As they went out of the store, Nancy had a feeling that she was missing something. But she remembered the clerk handing her the receipt and her credit card. She and Derek were about to cross the street when they both said, "Eugenia!"

They hurried back into the store, splitting up to circle the aisles. Nancy's heart raced and she called, "Eugenia! Eugenia!"

The girl was sitting under a rack of flirty spring dresses. "Hi, Auntie Nanny!"

"Eugenia! What are you doing there? It's very, very naughty of you to wander away from us."

"It's my house," said the child. "See, with clothes and shoes like the liddle room where I sleep."

Derek had come to her side. "The little room?"

"She's been sleeping in my closet," Nancy explained.

A prissy young mother pushing a huge pram overheard. She gave Nancy a look that would sour the milk she'd be breast-feeding her slobbery baby soon.

"She *wants* to sleep in the closet," Nancy said loudly. "I have an amazing and beautiful closet!" Nancy took Eugenia by the hand and said, "Honestly! Some people."

But Nancy felt a vague discomfort afterward, almost as if she'd done something as wrong as having visible panty lines. When Eugenia wanted to stay longer at the park, Nancy didn't tell her as she usually did that it was a workday, and when a nasty little dog snapped at the girl, Nancy said sternly to the owner, "All dogs are required to be on leash in this area! Either follow regulations or stay out of the park."

That night, while Eugenia was busy watching *The Little Mermaid,* Nancy called Sloane to make sure that she would be available to work at the Barbary Coast fund-raiser.

"Last Saturday in May, right?" Sloane said. "When my mother was alive, she was on the board and now I'll finally be able to go. How many bodies do you need?"

Nancy had forgotten that Sloane's mother passed away young. Perhaps that was why Sloane was so fanatical about mothering. "We need staff to cover the check-in table, special guests, swag, talent, crew, and caterers. I think we need at least eight besides us," Nancy said. "So, Sloane, how are your children?"

While Sloane talked about her boys in excruciating detail, Nancy organized the contents of her refrigerator. There were some new additions: yogurt, fruit, cheese, juice, cooked chicken breasts, baby carrots, and whole grain salads. The cupboards held graham crackers, dried fruit, and boxes of organic macaroni and cheese.

Sloane seemed to be winding down her monologue about an afternoon in the redwoods, so Nancy jumped in. "Did I mention that I'm watching my cousin Birdie's daughter, Eugenia? It's been an utter delight."

"How wonderful! I wish I had a girl. Maybe next time."

Nancy shuddered at the memory of Sloane's lumbering pregnitude. "Yes, girls are so effortless! Eugenia hardly says a word and she's content with everything."

"How long has she been with you?"

"About a week now. Birdie's taken Eugenia all over on her travels." "Travels" sounded nicer than "numerous shack-ups with international degenerates, artists, and combinations of the aforementioned."

Sloane was silent for so long that Nancy wondered if the connection had been lost. "Sloane?"

"Hmm, Nancy, you know I've met Birdie a few times."

"Yes, and?"

"She lives such an exciting life, and children thrive on stability. Little girls *aren't* quiet. They are very vocal and verbal and they can be so loud. They have no volume control."

"Maybe the ones you know, but Eugenia is a Carrington. I was a delightful child," said Nancy, and out of nowhere came the memory of how she'd had a screaming tantrum at her seventh birthday party because her mother served a fresh strawberry cake instead of the Barbie marshmallow cake Nancy wanted.

"I'm sure Eugenia's very sweet," Sloane said. "But it's possible that when she gets more comfortable with you, another little girl will emerge."

Nancy didn't appreciate Sloane's better-parent-than-thou attitude. "She's just here for a few days, but I'll keep that in mind. Must go now! Bye!"

Nancy tried to pay more attention to Eugenia's mood as they went through their bedtime reading, Claire Wilcox's *The Golden Age of Couture*. When she closed the book, Nancy said, "And that is how haute couture revitalized the economies of

Britain and France and restored hope and beauty after the atro-
cious shoulder pads and devastation of World War II."

"Auntie Nanny, can you sew?"

"Yes, and I used to make all the clothes for my dolls when
I was a girl. I sewed clothes for myself, too, but not as well as
your aunt Sissy." Nancy had even taken pattern-making classes,
but she only used the Bernina electronic sewing machine in
her laundry room for mending and altering clothes.

"Can we make a real cape?"

"I made a cape for my pony, so it should be no problem to
make one for you. Willoughby was very difficult to fit, and he
chewed up the delightful gingham hat I created for him. You
won't eat the cape?"

Eugenia giggled and said, "No!"

"That's good to know. Then I think we can work together."

"Auntie Nanny?"

"Yes, Eugenia?"

"Why does Derek go 'way?"

"He has to go home." Nancy imagined a sleek, masculine,
modern flat. Or a more traditional Edwardian apartment.

"Grammie says married people live together. Derek can
sleep here, too."

Her assumption took Nancy by surprise. "Eugenia, I'm not
married to Derek. Derek works for me."

"Are you going to marry him?"

"No."

"Are you sure?"

"Yes."

"Oh." Eugenia seemed very disappointed by this answer.
"Why not?"

"Because I am already married and I have a husband."

The girl looked skeptical. "He's not here. Mama lives with her husbands."

Nancy wasn't going to explain that those men were not husbands. "My husband lives in a big house. A giant house—a house big enough for a family of tacky, crude giants—with a monster-size wet bar in the bedroom. He lives there."

"I like Derek better."

"I do, too, but that's . . . I mean, Derek is very nice and stunning, but he's *staff*. One doesn't marry *staff*."

"I'm going to marry Derek."

Nancy didn't bother trying to explain the obstacles. "I hope you'll let me plan that wedding."

Later, when Nancy had tucked the child under the comforter in the closet, she asked, "Do you like sleeping here?"

"I like having my own liddle room. It smells good and I like the preddy things."

"Lit*tl*e and pre*tt*y. You are welcome to sleep here whenever you visit. Good night, Eugenia."

"Auntie Nanny, will you stay close?"

"Yes. Why?"

"Mama goes away when I sleep."

"I promise not to go anywhere. I'll be right out here."

Nancy stood at the doorway of the closet, watching until the girl closed her eyes. She didn't think Eugenia was *too* quiet. Some people were naturally quiet.

No one had heard from Birdie yet, and Nancy suspected that her cousin had flitted off to Greece. Why had Birdie kept the girl if she didn't want her? Why couldn't her clotheshorse cousin be bothered to buy shoes for Eugenia?

There were probably some obscure and childless members

of the family who would take in the child for a stipend. It's possible that there existed Carringtons who might even own a cow. She imagined Eugenia frolicking with a bovine companion on a farm somewhere in that vast unknown called America's Heartland.

Nancy's musings were interrupted by a phone call from her husband.

"Hello, Nance."

"Hi, Todd. How *are* you?"

"I miss you, sweetie. It's not the same here without you."

"How can you tell? That house is so big we always lost each other in it."

Instead of arguing, he said, "How's everything going? How's your new assistant?"

"Oh, Todd, he's fantastic! Thank you so much. He's smart and efficient. He writes down everything I say! He dresses exquisitely! You should go shopping with him and he can help you pick out attractive things." She heard a sigh at the other end of the line.

"Everything about me is wrong, isn't it? Maybe your assistant could help me pick out pajamas to wear when I go out to parties and get falling-over drunk."

Of course, Bill had showed him that picture. "Wait until you see the photos that are coming up. They show full boobage, although you always thought mine were too small."

He was silent for a minute, and then he said, "I know you're making this up, because Bailey told me you were working hard and exhausted when he saw you at Gigi's. He asked if it was okay to ask you out as a friend. I said sure, I'd be happy if he kept an eye on you. So what else is going on?"

He sounded as if he was fishing for information he already knew. Her mother might have ratted out the whole Eugenia situation to him. "Not much. I'm spending all my time planning Mrs. Bentley Jamieson Friendly's historical museum gala."

"Make sure you do an awesome job and really suck up to her. She's a great connection."

"Todd, I don't *suck up* to people. I cultivate relationships with people because they're fabulous." It was merely coincidental that fabulous people were usually well connected. "After all, I'm very close to Sloane and she hasn't a connection in the world."

He brayed out his har-har laugh. "How can you say that? Her father has advised presidents on transportation policy."

"But he's just a professor. Nobody cares about academics, and who reads his books? It's not as if he's Karl Lagerfeld."

"Who?"

She sighed. "Todd, there is a deep divide between us and I sometimes despair that you will never transcend your heterosexuality. Sometimes I think you don't even try."

"I don't want to 'transcend my heterosexuality.' Talking to you is impossible."

"I am a delightful conversationalist," she said. Even talking to Eugenia was more fun than talking to Todd. "I've got the kettle on. Talk to you soon. Bye."

She didn't miss him.

She made her last call of the night to her mother. They chitchatted casually about the weather and acquaintances. Her mother pointedly did not ask about Eugenia, so Nancy said, "Will you be home Saturday afternoon? I promised Eugenia that she could meet Willoughby."

"He's been a little wild lately."

"We won't take him out in the cart. We'll just feed him apples and stick daisies in his mane."

"I'll be here in the afternoon."

Nancy did the math: 30 minutes to get to the restaurant, plus 90 minutes prep, plus 120 minutes commuting back and forth to her parents, plus 60 minutes of visiting, plus 60 minutes for exigencies. "We'll be there just after one o'clock."

Nancy spent Friday cheerfully working on the fund-raiser. GP had sent her the prices of renting the sets, costumes, and entertainers, and Mrs. Friendly was happy with the proposal. Nancy mailed a signed copy of the insurance contract to the warehouse leasing agent and began writing up her detailed plan. The graphic designer dropped by and was thrilled with the piratey theme.

Bailey called in the late afternoon and told Nancy he had made dinner reservations at seven.

Nancy glanced at Eugenia, who was sprawled on the rug with her primitive drawings and meager possessions scattered around her. "I'll meet you at the restaurant," she said.

"You aren't trying to hide some secret lover from me, are you? That would wreck me."

"If I told you, he wouldn't be a secret. See you tomorrow."

After Nancy hung up, she realized that she needed a child car seat. She knew where to buy antique French ribbon, the Australian edition of *Vogue,* Limoges vegetables, and other essential things. "Derek, would you please find someplace that sells child car seats? I need one that won't clash with my Mini. Please have the store deliver it by noon tomorrow, no later."

After several calls, Derek put down the phone and said, "I

found a German model with excellent safety ratings, but no one can guarantee that you'll get it by noon."

Nancy took her eyes from the television, which was soundlessly playing a puppet show. One of the puppets would have made an amusing fake-fur bolero. "I suppose you'll have to go pick it up," she told Derek. "You can use my car."

"But madame . . ."

"Or else you can stay here with Eugenia," Nancy said. "I can't take her with me to buy a car seat *without* a car seat."

He looked as if he had been given a choice between drowning or hanging. Finally he said, "It's not far. We could *all* walk there and use the car seat in a taxi on the way back."

"I want to go with Derek!" Eugenia said.

Nancy looked at the girl's expectant face. "Okay, we'll all go."

twelve

tips for shopping success

It was a pleasant walk to Laurel Village, a neighborhood of shops and cafés. When Eugenia began lagging, Derek swung her up and onto his shoulders. "Hold on!"

Nancy had noticed that when she walked with her fabulous assistant and her puny ward, people smiled at them and said hello. She pretended to be equally impressed with their grimy spawn in label-laden clothing.

"Have you noticed how friendly people are when you're with a child?" she asked Derek, who still had the little girl on his shoulders, her small head resting atop his.

"I have observed that."

"They seem to think that we are all members of an exclusive

club, as if capitulating to a biological imperative is a major accomplishment."

"As always, you are right, Mrs. Carrington-Chambers."

"Still, it's rather nice when people are nice. I'm all for niceness. What about you?"

"I appreciate it when it is directed toward me."

"Well, who wouldn't be nice to you? You're so agreeable and gracious. I'm sure no one ever gets angry with you."

His face was averted but she caught that intriguing smirk again. "You would be shocked, Mrs. Carrington-Chambers."

"I'll never, ever get angry with you," Nancy teased, expecting him to respond quickly, but he was quiet. "Will I?"

"When that time comes, and it is inevitable, I think I shall be very disappointed in myself."

"Who's exaggerating now?" Nancy asked. "I'm not going to ask if I'll ever make you angry because I know I will. Todd shouts and says I'm impossible. Then he goes to a sports bar. How will you show your anger? Will you flare up, or will you smolder?"

Eugenia was slipping her fingers through Derek's espresso dark hair. "Mama yells and throws things at the fireplace. She broke a pitcher."

"Pic-ture," Nancy corrected.

"She broke a pic-ture and the vodka got all over."

"Your mother is very emotional," Nancy said. "Don't take it personally."

"What?" Eugenia said.

"Your mother is a very yelly person, like that dog in the park who was barking and barking because he thinks barking is fun. Your mother yells because she thinks yelling is fun. It's not your fault, okay?"

"Okay."

"Just remember, dogs like to bark, fish like to swim, Birdie likes to yell."

"That sounds like a song," Derek said, and began singing, *"Bugs like to bite, cars like to go."*

Nancy sang, *"Princesses like things pink, flowers like to grow* . . . Your turn, Eugenia!"

"Cows like to moo."

Derek grinned and sang, *"Nancy likes fine fashion, Eugenia likes her cape."*

"Derek likes . . ." Nancy began, and then wondered, what *did* Derek like? *". . . pirate ships, my mother likes handbags . . ."*

They found the children's store and bought a child seat. "This store is for babies," Eugenia said in disgust. "I'm not a baby."

"There are things here for nonbabies," Nancy said. "Shopping is like hunting. You have to be patient and look carefully at everything." They found Legos, colored chalk, and a book about farm animals.

When Nancy discovered haute couture paper dolls, she was ecstatic. "Oh. My. God. They've got every decade, from the Belle Epoque to the nineties! Lanvin, Schiaparelli, Ungaro, Worth, Ricci!" She grabbed one of each set.

When she went to pay, the clerk said, "Your little girl is very lucky."

"Oh, she's not mine," Nancy said. "She was left on my doorstep like a stray cat."

The clerk's expression froze and Eugenia said, "I'm not a cat. I'm a pirate."

Nancy smiled nervously and said, "It's a family joke. She's a pirate. She sailed her ship into our waters. Yo-ho-ho!"

Derek lugged the seat around as they stopped in the nearby

children's boutiques. Nancy steered Eugenia toward the racks of darling clothes, but the girl grabbed a boy's shirt with a skull and crossbones and wouldn't let go. "It's for our pirate party! You said yo-ho-ho!"

"I suppose I can't argue with that," Nancy said. "But only this once because it is a special occasion."

The only other shop Eugenia liked was the ribbon shop, where she picked out several lengths of ribbon and said, "This is for when we make my cape."

"Excellent planning, Eugenia," Nancy said.

Derek hailed a cab and tried to figure out how to put the child seat in the back. The cabbie got out and came around to help, saying, "I got three kids myself. How come you don't know how to use a car seat for your little girl?"

"She's not my—" Derek began and then he glanced at Eugenia. Then he said, "She's not a little girl. She's a pirate. Yo-ho-ho."

The cabbie shook his head and strapped in the seat, picked up Eugenia, placed her in it, and secured the seat belt. "Ahoy, matey," he said.

"You speak pirate very well," Nancy said as she slid in the backseat and told him her address.

"Why didn't you just say Château Winkles?" the cabbie said. "How's Miss Winkles?"

"As captivating as ever." Nancy looked at Derek and said, "It's a nickname for the building."

When they got to the apartment, the trio went to the garage and Derek wrangled the car seat into Nancy's Mini.

"You have a toy car!" Eugenia said excitedly.

"Yes, I guess I do, although I'm reevaluating my hatred of minivans."

"Can we go to dinner in your car?" asked Eugenia.

"We have macaroni and cheese for dinner." Nancy waited for the argument. But Eugenia sagged like a badly made soufflé and stared at the cement floor. "We also have cinnamon graham crackers. Yum, graham crackers! We can play with our fashion dolls."

Eugenia was not tempted by these delectable treats.

"May I suggest an evening of movies and takeaway at home?" Derek said, happily surprising both of his companions.

"A pirate movie?" Eugenia asked.

Nancy was so excited about spending the evening with Derek that she ordered a pizza on the phone. "They always taste like their cardboard delivery box, but just this once since it's a special occasion."

While they were waiting for the pizza, Derek dashed to the nearby video store and came back with four pirate movies. "I took longer because I stopped at the wine shop," he said, and handed Nancy a bottle of Barbaresco. "The shopkeeper assured me that it suits a pizza dinner."

Nancy and Eugenia had set places out on the cocktail table, "like a picnic," Nancy said.

Nancy opened the wine and they watched *Pirates of the Caribbean.* Eugenia sat between the adults and ducked her head toward one or the other of them during the scary scenes. "We can skip this part," Nancy said, but Eugenia wanted to listen.

The girl fell asleep halfway through the movie, and Nancy turned down the sound. "Johnny Depp is so sexy, don't you think?"

"Even in this film?"

"Oh, yes! That black guyliner is devastating. Have you ever worn it?"

"Guyliner? No."

"It would look fabulous on you. So would an eye patch. You've already got that mysterious look about you. Sometimes I want to do my eyes up with really thick black makeup."

"Like a pirate?"

"Yes, like a pirate wench. I would wear a ruffled blouse open to my belly button, breeches, and cuffed leather boots."

The girl sleeping between them tilted against Derek's chest. He said, "Where do you think her mother is?"

"No one's heard anything. She may have gone to Greece, but it's possible she's on the West Coast. She likes Baja. You probably think she's an awful person, but she's not really. Or maybe she is."

"What if she doesn't return?"

"Birdie's a homing pigeon. She always comes back, if only to aggravate her parents and extort money from them. It's not a question of if, but when."

"Who will watch Eugenia tomorrow night when you go out?"

"I'm taking her to my parents'. Not that they know yet." Nancy smiled. "We embrace the element of surprise in our family interactions. It's how we avoid the unpleasantness of saying no to one another. What is your family like?"

"My mum is lovely, but she never asks a thing for herself. My father left her when I was young, and she raised my brother and me by herself. Peter is happily married with two daughters."

"Do you ever wonder where your father is?"

"Occasionally. He did teach us one lesson—that a good man does not abandon his children." He put his arm around Eugenia and asked softly, "Her father?"

"Birdie has never told anyone," Nancy said. "Is it hard for your mother that you're gay?"

"I think she would be happy if I was married to a nice girl and had a family. Mind you, she thinks the world of Prescott."

"Derek, if things go well with the party and with other things in my life, this job might be permanent. Would you like that?"

"So many things are in flux now, Mrs. Carrington-Chambers. Let us see how things progress."

Nancy looked down at the sleeping child. "Do you know what I've noticed? She isn't as unattractive as most other children."

"Or as annoying. Most of them whinge constantly."

"I know. I hate that. Is Prescott waiting for you?"

"Yes, I'd better be going. Do you want me to take her to your room?"

"Please."

He gently picked up Eugenia, carried her into the bedroom, and laid her on the bed.

When Nancy walked him to the door, he said, "Enjoy your weekend."

"You, too." She hesitated. "Derek, you don't ever have to stay late—but Eugenia and I like being with you."

He looked into her eyes and said, "It's my pleasure, Mrs. Carrington-Chambers." He took her hand in his large, warm hand and held it for a long time. The tension between them was so strong, like those last moments of a date, just before a kiss, but this wasn't a date.

But maybe she was the only one who felt it.

Derek let go of her hand and said, "Good night, madame," and left.

While Nancy was capable of leaving her unsuspecting mother with a child, she couldn't leave her with a child wearing a towel. First thing on Saturday morning, Nancy took Eugenia to Nancy's favorite fabric store on Union Square to pick out material for an attractive cape. They went directly to the fourth floor, where the remnants were kept.

"Choose whatever you like," Nancy told Eugenia as she directed her to a table of small lengths.

Eugenia went through the piles, pulling out anything that was red.

A clerk walked behind the child, sighing loudly and rearranging the piles. The clerk looked at Nancy and said, "This isn't a playground. Are you looking for *something*?"

"Yes, we're looking for polite service. Even a child deserves that," Nancy said sweetly. "If you don't know where it is, you can direct us to your manager."

The clerk smiled tightly and went to Eugenia. In a much nicer tone, she said, "Let me help you find what you're looking for."

"We're making a pirate cape."

Eugenia couldn't decide on what she liked best, so Nancy bought prints and solids, muslins, wools for the winter, polished cottons, lush velvets, and even stiff oilcloth for rainy days.

The clerk suggested that they get Velcro to fasten the cape and metallics for emblems and sashes. She even helped them find big darning needles, yarn, and burlap so Nancy could teach Eugenia to stitch. Nancy bought brass buttons with little anchors because she associated them with buccaneers.

At home, she laid out red velvet, cut a rhomboid shape, and quickly stitched up the sides before attaching ribbon for decoration and Velcro at the collar. "It's not beautiful, but we'll decorate it and tailor it later and it *will* be beautiful," Nancy said as she put it on Eugenia. "I'm taking you to your uncle and aunt's house, my parents. Your mama took you there before."

"Can we see your pony?"

"Yes, you can meet Willoughby."

Nancy packed toys and books in one of her Froth totes and then drove carefully through the city streets. "I am following almost all the traffic laws," she said proudly to Eugenia, who was in the backseat sipping from a juice box. "Don't spill in my car. I'm only letting you drink this one time because it's a special occasion."

As Nancy headed down the Peninsula on the freeway, she remembered all those awful trips to the construction site with Todd and all the arguing on the ride back. She glanced in the rearview mirror at Eugenia and said, "You are an excellent travel companion."

Eugenia smiled and said, "I want to see the pony."

"So do I."

Nancy was always happy when she reached the woodsy hillside village where she'd been raised. She slowed down on the narrow road that twisted through ancient oaks. She turned onto a private dirt lane that led past an apple orchard to her parents' house. Every winter, when the rains came down, her parents talked about paving it, but then spring would arrive and their wish to keep outsiders away superseded safety issues.

Nancy parked on a level plateau by the tennis court and then helped Eugenia out of the car seat.

"Mama brung me here before."

"*Brought*, not brung. I knew you'd remember. Bring your book bag," she said, but left Eugenia's overnight case in the car.

"Where's your pony?"

"He's in his paddock near the stable, but first we're going to say hello to my parents."

Nancy loved the graceful Arts and Crafts brown shingle house that had been her great-grandparents' summer home. She led Eugenia to the carved wood and stained-glass door that opened directly into the airy living room, with its beamed cathedral ceiling.

Every detail of the room had been lovingly selected, from the exposed hardware to the custom-made tiles set in the brick fireplace, to the matte green jardiniere filled with fragrant lilacs.

"You can slide on the floor in your socks," Eugenia said.

Nancy looked down at the girl. "I always liked doing that, too." She took the girl into the rustic kitchen and called, "Mom?"

The back door was open so they went out to the weathered redwood deck. Hester was on a chaise with a tall tumbler in one hand and a hardback book in the other. On seeing her daughter and the girl, she closed the book, swung her legs over, and sat up. "Hello, Nanny. Good afternoon, Eugenia."

Nancy went to her mother and kissed her cheek. "Hi, Mom. Eugenia, come give your . . ." Nancy tried to figure out the relationship and said, "Give your aunt Hester a kiss."

After the girl did so, Hester said, "My, Eugenia, you're looking so pretty today. Is that a new cape?"

"Auntie Nanny made it. We got lots of cape clothes at the store."

"How lovely. Nancy, would you please bring out our lunch. Mina made sandwiches," she said, referring to the young woman who helped out on weekends when the housekeeper was off.

"Is she here now?" Nancy asked.

"She'll be back later. She went shopping."

As Hester asked Eugenia questions, Nancy went to the refrigerator to examine the contents. There was a platter of crustless sandwiches cut into diamond shapes, sliced melon, and a green salad. She carried them to the teak table outside and returned to the kitchen to fetch drinks.

When Nancy was getting ice for the lemonade, she checked the freezer, relieved to see that there was no vodka. She went back outside with the drinks and glasses.

Nancy marveled at her mother's ability to feign interest in Eugenia's conversation. Had it been like that when Nancy was little? She thought she must have been fascinating even as a child. "Where's Dad?"

"He's out on his boat," Hester said. "Or playing golf. He said something this morning, but I was half asleep. Your father works so hard, he needs his time to relax."

"He enjoys the outdoors so much," Nancy said as they all moved to sit at the table.

"We play in the park every day with Derek. He's teaching me football," Eugenia said as she lifted the top of a sandwich to examine its contents. "It's green inside."

"Do not perform a vivisection on your food, Eugenia," Nancy said. "It's my favorite, watercress and butter, and very delicious."

Hester took a long drink from her tumbler and said, "Who is Derek?"

"My assistant, Mom, remember? He's teaching Eugenia how to kick a soccer ball. May I pour you some lemonade?" Nancy ran her finger along the smooth frosty glass. "Is this a new pitcher?"

"Pic-ture," Eugenia corrected.

Nancy smiled. "I'm glad you're listening to me."

"Nanny, dear, please don't teach Eugenia to talk like you. I know you think it's funny, but it's very confusing. How is Todd?"

"Todd is fine. We had a delightful conversation the other day. He's thrilled that Froth is going so well." She poured a glass of lemonade and put it next to her mother's empty tumbler. Nancy talked about GP's theme for the fund-raiser, the warehouse location, and her success with Gigi's party.

Hester had only eaten a few bites of salad. "So nice that you're enjoying your business. You won't have time for it when you go back to running your house."

Nancy smiled and said, "How is the preservation group going?"

Hester's activities centered on ensuring that barbarians didn't destroy the local architectural heritage. She became animated as she described an ongoing legal battle with a tech mogul who had purchased a property that had been the primary residence of raccoons for the last half century. "He tried to remove all the copper ornamentation—even the sconces!"

"He's a monster," Nancy agreed. "Although Todd thinks anything new is better than anything old, except for money, and then he likes both new and old."

"Nancy, if you bring up that wet bar again, you'll give me a migraine. Todd means well and does his best, considering."

"You're right. He means well." Nancy couldn't look at her watch because it might make her mother suspicious. "I promised Eugenia that she could meet Willoughby," she said, and stood. "We'll help you clear. Come on, Eugenia."

They carried the dishes to the kitchen and then Nancy took an apple from the fruit bowl. She cut it into pieces so Willoughby wouldn't choke.

Eugenia jumped and skipped all the way to the corral up the hill. "Can I feed him?"

"Yes, and I'll show you the right way to do it so he won't snap."

The black-and-white miniature horse was in the corral with his companion, an old sheep named New Marianne. Nancy's mother had named the horse and the original Marianne when she'd gone through one of her book club phases. "Hi, Willoughby!" Nancy said, and he came up to the gate with a toss of his head and a snort.

Nancy demonstrated how to give Willoughby a snack. "You have to keep your hand flat and let him come get it politely. I'll do it first and if he's too frisky, he doesn't get any more. Good behavior is rewarded."

The horse didn't try to nip and accepted a scratch on his nose. Eugenia held her hand through the gate and the horse took his treat.

"Very good, both of you!" Nancy said, pleased.

Eugenia wanted to stay, but Nancy said, "We'll come back later. I have to go to the house now."

Her mother was no longer outside. Nancy took the girl and the tote bag of books to the living room and said, "Stay here and be a good girl while I talk to your aunt Hester."

Nancy went upstairs and found her mother in her spacious dressing room, a tumbler of ice and clear liquid in her hand. With her free hand, she was sorting through dresses. One wall held an astonishing collection of brilliantly colorful handbags, totes, clutches, and satchels.

"Mom, would you please watch Eugenia tonight? I'll bring in her things from the car, and I'll pick her up tomorrow. I've got to take care of something tonight."

Hester pulled out a teal silk cocktail dress. "I wish I could, Nanny. We're going to an anniversary party tonight."

"You didn't mention it when we spoke yesterday. You said you'd be home."

"I said I'd be home in the afternoon," Hester said with a very convincing smile. "If I'd known that you needed a baby-sitter, I absolutely would have canceled. It's not too late. I'm sure they'll understand, even though it's a small party. Your father can go without me. I'm feeling a little tired anyway. I was going to catch forty winks."

Hester dropped the dress on a bench and took unsteady steps toward her bed. "You can leave Eu . . . Eu . . . the girl, and when Mina comes back, she'll help. Just let me close my eyes for a few minutes and rest."

Nancy took the tumbler from her mother's hand and set it on her glass-topped vanity table, where it would be out of reach. Then she guided Hester to the bed. "Don't worry about it, Mommy. It's not important. You get your rest."

When Nancy had covered her mother with a soft cashmere throw, she went to the closet and did a quick search. She found an almost empty bottle of vodka in a chocolate brown suede boot. Then she went to the bathroom and emptied the vodka in the sink before she filled a tumbler with water and got two aspirins from the cupboard.

When she came out of the bathroom, she saw Eugenia hopping from foot to foot at the open doors to the dressing room.

"Eugenia, do you want a pirate bag? Choose one you like." Nancy went to her mother. She slid an arm under her shoulders and raised her up.

Hester's eyes fluttered open. "I'm sorry I'm so tired."

"It's all right, Mommy. Here, take these and have some

water." Nancy gave her mother the aspirin and made sure she drank most of the water. She kissed her mother's warm brow and smelled her girlish L'Air du Temps. "Go to sleep now."

As she watched Hester's face go slack, Nancy pressed her lips tightly together, feeling a rise of emotions she couldn't think about right then. "I love you, Mommy," she said, but Hester was already asleep.

"My mama likes naps, too. She says, 'Be quiet, Mama's tired.'"

Nancy turned to see Eugenia looking at the sleeping woman.

"Some mothers like naps," Nancy said in a hushed voice. "Did you pick out a pirate bag?"

Eugenia looked at the shelves and pointed. "That red one."

"Your taste is improving," Nancy said as she held up the girl so she could pluck a shoulder bag of glossy, butter-soft scarlet leather off a top shelf. Nancy chose a stunning deep purple tote for herself and then said, "We have to go back now."

"Can we take Willoughby with us?"

"No, he doesn't like stairs, and he likes being with Marianne." Nancy collected the vodka bottle from the bathroom and slipped it in the purple tote so she could dispose of it.

Then she gathered Eugenia's things and got her into the car seat. An older Honda drove up and parked beside the Mini, and Nancy waited until her mother's weekend helper got out. "Hi, Mina!"

"Hi, Nancy. Leaving already?"

"I couldn't stay long. Thanks for the yummy lunch. But you didn't have to cut the crusts off."

Mina opened her trunk and took out a bag of groceries. "You're welcome. I fed the crusts to that wily Willoughby."

"He was a complete gentleman when we visited. Oh, my mother is napping now. Would you mind checking on her in a few hours? I know she's going out tonight, and I'm sure she doesn't want to oversleep."

"Sure, Nancy." The woman looked somber and said, "I always try to look out for her."

"Thanks, Mina. My sisters and I appreciate how helpful you are."

As Nancy drove back to the city, she considered her options and was calling Sloane even before they hit the freeway. "Sloane, how are you?" she said cheerily.

"Almost out the door, Nancy. So good to hear from you so soon again."

"I don't want to keep you, but I was wondering if you were available tonight. Because I need someone to look after my niece, Eugenia."

"Oh, how nice that she's still with you! We're having a campout at Lloyd's co-op preschool. We'll be going for a star-watching night walk, roasting marshmallows, telling stories, and having sing-alongs. She's welcome to join us."

Nancy looked in her rearview mirror. Eugenia was staring out the window and singing softly to herself, and Nancy made out, *"Nanny likes blue, cows like to moo . . ."*

Nancy thought about the girl being abandoned with a horde of strange, grubby children, sticky with burnt marshmallow. She thanked Sloane and said, "It's probably best if someone comes to my place. I'm sure I can find someone else."

"We'll get the kids together soon. You can come to my house for a playdate."

"Absolutely," Nancy said, while thinking, *Ugh!* She called Milagro, but she was out of town. Finally she called Derek.

"Mrs. Carrington-Chambers, what a surprise to hear from you."

"Oh, Derek, an emergency has come up! I know it's your day off, but can you come immediately? It's absolutely critical!"

"Are you all right? Is Eugenia all right?"

"Yes, but I need your help. I'm driving home right now. Can you be there in an hour?"

thirteen

the dangerous allure of impulse

*N*ancy and Eugenia stopped at a drugstore and bought Disney movies and then went to a gourmet burger shop and got dinner for Derek and the child. "Desperate times call for desperate meals," she told Eugenia, who was saying "Hot, hot, hot!" as she ate sweet potato fries from a paper bag.

"Leave some of those fries for Derek."

Nancy's assistant opened the front door of her apartment as they came up the stairs. "Mrs. Carrington-Chambers, what can I do to help?"

"Would you stay with Eugenia tonight? My mother wasn't able to help because she's going out. Isn't my new tote a fab color? Do you like Eugenia's pirate bag? I picked up burgers and fries. I know you like buffalo meat. I got yours with bacon and cheddar cheese."

She saw an expression—relief?—cross his face now that he knew he could be the solution to her problem.

"Madame, you called me to babysit?"

"I've exhausted every possibility. My friend Milagro is away, and Sloane wanted to throw Eugenia into a rabble of unwashed muffigans, in a situation that sounded scarily *Lord of the Flies*-ish. I desperately need to go out and repair my reputation."

"If you really require me to be here . . ."

"I really, really do."

Eugenia tugged at Derek's jacket. "Auntie Hester had to take a nap, like Mama does after she goes to a party. We got *Peter Pan* with pirates and a crocodile."

Derek's expression softened as he looked down at Eugenia. "You did, did you? Is that a new cape you're wearing?"

"Auntie Nanny and me sewed it."

"Aunt Nancy and *I*," Nancy said. "Eat your hamburger first, before it gets cold."

"I'm not hungry. Derek, we ate green sandwiches and saw Willoughby. Auntie has a toy horse and a toy car."

Derek smiled. "She likes toys, I guess."

"Do you like toys?"

"Derek likes boy toys," Nancy said, and winked at her assistant.

Nancy had wanted a leisurely bath, but she had to do with a quick shower. She dried her hair so that it was loose and wavy and put on her makeup. After pulling on a nude minicami slip over her nude thong, she walked into her room and opened the door to her closet. She'd planned on wearing a light dress, but a chilly wind had come in with the fog. As far as she was concerned, goose bumps were as unattractive as cellulite.

"Derek," she called. "Come help me."

He came into her bedroom and stopped in his tracks when he saw her. "Yes, Mrs. Carrington-Chambers?"

She pulled out the filmy spaghetti-strap dress in question. "Is it too cold out for this?"

"It is indeed a little brisk, madame."

"What do you think I should wear?"

"I think you look fantastic as you are now," he said in a husky voice.

"Stop teasing. Be serious."

He came to the closet. "Have you a black leather catsuit in there?"

"I wish! A skirt, or a dress, or pants? I can't look too datey, but I don't want to look hopeless."

"Men enjoy a girl in a dress. They like the femininity of a dress, and your legs are awe— fabulous."

"I take the stairs so often, I'm practically French." Nancy brushed back the clothes with her hand so he could glimpse them.

"That one," he said. "The . . . what is that color?"

"Coral." She pulled the sleeveless dress from the rack and held it in front of her. It had a low, square neckline and a ruched bodice that accentuated her slight curves. "You think it's too much for a first nondate? I bought it hoping that Todd would take me dancing, but he thinks only girls dance, preferably in high heels and a G-string."

Nancy slipped the dress over her head, adjusted the straps, and stood in front of Derek. "Does it work?"

He stared for a few seconds and there was something about

the way his blue eyes looked at her that made her almost shiver. Then he said, "You look smashing, madame."

Nancy had never been told she looked smashing before. "It's so nice to have a man who can offer real girlfriend advice."

"Derek!" called Eugenia from the other room.

"Eugenia awaits," he said as the girl scuffed into the room waving ribbons like streamers in her hand.

"Can Derek come back and watch *Peter Pan* with me?"

"I'm sure he'd find that much more interesting than watching a girl prance around in her underwear."

"It was no great hardship, madame."

"Now you're the one being too nice. Would you call a cab for me? I don't know if we'll go anywhere after dinner, but I'm sure it won't be too late."

"Mrs. Carrington-Chambers, if you are enjoying yourself with your friend, I don't mind staying. Will you have your mobile if I need to ring you?"

"Yes, but I know you can handle anything, because you're fabulous." She went up on her toes to kiss his cheek. He always felt so good that she wanted to rub herself all over his smooth, muscley body. She must be lonelier than she thought.

After she finished getting herself together, she took a highly critical look in the mirror, searching for any imperfections. She took off a necklace and put on a gold cuff bracelet and dangly gold earrings, then said good night to Derek and Eugenia.

The cab was double-parked in the street. Nancy gave the driver the address to the restaurant and said, "I want to arrive exactly at seven fifteen." She didn't want to arrive before Bailey, and he was the sort of fellow who made girls wait.

Nancy was glad to see her tall friend standing outside the brick building talking on his phone. When he spotted her getting out of the cab, he put the phone away and helped her out.

She touched his black leather zip-front jacket to confirm that it was lambskin. She liked the textural contrast of the leather with his jean-cut, sanded corduroys. His finely woven gray-and-black-striped shirt showed that he had a more serious side.

"Nancy!" He kissed her cheek and she noticed that his cologne was an acrid sports scent that Todd and his pals favored.

"Bailey, I hope I haven't kept you waiting."

"Not long. You look amazing." Despite the evening breeze, Bailey's sandy hair remained in place.

He held the restaurant door open for her, the hostess came forward, and they were escorted to their table. When she was drinking her Bitter Widow and he had his Salty Dog, he said, "I've been waiting a long time to get you alone."

He waved to a couple at the bar and said quietly to Nancy, "She's a lobbyist for the shipping industry, and he's a high-tech headhunter."

Most of the meal was like that. Bailey would smile and say something complimentary, while always aware of the shifting crowd around them. She admired the way he kept his gaze on her and asked her questions in his gravelly voice. She liked the way his brushed-back hair showed off his slight widow's peak. "What are you thinking?" he asked between courses.

"I like your outfit. Todd thinks dressing up means putting on a clean polo shirt and long pants."

Bailey laughed. "He wears suits for meetings."

"But resentfully. He comes home with his tie shoved in his

pants' pocket." There was so much she wanted to ask Bailey: What product did he use on his hair? Did he have a skin care regime? Had the *poutine* tasted as divine as it looked?

"Speaking of Todd," Bailey said.

"You told him we were going out and explained that that Rich Bitches photo was not what it seemed."

"Yes," he said. "Was that all right?"

"I was glad to find out that at least one person wasn't eager to think the worst of me."

"Todd said no one would believe that you were toasted since you're a stickler for proper behavior."

"Those who don't believe that I'm a slut think that I'm a priss. I don't know which is worse."

"I don't think you're either, Nancy. I admire a woman who has standards," Bailey said. "How is Froth going? I heard you're going to drag the Barbary Coast party out of the Stone Age. I go every year, because Mrs. Friendly is definitely someone I need to get to know, but if you're going to be there this year, I may even have fun."

"Bring your checkbook," she said. "It's going to be spectacular."

"What are you doing?"

"It's all under wraps for now. GP is helping and my assistant, Derek, has been invaluable."

"Is Derek that guy looking all Hugh Hefner in the pajamas at Gigi's?"

"All the gentlemen were in pajamas. Derek doesn't look like Hef. Derek is tall, handsome, has exquisite taste, and couldn't be less interested in Barbie-trons."

"I've been to the Playboy Mansion."

"I don't want to know. I'm losing my appetite now, thinking of the fetid bacterial swill in that grotto."

"It was just business," he said with a smile. "Most of my contacts are here, but I have to go to SoCal to establish myself."

"For an eventual run at statewide office?"

"As California goes, so goes the nation," Bailey said. "I haven't decided if I *want* to hold office. A consultant not only makes a better living than an elected official, but we've got more flexibility."

"Do you aspire to be a puppet master?"

"If I held office, I wouldn't be anyone's puppet," he said with a grin. "Of course, bachelors rarely get elected above the county supervisor level. People don't trust us."

"Should they?"

"No one should ever trust a person whose career depends on popularity."

"I didn't realize you were so cynical."

"I'm a complete optimist or I wouldn't be trying. My life is all about trying to do the things people tell me are impossible."

"Bailey, please don't make me listen to your stump speech. I'm sure it's brilliant."

He laughed. "Most people are riveted by the narrative of my rise from genteel poverty. Of course, it's easy to climb when that's the only direction available. Your situation is more challenging."

"I'm glad my parents held me to high standards," she said. "They are delightful people, even though now, with Todd . . . They've been concerned."

"Todd knows you can't stand living at Villagio Toscana, especially with half the development empty. If I had the money, I'd buy adjoining lots and wait out the market," he said. "The house is another thing. Do you break up a marriage over bad architecture?"

"I don't know, but I think excellent architecture can keep a marriage happy. My parents' Craftsman is a gem." Nancy was dying to see the ramshackle mansion that Bailey was renovating, and she asked, "How is your fixer-upper going? Will anyone ever see it, and does it have good bones?"

"Spend tonight with me and I'll give you a tour in the morning."

"So sorry, but I have a meeting with Derek and I can't cancel it."

"You have a meeting with Derek tonight, or tomorrow morning?"

"Yes," she said, and laughed.

"Should I be jealous of him?"

"Absolutely. He's like a best girlfriend and a stunning man all rolled into one. He can dish about style and get things off the top shelf. He helped me dress this evening."

"I can help you undress."

"I can do that myself. I've always wanted to have a maid who arranged my hair and wore a white lace cap and called me Miss Nancy. I don't suppose you have a maid's uniform."

"No, you have to play dress-up with your assistant. My interests are strictly masculine." Bailey's leg stretched under the table so that it was next to hers.

She was enjoying Bailey's flirting even though she didn't know if he was really interested in her. "You agreed that we'd have dinner as *friends,* and you told Todd that you were taking me out as a *friend.*"

"I'd have an easier time treating you like a friend if you weren't so damn pretty."

"Let's talk about something safe. Tell me about your boat."

Bailey had bought the sailboat at a ridiculously low price from one of his many benefactors. As he discussed the repairs it needed, she studied his face. There was no doubt that he was handsome, but no particular feature stood out as either good or bad. His nose was thin and she wondered if he'd had rhinoplasty.

Bailey said, "I'm really lucky to have a friend who helped me acquire it."

"You were able to buy your house through a friend, too, weren't you?"

He tilted his head and studied her. "Yes, if it wasn't for my friends, I'd be scrounging to get ahead in some crappy job, and living in a crappy apartment."

"I'm not criticizing you, Bailey. I think you're lucky that people like you so much," Nancy said. "Poor Todd just gets on the wrong side of people and even when he's got a good idea, he has to fight for it."

"Like that sports medicine business."

"Exactly. He put his whole heart in it and it's a growth field. It should have done better," she said, thinking of how depressed Todd had been when the business had foundered. She remembered that it was Bailey who'd suggested the investment. "You were involved in that, too, right? I hope you didn't lose too much."

Bailey smiled and said, "I'm surprised that didn't work out for Todd. I'm going to try to work with him, Nancy, on his people skills."

"I'm sure that would help him."

"Anything for a friend. Would you like to go out on my boat sometime?"

Nancy thought of how much fun she'd had when she was about Eugenia's age, going out with her family. "Perhaps in June, after the fund-raiser." If Eugenia was still here, she'd need a life jacket.

"Promise?" Bailey asked, but he was looking at someone across the room and lifting his chin in greeting.

Nancy wanted him to understand that he couldn't just take her out to fill a seat, so she said, "Thank you for a lovely dinner," and picked up her pewter metallic clutch.

He looked surprised even though his forehead was strangely immobile. "Don't you want dessert or coffee? It's still early."

"Is it? I haven't been keeping track of time."

"Have I bored you?"

"Yes, terribly. It's been unendurable." She turned her head to hide her smile.

He laughed and reached for her hand. "I thought we could go out somewhere else. We could hit a club."

"That's what people do on dates."

"To hell with my promise. I want this to be a date."

Nancy said, "A married lady doesn't date, Bailey."

"A married lady could go to a group event, couldn't she? A friend is having a party. We could go to that and be surrounded by a hundred chaperones and stand at least a foot apart when we dance."

"If you really want me to, I could go, as a friend."

"I really, really want you to."

They left the restaurant and walked a few blocks until they reached a hybrid SUV. "The mileage is very good," he said a little apologetically.

Bailey drove south of Market to a mess of industrial buildings, some of which had been converted to restaurants and nightspots. Nancy was disappointed by the hoboish crowd outside the clubs. Where was the glamour?

When they reached the warehouse where the party was being held, valets were out front, and a few decently dressed people milled about. Bailey got out of the car, tossed the keys to the valet, and ran around to open the door for her.

"Hey, Bailey," one guy called out.

"Stuckler, what's up," Bailey responded, and then said quietly to Nancy, "Kirby Stuckler, big in winter sports equipment fabrication."

The doorman, tapping a clipboard against his thigh, said, "Hey, Bailey, how's it going?"

"My man," Bailey responded, and Nancy admired his man-of-the-people ease in exchanging a fist bump and a slap on the back with the guy while remembering to tip him.

Once off the dirty street and inside the warehouse, Nancy felt more comfortable. Bailey took her through an entry hall curtained with billowing white parachute silk and into a vast room where individual bamboo cabanas surrounded a dance floor.

In minutes they were lounging on the cushioned benches of a cabana as guests of Bailey's friend, who produced corporate videos. She looked at the dance floor and saw skinny, gawky GP coming toward her with a big smile.

"Hey, princess! I didn't know you'd be here." He joined them and suddenly she started seeing old friends and acquaintances. The band was playing swing music, bottles of champagne appeared, people were moving from cabana to cabana, people were dancing, and she felt the way she used to feel.

She felt like Nancy Edith Carrington, the cutest and most popular girl in the room.

"Nancy! Nancy!"

She searched through the crowd and spotted Junie Burns, whose transformation was even more obvious in party clothes. Junie's flippy skirt hid her hip problem and a delicate halter drew attention to her attractive shoulders. "Junie!"

Junie was flushed prettily, and Nancy thought this party must be very exciting for someone like Junie, who rarely got out of the office.

"Junie, you were supposed to call me! Especially if you have time to get out."

"I came at the last minute," Junie said as she looked around at Nancy's group. "Oh, Bailey!" she called, and waved back to him. Then to Nancy she said, "Are you here with anyone?"

"No, just Bailey. It's part of my get-out-and-promote-Froth strategy. Todd thought it was a good idea when Bailey asked him. Are you here with anyone?"

Junie shook her head. "No, just seeing friends."

"That's what I love about the city. Everyone can go out and just be friends. It's not all coupley." Nancy wanted to ask Junie how Lizette's party had been, but she wasn't going to let it get back to Lizette that she cared in the least.

Nancy mingled with everyone while Junie was nearby, so her friend wouldn't get the wrong idea. But when GP asked her to dance, she said yes, because not even Junie could misinterpret that.

After he stepped on Nancy's feet a few times, she said, "Do you even know how to swing dance?"

"How hard can it be?" he said, and counted, "One, two, three, one, two, three . . ."

"I am ebullient about the fund-raiser. Do you have any updates?"

"I'm meeting someone next week who will, one, two, three, help me with the actors. Did you read Asbury's history of the Barbary Coast?"

"Yes," she said, because she had looked at the cover before putting it on the bookshelf. "You really rescued us with your concept of an *authentic* theme."

"I'm stoked that you're okay with that."

"Of course I am," Nancy said. "Why wouldn't I be? I want it to be exactly the Barbary Coast that Asbury describes so vividly."

"Totally. I'm getting pretty good at this," he said, dipping her.

"Whoo!" The champagne made it all so much fun.

Then Bailey tapped her partner's shoulder and said, "May I cut in?"

Nancy was whirled around into Bailey's arms. He held her close and smiled.

He danced well, a necessary skill for someone who is welcome as an extra man at parties.

She asked, "What happened to dancing a foot apart?"

"It's not really dancing unless I can feel you next to me," he said, pulling her closer.

She swayed with him to the music and realized how much she'd missed dancing. "A few more minutes, but then I should go."

But a few minutes turned into "a little longer," then "not quite yet," and then everyone went for drinks at a raucous bar that was playing her favorite arias on its classic jukebox. Local actors and performers began showing up, including a troupe of burlesque dancers.

Bailey was caught up in a discussion about city zoning law

with a restaurateur, so Nancy excused herself and made her way to the most stunning of the dancers, a tall, buxom brunette, who sat in one of the red booths. She wore a red velvet costume, trimmed in white and blue, a pillbox hat with an explosion of snowy ostrich plumes, and red boots.

Nancy sat beside her and said, "Love the look. What's the inspiration?"

"Jackie O and Wonder Woman, but I don't think anyone but me gets it."

"I love Jackie O. She had a deep understanding of her own style, moving from those simple Oleg Cassini sheaths to Valentino and Carolina Herrera as her life progressed."

"Is style really a reason to admire someone?"

"Knowing your style means knowing yourself and knowing how you want the world to perceive you. Jackie's style showed an appreciation for beauty and the art of fashion."

"You're right," the dancer said. "But I wonder what her life would have been like if she hadn't had to be the good girl."

"And why Wonder Woman?"

"That was my boyfriend's idea. Ex-boyfriend, actually. He broke up with me today. The empowered beauty, but I think he just had the hots for Wonder Woman when he was a kid."

"I didn't realize the costumes had so much backstory."

"I'm writing my master's thesis on the politics of feminist identity and gender in popular performance." She held out her hand and said, "I'm Melanie, by the way."

Nancy shook her hand and said, "Nice to meet you. I'm Nancy."

"Nancy!" Melanie shook her head, the plumes on her hat fluttering.

"What?"

"Sorry, the ex-boyfriend works for someone named Nancy. He said she was crazy, but I suspected that something was going on." She shrugged. "Then he says he's in love with her and dumps me."

"Ouch. You must meet a lot of men, though."

Melanie nodded. "I do and that's how I knew this one was special. He's a reporter, an *unemployed* reporter like the rest of them, and he and Nancy Fancy were collaborating on some hush-hush research project."

"That can't be a real name," Nancy said, laughing.

"I think it was just his little nickname for her, but I did know a real Candace 'Candy' Caine, C-A-I-N-E."

"I know Binky Winkles and a gay man whose last name is Bottomsley," Nancy said.

"That guy is named Whiteside," Melanie said, indicating Bailey. "I saw you with him. He's been at some of the business gigs I do, but he always leaves before anything gets out of control. A careful type."

Nancy pulled a Froth business card out of her clutch. "I plan events and often hire performers. I'm swamped right now, but call me in a month and we can talk."

Melanie took the card and tucked it in her cleavage. "Nancy Carrington-Chambers. Now, that's *fancy*. Thanks. I'll be in touch." She yawned. "Sorry. I'm usually in bed by one and it's already half past."

"That late? I've got to get home."

Nancy returned to Bailey's table and told her new acquaintances, "I really, *really* have to go. Bye, bye!"

Bailey was saying "But . . ." as she blew kisses and exchanged promises to see everyone soon.

He held out her jacket for her and she rushed out the

doors and into the night. Nancy breathed in the refreshingly cold night air, smelling those city scents she loved: the salty breeze from the waterfront, faint garlicky food aromas from the closed Italian and Chinese restaurants, yeasty baking bread, and the rich, bitter scent of roasting coffee beans.

Nancy liked the sound of her heels clicking on the sidewalk, the darkened storefronts, a burst of laughter in the distance. She felt free and she wished she could stay out all night.

Bailey slipped his arm through hers. "You are always rushing away from me."

"You seem to think everything is about you, Bailey."

They had arrived at his car and he stopped and turned to her. "It's just that I thought we connected tonight."

"Bailey, I'm sure you *connect* with a lot of girls."

"No, I *date* a lot of girls."

On the short drive home, he talked casually about the people they'd seen during the evening. He pulled into the driveway of her building and said, "How is Binky Winkles doing?"

"She's as scintillating as ever."

"I always like seeing her. She's such an icon."

"We're honored to have her in the building."

Bailey got out of the car, went around, and opened the car door for her. They walked to the front entrance of Château Winkles. "Thank you for going out with me," he said. "When can I see you again?"

She looked up at him, very much aware of his appeal. It wasn't just his looks, but his confidence and ease. She wondered what he was like in bed. "I really am busy, Bailey, but call and I'll check my calendar."

"I've had a crush on you forever, you know."

"I didn't," she said, and then remembered small gestures and looks that he'd given her when they were out with Todd and other friends.

"I didn't want to seem obvious since I felt pretty pathetic and hopeless, lusting after my bro's girl," he said. "Good night, Nancy."

He put his hands at her waist and leaned in to kiss her. She turned her head so that his lips landed on her cheek. She again smelled the harsh sports cologne. It would be an easy fix.

"Good night, Bailey."

Once inside the lobby, Nancy took off her shoes and walked quietly upstairs. She felt exhilarated. She felt sexy and pretty and young again.

She opened her apartment door and peered into the living room, but it was empty. She looked into the bedroom and, because the closet door was open and the closet light was on, she could see Derek asleep in a T-shirt and jeans atop the matelassé coverlet on the bed, a blanket partially covering him.

She tiptoed to the closet and saw Eugenia sleeping on her side, her fingers gripping the terry-cloth cape.

Nancy left the closet door a little ajar, then turned toward the room. Derek's jacket and shirt were carefully draped on the back of a chair and his shoes were on the floor, neatly aligned. Should she wake him so he could go home? But it was late. Nancy quietly went to the bathroom to wash up and brush her teeth before returning to the bedroom.

Derek was so beautiful with his dark hair falling over his forehead, his features more stark and masculine in the shadows. Nancy slipped off her dress and slid under the covers.

Derek shifted toward her and his arm reached out and

around her. She reached to him, too, incapable of resisting the urge to touch the fine pima cotton of his shirt and feeling the firm flesh beneath.

When she was with Derek, she didn't have to be anyone else, or be careful about what she said or did, or wonder what he wanted from her. Nancy was filled with appreciation and perhaps, too, the mix of drinks and the excitement of the night.

So when Derek opened his eyes and gazed at her dreamily, she gazed back. And when he pulled her to him, she reached for him. And when he put his mouth on hers, she opened her lips. And when his hands pushed away the blankets between them and ran down her back to her hips, she moved her bare leg over his.

And when he said, "Oh, Mrs. Carrington-Chambers," she said, "Oh, Derek."

He pulled her atop him and his kisses were enthusiastic, and Nancy felt a rush of affection and pleasure that she'd never felt when Todd's rough mouth clamped on her or his big, meaty hands groped her.

The scent of Derek, his taste, the way he felt, was intoxicating.

Derek stopped kissing her. She could feel his chest rising and falling beneath her. Something else was rising, too. He said, "I don't want to wake her."

Nancy raked her fingers through his hair. "The laundry room."

She got up and walked on tiptoe there. He was close behind. He shut the door and then he pulled off his T-shirt, exposing his muscled torso. She lifted off her minicami, a little shyly, relieved that he wasn't in any position to compare her breasts to another woman's.

He explored her body with a novice's wonder, and she gasped with pleasure at his beginner's luck in finding her most sensitive places, places in her body that she didn't even know were erogenous.

She impatiently unbuttoned and unzipped his jeans, stroking him and making him groan. Although she didn't want to think about anything or anyone else, she said, "Will Prescott mind?"

"You're a woman, so it doesn't count as a shag. What about your husband?"

"You're gay, so it doesn't count." She ignored the logical inconsistencies of this reasoning and admired his slim-fit, black cotton oxford boxers. They were more perfect than she had imagined. Then she pulled them down and admired other things about him.

fourteen

seek hallmarks of quality

The next morning, Nancy awoke to someone prodding her arm. "Let me sleep a little longer, hon. Then you can do anything you want with me."

"Can we go to the park?"

Nancy opened her eyes to see Eugenia standing by the bed, already dressed and wearing her new cape. "Where's Derek?"

"Making a cappuccino for me. We ate Count Chocula."

"You're too young to drink coffee. You can have steamed milk. Go back to the kitchen and tell Derek that I'll be there after my shower."

"Then can we go to the park?"

"Later, but only because it's a special occasion."

When Eugenia trotted off, Nancy scrambled for clothes. She saw Derek's jacket still on the chair. His wallet, keys, and phone were on the seat of the chair. It wasn't the sleek black wallet she'd seen before. It was worn brown leather with frayed edges. She picked it up and then thought, *A lady does not snoop*, and returned it.

She showered and dressed in a short black-and-white print dress, a turquoise cashmere sweater, and black flats. As she fixed her hair, the diamonds of her wedding rings glinted on her finger. She pulled them off, thought a moment, and put them back on. She was still married.

Then she went to the kitchen, where Derek was in his T-shirt and jeans, looking very sexy. It was too bad he was . . . Derek. She wanted to wrap her arms around him, but Eugenia was watching, so she said, "Good morning, Derek."

He handed her a mug and said, "How are you feeling this morning, Mrs. Carrington-Chambers?"

"Remarkably invigorated," she said. "You?"

"Fabulous," he said, that smirk playing on his lips and making him look rakish and *different*.

Eugenia was sitting at the kitchen table, blowing bubbles into her milk with a straw.

"Eugenia, do not play with your food," Nancy said. "If you are finished, put the cup on the counter."

"Derek, do you live with us now?" Eugenia asked, then blew more bubbles into her milk.

Nancy exchanged a look with her assistant and said, "Derek does not live here. He has his own place. He had to stay late to watch you. Now, if you're a good girl and spend some quiet time looking at your fashion magazines, I'll make another cape for you later."

"Okay," Eugenia said. She left her cup among the milk splatters on the table and got off the stool. "Derek, if you live here, you can share the little room with me and we can draw more stories."

"That's very generous of you, Eugenia. As your aunt Nancy said, I already have a place to live."

"Don't you like us?"

He grinned and said, "I like you very much. But this apartment is too small for all of us."

She looked at the two adults. "No, it's not."

Nancy said, "Eugenia, please do as you're told."

Eugenia scrunched up her face and said, "Huh!" and stomped off.

"Did you see that?" Nancy asked. "She gave me attitude!"

"I saw." He went to Nancy and put his arm around her waist. "I like you this way, not so done up."

She looked into his *l'heure bleue* eyes. "People expect me to look pulled together. Am I the first woman you've been with?"

"You were shagtastic. What now?"

Nancy got scared that he was going to tell her he didn't want to see her again. "I don't want you to do anything that you don't enjoy."

"Did it seem as if I wasn't enjoying myself?" His hands dropped lower onto her hips. "I assure you, I enjoyed myself more than I ever thought I could."

She laughed, and then thought of the complications. "So long as we remember that this is an extension of our friendship. After all, you have Prescott and I'm married."

"My relationship with Prescott is really just a friendship at this point. It's an important friendship, but there's no . . . we don't have a physical relationship."

"You don't need to explain." Nancy wondered if he would ever tell her about the mysterious Mel, or if there even was a Mel.

"Prescott wouldn't understand, so . . ."

"Gossip would hurt me, too. It will be our secret, something we can enjoy privately, because I'm married."

"And I'm gay." His hand reached down to her leg and wandered under the hem of her dress. He began stroking her thigh in a way that made her want him right then and there. "Yet I fancy you."

Nancy laughed and jumped back. "Not now! Eugenia might come in."

"As always, you are right, Mrs. Carrington-Chambers."

"It's silly, isn't it, how Eugenia thinks we can all live together."

"Children live in a fantasy world where anything is possible."

"Fortunately, we can be realistic about this. I don't want it, us, to interfere with Froth and business."

"Of course not. But as it is my day off . . ." He gave her a long, lingering kiss before saying "Good day, Mrs. Carrington-Chambers."

"Bye, Derek."

He got his things from the bedroom, and then she heard him saying bye to Eugenia and leaving.

She felt dreamy and satiated, so she didn't mind lingering at the park with Eugenia. Since she'd been playing outdoors so much, the girl's hair had taken on amber tones that shone in the sunlight, and her complexion had become rosier. Later, as promised, they made another cape. Eugenia picked out a pink and purple daisy print, big brass nautical buttons, and silver lamé for an appliqué.

"That sounds a bit much," Nancy said as she smoothed the fabric out on her sewing table.

"I want it like that!"

Nancy noticed a more strident tone in her ward's voice. Eugenia's leaf brown eyes shone, and her little pink lips were firmly set.

"I seriously question this decision, but I believe you must be allowed to follow your own creative muse. Don't come crying to me if you are mocked in the school yard."

"Auntie Nanny, when do I go to school?"

"Your mother will decide. I loved school. I was a delightful kindergartener. I always colored neatly within the lines and knew the name of every crayon color in the big box. Carnation Pink and Aquamarine were my favorites."

"Do you have crayons?"

"We'll get some and I'll teach you the names of all the colors."

"I need to color the stories I made with Derek."

"Where are the stories?"

"I'll get them." Eugenia skipped out of the room and came back with a manila folder. There was a drawing of a ship on the high seas and ornate lettering that said "The Adventures of Pirate Girl." "We made the story but I need to color the pic-*tures*."

Nancy opened the folder and saw several sheets of paper with a clever cartoon version of Eugenia as a pirate. Dialogue balloons boldly announced explosions and exclamations as the heroine faced a sea of sharks, battled enemies, and steered her ship in a storm.

"I told Derek what to draw," Eugenia said. "He's going to make a book for me."

"This is a terrific story, Eugenia. I didn't know Derek could draw like this." There was still so much Nancy didn't know about him, so she didn't understand why she trusted him so instinctively.

"He showed me how to draw a shark with big teeth." Eugenia sat on the floor with a pen and began adding to Derek's illustrations.

"Eugenia, you better not get ink on my rug."

"Huh!"

"And don't you 'huh' me, missy."

As Nancy made a cape pattern and cut out the cloth, she realized that her evening out with Bailey had dimmed after her experience with Derek. Sex with Todd or anyone else had never been as good. Perhaps gay men were more attuned and sensitive. It was a pity they weren't interested in women, because they had so much more to offer a girl than any of the straight men she knew.

Nancy felt a desperate need to talk to someone about what had happened. Milagro could keep a secret and was generous with her affections so she wouldn't judge.

Nancy phoned her friend and arranged for her to come for dinner on Wednesday. "Come at five, because I want you to meet my fabulous assistant," Nancy said.

"Will you feed me something besides expensive water and cocktail olives, or should I bring something?"

"My kitchen is a Copacabana of gourmet foods," Nancy said as she opened the cupboard to make sure she had a box of organic mac and cheese. "Bring a large box of crayons. My niece, Eugenia, is still here. Her twin passions are pirates and cows."

"Cows are overrated, but I love pirates."

"It is a universal dream to dress like a pirate," Nancy said.

"Truer words were ne'er said. Crayons, it is, but I'm going

to throw away the Peach one. There has never been a 'peachy' complexion that color and it skips badly when you try to use it."

"You're thinking of Burnt Sienna, which is flawed in some unfixable way, possibly at the molecular level. See you Wednesday."

While Eugenia was splashing in her bath that night, Nancy sat on a low stool. Water glistened on the child's smooth skin, and her wet hair clung darkly to her scalp. Her nose wasn't bad. It was a Carrington nose.

"Can I get a pirate ship, Auntie Nanny?"

"It won't fit in the bathtub. Pirate ships are huge."

"Not a real one!" Eugenia giggled. "A toy one."

"Wouldn't you rather have dolls? We could make pretty dresses for them."

"No."

"But all little girls like dolls."

"I'm a pirate. I like pirate toys, like swords. Can I have a sword?"

"When you're old enough. You could take up fencing. It's like sword fighting and the fabulous costumes inspired a whole line by Jean Paul Gaultier."

"Okay. I want a *shiny* sword."

Eugenia played in the tub for an hour while Nancy reminisced about her night with Derek, but she noticed that Bailey didn't call. That's how it was with straight men—they always had a strategy. But Bailey probably hadn't pursued anyone who'd absorbed Sun Tzu's many tactical lessons.

The next day Nancy wore a deep violet blouse with a short gray skirt, charcoal tights, and brown riding boots so she could show off her legs. Not that she had to dress to impress Derek.

He came in wearing his business casual: jeans, a button-down shirt, and a blazer. Nancy would have been happy spending the day looking at him.

Eugenia came from the kitchen and threw herself at him. "Derek!"

He laughed and lifted her up in a hug. "Good morning, Eugenia. Are you happy to see me?"

"Yes! We made a new cape and Auntie Nanny is going to teach me crayon colors and I'm going to color our stories!"

"That sounds very exciting. You can show them to me later." He swung Eugenia around before putting her down.

"Hi," Nancy said. "I love that shirt on you."

"Thank you. Would you like your cappuccino now, Mrs. Carrington-Chambers?"

"I'll come to the kitchen with you." Turning to Eugenia who was looking at a picture book about Blackbeard, she said, "I'll call you when your breakfast is ready."

Nancy followed Derek down the hall and said, "I'll fix her a dish of fruit and yogurt." In the kitchen he went to the refrigerator, took out the milk, and handed her a container of vanilla yogurt.

While he measured coffee beans into the burr grinder, she spooned the yogurt into a dish and sliced strawberries into it. "We're so efficient together," she said.

"Like a well-oiled machine," he said with a wink.

"Are you talking dirty to me?"

He picked up one of the strawberries and held it to her mouth, saying, "Would you like me to?"

She ate the strawberry and felt her cheeks grow warm. "I didn't know you could draw so well. I love 'The Adventures of Pirate Girl.'"

"American comic books were one of my boyhood obsessions."

"What were your other obsessions?"

"What were yours?"

He was standing only a few inches from her and she realized that it might not be easy to keep work and platonic sex separate. Then the intercom buzzed.

"Maybe it's Birdie," she said, and they looked at each other, neither one needing to say what they were thinking about the girl going back to her mother.

Nancy went to the intercom by the front door and said, "Yes?"

"Delivery for Nancy Carrington."

"I'll come down," Nancy said. She turned toward the kitchen and called out to Derek, "It's a delivery! Deliveries are always good." Maybe Bailey was sending flowers. Nancy took the steps down quickly and opened the Château's front door to a man in a brown uniform with a very large flat parcel wrapped in brown paper.

"Morning. I need a signature."

Nancy signed for the package, thanked the deliveryman, and took it upstairs to her apartment to examine it. It was light for its size and the package had customs labels in another language. Nancy had an unpleasant sense of foreboding as she walked into her apartment.

"Open it! Open it!" Eugenia said, dancing around. "Is it a birthday present?"

"No, it's not my birthday." Nancy put the parcel on her writing table and cut through the wrapping with scissors. She tried not to panic when she saw the Greek lettering on the layers of newspaper wrapped around the flat object inside.

Derek came into the room just as Nancy removed the final layer of paper from the object.

It was a painting of a beautiful naked woman on a balcony. She was leaning back against a white balustrade and in the background was a cobalt blue ocean.

Eugenia said, "Mama!"

Nancy turned the painting over and found a thin sheet of notepaper taped to the wood frame. "It's from Birdie. She's in Greece."

"Read it!" Eugenia said excitedly.

Nancy skimmed the letter first and then said, "Your mama says, 'Dear Nanny, I was so busy that I didn't have a chance to call you before my flight. Give all my love to Eugenia. I know she is having a wonderful time with you. Kisses.'"

Eugenia reached out to touch the frame. "Put Mama on the wall."

"I'll have to find the right place for her." Nancy looked at the painting and had to admit it was good. She saw a scrawl in the corner that she guessed was Yannis's signature. "Time for your breakfast, Eugenia. Come to the table."

When the child was eating her meal, Nancy called Derek into the hallway.

"Yes, madame?"

She was still holding the note. "That isn't all Birdie said. 'Take care of my angel. Yannis and I will be exploring the world's wonders and the wonders of each other's body.' Eww. She always gives too much information."

"The painting looks well executed."

"When you sex up enough artists, you occasionally find one with talent."

"What are you going to do?"

"I can't have Eugenia spending her days coloring until Birdie trades in Yannis for the next creep waiting to explore her well-charted geography."

"Now may be the time to engage a nanny."

"Then there would be another person cluttering up the apartment. Sloane may know where we can park Eugenia during the day. Um, somewhere educational and enlightening."

So Nancy called Sloane, who was eager to help. "I'll look into it right away. Do you have any preferences? There are co-op preschools, Montessori, Walden, language-intensive, art based, and—"

"I'd like someplace where Eugenia will learn manners, good posture, and how to color. Where she can play outside. A pirate-themed facility would be ideal, particularly if they have a pet cow."

"I don't know if there are any—"

"Wonderful! Call me back!" Nancy hung up, glad to have delegated the task to someone who cared about the minutiae of child rearing.

Nancy called Frilly and told her about Birdie's gift and letter. "Aunt Frilly, it might be weeks before she returns. Are you having any luck convincing Uncle Robert to take Eugenia in?"

"Not yet. He says it would be enabling Birdie's irresponsibility, so we can't do anything."

"That might be appropriate if Birdie was a heroin addict, but there is another person to consider in this situation."

"Eugenia."

"No, me. You keep working on Uncle Robert and I'll see if I can find child care. Do you think you could contribute toward this?"

"You *do* get that apartment rent-free, Nanny."

"All right, fine."

Nancy didn't know what child care would cost, but she did something she very rarely did: call her father at work.

His longtime assistant answered. "Julian Carrington's office."

"Hi, it's me."

"Hello, Carolyn."

"No, it's me, Nancy. Who's Carolyn? May I please speak to my father?"

"Oh, I'm so *sorry* about that. I don't know what I was thinking. I swear my mind is going. I apologize. Please forget that I got so confused. Just a moment and I'll see if he can talk."

Nancy thought her apology was excessive, but her father preferred his assistants to be obsequious.

There was a click on the line and Julian said, "Nancy! To what do I owe the honor?"

"Hi, Dad, I hate to bother you at work, but there is this urgent matter. Birdie wrote to me from Greece. She wasn't clear on when she'll be back, and I've taken it upon myself as a family responsibility to provide child care for her daughter, Eugenia."

"That's a welcome change from your usual attitude. Caring for a child is one of life's great rewards."

Nancy remembered how her father always came to say good night to her when he finally returned from work in the evenings. "You can say that because I was a delightful child."

"Actually, Nanny . . ."

"But let's not talk about me. Uncle Robert refuses to contribute to the care of his granddaughter. There's food, clothes, crayons, pirate shirts, a car seat, and whatever a day care costs until Birdie comes home again. It all adds up."

She expected him to offer to transfer funds into her checking account.

Instead, he said, "You're a married woman now, Nancy, and we've provided you with more than enough to cover a child's expenses for a short time."

"Yes, but my cash flow is tied up in Froth right now and I'd prefer not to withdraw from my shared account with Todd. Also, that awful house is still a drain on my income—"

"Who is responsible for that?"

"Todd was the one who—"

"Todd was the one who tried to work with your exorbitant plans," Julian said. "Times have changed, the world has changed, and we all have to make adjustments. That includes you. Is there anything else?"

She resented the way he spoke to her, but a lady didn't rebuke her father, so she said calmly, "Mom seems really *tired* every time I see her."

Julian sighed. "You know how she lets her nerves get the best of her, even though someone's always helping around the house. I've got another call coming in. Bye, Nanny."

fifteen

the timeless charm of classics

Sloane got back to Nancy that afternoon. "I have wonderful news. There's a temporary opening at Three Bridges Preschool, which is only a few blocks from the Château. One of their children is going for a month abroad with his family. It's a terrific school and I told them how invested you are in progressive care for the whole child."

Nancy didn't know what that meant, but said, "Yes, that's right. The whole child, very progressive."

"They can see you and Eugenia there tomorrow at ten. That way you can observe a regular morning."

"Fantastic. I will take the whole child there."

After Sloane had given Nancy the address and contact

information, Nancy said, "Thanks for helping, Sloane. I wouldn't have known where to begin."

"I'm glad you came to me. It must be a treat to spend time with Eugenia, since your sisters' families live so far away. How are your sisters?"

Nancy hadn't talked to them in months. "They're wonderful. Once my schedule lets up, I'm definitely going to see them. I'll give you a report back on our visit to the preschool."

Nancy was sitting on her bed, thinking about the complications of family, when Eugenia came running in, brandishing a cardboard sword.

"Look what Derek made!"

Nancy saw the glee in the little girl's face and shouted, "Oh, no, a pirate's in my room!" and started running.

Eugenia chased her and soon they tumbled on top of the bed, laughing. Nancy stroked the girl's fine brown hair and inhaled her clean child's scent and said, "Guess what? We're looking at a school tomorrow."

"Are you coming?"

"I'm coming with you to look at the school. We'll meet the children and decide if we like them or if they should walk the plank."

"And sharks will eat them!"

"And crocodiles," Nancy said. "Now you have to play quietly so Derek and I can do our work."

When five o'clock came, Derek put on his jacket and said, "Prescott is making dinner."

"I'll walk you out," Nancy said, thinking that maybe they could share a friendly kiss on the stairs.

"Me, too." Eugenia got up off the floor and picked up her sword.

They walked down the stairs together, and the adults kept the conversation businesslike. When they reached the lobby, the front door opened and Miss Binky Winkles tottered in, lugging a bag of groceries.

Derek quickly went forward, saying, "Allow me to take that for you, madame."

"It's miss, young man. I'm still available."

He laughed as if it was funny, and Nancy pasted a smile on her face and said, "Good evening, Miss Winkles."

"Hello to you, Girl Carrington. Introduce your friends."

"Miss Winkles, this is Derek Cathcart, my assistant, and this is Eugenia, my niece."

Miss Winkles took a long look at Derek, then Eugenia, who was still holding her sword. "She's one of your sisters' daughters?"

"No, she's Roberta's daughter."

"Oh, *that* one! Well, she's got her mother's looks. Let's hope she's got more—"

"Miss Winkles," Nancy cut in. "Would you like Derek to help you take your groceries up?"

"Yes. What did you say your full name was, young man?" Miss Winkles asked as she went to the elevator and pushed the call button.

"Derek Cathcart."

"Where are your people from?"

"England."

"Hmm, you're sure you're not from around here?"

"Yes, I'm sure," he said.

"You're the spitting image of one of my sister's beaux. A handsome devil, that one. A flimflam man and a terrible womanizer. His name was Tom Drexler, or Dave Drexler, something like that. Do you have a grandfather by that name?"

"Not on my father's side, Miss Winkles, and my mother was adopted, so we don't know that side of the family history."

As Derek and the old woman got in the elevator, Eugenia slipped in with them. Nancy heard her say "I want to push the button!" as the doors closed.

Nancy went to her apartment and waited for Derek to bring Eugenia back. Twice she went to the front door. Then she put away the girl's toys and papers and polished the dining room table.

She was vacuuming, so she didn't hear them come back in.

"Bye, Derek," Eugenia said. She closed the door and skipped into the living room, swinging her sword.

"Where have you been all this time?"

"Miss Winkles has a spyglass! She can see pirate boats from her house."

"It's an apartment, not a house," Nancy said. She'd always wanted to see it. "What does it look like?"

Eugenia pursed her lips in concentration. "It has lots of things all over and lots of pic-*tures*, but not as pretty as the one of Mama. Can we put it on the wall?"

"I don't know that it really goes with any of my things."

"I *want* to look at Mama!"

Half an hour and many tears and high-pitched screams later, Nancy propped the painting at the back of her bedroom closet where Eugenia could see it at night. Birdie's green eyes stared at her, bold and sensual, from between the formerly perfect racks of clothes.

When Nancy finally tucked Eugenia in that night, she felt

as worn out as she had after an argument with Todd, but much more forgiving. She said to the girl, "A lady does not throw temper tantrums. I want you to be on your best behavior tomorrow when we visit the school, okay?"

"Okay. Night, Auntie Nanny," Eugenia said, and reached up and gave Nancy a kiss on her cheek.

"Good night, baby," Nancy said, and kissed the child's forehead. She glanced up and saw Birdie's self-satisfied gaze staring out from the painting.

Nancy's phone rang late that night. She glanced at the incoming number and saw that it was Bailey. A gentleman did not request booty calls, so she didn't answer. He left a message asking her to go out on Wednesday.

However, Wednesday was not a significant date night, and Nancy had already arranged to see Milagro. A lady did not cancel on girlfriends to go out with a man.

On Tuesday, Nancy put on her preschool interview clothes: a gray and ivory thin knit cardigan, skinny black cords, and ebony ballet flats with ivory ribbon trim.

Derek arrived as she was telling Eugenia, "If you wear that shirt, people will think you're a boy."

"I want to wear my skull shirt!"

"How are you this morning, Mrs. Carrington-Chambers?"

"I feel like I'm trying to wrestle snakes into leg warmers," she said. "I'm suffering from caffeine withdrawal."

"I can help with that." He smiled at her and said, "You look full of mischief today."

She said, "I'm ready to play on the swings if they have a set. I have excellent technique."

"I hope you will demonstrate later."

Eugenia took advantage of Nancy's momentary distraction

to grab the skull-and-crossbones shirt, run into the bathroom, and slam the door.

Nancy went after her, saying, "Eugenia whatever-your-middle-name-is Carrington, come out of there this minute!" and she could hear Derek laughing as he went into the kitchen. "It's not funny!" she called to him, but she was smiling.

At ten o'clock Nancy arrived at the preschool, which was only a few blocks from her apartment, with a child wearing a skull-and-crossbones shirt and a purple, pink, and silver lamé cape. She didn't have to look at the address to know she was at the right place. She could hear the nerve-rattling children's voices from the sidewalk.

Three Bridges Preschool was in a renovated one-story building with half-barrel planters of lettuces, sweet peas, and pansies out front. Nancy rang the doorbell and a middle-aged woman with cropped gray hair came to the door and said hello. She had that no-makeup and Levi's jeans look that Nancy associated with people who went camping and made their own bread.

"Hello, I'm Nancy Carrington-Chambers and I have an appointment with the director."

"Hello, Nancy. I'm Madeline Kanbar." She shook hands and then bent to say, "You must be Eugenia."

"Hello."

"You can call me Mrs. Kanbar. Please come in."

Mrs. Kanbar led them on a tour of the preschool, showing them the art, music, cooking, reading, and nap areas. Nancy was impressed with the extensive collection of dress-up clothes and spotted a Pucci scarf on a hat rack. The backyard had a jungle gym, tricycles, toys, and benches and tables.

Small ruffians ran everywhere, occasionally stopping to stare at Eugenia. Nancy didn't bother to listen closely to Mrs. Kanbar's history of the center, since Sloane had already vetted it.

They went to Mrs. Kanbar's office and she said, "At ten thirty, we have circle time and then go into groups for the day's projects." She handed Nancy a sheet of paper and a pen and said, "If you're interested in the temporary spot, you'll need to fill out this form and give a deposit."

"We're definitely interested. It seems very progressive and I love your whole-child philosophy." Nancy quickly filled in the form, but was stumped at certain areas. "Eugenia, when is your birthday?"

Eugenia shrugged.

Mrs. Kanbar looked surprised. "You don't know her birthday?"

Nancy smiled and said, "Her mother left her with me like . . . a delightful surprise! She's traveling now. But Eugenia is almost five, so I'll just do the math . . ."

"Are you sure?" Mrs. Kanbar asked.

"Of course! She told me."

The school director looked at the child and said, "Eugenia, how old are you *really*?"

The girl held up five fingers and then four.

"I thought so," Mrs. Kanbar said. "We'll say four, but a big-girl four."

Nancy wrote a check for the deposit, which was far more than she'd anticipated, and handed it to Mrs. Kanbar, who placed it in her desk.

"Eugenia, can you draw a picture for me?" Mrs. Kanbar asked, and gave a piece of paper and a crayon to Eugenia. She said to Nancy, "Let's talk in the hall."

Nancy followed her there, saying, "I hope her age is not a problem."

"Not at all. I've known Sloane for some time and I value her opinion. She explained your unusual situation, otherwise I wouldn't take a child without proper permission from her legal guardian. It puts the school at legal risk."

"It's nothing I planned," Nancy said, wondering why she felt as if she was the one doing something wrong. "Her mother is unavailable."

"Eugenia's very lucky to have an aunt who cares so much."

"Yes, well . . ."

"Our regular program begins at nine, but we have early drop-off from seven thirty."

"Nine is fine."

They stayed for part of circle time, and Eugenia was bouncing with excitement on the walk home.

Nancy said, "Hold my hand while we're crossing the street. I can't believe you fibbed about your age." She was exasperated when Eugenia didn't respond. "Time passes quickly enough. Enjoy this idyllic year of your life. The big oh-four." She liked the warmth of the tiny hand in her own.

"Auntie Nanny, Miss Wiggles said I should have a kitten. She had a kitten when she was a liddle girl. Can I have a kitten?"

"Miss Winkles has a lot of ideas. You can ask your mother about a kitten."

"A kitten can sleep in my liddle room."

"Lit*t*le. A kitten would shred my clothes with its diabolical claws. No."

"I will watch it and say 'No!'"

"I'm saying no now. Did you like the school?"

"Mrs. Candybar smelled like lemons, not chocolate. Where were the candy bars?"

"I'm fond of citrusy colognes and hers was lovely. I don't know if she gives out candy bars. She probably thinks parents should give candy bars." Nancy saw Eugenia's disappointment and added, "Aunts can give candy bars, too."

"A boy said he liked my cape."

"It is stunning. Capes are both an underused and misused garment. They're unique in that the lining is as important as the exterior. You can swirl one, or throw an end over your shoulder dramatically. It can be short, a capelet, or long. Floaty or heavy. It's very versatile."

"You can wear a cape, too, Auntie Nanny."

"You get more interesting every day, Eugenia."

Derek was just getting off the phone when they returned. "How was the school, Eugenia?"

"Mrs. Candybar showed us the play yard and Aunt Nanny is going to give me candy and when can we get my kitten?"

Derek looked at Nancy, who was shaking her head no. He said, "The designer's messengering invitation samples this afternoon, and the contract for the warehouse will be ready for you to review tomorrow. GP called and said the sets will require two full days to set up."

"It's getting exciting, isn't it?"

He smiled. "I can see why you enjoy it."

After lunch, when they'd run out of breath kicking the soccer ball in the park, Nancy and Derek sat in the sun, which had finally made an appearance, and watched Eugenia practice tumbling. There was no one else around and Derek's hand moved to take Nancy's.

She smiled. "I've been holding hands more these last few weeks than I have all of my adult life."

"Don't you hold hands with Mr. Chambers?"

"Oh, please. Todd thinks hand-holding is gay. His buddies got more hugs and ass slaps than I ever did. What about you and Prescott?"

"He isn't as cozy as you. He does make an excellent mushroom risotto."

"Todd doesn't cook. He had a giant outdoor kitchen built and promised he would grill, and he did it a total of three times. He preferred a conflagration to technique. Everything was burnt on the outside and raw on the inside."

Nancy looked down at Derek's large, lovely hands and thought of where and how he had touched her. She said, "We always talk about me, and never about you. Tell me about your life."

"A life in service is not very exciting, madame."

"Your drawings are wonderful. Did you study art?"

He laughed and said, "I spent many an hour in the comic-book shop and I took classes. I never found the right story to tell."

"You don't seem to have any trouble telling the Pirate Girl story."

"I merely carry out Eugenia's dictates," he said, and rubbed his thumb on her wrist, sending tingles up her arm.

"Tell me about your family. I know you said your mother raised you and your brother by herself. How did she do that?"

"She worked as a medical secretary and became an office manager. Peter and I would like her to retire and move in with his family."

"Are you close to them?"

"Yes, but I had to go where I could find work, Mrs. Carrington-Chambers."

"What is your mother like?"

Now he smiled. "Very affectionate and loving, but firm. She was adopted by an older couple and keeping us together as a family was very important to her."

"So you were poor?"

"Not as poor as many. We had food and a roof over our heads and our mates. We were happy playing ball or having a swim."

"I think you must have been a well-groomed, beautifully mannered boy who loved school trips to the museum."

He smirked. "I will not disillusion you, Mrs. Carrington-Chambers. I think you were an idiosyncratic towheaded girl who demanded to have everything exactly as she wanted it."

"I was a delightful child!" she said, and laughed. "What is Miss Winkles's apartment like?"

"It is like a curiosity shop. I enjoyed the adverts with the Winkles Triplets. Everything was three times as fast, or three times as good."

"Or three times as fun, if you believe the rumors. Miss Winkles always has something snarky to say about *my* family, but I heard that she and her sisters would pass men around like the flu."

Nancy was leaning against Derek, drowsy with warmth and happiness, when a couple approached the park. She pulled her hand away from his and got up suddenly. "Time to go."

But when they got back to the apartment, and Eugenia was napping on the sofa, Nancy and her assistant went to the kitchen and closed the door. She said, "Just this once."

"Because it's a special occasion," he said as he urged her back over the small table.

"We eat at this table," Nancy said.

"The laundry room?"

They kissed and touched as they walked down the hall and left the door ajar. She'd gotten his trousers down and he had unsnapped her bra when she stopped suddenly. "Did you hear that?"

"No. What?" His lips were on her neck and his hands came up to her breasts.

"I thought I heard Eugenia."

"She's fine. She's sleeping."

But Nancy had already grabbed her sweater from atop the washing machine and was putting it back on as she left the room. She went to the living room.

Eugenia's eyes were closed and she breathed evenly. Nancy arranged a light blanket around her. "I guess she was just dreaming," she said to Derek, who'd pulled on his trousers and joined her.

"Can we go back?"

"She'll be in school tomorrow. We can wait," Nancy said, even though she didn't want to wait.

Nancy didn't call Bailey until seven in the evening, when she hoped he would be out to dinner and not pick up. She left a brief message, saying, "Thank you for your invitation, but I'm afraid I'm not available on Wednesday. Ta-ta!"

He called back five minutes later. She answered on the fourth ring.

"Hi, Nancy, it's Bailey. I just got your message."

She didn't respond.

Finally he said, "I guess I should have called earlier. I had a great time on Saturday."

"It was nice," she said calmly, and then more enthusiastically, she added, "It was so much fun dancing with GP. I've loved him forever, and I finally got to chat with Junie, who's been completely tied up with work. You know her, don't you? She's really lovely."

"Yeah, we've met," Bailey said. "When can we go out again, Nancy?"

"Why don't you tell me what your availability is and I'll check my schedule?"

"Friday," he said. "There's a dinner party—"

"Oh, I'm sorry. I'm busy Friday." She wondered if she could get Derek to watch Eugenia again. He and Prescott were probably busy most weekends.

"Saturday . . ."

"No, that doesn't work for me. How about next Tuesday?"

"Tuesday? Great. I'll find something special to do."

The next morning, Eugenia crawled into Nancy's bed with a picture book. She snuggled close to Nancy and quietly turned the pages. Nancy put her arm around the sweet little body and nuzzled her fine hair and warm cheek. "Why are you up so early?"

"I have to go to school."

Nancy glanced at the clock. It was six fifty. "We have lots of time. We have more than two hours. Be patient. You have to learn to wait."

"I don't want to wait."

"Neither do I, baby, but sometimes you've got to wait for good things. You should always do something productive while you wait so it's not a waste of time. Would you like me to read to you?"

Eugenia nodded and handed Nancy the pirate book.

Later, when Nancy dressed, she did something she never did—change her clothes over and over again because she didn't know what was the right attire for a prelunch mini-sexathon with a gay assistant.

She settled on a black lace bra and matching thong under a demure black sheath dress with a satin trim at the waist. It was feminine and chic without being too scarily girly for him. Since she was walking to the school, she wore midheeled shoes, and hoped she didn't look nunish.

Or maybe he would like that. Maybe he wanted to be scolded and spanked. She'd never had the urge to spank Todd, but she'd frequently wanted to slap him.

Eugenia wanted to run all the way to Three Bridges. She'd dash ahead, her red cape flying back behind her, and then Nancy would call out, "Come back!" and "Don't go past the corner!" and "Wait right there, missy!"

Other kids were arriving with their parents and au pairs. Nancy examined the children carefully, trying to suss out potential biters, hair-pullers, or chronic nose-pickers. She saw several shady characters. She held Eugenia's hand and said, "You don't *have* to go to school here."

"I want to," the girl said, and ran to a cluster of children playing with a rubber ball.

Nancy watched anxiously as Eugenia hung at the periphery of the group.

"The first day is always harder for the parents than the kids," a voice behind her said.

Nancy turned to see Mrs. Kanbar. "Hi."

"Would you like to stay and watch for a while?"

"If it's okay . . ."

"Of course. We have an open-door policy for parents, and there's a fresh pot of coffee in the kitchen."

So Nancy had a mug of surprisingly good coffee and stood

back observing the kids. Eugenia and another little girl sat on a brightly colored rug, playing with stuffed animals and plastic blocks.

When Nancy looked at the big, round school clock on the wall, she was surprised that an hour had passed. She found Mrs. Kanbar and said good-bye. "Be sure to call me if there are any problems."

"She's doing fine. Some children have more difficulty than others adjusting to new environments."

"Oh, her mother drops her off different places, so Eugenia's used to that," Nancy said.

"Children do best in a stable home," Mrs. Kanbar said, echoing Sloane's comment. "See you this afternoon."

As Nancy walked to the door she heard the thump-thump of feet running, and then arms clamped around her thighs. She looked down to see Eugenia's worried face. "Yes, baby?"

"You're coming back?"

Nancy crouched down to look in the child's face. "I'll be back to get you after you have lunch and playtime today."

"Promise?"

"I promise." Although Nancy thought public displays of affection were overdone, she kissed the girl's warm cheek.

As Nancy returned to Château Winkles, she felt anxious, a combination of leaving Eugenia among unknown children and excitement about being alone with Derek.

He was sitting at his desk when she arrived. In a black suit with a white shirt, he looked as if he had stepped out of a European commercial for an expensive car or watch.

"Good morning, Mrs. Carrington-Chambers. Did all go well at the preschool?"

"Eugenia was playing when I left. However, many of the children looked like incipient criminals."

She didn't know what to do, so she sat on the sofa, crossing one leg over the other as gracefully as she could. "When I was a child, I arranged my toys by size and type. I changed my clothes if I got a speck of dirt on them. I never sassed my parents, or stole, or cheated on tests. I was a perfect little girl."

"Too perfect?" he asked. He stood up and came to her. He sat beside her, his thigh against hers. "And now you're being rather wicked."

"A *little* wicked," she said, and he pressed her back and began kissing her eyelids, her cheek, her neck.

She said, "Not on the sofa! This fabric isn't Scotchgarded!"

"Not the laundry room again?"

"The bed?"

Derek carried Nancy to the bedroom, which was so romantic that she didn't say anything when her foot banged on the door frame. As he laid her on the bed, she asked, "I need to know—do you want me to spank you or anything?"

His eyes widened and he grinned. "Wicked *and* saucy! Do you *want* to spank me?"

"Not really, but I just thought . . . I don't know what you like. Since this is something new to you."

"Then I think you should teach me precisely what pleases you." He took off his jacket and placed it neatly over the chair, then slipped off his tie and hung it there also.

Her sex life had been comprised of trying to please men and she was thrilled by the idea of having a man do what she wanted. "Take off your shirt and come here."

* * *

Later, he fell back on the bed, breathing fast. He asked, "How was that?"

"Incredible." She expected Derek to either get up or move to the far side of the bed and fall asleep, but he put his arm around her and stayed close. "You're amazing for someone who's . . . for whom it isn't a natural inclination," she said, and then insecurity kicked in. "Did I . . . was I all right?"

"More than all right. You're totally aw— awfully fabulous. You must know that."

She laughed nervously as she stroked his chest. "Todd says I'm uptight. But I think he got all his ideas about sex from porn. I kept telling him to stop trying to shove things in me. I'm a girl, not a vase. Do men really like that?"

"Different men like different things."

"I'm sure you know more about that than me. I mean, you are one and you've probably had your share of relationships."

"There've been a few, never one with anyone like you."

"When I met Todd, I was only nineteen. I'd had boyfriends before, but he seemed so experienced by comparison. We took a break when he was getting his MBA, and I went out with other guys and I kept thinking, *'Is this it? Is this what love is supposed to be?'* It wasn't any better, so I went back to Todd. He told me my problem was that I had to loosen up."

"Mrs. Carrington-Chambers, you seemed wonderfully limber to me."

"It's those years of dance class," she said. "May I tell you something I haven't told anyone else?"

"I don't . . ." he began. "I wouldn't trust myself with a confidence that could hurt you, madame."

She looked into his twilight blue eyes and needed to tell him. "Last November, I met a man, Anthony Harper, when we were both looking at the same print collection at MOMA. Todd was never home, and I was lonely and angry. Anthony was divorced, older, and sophisticated. He invited me to lunch and he told me that I was beautiful and smart. I knew it was a line, but I was grateful to hear it."

"You *are* beautiful and smart."

"Not smart enough. I went with him to his condo," she said. She watched Derek's face, but his expression stayed the same. "Sex with Anthony wasn't any improvement over sex with Todd. I felt nothing, but he seemed happy."

"Men think all sex is good sex," Derek said.

"Afterward Anthony said, 'I knew you were ready to drop your panties when I met you.'" Nancy still felt ashamed and blushed. "He laughed as if it was a joke, but I knew it was an insult."

"That's a nasty thing to say."

"I saw him a few more times during the next few weeks. I hated Anthony and I hated myself more, and I was terrified someone would find out. I ended it before Christmas."

Derek kissed her brow and said, "It's over now and forgotten. I've forgotten it."

"I wish I could. In March he called and asked me to go with him as a friend to see an exhibit of antique glass. I thought if I said no, he'd tell people about us."

"You felt threatened?"

"He never said anything overtly, but there was an undercurrent," she said. "We met at his friend's art gallery. Anthony came up behind me suddenly and I dropped a nineteenth-century glass bowl I'd been looking at. It shattered into a hundred pieces and I was horrified, but he just smiled and said, 'That will cost you, rich girl.'"

"Could he have startled you intentionally?" Derek asked.

"It's possible. I told Anthony that he shouldn't call me again, and he said, 'You're a lousy fuck anyway.' I left a blank check with the gallery, which was stupid, but I wasn't thinking straight. They never cashed it. I guess their insurance took care of it. When I learned he'd lost his job and moved to Florida, I was so relieved."

"Anthony was lying. You're a brilliant fuck and I'll pummel to a bloody pulp any man who says otherwise."

"Brilliant like mashed peas?"

"Brilliant the American way. Brilliant in every way."

"It's because I have a brilliant student."

His fingers trailed down her body and he said, "I believe I'm ready for another lesson, madame."

sixteen

style takes risks

Long before it was time to pick up Eugenia, Nancy found herself checking the clock. Finally she said to Derek, "I think I'll go a little early. Would you like to come for a walk?"

On the way there, she had to stop herself from touching him. Not in public.

Eugenia was ecstatic when they picked her up. She chattered about everything they'd done and the children she'd met. "Leda is my friend. She has a cat *and* a dog. Can she come play at our house? Can I have a cat?"

"What else did you do?"

"I learned a song about a frog on a log. I went on the

swings and Mrs. Candybar pushed me. We had orange juice and spa, spa . . ."

"Spaghetti?" Derek guessed.

Eugenia nodded. "And we read stories."

She reached up to Derek and said, "Give me a ride."

"Please," Nancy said.

"Please."

Derek picked her up and put her on his shoulders. They were smiling and talking about the school when a young woman came from the opposite direction. Nancy recognized her as a waitress from their regular bistro.

"If it isn't my favorite family," she said. "Enjoy the afternoon."

"You, too," Derek and Nancy said in unison, and then looked at each other.

All day, Nancy felt as bubbly as a bottle of champagne. She loved the revised invitation mock-ups that the graphic designer brought by, incorporating a historical line drawing of the Barbary Coast.

As the designer was about to leave, he said to Derek, "I didn't recognize you at first with all your clothes on. I guess I don't focus on faces."

Derek said, "I'm sorry, but I don't catch your meaning."

"Haven't I seen you at the gym with that hot guy with the reddish brown hair and the great abs? Your boyfriend?"

"Yes, you may have," Derek said, and Nancy was surprised to feel a stab of jealousy.

When the designer left, Nancy said, "You don't have to be careful about mentioning Prescott."

"Who is Prescott?" Eugenia asked.

"Prescott is Derek's special friend," Nancy said. "He lives with him."

"Huh!" the girl said. "I don't like him."

"That's very rude, Eugenia," Nancy said, but she didn't scold further. "Derek, I'm going to run the invitation design over to the Saloon. Is it all right if I leave Eugenia here with you for about half an hour?"

Eugenia ran to Derek and took his hand.

"Yes, madame, I think we can manage."

Nancy wanted to get back so quickly that she practically ran all the way. She was out of breath by the time Greene opened the Saloon's massive front door.

"Good to see you haven't brought that shiftless bastard," he said, and left.

Nancy asked one of the maids where she could find Mrs. Friendly, and was led to an ornate parlor, where Mrs. Friendly was listening to a young woman read from a book. She smiled at Nancy and said, "I'll be damned glad when my surgery's done and I can read by myself again."

"I brought by the design for the invitation."

The older woman said, "Doesn't do me any good. I'm sure it's fine. I always used to write notes to the major donors, too, but I can't do that now."

"That would be a very nice touch," Nancy said. "I happen to have a friend who is quite skilled at imitating handwriting. If you have a writing sample and a stock of note cards, I'll take care of sending out personal messages to the special guests."

"Is this a person who can be trusted with my personal stationery?"

"Yes, she's a dear friend of Gigi's and mine."

Nancy returned to the Château with a box of Mrs. Friendly's engraved note cards and a writing sample. Eugenia flung

herself at Nancy as if she'd been gone for years instead of minutes and said, "Let's make capes."

So they spent two hours drawing, cutting, and sewing.
Nancy's cape was the same blue as Snow White's dress. Derek
opted for Sherlock Holmesian brown tweed, and Eugenia
chose a bright yellow and red pop-art graphic.

Nancy was more cheerful than she could ever remember
being. She was sure now that leaving Todd had been the right
thing to do.

The next morning, Nancy and Eugenia were up early and
eager to go to Three Bridges. They held hands and skipped half
the way there. Nancy dashed back to Château Winkles.

She hoped Derek was in the mood. He was. She felt so
completely uninhibited with him that she did things to him
she'd never even thought of doing to Todd. She wasn't coloring within the lines anymore, and when Derek was slick with
sweat and gasping, Nancy laughed and said, "You've gotten
one hundred percent on the oral portion of our test. Now
we'll move on to the in-depth section of the exam."

Milagro arrived just before five, a large canvas bag slung over
her shoulder, looking very sexy in that ethnic way of hers in a
magenta cotton dress and lots of silver bangles, her glossy black
hair falling in loose curls over her shoulders.

"Milagro, this is my assistant, Derek. Derek, Milagro and I
were college roommates."

"Hey, Derek," Milagro said, her voice automatically going
all low and flirty. "Are you keeping Nancy from following her
silliest whims?"

"I find Mrs. Carrington-Chambers's whims to be inspired,"
he said, a smile edging his lips upward.

"In other words, you're aiding and abetting her. Excellent. Do you know that she wants to establish a federal agency that could fine people for fashion crimes?"

Derek glanced at Nancy and said, "What a remarkable notion. It would not only generate revenue, but discourage the American tendency toward sloth as well."

Nancy said, "It's all because of Casual Friday. It's spread a plague upon the populace. What is wrong with adults dressing like adults? There is no reason for anyone over the age of five to wear any item with an elastic waist."

"You're so strict about these things," Milagro said. "Did you tell Derek your idea that everyone should have his or her own runway music?"

Eugenia was hopping from one foot to the next and staring at red and yellow feathers peeking out of Milagro's bag.

Milagro looked down at her and said, "Who is this jumpy little peanut?"

"Mil, this is my cousin's daughter, Eugenia. Eugenia, this is my friend Milagro. You can call her Miss Demeanor."

"Hi, Eugenia. I have something for you."

"What?"

"Say hello back," Nancy said. "Honestly, I feel like the etiquette police, and that's another agency I'd be thrillified to establish."

"Very nice meeting you," Derek said to Milagro. "Good night, ladies."

Milagro put her bag down on the desk and began rummaging through it. As soon as the women heard the front door close behind Derek, Milagro said, "Oh my God, he's *scorching* hot."

"So it's not just me. I'll tell you more when the Lilliputian is elsewhere."

"What do you have?" Eugenia asked, pulling at Milagro's hem.

"I have a big box of crayons, coloring books, and your . . ." She looked at Nancy expectantly.

Nancy sighed and said, "Auntie Nanny."

Milagro grinned wildly. "Your *auntie Nanny* told me you liked pirates so I got this for you." She pulled a colorful stuffed parrot made of felt from her bag. "If you pull the string, it talks pirate talk."

Eugenia clapped her hands and reached for the toy.

"Say thank you, Miss Demeanor."

"Thank you!"

"You're welcome."

Eugenia sat on the floor playing with her toy parrot, and Nancy said, "Come on. Let's get dinner together."

"I brought provisions. Cheeses, crackers, sliced meats."

They went to the kitchen and Nancy said, "I told you I'd have food. Your hair looks fab. I'm glad you're finally taking my advice about hot rollers."

"You were right about the hair rollers. You didn't tell me the kid was so cute."

"Eugenia? She's not as ghastly as the majority of children. Her vocabulary is sadly limited, and you saw her cape. She chose that pop-art pattern despite my passion fruit arguments against the pop-art movement."

"Do you hate pop art, too?"

"Not in large pieces on vast white walls, but the body is a much smaller canvas and print should be proportional." Nancy took a bottle of Bandol rosé out of the refrigerator and opened it, while Milagro took packages out of her tote.

"Is that in your 'Theory of Style'?"

"Not yet, but I'll be sure to add it."

Milagro arranged the food on a platter and said, "You always make me think of *The Spoils of Poynton*."

"Because I'm spoiled?" Nancy poured the wine into two of the etched pink tumblers.

"It's a novella by Henry James and there's a character who can't sleep all night because she's in a room with terrible wallpaper."

"She sounds like someone I'd like." Nancy filled a pot with water and took a box of macaroni and cheese from the cupboard. "Derek calls this macaroni cheese, no 'and,'" she said as she put the water on the stove to boil and picked up a wineglass. "*À tes amours*."

"*Salud*. Are you doing the horizontal hokey-pokey with him?"

Nancy choked on her wine, and Milagro said, "I thought so. He's eminently hokey-pokeyable. He's bossa novalicious."

When Nancy finally stopped coughing, she said, "He's gay."

"Yeah, and I'm very frequently ecstatic, too."

"By which I mean he's a homosexual."

"My gaydar swung decidedly to the hetero side of the gauge."

"Your gaydar is proven to be unreliable, since your very presence is like a magnet near a compass."

"Oooh, who took 'Science for Nitwits'?"

"We both did and I'm the one who got the A."

"Then you understand the need for empirical proof. How do you *know* he's gay?" Milagro asked.

"I ran into him shopping for organic vegetables with his hunky boyfriend one Sunday. They were going to a rockers and rent boys tea dance."

Milagro sipped her wine. "That's very damning evidence. So why are you having sex with him?"

"I never said—"

"You have a hickey on your neck."

Nancy slapped her hand to her neck and Milagro said, "Psych! I was just guessing because you look so happy and *gay*. And he gave you a look before he left. A 'Your hoo-ha is as exquisite as an exotic orchid' look. All Georgia O'Keeffe–ish."

"A lady doesn't discuss her hoo-ha or its appearance except with her discreet aesthetician. Okay, so what if I was affectionate with him?"

"One girl's affectionate is another girl's ooh, baby, baby. Dish!"

"It just happened and he was like, it was incredible," Nancy said, flustered and excited. "It was the most amazing thing ever. It was to sex as truffles are to toadstools, so superior that it is not recognizable as being in the same genus."

"You *were* sleeping with Toad for all those years. Ugh. I read a novel by Leon Edel and he described a character as having hands like hams in his gloves and that's what I always think of when I think of Toad. I never understood how you could let him touch you."

"And I never understood how you could sex up every cute waiter who remembered to refill your water glass."

"Consideration like that is appreciated in the bedroom as well as in a nightclub bathroom, wherever one may be at the time," Milagro said. "Derek's really gay? Not bisexual, confused, or polymorphically amorous, which is the new skankoholic?"

"He's *really* gay. My graphic designer recognized Derek from seeing him with his boyfriend at the gym."

"Hmmm." Milagro popped an olive in her mouth. "We should make a salad. Do you have greens?"

"There's oak leaf lettuce in the fridge. What was that 'hmmm' for?"

Her friend considered before saying, "Nancy, Derek's gorgeous, agrees with your fashion edicts, and he's clever. If he's *really* gay, you shouldn't become attached. Because you can boink them on occasion, but you can't rewire them, no matter what anyone says."

"I'm not attached. I'm just very, very fond of him. I feel like I'm catching up on all those orgasms I didn't have, as well as the ones I didn't especially enjoy, over the last several years."

Milagro nodded. "It's all contextual and your context was Toad. But what if you fall for Derek, Nancy-pants? Will your heart break when he realizes that no matter how assiduously he tends the garden, a penis will not sprout from your nether regions?"

"But I *won't* fall for him, will I? He's gay and he's staff and I understand the limitations perfectly. Besides, I went out with Bailey Whiteside, and we're going out again next week."

"Why, Nancy, why, why are you going out with another self-important prick?"

"Bailey's not a prick. He's ambitious, smart, and fun. While you've been partying hither and thither for years, I've been stuck out in the middle of nowhere. Bailey's a good escort, and Todd knows we're going out as friends."

"That's even weirder," Milagro said. "And what if someone finds out about you and Derek? Doesn't your prenup have a fidelity clause?"

"You're assuming that A, I'm getting a divorce, and B, someone would find out. I haven't decided a thing yet. Although now that I know what sex can be like, I realize that Todd and I can improve things," Nancy said.

"My brain is now frying with the image of naked Todd and a sex manual. Eww and eww. I'm scarred for life."

"As to the second part of the problem, Derek won't tell. It would ruin his relationship with his boyfriend."

"So basically I need to tell people you're having an affair with Lizette, which you're not, and pretend you're not having the one you are?"

"Yes."

"Okay. You're a fascinating woman, Nancy Edith."

"Thank you and thanks for bringing the presents for Eugenia."

"No problem. How long do you get to keep her, Auntie Nanny?"

"Don't call me that. I have her until my cousin decides to come home to shake down her parents."

"If Birdie's as bad as my mother Regina, you should keep Eugenia. I'm dead serious. I would have loved if some wacky and glamorous aunt had taken me from my mother Regina."

"Your mother Regina is a sociopath. Birdie's a free spirit."

"Why isn't Sissy watching her?"

"Sissy has issues about Birdie. It's complicated."

"How interesting to learn that there are branches of your family that have actual problems. Yours is like one of those perfect TV families, pearls on your mom, your dad with a pipe in the study, and everyone is always so nice and saying 'Lovely, lovely' all the time."

"I'm very lucky," Nancy said. "How would you like to do some forgery for me?"

seventeen

fit that flatters

$\mathcal{N}$ancy's mornings with Derek were like a holiday; she knew they couldn't last, so she savored every moment. She was lying in his arms, running her finger across a scar on his leg, and she said, "I was afraid you were too perfect. What is this from?"

"My brother, Petey, dared me to ride my bicycle down a flight of stairs."

"So you were the kind of boy who did things on dares?"

"I admit nothing," Derek said.

"I'm going out to dinner with Bailey next week. I'll ask Sloane to watch Eugenia. You don't mind, do you?"

"It's not my place to object."

"I'm not talking about you as an assistant, but as my friend."

"As your friend, I'd like you to be with someone who makes you happy."

She'd had more joy in the six weeks after leaving the House of Horrors than she'd had in all her years with Todd. "Bailey's entertaining and he's got a good future. We're just friends for now, but you've shown me that things can be better with someone besides Todd. Maybe Bailey is that someone."

"How will you know?"

"Do we have to talk about other men now?" She nestled closer to Derek. "You're the only man who likes me just for me."

"May I ask you something, madame?"

"Anything."

"What would you do if you found out a man you cared for wasn't what he seemed?"

She propped herself up on one arm. "Are we back to Bailey? It's sweet of you to worry. I know he's ambitious and calculating, but he's also a good partner for someone who wants to live a more dynamic life."

She looked into Derek's lovely face. "I know this will have to end when you get tired of my girl parts, but I really want to enjoy it while we can."

"I'm not tiring of you."

She laughed and said, "Do you know that Milagro even asked if I was sure you're gay. Can you believe that?"

He hesitated, then said, "It's easy to see what you want to see. What did she mean when she said that you thought everyone should have their own runway music?"

"We should each have a song that we imagine when we're

walking down the street and the wind is blowing back our hair because life is the ultimate runway, even though life doesn't let us walk in slo-mo."

He laughed. "I'll add that to your notebook. What's your song?"

"It varies. Lately it's been 'Walking on Sunshine.'"

"Do I have one?"

She rolled on top of him. "Sometimes you look so serious, I think it should be 'Behind Blue Eyes,' but you're not a bad man, so maybe it's Tom Jones's 'Sex Bomb.'"

He clutched her hips and said, "I'll try to live up to it."

A knock on the front door startled both of them.

"Who could that be?" Nancy asked, getting out of bed and reaching for her clothes. "Maybe Birdie got in the building. Can you answer it?"

Derek was already pulling on his boxers. "Yes." He was stepping into his trousers when there was another knock.

Nancy dashed into the bathroom and heard him call out, "One moment, please!" The phrase "whore's bath" came to mind as she cleaned herself with a washcloth and threw her clothes on. She ran a brush through her hair, dabbed on lip gloss, took a few slow breaths, and walked out.

When Derek heard her coming, he stepped away from the open front door and said, "Miss Winkles has come to invite us to tea."

The old lady gave Nancy a knowing look. "Not you, Girl Carrington. I can see how extremely busy you are."

Derek said, "I was just explaining that my fountain pen had splattered on us, and we were trying to clean up my jacket and—"

"And your socks," Miss Winkles said, looking down at his bare feet. "When you get the ink out of them, you can bring Eugenia up to tea at three o'clock. I told her she could look at my photo albums and through the spyglass. See that you arrive promptly."

He said, "Miss Winkles, I appreciate your kind invitation, but I have tasks . . ."

"Oh, I'm sure Girl Carrington can spare you for half an hour."

Nancy smiled and said, "Of course, Miss Winkles."

Miss Winkles left and Derek shut the door. "She knows."

"Binky Winkles is famous for having a bad opinion of everyone. Why does that crone remember Eugenia's name and not mine?"

"Would you like me to find out?"

"Yes. We'll buy some flowers for you to take to her and you can disarm her with kindness."

Eugenia was thrilled with her invitation from Miss Winkles. She had brought home a painting that she wanted Nancy to put up. "It's a boat," she said, and indeed there was a brown splotch on blue splotches that could've been water.

"Very aquatic. Thank you, Eugenia." Nancy used a magnet to add it to the collection of drawings on the refrigerator.

"That is a splendid painting," Derek said.

"I'll make one for you and one for Miss Wiggles. I need paint."

"Miss Winkles," Nancy corrected. "Use the crayons Milagro brought you. Paint is too messy."

"Crayons are for babies."

"Crayons are not for babies. Great artists have used crayons. *I* used crayons. Derek, did you have crayons in England?"

"Crayons are international favorites."

Nancy mouthed "Thank you" to him. "See, Eugenia, everyone loves crayons."

The girl squinted and said, "I'm going to ask Miss Wiggles if she has paint."

When Derek and Eugenia went upstairs to tea with Miss Winkles, Nancy decided to call her mother. She felt more comfortable doing it without anyone overhearing her conversation.

The housekeeper answered and said she'd call Mrs. Carrington to the phone.

A few minutes later, Hester said groggily, "Hi, Nanny. I was napping."

"I haven't heard from you in ages. How are you?"

"Wonderful, dear. Has it been that long since you visited? Time slips away somehow."

"How was the anniversary party?"

There was a pause and finally Hester said vaguely, "The dinner party? Lovely. Always so nice to see friends. How are you doing? Is the girl still with you?"

"Yes, Eugenia is still with me. Didn't Daddy tell you that Birdie sent me a letter from Corfu? That and a naked painting of herself."

"Good heavens."

"It's a good painting, but *unnecessary*. What have you been doing?"

"Did I tell you we got an injunction against that dreadful man who wants to do *new construction*?"

As Nancy listened to Hester describe the intricacies of the legal process, she thought not for the first time that her mother should have gotten a job that took her out of the house.

"I'm so glad you are doing something to preserve the character of the neighborhood," Nancy said. "Eugenia is having tea with Binky Winkles. Miss Winkles has *never* invited me up to tea and she always calls me Girl Carrington, but she knows Eugenia's name."

"Well, Nanny, you might try to be a little nicer to her."

"I am nice! I smile and ask how she is and hold the door for her. I'm a delightful neighbor. Have you heard from Blaire or Ellie lately?"

"Your sisters haven't called in, I can't remember. The time difference makes it hard for them to call."

"It's like they've forgotten we exist."

"Nanny, they're busy. Blaire e-mails me whenever she can and Ellie sends cards and gifts."

They talked awhile longer about Nancy's events business and then Nancy realized that her mother was responding with rote expressions of "That's nice" and "How lovely," so she said, "Mom, get your rest, okay?"

"Thank you, darling. Come visit soon."

"We will."

Nancy was wondering if she should go upstairs and rescue Derek and Eugenia when she heard their footsteps pounding down the stairs and Eugenia's high-pitched laughter.

Eugenia ran into the living room grinning wildly, her eyes gleaming. There was a smear of pink frosting on her face. "We raced and I won!"

Derek came a second later, laughing. "You were supposed to wait until I counted to three."

Nancy said, "I want a full report. Eugenia, did you have a nice time with Miss Winkles?"

"Yes!" Eugenia shouted. "We ate cupcakes and sang songs. She is going to teach me to play the piano."

"Really?"

"Miss Winkles has a sweet, light voice," Derek said. "She had me bring boxes of photographs down from a closet because she thinks I look like someone she knew."

"Everybody thinks you look like someone, but I don't find your looks common. Eugenia, what did you see through the spyglass?"

"I saw boats and a pirate island. Miss Wiggles says I can visit every day and play piano."

"Did she? That was very nice of her. Don't touch anything until we've washed your hands," Nancy said, thinking that she would have liked a cupcake, too.

As Derek was leaving for the day, Nancy slipped into the entry hall with him. "Did you find out why Miss Winkles calls me Girl Carrington?"

"She said she'd tell me next time." He looked through the doorway and made sure that Eugenia was not looking. Then he pulled Nancy to him and kissed her. "Until tomorrow, Mrs. Carrington-Chambers."

"'Night, Derek."

She closed the door and turned to see Eugenia looking at her. Nancy didn't know how much the girl had seen. The girl pulled the string of her stuffed parrot, which let out a recorded squawk of "Scurvy dog!"

"Eugenia, we are going to clean all that sticky frosting off your face and hands. Come along."

"Scurvy dog!" Eugenia shrieked, and ran out of the room, clutching her parrot. "Scurvy dog! Scurvy dog!"

When Nancy had caught the girl and put her in the bathtub to play and calm down, she asked, "Why do you like pirates?"

Eugenia poured water from one plastic yogurt container into another. "Do you want yummy tea?"

"Yes, thank you." Nancy took the container and pretended to drink. "Delicious. Is it because pirates wear big boots?"

"Do you want more tea?"

"Yes." Nancy handed the cup to the child, who poured the water back in the tub and filled it again. "Is it because pirates have swords?"

"Hmm." Eugenia was playing and didn't seem interested in Nancy's question.

Nancy washed the girl's hair with the Kiehl's baby wash she'd bought. She made sure to rinse the soap out from behind Eugenia's small pink ears and to clean her fingers.

Eugenia suddenly said, "Pirates take their house with them all the time," and then she submerged herself and blew bubbles, her fine hair floating out behind her.

Nancy ached thinking what it must be like to be Eugenia, without a home of her own.

Nancy had just put Eugenia to bed when her phone rang. It was Todd.

"I'm out front," he said. "Can I come up to talk?"

"Oh," she said, looking around at the toys scattered on the floor. "Yes. Just give me a minute to put some clothes on."

She picked up all of Eugenia's things and threw them in the laundry room. She ran to the bathroom and touched up her makeup. Then she went to the entry hall and buzzed the front door.

Nancy smoothed her skirt as she waited for Todd to come out of the elevator. He was wearing clothes that she'd put aside to give to charity: a blue-and-white-striped shirt with a white collar and cuffs and those pleated trousers that made his hips look wide.

"Hi, Nance."

"Hi, Todd."

They looked at each other for a moment and then he leaned in to kiss her cheek. "Can I come in?"

"Of course." She let him in, wondering what he wanted.

He glanced around the apartment and said, "It looks better without all that pink stuff."

"I liked the pink, but the room serves a dual purpose now."

"Yeah, well. So how's Froth going?"

"Really well. Thanks for asking. How's everything with you?"

"Good. A little lonely around the house. I miss having you around. I cut the cleaning people down to once a week, but they don't do things right without you to supervise them. Do you have something to drink?"

"Would you like water or a glass of wine?"

"Wine would be awesome."

Wine would be awesome. She went to the kitchen wondering how she ever could have lived with this Visigoth.

When she returned he was standing by the fireplace, his hands jammed in his pockets, even though she'd told him a thousand times that it stretched and bagged the gabardine.

She handed him the wineglass.

"You're not going to have a drink with me?" he asked.

"I don't really feel like a drink now."

"Bailey told me you're going out again."

So that's why he'd come. "Just as friends."

"That's cool. He's already promised me that nothing will happen. I'm glad he's watching out for you."

"It's so nice that you two are negotiating my honor. Maybe you could give him the spare key to my chastity belt."

"It's a guy thing, Nance. You wouldn't understand, because with females it's always competition and backstabbing."

"That is so sexist. I don't have those relationships with my girlfriends."

He let out a loud har-har-har. "How many times have you said that Lizette is tackier than hot asphalt or Junie dresses like she's sold her soul to a chain-store Lucifer?"

The phrases sounded vaguely familiar. "I was trying to help them. They needed my guidance."

"Yeah, you only do it out of kindness, telling everyone how inferior they are. All your bridesmaids paid you back, didn't they, dropping you when Villagio Toscana tanked? But I didn't come here to argue, Nance."

A lady didn't beat her husband to death with an Edwardian fireplace poker even when he was distorting reality to make her look bad. "So why *did* you come here?"

He moved close and she could see the uneven edge of his haircut and the roughness of his skin. "I told you: I miss you. For better or for worse. We can make it through this rough patch." His free hand went to her waist.

All she could think was, *Hands like hams.* "Todd . . ."

"When was the last time we had sex, Nancy? You haven't let me near you since Christmas."

"You were always at work or the gym or with your buddies," she said, remembering how relieved she had been when he arrived home late enough for her to pretend to be asleep.

"I was working for you, for us. I love you. I always have." His ham-hand pulled her closer, as his bleached denim eyes stared morosely at her. "Don't you feel anything for me?"

He was her husband and she thought that she'd loved him. "I still have to figure out what I feel. I thought I had three months to think about it."

"Three months to stay here, not to give up sex." He twisted so he could keep hold of her while gulping down the rest of the wine. "Let's get busy."

She didn't turn fast enough and his mouth landed on hers. She felt the familiar lump of tongue jammed between her lips and Todd made a small grunt of excitement.

She tried to pull away, but he said, "Come on, baby."

"I'm not a baby. I'm a big girl." The indignant voice came from the doorway.

Todd let Nancy go and said, "Who is that?"

Eugenia, in her purple kitten jammies, glared at him and went to Nancy, half hiding behind her and grabbing onto her leg.

"This is Eugenia, Birdie's daughter," Nancy said. "You met her when she was a baby. But she's not a baby now. She's a big girl."

"Why is she here? Where's her mother?"

"Eugenia's visiting me."

"I live in the liddle room," Eugenia said. "Who are you?"

Nancy looked down and said, "This is Todd. He's my husband. We're married."

"Huh! What about Derek?"

"I already explained that I'm married to Todd. Derek works for me."

"I love Derek."

"Of course you do, honey. We all love Derek. He's fabulous," Nancy said, and picked up the girl. Looking at Todd, she said, "I've got to get her back to bed. Do you mind locking the door when you leave?"

Nancy knew that Todd was angry, because his face went red and his thin lips twisted.

"If that's how it's going to be," he said. "Good night, Nance."

As he left the room, Eugenia looked over Nancy's shoulder and shouted, "Bilge-sucking blaggard!"

"That's not a nice way to talk to your uncle," Nancy said as she tried not to laugh.

eighteen

get the runway look

*E*ugenia wanted to take her Pirate Girl story to show-and-tell; Nancy put it in an attractive binder and Eugenia talked all the way to Three Bridges about the next chapter that she was going to write.

"It sounds amazing," Nancy said. "Take care of the drawings and bring them back so you and Derek can keep working on them."

After kissing the girl good-bye, Nancy stopped at the florist and the patisserie.

"Honey, I'm home!" she called as she went through the door. She went to Derek at his writing table and gave him a kiss. "Americans say that as sort of a joke. It's in all the television shows. What do you say?"

"We say, 'What's for tea?'"

"I brought croissants for us."

"I brought something, too." He picked up his leather shoulder bag from behind his chair, opened it, and took out a video camera.

"Oh, no! I'm telling you the same thing I told Todd. A lady does not let herself be photographed in her birthday suit unless Annie Leibovitz is behind the camera, and you, sir, are no Annie Leibovitz."

He laughed and said, "Mrs. Carrington-Chambers, I should never think of putting you in that position, unless you specifically requested it. Actually, I have another idea. We'll wait until we pick up Eugenia."

"We aren't going to be like those appalling people who tape every moment of their offspring's existence—not that she is our child."

"I should hope not, Mrs. Carrington-Chambers. We are cut from a different cloth, although Eugenia *is* wonderful."

"We're making a movie?" Nancy asked as she put down the bundle of flowers and the bag of pastries.

"You have to wait," he said. "Perhaps I can distract you." He smirked as he slipped his hand under her fuzzy lilac sweater.

"Before coffee?" she said, laughing.

"I'll do my utmost to ensure that you stay awake."

He was true to his promise.

Afterward, when she was about to dress, he said, "I want to select what you wear."

"Are you up to the task?"

"Women's clothes are not my speciality, but I will try my

best." He chose a pair of black boots, skinny resin-coated jeans, a skintight charcoal sweater, a black trench, and a long sea green silk chiffon scarf.

"That is rather dramatic," she said. She'd never worn the jeans before because she thought they might be too sexy. "If we're going to rob a bank, I'll need a beret like Faye Dunaway in *Bonnie and Clyde,* one of the great fashion movies."

"What are the others?"

"*Annie Hall,* but in a bad way. All Audrey Hepburn movies. Movies with costumes by Edith Head. Movies with costumes by Kym Barrett, who did *The Matrix* and *Romeo + Juliet.*"

"That's all?"

"Danilo Donati's costumes and Travis Banton, who de-signed Marlene Dietrich's most famous looks. Giorgio Armani's costumes for *American Gigolo* and *The Italian Job,* which fea-tured gorgeous clothes, Mini Coopers, *and* a robbery. That brings us full circle."

"Well, that's it then—we must commit a robbery."

"Put it on the calendar after the gala." She pulled on the boots and stood up.

Derek adjusted the scarf around her neck. "One last detail." He reached into his pocket and took out a small box tied with a red ribbon. Handing it to her, he said, "For you. I thought of you when I saw it."

She unwrapped the box, lifted the lid, and saw a petite and exquisite yellow guilloche butterfly pin nestled in tissue. She took it out and looked at the way the translucent enamel cap-tured the light. "It's beautiful!"

"It's vintage from Norway." Taking the brooch from her, Derek pinned it to her scarf. "You're very lovely, the prettiest girl I know."

"That was not your initial impression. You said I was pleasant-looking."

"Did I? I meant pleasantly super, because I think you are super."

"You know the crazy thing? Last night, Todd came by and I kept comparing him to you."

"Did you . . ."

"A lady doesn't discuss these things, Derek, and no, I couldn't even tolerate him touching me."

"I'd be gutted if you had," Derek said, "although it is not my place. He's your husband."

"What does it mean when a lady's husband can't compare to her fabulous assistant?" Nancy looked at Derek and felt things she'd never felt with anyone else. She wondered if he might feel them, too, behind those blue eyes.

Derek put on a long, slate-colored duster over his suit and carried the leather bag with the video camera. Nancy's scarf blew in the breeze as they went to pick up Eugenia at Three Bridges.

The girl ran to them and said, "Mrs. Candybar liked my pic-tures and is sharing them." Her cape fluttered in the wind as she brandished a stick that had a shorter stick bound cross-wise to it with red yarn. "I made a sword," she said and she whacked a fence as they passed.

"Do not hit things with that weapon, Eugenia," Nancy said. "Derek, where are we going?"

"To that stretch of flat sidewalk," he said, indicating a tree-lined block.

"Can we have a sword fight?" Eugenia asked. "Find a big stick."

They had arrived at their destination, so Nancy looked up and down the block. "Color me bewildered."

"Go to the corner and then come back doing your best runway walk."

"Really?"

"Really."

"I'll feel silly doing it." She grinned and said, "But silliness is greatly underappreciated. Remember to put that in my notebook. We'll say, 'Silliness is to life as bubbles are to champagne. Essential and uplifting.'"

"I'd like to see the sexy, devastating side of you now," he said, reaching out and quickly touching her hand.

"Then I'll channel my inner Inès de la Fressange." Nancy walked to the end of the block and returned with a strut, tossing her hair, narrowing her eyes, and exuding as much sultriness as she could summon while Derek taped her.

After Nancy had had three tries, Eugenia shouted, "My turn, my turn!"

The girl marched down the sidewalk with jabs toward invisible enemies and cries of "Ahoy!" Nancy thought her cape flowed beautifully. When the child finished her runway walks, Nancy reached for the camera and said, "Now it's your turn, Derek."

"It's not necessary, Mrs. Carrington-Chambers."

"Then why did you bring the coat? I'm afraid I must insist."

He went to the end of the block and came back as she shouted encouraging things like "Smolder for me!" and "Be fierce!" and "You're a beast!" which made him laugh and then they had to start over.

Eugenia recruited a man walking down the street to tape

the three of them walking together. The man handed back the camera, saying, "It's always good to get the family videos when the kids are young. They grow up so fast."

As the trio walked toward the Château, Derek said, "I'll edit and add music."

"We can watch them on movie night. That is, if you're free some night."

"Can we have a sleepover?" Eugenia said. "Derek, stay for a sleepover!"

"Perhaps this weekend."

He and Nancy exchanged a look and she thought how nice this was, how much fun it was to be with him. And Eugenia, of course, she thought, as Eugenia thwacked a fire hydrant with a shout of "Avast, matey!"

"If Prescott wouldn't miss you . . ."

Derek looked a little downhearted. "Prescott is spending the weekend visiting his ex in Mendocino."

Nancy put her hand on his arm. "Are you okay with that?"

"It is to be expected considering our situation."

"We could go somewhere, too," Nancy said. "We've got a place at Stinson Beach. It will be nice to get away now because things will be crazy until the gala is over."

"The little pirate would enjoy the ocean," he said.

When they were back at the apartment, Nancy excused herself and went into the bedroom to call her mother. "I thought I'd go to the beach house this weekend, if it's available."

"You may as well use it. I haven't been there all year."

Nancy thought about her mother's life and said, "Would you like to come with us? I mean, it's just Eugenia and my assistant and myself."

"Your assistant is going?"

"He's very good with Eugenia and she adores him. I think you'd like him, Mom. His taste is impeccable and he shares my passion for fashion."

"It's sweet of you to ask, but on Saturday I've got a show-room sale for a designer who specializes in period wallpapers, and your father and I have a brunch on Sunday. You have a good time."

So on Friday evening, Nancy, Derek, and Eugenia packed up the Mini and drove across the Golden Gate Bridge, north through the woods, and on the spectacular serpentine road along the coast. "I don't feel good," Eugenia said from the backseat.

"You'll feel better if you pick a spot far ahead and stare at it," Nancy said. "It's just a little ways more."

"Carly barfed at circle time today."

"We don't say that, Eugenia. We say 'Carly was ill.'"

"Her ill was orange and smelled bad and she cried. She eats Play-Doh."

"Thank you for sharing, Eugenia. Only a little farther."

"We can sing a song," Derek suggested, and started with "Row, Row, Row Your Boat." By the time they were finishing "Old McDonald," the sun was about to set and they'd arrived in the quaint town.

"We have to hurry," Nancy said, and turned down a private drive that led to a carport next to a gray wall. "Everyone grab something." They picked up overnight bags and bags of food and DVDs, and Nancy led them around the wall.

The pale gray beach stretched in front of them, the Pacific Ocean rolling in with a low roar, and the wind whipped at their hair and clothes. To their left was an elegant house with floor-to-ceiling glass windows facing the beach. Nancy said, "Now, *this* is how modern should be done."

She keyed in the security code on the alarm panel and they walked into the house, tracking sand with them. The first floor was one vast open space decorated in whites, soft grays, and shades of blue-gray. There was a fireplace at the far end, a kitchen at the other, and a wide industrial steel staircase. The space was furnished with streamlined low sofas, square occasional tables, and a long bleached wood dining table.

"Take off your shoes!" Nancy said. "Hurry."

They left their shoes at the door and went outside onto the cool sand. Nancy rolled up the cuffs of Eugenia's pants and Derek rolled up the cuffs of his jeans.

Nancy said, "Eugenia, you can only get your feet wet and you have to watch out for the jellyfish on the beach. They're clear and they sting. I'll race you!"

As the three ran to the edge of the waves, Nancy and Derek exchanged looks and slowed down so that Eugenia reached the water first.

"I win, I win!" she cried. "It's cold! Where are the pirates?"

"We're the pirates!" Derek shouted, and dashed to pick up a driftwood branch that he gave to Eugenia. He found another branch and he and the child had a sword fight while Nancy danced at the edge of the waves with a long seaweed streamer.

The sun dipped on the horizon, tinting the sky and clouds orange and gold. "Make a wish," Nancy said. "Let's all make a wish."

"I want a real sword," Eugenia said.

Nancy wished that she could find a way to stay as happy as she was at this moment, but she didn't say her wish aloud. She turned to Derek and asked, "What did you wish?"

"That things weren't as complicated as they are."

So he was thinking about Prescott. She reached for his hand, cool in the chill of the evening, and said, "We'll figure them out."

They washed their feet off in the warm water of the outdoor shower by the spa on the enclosed private deck and went into the house.

Nancy assembled a dinner with the food she'd bought at a deli and opened a bottle of champagne while Derek and Eugenia built a fire. After dinner they roasted marshmallows and made s'mores. Eugenia laughed when Derek grabbed Nancy's hand to lick melted chocolate off her fingers.

They watched *Muppet Treasure Island* and Nancy noted, "Miss Piggy always looks amazing. Like Audrey, she's iconic with her long blond fall and pearls."

"Can we hunt for treasure?" Eugenia asked.

"Yes, tomorrow, but now you've got to go to bed."

They put Eugenia in the smallest bedroom so she would be cozy. "You can listen to the ocean sing to you all night," Nancy said. "If you need anything just call and I'll come." She and Derek kissed the girl good night and left the door open so she would have light from the hallway.

Nancy felt odd about sharing her parents' suite with Derek, so she took him to the room she usually stayed in. She was standing by the window watching the reflection of the moon on the water when he came up behind her and put his arms around her.

She leaned back to him and said, "I like our mornings together, but it's nice to be able to spend the night with you."

"I think so, too."

They just stood like that, thinking their own thoughts, and Nancy's included a desire to brush her teeth, because she wanted to wrap herself around Derek and kiss him until he was breathless. "I'm going to get ready for bed."

When she went through her cosmetics case, she realized she'd forgotten her toothpaste and walked to her parents' room.

She put on the lamp and saw the king-size bed facing the windows. She wished her mother would come and enjoy this place more often. Nancy went into the bathroom and opened a drawer on her mother's side of the vanity. She took out the toothpaste and was shutting the drawer when she saw something interesting. She picked up a bottle of Bobbi Brown face lotion. There were other unfamiliar skin care products and a pretty metallic lip color.

But Nancy's mother only used lotions that were formulated for her by her dermatologist, and Hester thought that metallic lipstick was unattractive on women over forty.

Nancy went into the bedroom and opened dresser drawers. She found a black bikini and Stephen King paperbacks. Her mother only bought hardback books and her father didn't read fiction.

"What are you doing?" Derek was standing at the door.

"Nothing," she said, and realized that she was holding the bikini top.

Derek smiled. "Is that yours?"

"I don't know whose it is. My parents sometimes let other people stay here. Someone must have left her things."

"I often leave things behind when I stay somewhere."

"It could even have been Birdie, because she's got access to this place and she's so careless. Oh, the thought of her in my parents' bedroom . . . how unpleasant . . ."

"Mrs. Carrington-Chambers, please stop thinking about other people and come here."

She went to him and he took her hand and walked her

back to the bedroom. He stroked her cheek and said, "I'm mad about you, Mrs. Carrington-Chambers, and now I'm going to make you forget your name." Then he kissed and caressed Nancy until she couldn't think about anyone else, or anything else but being with him at that moment.

The next day, they bundled up and went for an early morning walk on the beach. Nancy showed Eugenia jellyfish and they collected small shells and found tiny crabs.

As the day warmed and the fog burned off, Eugenia met a family with children. She built sand castles with them while Derek and Nancy watched drowsily on a blanket.

At noon, they called Eugenia to them. The mother of the other children said, "You've got a wonderful little girl."

Derek said, "We think so. Your kids are nice, too."

They washed sand from their feet and put on their shoes. Nancy dashed upstairs to put on her butterfly brooch, Eugenia got her sword, and then they walked together to the cluster of shops and cafés.

"It was very generous of you to compliment those children," Nancy said.

"One tries to be polite," Derek said. "Eugenia, there are too many cars here. Hold my hand."

As they crossed the highway, now crowded with tourist traffic, Nancy caught their reflection in the window of a surf shop. In shorts and T-shirts, holding hands, they looked like they belonged together. Dressed so casually, Derek looked less *fabulous,* yet more incredible.

They went to the market in the handsome old white building and picked up groceries for lunch. Derek said, "Let me get this," and shooed Nancy away from the register.

She and Eugenia waited for him on the porch out front.

"Hey, Nancy," said a gravelly voice.

She turned to see Bailey and his slightly older companions. Bailey was wearing a yellow Lacoste polo, madras shorts, and leather thongs. His calves looked a little thin, but she was used to seeing Todd's thick, muscular legs and Derek's naturally athletic limbs. Nancy wondered whether Bailey was wearing madras ironically, or not.

"Hi, Bailey. What are you doing here?"

"We're doing some bodysurfing," he said to her. His friends waved to someone farther down the street and he told them, "Go ahead. I'll catch up in a minute." When they'd left he smiled down at Eugenia and said, "Who's this little angel?"

"This is my niece, Eugenia. Eugenia, say hello to Mr. Whiteside."

Eugenia ignored them and whacked at a post with her sword.

"I'm trying to civilize her," Nancy said.

"Are you here for the day? Is your niece staying with you? Because, if not, I've got a room in the house we rented." He put his hand on Nancy's arm.

"I'm staying at my parents' place."

"Derek lives with us," Eugenia said with a belligerent glare at Bailey.

He looked puzzled and said to Nancy, "Your assistant?"

"Derek doesn't live with us," Nancy said, nervous that Eugenia would say something even worse. "He helps me with Eugenia and I thought it would be a treat for both of them to come here."

"So this is what you meant when you told me you were unavailable tonight. Someone, me for example, might get the wrong idea about you and your assistant."

Nancy was afraid that her sexual satisfaction was obvious. "That's absurd. It's a working weekend. It's preposterous to think that I'd be involved with him."

"Because he's gay?"

"Yes, gay and he's *staff*. We Carringtons know enough not to get involved with the help, Bailey, but we appreciate their assistance with chores and drudgery, and a child is nothing if not drudgery."

Eugenia ran toward the store's doorway and Nancy glanced over to see Derek standing a few feet away, holding the bag of groceries. The expression on his face was unreadable.

Nancy felt a painful mix of fear and guilt. How much had he heard? "Derek!" she said. "You remember Bailey Whiteside. You met at Gigi's party."

"Hey, how's it going?" Bailey said, with an upward tip of his chin.

"Good afternoon, Mr. Whiteside. Mrs. Carrington-Chambers, I'll take these back to the house and prepare lunch. Would you like me to take Eugenia for you?"

"Yes, thank you."

Eugenia grabbed Derek's hand and they walked away, the small brown-haired girl and the lanky dark-haired man.

"Well, that was awkward," Bailey said. "But the English are much more honest about class divisions. If he's babysitting, do you want to come for a barbecue tonight?"

"Thanks, but I promised Eugenia that I'd watch movies with her. I'll see you on Tuesday."

Bailey leaned over and kissed Nancy on the lips while she stood stock-still. "Can't wait," he said. "Maybe you can get that guy to watch her all night."

"Nice try, Bailey." She smiled, but all she could think about was getting to the house and explaining to Derek. She was so upset that she almost walked into the local man who took care of the house for her family.

"Hi there, Nancy."

"Hi, Lowell."

"Your mom called and said you were coming this weekend. I stocked up the firewood. Anything you need?"

"No, everything is fine. Thank you." She took a step away, but Lowell didn't seem to notice her urgency.

"Are you cooking? Because I just had the oven fixed. The temperature gauge was off. It should be fine now."

"I'm not using the oven. Thanks for telling me."

"Have you seen the kitten?"

"What kitten?"

"A mama cat had her babies under the deck. I got all but one of them and found homes, but one is still hiding there. Little stripey thing. I leave food."

"I haven't seen any kittens. Maybe you could call someone to trap it." How much longer would he trap her here?

"Might do that. Well, you got my number if you need anything."

"Yes, thanks so much, Lowell. You have a good weekend."

"You, too."

When Nancy finally reached the house, her heart was racing. Far from doing anything wrong, she'd diverted Bailey's suspicion.

Derek was in the kitchen making sandwiches.

"Hi!" she said with more cheer than she felt. "That was close. I think I managed to throw Bailey off our trail."

"No need to explain, madame. You said nothing that wasn't true." He smiled politely, but it wasn't his usual smile, the one that carried to his eyes.

"You know I am very fond of you, Derek." She looked at the perfect line of his nose, his cheekbones . . .

"Thank you. Would you like to eat in or outside?"

"On the back patio. It's warm there." She watched as he sliced the sandwiches in half and put them on a platter. "Are you sure everything is all right?"

"Between us, yes. But Prescott called a few minutes ago. He's returning home and he'd like me to be there tonight. If you have no need of my help with the drudgery or chores, I'll find a bus back to the city."

"I didn't mean it that way. Please, Derek, you know me better than that." Nancy wanted to throw her arms around him and ask him to forgive her and have everything be the way it was that morning.

"But I'm afraid, madame, that you don't know me at all."

As Nancy looked at his cold expression she realized that she'd fallen for a man who could never love her and then, for the first time in her life, Nancy's heart broke. She blinked back tears and composed herself. "I'll give you a ride if you want to go."

"Yes, I'd like to."

"I'm happy that you and Prescott are working things out." Her voice sounded shrill to her own ears. "We'll have lunch and go. Where's Eugenia?"

"She's playing on the patio."

"I'll take out our drinks."

Nancy's hand trembled as she poured lemonade for them. She carried the drinks to the back door. Thankfully, the cover was secured atop the spa. She hadn't even thought of all the dangers that lurked in everyday life.

Eugenia was lying on the deck, her little legs kicking as she tried to wiggle under the crawl space of the house.

"Eugenia, what are you doing? Get out from under there."

The child grunted in her effort to squeeze farther under the house.

"Eugenia Carrington!" Nancy put the drinks on the teak table and went to the girl. "Come out of there right now." When Eugenia continued her wiggling, Nancy gripped her waist and pulled her out.

Eugenia was holding a striped kitten and smiling triumphantly. "Look what I found!"

The kitten twisted and scratched Eugenia, but the girl kept holding it.

"Let go of that thing! It's probably got diseases."

"No!"

"Give it to me." Nancy really didn't want to touch the cat, which was obviously feral.

"No! You said I could have a kitten."

"No, I didn't. I said you could ask your mother." Nancy tried to take the kitten from Eugenia, who shrieked, "No!" and darted away. Nancy followed and they both crashed into Derek, who was coming out of the house with their lunch.

The tray of sandwiches clattered to the deck, and Eugenia deftly squeezed past Derek into the house and up the stairs.

"What was that?" Derek said as Nancy rubbed her arm.

"She found a wild kitten under the house. It's probably carrying bubonic plague." Nancy chased after the girl with Derek right behind.

The door to the bathroom was closed and Nancy heard water running. She tried the doorknob, but it was locked. "Eugenia, open this door this minute."

"Go way!"

Nancy looked at Derek and said, "That tub is big enough for you to drown in."

"Have you been plotting my demise?" he said. "The lock is simple. Stay here and I'll find something to jimmy it."

"Try the utility room. There are tools there." Nancy banged on the bathroom door. She heard the cat yowling and Eugenia's own animal noises. "Don't you drown that cat, missy, or you'll be in serious trouble. You'll never eat pudding again. Eugenia!"

Nancy heard things clunking to the floor. "Eugenia! Did you break something? What are you doing in there?"

Derek was back in a few minutes with a small screwdriver. Nancy stepped aside as he put it in a small hole in the knob and fiddled with it. He turned the handle and the door opened.

Eugenia, her clothes drenched, was in the tub with the water running. She held the angry, soapy kitten and said, "Now you are all nice and clean." Containers of bath products were on the floor, and a shampoo bottle had spilled its fragrant contents on the tiles.

Derek turned off the water and Nancy hauled Eugenia, still holding the kitten, out of the tub. Nancy wrapped the animal in a towel and handed it to Derek. She clutched the wet child to her. "Don't you ever scare me like that again!"

After Nancy had washed and dressed Eugenia's scratches with antibacterial ointment and dressed her in dry clothes, she went to find Derek. He'd made a collar and leash for the cat with a length of nylon cord and tied the creature to a chair leg.

"My kitten!" Eugenia said.

"She found her treasure after all," Derek said.

"I am not keeping that thing. Do you and Prescott want it?"

"Prescott is allergic to moggies."

The adults were both somber as they salvaged lunch. Nancy tore at the crusts on her sandwich to make it seem as if she'd eaten a few bites. Then she and her assistant packed their things, put the kitten in a cardboard box with air holes poked into the top, and buckled the child in her carseat.

The drive home seemed to take forever and not just because of weekend traffic. Eugenia was happy in the back with the cat beside her, but Nancy and Derek were silent for most of the journey.

Maybe Derek wasn't angry with her, but preoccupied with the thought of seeing his wayward lover again. The thought of Derek with someone else . . . Derek kissing someone else. Derek laughing in bed with someone else. Nancy felt sick. It was the curvy road. She focused on driving and kept quiet.

When they got to the city, she said, "You know, I've never seen where you live."

"It's best if I go there by myself today. I'll take the bus from the Château."

"I am going to show Miss Wiggles my kitten," Eugenia said.

"You are not keeping that animal."

"You promised."

"I did not."

Eugenia began kicking the back of the passenger seat and Nancy wondered how they had gone from an idyllic morning on the beach to this. "Eugenia, you're going to have a time-out when we get home!"

Derek helped Nancy unload the car and carry the things

upstairs. "Thank you for the holiday," he said. His blue, blue eyes didn't meet hers. "I shall see you Monday morning."

She wanted him to stay. She wanted him to smile at her and like her again, and call her Mrs. Carrington-Chambers in that teasing tone. "Last night . . ." she began, but what could she say? "I hope everything goes well with Prescott."

He nodded and left. Nancy heard a ripping sound. She looked around the room and saw the kitten climbing on her custom drapes while Eugenia giggled.

Nancy could have screamed. She wanted to scream. But a lady doesn't scream when her unexpected houseguest destroys her furnishings and the gay object of her desire returns to his boyfriend.

nineteen

must-haves for luxurious living

$\mathcal{N}$ancy made scrambled eggs for dinner. Even the cat ate them. Nancy was so worn out that she went to bed at the same time as Eugenia. She could hear the kitten mewling faintly in the laundry room. It stopped after an hour. Derek and Prescott might be going out to a club now, or having a romantic dinner by candlelight.

Prescott was probably looking into Derek's *l'heure bleue* eyes and planning their future. Nancy should be thankful that this thing with Derek had stopped now, before she became too entangled with him. Because he was gay and he was staff. Somehow that wasn't important anymore.

She put the beautiful butterfly pin in the drawer of her writing desk because she wanted it to be close to her.

On Monday, Derek came to the apartment and went about his job as if they'd never shared any intimate moments. He made a cappuccino for her, but not for himself, and sat at his desk, methodically going through his tasks for the fund-raiser.

Nancy tried to keep her voice normal as she called the caterer and the photographer and set up meetings. Sometimes she glanced over at Derek, but he kept his eyes on his computer.

GP stopped by to say he'd hired people from a welfare-to-work program to act as costumed extras at the event. He talked excitedly about giving people employable skills, but Nancy had a hard time following the conversation with Derek sitting silently across the room.

Nancy said, "It will be so fabulous to see the grit and depravity of the Barbary Coast," but her "fabulous" sounded hollow to her own ears and she said, "If you'll excuse me, I'll get water for us. GP, do you like sparkling or flat?"

Derek stood up and said, "I can—"

"No, I'll do it," Nancy said. "Sparkling is better. It's more cheerful."

She went to the kitchen, opened the refrigerator, and stared at the contents without seeing. The cold hit her and she grabbed the closest tall bottle, which was shoved in the back behind the juice bottles and milk.

She poured the water into three glasses and added ice cubes and slices of lime. She dropped neon-bright straws in the glasses and carried them out. When she was in the dining room, she heard GP talking to Derek and paused to readjust the slippery glasses.

GP's voice was clear. "Nancy saved me, you know."

There was a low rumble of Derek's reply.

Then GP spoke again. "No, really. I had, like, no social skills and my family had gotten buckets of money, but I didn't know how to act with these rich kids. My roommates used to torture me every fucking day. I was going to drop out, but Nancy started talking to me. She'd come sit on my bed and talk about her classes, clothes, movies. She told me that I was her tech czar and had to update her gadgets."

This time she heard Derek saying, "You served a purpose for her."

That's how he saw her, as using people for drudgery and chores.

GP said, "Yeah, I thought so, too. That's what she wanted me to think because it made me more comfortable when I felt useful. But when other people saw that Nancy was my friend, their whole attitude changed. Even my jackass roommates started including me in things."

Nancy moved a chair loudly so they would hear her coming and then took the water into the living room.

GP showed her his schedule for delivery of the sets and props and ran down numbers with her. As he was leaving, he said, "I'm going to make this totally kick-ass for you, princess. Just you wait and see."

Then she was alone with Derek. She tried to keep everything professional, but just before she left to pick up Eugenia she said, "I hope things went well with Prescott."

"Indeed. I understand precisely where I stand with him and that is very reassuring."

"Good, wonderful. I want you to be happy, Derek," and she felt more grief at losing the man she never could have had than at leaving the one she'd pledged her life to.

Eugenia was so eager to return to her kitten that she rushed back to Château Winkles and didn't seem to notice that the mood had shifted.

"His name is Blackbeard," she told the adults. "He has little swords in his paws." She and Nancy took the kitten to the vet for shots and bought a travel case, food, a sandbox, and toys.

By Tuesday afternoon, Nancy was anxious to see Bailey, thinking that he could be the bracing tonic of heterosexuality that would cleanse away her fervid longing for Derek. Sloane had already agreed to watch Eugenia and even offered to watch the kitten.

Blackbeard didn't like his travel case and mewed loudly all the way to Sloane's house in the Avenues. Nancy found these neighborhoods depressing. They were as foggy as hers, but the fog seemed dirtier. The houses were smacked side by side and some were covered with layers of grime from car and bus exhaust.

"No *hors de* control antics with Miss Sloane," Nancy said. "Do what she says and say please and thank you."

"Okay."

"She's a very nice lady and her boys are well behaved."

"Okay."

As Nancy and Eugenia stood on the stairs to the taupe house, the child said, "Auntie Nanny, will you come back for me?"

"I will always come back for you, Eugenia. But I'll be out late, so I'll pick you up tomorrow morning to take you to school. You can have a slumber party."

"Like with Derek?"

"Yes, but don't tell anyone about that. It's a secret. Adults don't have slumber parties."

"Mama does with her bed-friends."

The door opened and Sloane stood there flanked by two curious boys with curly brown hair and freckles.

"Hi, Mrs. Chambers," they said, and hugged her.

"Hello, boys. This is my niece, Eugenia. Eugenia, one of these children is Lloyd and the other is Dobler. I can never tell which is which."

One said, "I'm Dobler," and the other said, "No, I'm Dobler!" and they shoved each other.

Sloane said, "Come in, Nancy. The boys were so happy when I told them you were coming."

"I think they are dreadful children," Nancy said, and mussed the hair of the smaller child, who asked, "Did you bring me a present?"

"Why would I do that? Is it Christmas? Is it your birthday?"

"We brought toys," Eugenia said. "And I brought my cat. His name is Blackbeard."

Nancy pulled the gifts out of her tote bag for the boys. They ripped through the wrapping and Nancy said, "You're really little monsters, aren't you? The store clerk told me that boys like grotesque robot things."

"Thank you! Thank you!" the boys shouted.

"Nancy, you spoil them. You don't have to bring presents every time you see them."

"Children have such undeveloped little brains, it's the only way I can make sure they'll remember me when I'm in a home and need someone to tell the nurse to turn me over once a day."

Sloane laughed. "You say such awful things. Where are you going tonight?"

Nancy looked at Sloane's living room. Toys were everywhere and photos of the boys were displayed in cheap Plexiglas frames. The olive green wall-to-wall carpeting was worn and faded. A dining table was set up for a tea party with plastic cups and saucers and a plate of crackers with peanut butter.

"I'm having dinner with Bailey Whiteside and maybe we'll go to a club. I guess you were gone before he showed up at Gigi's party. Do you know him?"

"He was a friend of my husband's." Sloane continued to smile, but she seemed uneasy. She rarely mentioned the man who had abandoned her. "They shared an apartment in Boston for a year. We all used to go out together. We even took trips together."

Nancy couldn't imagine homebody Sloane larking around with Bailey and his crowd. "Todd met Bailey through mutual friends when Todd was in biz school, but I didn't know you were close to Bailey, too."

"It was a long time ago. I feel like a different person now with my boys. It's been so long, I'm sure Bailey's different, too."

Nancy thought that the desparkling effect of motherhood must surely be more dramatic than whatever changes Bailey had gone through. "I'll come get Eugenia at eight thirty tomorrow."

The children were running through the house and shouting. Sloane smiled and said, "I thought you told me she was quiet."

"She *was* quiet. But lately she's becoming very obstinate and outspoken. It's not very ladylike."

"She must be feeling safer."

Nancy called, "Eugenia, I'm going now. Adieu." Eugenia ran over and Nancy obligingly bent over to give her a kiss good-bye.

The girl whispered, "You'll come back?"

"I told you I would. I promised and I keep my promises."
Well, with a few exceptions. "I'll see you tomorrow morning."

Nancy went home and cleared Eugenia's plastic toys out of
the bathtub and set them in a red bin. Once in the shower, she
picked up her bottle of fig apricot body gel and squirted some
onto her bath mitt. Nothing came out. She squeezed harder
and then shook it. It was empty.

She reached for a tube of nectarine blossom and honey gel.
Empty. She opened the container of almond body scrub. Soapy
water splashed out of the jar. The only things Eugenia hadn't
plundered were the haircare products on a high shelf. The
child's mischief made her smile, but otherwise she felt as if she
were getting ready for a job interview, not a date.

Nancy put on a body-skimming jungle green V-neck dress
with skinny shoulder straps and teal suede heels with cutouts.
She wore delicate, dangly gold and smoky quartz earrings and
a trio of thin gold bracelets.

Bailey buzzed the intercom and Nancy told him she'd be
right down.

In her bedroom, she reached for the bottle of L'Heure Bleue
and stopped. Then she dabbed on her old scent and wished
that Junie Burns hadn't hijacked it. Nancy topped the outfit
with a dandelion yellow cropped jacket that her cousin Sissy
had made for her.

As she walked down the stairs to the lobby, she thought of
Junie and the other so-called friends who hadn't bothered to
call her.

Bailey was in the lobby chatting with Miss Winkles. He was
attractive in a narrow gray jacket, pale gray shirt open at the
collar, and charcoal jeans. These were nice neutrals.

Miss Winkles, in one of her lumpy knit suits, said to Nancy,

"I thought this one was your handsome Derek at first, but he's just a Whiteside."

"Is there anything wrong with that?" Bailey asked with a flash of teeth.

"My sister, Dody, made the mistake of going out with a Whiteside. We called him 'the Mouth-Breather,'" Miss Winkles said, and walked to the elevator doors. "Girl Carrington, tell Derek to bring Eugenia to tea and her piano lesson tomorrow. I need him to fix a shelf for me."

"Miss Winkles, Derek is extremely busy right now."

Miss Winkles gave her a threatening look, so Nancy said, "But I'm sure he can make the time to help you."

"Good," Miss Winkles said, and got in the elevator.

As Nancy and Bailey went to his car, he said, "You look very pretty tonight. Is Miss Winkles becoming senile?"

"Miss Winkles is as effervescent as ever," she said as he held the car door open for her. After he got in and started the engine, she asked, "Where are we off to?"

"A private party at a new restaurant. Is your niece still with you?"

"She's spending the night with Sloane and her boys."

"Sloane?"

"Sloane Seitz, Lewis's wife. Don't you know her?"

"Oh, *that* Sloane. Yeah, I knew Lewis before he bailed. Good guy, but weak."

"I never met him."

"He let his habits get the best of him. I wonder where he is these days. Did Sloane say?"

"No. She only told me that you were friends and used to go out together. I can't imagine Sloane partying. She's such a professional mommy."

"She was nice. Too bad she married a loser."

His tone reminded her unpleasantly of Todd. "He was your friend."

"I was pretty kicked back in those days and I thought he was a cool guy. But when I saw where he was headed, I had to cut ties. Let's talk about us."

She glanced at his nice, if not exceptional, profile. It wasn't his fault that he wasn't Derek. "I am still married, and I need you to respect that, Bailey."

"I'm trying to, Nance, but if it's over with Todd, I'd like to know."

Nancy stared at her hands and noticed that her enamel had chipped on two fingernails. "I'll tell you if that happens."

Bailey pulled to the curb in front of a South of Market restaurant, got out, and handed his keys to the valet. Another valet opened the door for Nancy.

Bailey took her arm and led her inside. "Bailey Whiteside and guest," he told the hostess.

She checked his name and then said, "Enjoy your evening."

The restaurant was already full and Bailey looked over the crowd. His eyes fixed on a man sitting at the end of the bar, looking out of place. Bailey dropped his head and said quietly, "Linus Boschert. Northern European development chief of a telecom, but he's here for two months. Let's make friends."

They talked to the newcomer, shared wine and hors d'oeuvres, and Bailey introduced Linus to a pretty young architect.

"That was nice of you to make him comfortable," Nancy said.

"It's good to have friends in the right places. I can use a place to stay if I visit Geneva."

"There are already places for that. They're called hotels. I recommend the Beau-Rivage."

"Why spend money on a room when I can stay with someone for free and develop a connection at the same time?"

"You're the most openly ambitious person I know, Bailey."

"Thank you. Who shall we talk to next?"

Nancy ran into a friend of GP's who asked her about buying a table at the Barbary Coast fund-raiser.

"I'll messenger an invitation to you tomorrow. It's for a wonderful cause—carrying on the great legacy of the pirates who founded our city."

As they moved to talk to another group, Bailey said to her, "Did you say that pirates founded our city?"

"It is a universal dream to dress like a pirate," she said, but Bailey didn't seem to find her comment funny. "You still haven't responded to your invitation."

"I wanted to make sure you would be my date."

"I'll be working the whole time," she said, "but I'll put you down for two tickets."

People came in and out of the party, and she talked and exchanged business cards with them. Then a band appeared and there was dancing, and four buff, bare-chested men carried in a stretcher with a tub-shaped ice sculpture filled with bottles of vodka and caviar.

In the ladies' room, a dermatologist gave shots of Botox, and girls exchanged prescription drugs. Nancy politely accepted Percocets that she put in her plum eel-skin clutch.

When she came out, Bailey was waiting for her.

"Do you have time to come see my place?"

"Tomorrow's a workday."

"Walnut paneling and those plaster decorations that look

like scrolls and leaves. I promise not to take advantage of the situation."

Nancy tilted her head and said, "I've always had a weakness for a fine cartouche."

Bailey's mansion was the classic worst-house-on-an-amazing-block investment. Nancy took one look at the dilapidated exterior and saw the grand dame it had once been. "You don't have mice, do you?"

"Not anymore. It's been empty for the last decade and before that it was rented out to a family."

"You mean cult."

"Is there a difference?" They walked up the stone steps to the beautiful carved wooden doors. Bailey said, "It took me a month to strip and refinish these doors. The place is a mess, but most of the original architecture is intact."

He turned on lamps that weren't bright enough to illuminate the recesses of the large rooms. Their footsteps echoed as Bailey led her to a long hall and into a furnished room.

"I'm living in the dining room for now." A trio of chandeliers hanging from the water-stained ceiling sparkled as if they'd been recently cleaned, but the parquet floor needed to be refinished. The room was divided into sleeping, eating, and work areas.

"This has so much potential," Nancy said. She had a vague recollection of saying the same thing to Todd when they looked over the lot they'd purchased. "You should talk to my mother. She knows all about historical restoration. Tradition is important to her."

"At first I was planning to flip this, but if I married the right woman, someone who could appreciate this house, I'd want to stay." He gave Nancy a meaningful look and she blushed.

She said, "She'd have to be the sort of woman who could envision what this will be. She'd need to keep watch over every detail, so that the renovation would be true to plans."

They talked for more than an hour about the house, and when Bailey suggested she stay the night, she said yes. She slept in his T-shirt on the big brass bed, and he took the sofa.

He kissed her softly, and, even though she kept her mouth closed, the contact made her uncomfortable.

"Good night, Bailey."

"Sweet dreams, Nancy."

When she heard his breathing slow in sleep, she felt relieved that she'd escaped any pressure for sex.

When Nancy awoke and saw how bright the morning was, she leapt out of bed, saying "Damn, damn, damn!" as she gathered her things.

Bailey sat up on the sofa and rubbed his neck. "What's the matter?"

"I was supposed to pick up Eugenia ten minutes ago. Could you give me a ride home, or call a taxi?"

"I'll give you a lift."

She ran to the bathroom, dressed, and swished toothpaste around in her mouth. Her curls had flattened, so she found a can of foam mousse and attempted to revitalize them.

Bailey said, "Calm down. You're only a few minutes late. I can drive you to Sloane's and we'll pick her up."

"You don't have a car seat."

"I'll drive carefully. It's only this one time."

"Every time matters." Nancy called Sloane to say she was running late.

Bailey made light conversation on the way back to Château Winkles, but Nancy couldn't concentrate. She pecked his cheek, and when he said "I'll call later," she answered, "Yes, lovely. Thank you for everything."

She got her car and could have made it to Sloane's faster, but she'd actually started abiding the traffic laws. Nancy parked across the driveway, and as she walked up to Sloane's house, she saw Eugenia's face pressed up against the front window.

Nancy waved wildly and Eugenia grinned and then disappeared from sight. The door opened as Nancy walked up the steps.

Sloane said, "Look who's here!"

Eugenia was jumping and saying, "Auntie Nanny!" and Nancy grabbed her in a hug and lifted her.

"I told you she was coming," Sloane told the girl. "Your aunt is someone you can always count on because she loves you very much."

"I'm sorry I was late, baby. Where's Blackbeard?"

"Lloyd has him."

"Go get him so we can put him in the case. Blackbeard, not Lloyd. He won't fit in the case."

When Eugenia left, Nancy said, "I'm so sorry!"

"It's all right. I hope you had a nice evening."

"I did! We went out and then Bailey wanted to show me the house he's renovating and it got late . . ."

"Bailey always was fun. Did you mention me?"

"I did. He said you'd all been friends, but he knows how busy you are with the kids."

"Different paths," Sloane said. "We had a great time here. Eugenia's welcome to come anytime."

Nancy packed up the kitten and the child, dropped Eugenia off at preschool, and went back to her apartment. She had done absolutely nothing wrong. Nonetheless, she felt walk-of-shameish as she came in the door of her apartment, carrying Eugenia's bag and the cat carrier. Derek looked up from his work to see her in last night's clothes.

"Good morning, Derek," she said as she opened the case to let the kitten out. "I'll be a few minutes. Any deliveries this morning?"

"Good morning, madame. The caterer sent the final menu."

"Good. I'm dying for a cappuccino." She tugged at her dress, but the wrinkles were obvious.

"Certainly, madame."

His coolness was infuriating. "Do you notice anything different about me?"

Derek's unreadable gaze assessed her. "You have done something different with your hair, Mrs. Carrington-Chambers."

"Yes, and I'm wearing a cocktail dress."

"So you are. If you will excuse me . . ." He stood and went to the kitchen.

She followed him. "It is really horrifying that you don't seem to care where I've been. I could have been kidnapped by thugs and held for ransom all night long."

"Forgive me for being so insensitive. *Were* you kidnapped and held for ransom?"

"No. I went to a party with Bailey, then it got late, and then . . . well, never mind. I would be terrified about you if you came in late one morning with bad hair."

"It is unnecessary for you to worry about me, regardless of my hairstyle."

She grabbed his arm, surprising herself and him. "Derek, why are you being this way?" She looked into his eyes and felt her own welling up.

His expression softened. "We went too far. We have to step back. You know that." Then he lifted her hand from his arm and held it up to display her wedding rings. "These men give you diamonds. What can I give you? There's no place for me in your personal life and no place for you in mine."

He let her hand go. Her throat had constricted and she couldn't answer to tell him that his one butterfly brooch meant more to her than all the diamonds at Tiffany's.

"Mrs. Carrington-Chambers, I'm glad you've found someone more suitable to your lifestyle," he said more formally. "But I would rather you did not trust Whiteside. He seems somewhat dodgy."

"You don't even know him."

"Maybe not, but he's a friend of your husband's, isn't he?"

"If you mean that he's one of *us*, yes." She swiped at her eyes and said, "You're just jealous of him because he's successful and everyone adores him and he's got a great future. Just because Prescott cheats on you, don't assume that everyone is untrustworthy!"

"Don't you see the irony in that, Mrs. Carrington-Chambers?"

"You bastard." She grabbed a paper towel and blew her nose. "I'm going to go to my bedroom and when I come out, I want to pretend this never happened. I want to pretend *we* never happened. You just do the job you're paid to do. Is that clear?"

"As you wish, Mrs. Carrington-Chambers."

She closed the bedroom door and tried to control herself. A lady didn't sob and argue with the help. Nancy went to the closet and turned on the light. She'd left shoes scattered on the floor, and Eugenia's bed was a tumble of blankets and toys. There was a bad smell that the delicate aroma of room spray couldn't cover.

Nancy shifted aside the skirts on a lower rack and saw a brown cat turd near the wall. She stepped back and something crunched underfoot. It was a crayon in the shade of Jazzberry Jam. Against the closet wall, Birdie stared out from the painting, looking self-satisfied. Nancy thought that this was what the *Mona Lisa* had been smiling about—a cat turd in someone's else's closet.

When Nancy returned to her writing desk much later, her eyes were red, but she was impeccably dressed in black and white. Her cappuccino, sitting on the counter, was cold and the foam was as deflated as her spirits.

Derek and she only spoke when they needed to exchange information. What were suitable centerpieces? He would check the records at the Historical Society. Where would the actors change clothes? She'd call the property manager.

He didn't go with Nancy to pick up Eugenia, but when the child came back from preschool, he was as warm to her as he'd always been.

"Oh, I almost forgot," Nancy said. "Miss Winkles invited you both to tea and a piano lesson for Eugenia. Derek, I believe she has some tasks for you, and I can talk to her about that."

"I enjoy helping Miss Winkles, madame."

"Can I take Blackbeard?" Eugenia asked.

"Yes, and I hope he makes her as happy as he's made me. Also, don't let that animal in my . . . in your little room, and do not leave your crayons around. You must put them back in the box after you use them."

Eugenia flopped her head to one side and then the other and said "Duh!" in a way that was so silly that Nancy found herself smiling.

While they were gone, Nancy tried to rid her closet of the

awful smell. She cleaned, she disinfected, she spritzed. She had just put Eugenia's blankets in the washer when Bailey called.

"Hey, gorgeous," he said.

"Hi, Bailey."

"Will you please go out with me on a Friday? Or Saturday?"

"What's wrong with Tuesdays?"

"It says you don't think I rate a weekend date. You're damaging my credibility as an eligible bachelor."

"I may be available on Saturday. I'll have to see if I can get a babysitter."

"When will I have a chance to get to know Eugenia? I'd like to meet her mother, too."

"I'll introduce you to Birdie as soon as she flutters into town," Nancy said. "I'm sure I'll find a babysitter."

"Great. I'm planning something special," he said. "I know it's early days, but Nancy, I can see a future with you. I always thought we had a connection, and it grows stronger every time I see you. I hope I'm not scaring you off."

"No, you aren't."

When Nancy finished the call, she closed her eyes and tried to think through the sorrow of losing Derek. She couldn't imagine going back to Todd and living in that house. She didn't want him to touch her and she couldn't stand the idea of bearing Toddlings.

Bailey had made his intentions clear, and she liked him. Things would only get better between them. If she got divorced, she could go on real dates with Bailey. Her parents would be upset initially, but her father would be able to see the value of an association with the Whiteside family.

When Nancy opened her eyes, she was resolved. She picked up the phone and called her attorney, Renee. "I want to move forward with the divorce. I'd like you to get all the papers in order so that we can file them as soon as I get confirmation on one personal matter."

"It's your call, Nancy, but if Todd broke the prenup, I think we should ask him to reimburse you for the total cost of the house, *including* his contribution," Renee said. "California doesn't allow sanctions against infidelity, but it will be very useful as leverage and that way you'll get something from the time you've spent with him. Always ask for more than you'll settle for."

"He hasn't done anything. It's me. I should have listened to my father and not cashed out my wedding stock to throw into that disaster. If Todd wants to keep it, I'll consider an offer based on half its current market value."

"I want you to sleep on that, okay, because decisions like this shouldn't be based on impulse or emotions," Renee said. "Now, if Todd contests the prenup, I need to know if there's anything, absolutely *anything* he can use against you. Forewarned is forearmed."

"You don't have to worry, Renee. I've been a delightful wife."

"I'll have my secretary send you an invoice for the retainer and a form to fill out with your shared assets."

"Thanks, Renee."

Now Nancy needed to know if Bailey was as serious about a future together as he seemed.

twenty

creating your signature look

*E*ugenia couldn't wait for her next sleepover at Sloane's. She drew designs of capes for Lloyd and Dobler, triangles and squiggles. Nancy spent Saturday morning making garments from the drawings while Blackbeard played with the scraps of cloth, and they all listened to the soundtrack for *The Sound of Music.*

"We'll have to watch *Mary Poppins,* where Julie Andrews plays a British nanny, who sings and does magic."

"Like Derek," Eugenia said.

"Derek doesn't do magic."

"Yes, he does. He can change his voice when he's Rick."

"That's not magic. It's Derek, not Rick." The thought of

him made her ache. "Julie Andrews was in another movie where she plays a woman pretending to be a man, and she has to decide if she wants to keep pretending and be successful, or if she wants to be honest and happy with the man she loves."

"Like Rick and you pretend."

"What do you mean, Eugenia?" Nancy asked, nervous that the girl, who had seen too much with her mother, had seen something here.

"Lloyd needs a shiny star on his cape," Eugenia said, and pointed at a length of metallic fabric.

Sloane's boys were overjoyed with their superhero capes.

"Nancy, those are wonderful!" Sloane said. "You made them?"

"It was a team effort. Eugenia drew the designs and I executed them."

"I think you did more than that," Sloane said. "Will you be seeing Bailey again?"

"I know it's a little strange, because he's Todd's friend, not that anything has happened, but we've got so much in common. We both love going out, parties, living in the city, classic architecture, and networking. He dresses as well as a straight man can dress, and he pays attention to me," Nancy said. "There's mutual respect."

"Do you think things will become serious?"

"There's a chance of it. Todd and I haven't been happy with each other for years. You must have gone through the same thing with Lewis."

Sloane checked to make sure the children weren't nearby. "Todd isn't a compulsive gambler."

"He's gambled on investments. Not all of them have been successful, but the higher the risk, the higher the payoff.

Bailey's made some of the same investments, but he's done well."

"Some people are like ducks," Sloane said. "When the waters flood, they float on the surface. Others go under."

Nancy patted her friend's shoulder. "But you're doing wonderfully now, Sloane. I'll see you at noon tomorrow. Oh, I wanted to mention that Froth is going so well that I can give you a raise, ten percent, now that we're taking on bigger projects. And, here," Nancy said, and handed Sloane an envelope.

"What's this?"

"Gigi mentioned that you were especially helpful at her party and sent a little something extra. See you tomorrow."

"Give Bailey my best, will you? It would be nice to see him again."

"I'll tell him. You can catch up with each other at the fundraiser." Poor Sloane, dreaming of past excitements.

Bailey had told Nancy to wear jeans, but hadn't told her what they were doing, so she packed a satchel in case she was out for the night.

He picked Nancy up at the Château and said, "I wanted you to see my house while it's light out. Where's Birdie's daughter?"

"I call her my niece because it's simpler. Eugenia's with Sloane and her boys. Sloane says hello."

"I'm glad you could find a babysitter. Birdie's lucky to have someone as responsible as you to help out. I think the best families are like that, always knowing the importance of supporting one another."

She was pleased that he appreciated her reliability. "I'm not usually one of those mothery people, but Eugenia's very creative and fascinating," she said. "Oh, here we are. It looks so different in the daylight."

"Worse, I know. Good restoration is actually harder and more expensive than new construction. My friends think I should have demolished it and started fresh, but how could I tear down this old beauty?"

Bailey turned into the long cracked driveway and drove around the mansion. He parked by a dilapidated carriage house.

The garden was overgrown with shrubs and weeds. The yellow fruit of an overgrown lemon tree was the one spot of bright color. "This is an enormous project," Nancy said.

"Things that come too easily often aren't worth anything," he said, and stared into her eyes. "I don't mind working hard for something worthwhile, for quality."

She smiled and said, "Take me on a top-to-bottom tour." If she'd said this to Derek, he would have given her one of his sexy grins, but Bailey led her in through the servants' entrance.

"The staff quarters are that way," Bailey said, pointing to a hallway. "Here's the kitchen."

"Oh, my," Nancy said. The large, airy room still had its original green and white tiles, deep porcelain sinks, and coved ceiling. "Show me more."

She exclaimed about everything from the brass heat registers to the carved oak banisters on the main staircase. A few floors were rotted, but others were undamaged under nasty old carpets.

In the cool shadows of the wine cellar, Bailey said, "I haven't shown the house to other girls. They wouldn't understand what it means to me and what it can be. Let me show you the view."

When they had reached the third floor, Bailey led her to a walnut-paneled room with a massive arched window. The sun was setting, washing the fog golden, and Nancy thought of the sunset she'd seen at the beach.

Bailey took her in his arms, and she expected to feel desire, but the only lust she felt was for the house. For whatever reason, his kiss was pleasurable. On a scale of one to ten, with Todd's kissing being almost five and Derek's being eleven, Bailey scored a solid seven. She wondered what her kissing rated, and she opened her lips and made an extra effort.

Bailey had set up dinner in his living area. Nancy was pleased by the gleam of silver candlesticks, crystal wineglasses, and the heavy old silverware. He'd bought a roasted chicken, salads, side dishes, and a chocolate torte. "I hope you don't mind cold food," he said.

"I can't believe you did all this for me."

He poured white wine into two glasses. "It's just the beginning, Nancy."

After a leisurely dinner, Bailey built a fire outside in an old brick barbecue that was as large as a sarcophagus. He brought out a boom box and played a mix of songs that he said he'd made for her. They were softer ballads, the kind of music guys thought women liked.

They slow-danced on the cracked stone terrace and he talked about himself. "Our house was almost as bad as this. My parents managed to keep the exterior looking okay, but the inside was falling apart, so we never had anyone over. Things broke and rotted. We were all living in a few rooms."

"It sounds quite Gothic," she said. "Did you have ghosts?"

"Yes, ghosts of family ambitions that were murdered and buried somewhere near the lilac garden," he said. "My parents couldn't imagine doing anything as undignified as getting jobs that would pay real money. Dad wrote his histories about obscure naval battles, and Mom's idea of living within our means was to become a docent at all the museums so we could get free passes."

"You've met my father," Nancy said. "He believes that art is fine for people who can't do anything else. He thinks I rebelled against him by not going into business with him."

"Did you?"

"No, I really wanted to care about business and money, but it's all theoretical, a game, and I never could see the beauty in it," she said. "I'm sure I've disappointed him."

"You shouldn't feel that way, because I think you're amazing, Nancy. If we were together, I'd encourage your event-planning skill set, because it can be a powerful tool," he said. "I don't want a little wifey sitting at home. I want someone who'll be my partner, and we'll be a force."

"Politics are vicious, Bailey."

"Not if you're careful, and I'm always one step ahead of the other guy."

They drank cognac in front of the dying embers of the fire, and she thought of how romantic Bailey was. She tried to enjoy his kisses, but when his hands began sliding under her clothes, she drew back. "I'm sorry, Bailey. I'm not ready for that now."

He let out a long breath and said, "Do you think you will be ready sometime, with me?"

Nancy nodded. "Please don't tell anyone, but I called my attorney and asked her to draw up divorce papers. You were part of my decision."

"Awesome! I'll keep your secret about that and about us if

you want more," he said. "I can't wait until I get you into bed with me."

Nancy stared at the tall, handsome man and imagined lying in luxurious linens with him while they pored over the latest issues of *House Beautiful*. "Neither can I."

She stayed awake in the brass bed long after Bailey had gone to the sofa and turned out the lights. She could see herself living here as clearly as a magazine layout. The corner bedroom would be set up like a Parisian apartment with antique furniture in a honey and lavender color scheme. The master bath would have a tiled arch over the deep free-standing tub. A rustic farmhouse table would be set by the brick barbecue for outdoor dining.

The old carriage house could be converted to offices that she could share with Derek, and Eugenia's room would have a pirate theme, naturally, and a ladder and a loft. But Derek and Eugenia wouldn't be here. It would be too uncomfortable to have him here with Bailey, and Birdie would eventually come for her daughter.

But Eugenia could visit sometimes and Nancy could find another amazing assistant. She'd throw herself into Bailey's whirlwind life, helping to manage his political campaigns. They'd be a power couple, and if they ever had children, people would stop to admire their family. Her parents would be impressed with her success, and her friends would clamor for her favor.

She realized that it was the same cliché dream she'd had before she'd married Todd.

The next morning, Nancy stayed in bed while Bailey made breakfast. He squeezed fresh orange juice and said, "Would you mind getting the newspapers? You can wear my robe."

Nancy slipped on the navy robe that was hanging on the bedpost. "I'll be right back."

She went to the front door, cracked it open, and looked out. Two papers were within reach, but one was in a dead shrub. As she dashed out and grabbed it, someone said, "Nancy?"

She turned to see Junie Burns in Lycra running capris and a matching top. Nancy held the newspapers in front of her. "Oh, hi, Junie."

"Just out for my morning run," Junie said, her breath coming fast. "This is Bailey's house."

"I'm just . . ." Nancy held the papers up as explanation.

June looked at her scornfully. "I used to think you deserved Todd. I thought you were better than me and that's why you got a guy like that." For the first time since Nancy had known her, Junie's voice was firm. "But you didn't even appreciate what you had. You just chewed him up, spit him out, and now you're moving on."

"This isn't what it seems," Nancy said, wondering what had happened to the meek, admiring girl she'd known.

"You're the one who believes appearances are everything, Nancy, and I know what I'm seeing." Junie shook her head. "Don't *ever* call me again."

Nancy stood stunned while Junie ran off. Then she went inside the house and to the dining room.

Bailey saw her expression and said, "What is it? Is anything wrong?"

"Junie Burns was on a run when I went outside. She thinks that we . . ." Nancy still couldn't believe that Junie had turned on her. "She was really nasty and bitter. She's going to tell everyone that we slept together."

"No need to freak, Nance. Everything's still cool between

me and Todd. I'll call and tell him you crashed here, but nothing happened. Everyone knows that Junie's been jealous of you for years, so it's not like Todd's going to listen to a thing she says. Come have breakfast."

When Todd didn't call her that afternoon or evening, Nancy hoped that Bailey was right.

On Monday, Nancy tried to focus on her work, but her confidence had evaporated and she found herself second-guessing all her decisions. Too often she caught herself staring at her beautiful, aloof assistant and thinking that if he gave her a comforting hug, she would be able to clear her mind and figure things out.

Sometimes their eyes met and she felt a wave of sorrow and longing that seemed to grow stronger every day.

When Nancy received her attorney's statement, she wrote out a check for the retainer. She used a pen with green ink because green is the color of hope.

She went out with Bailey on a few nights while Sloane babysat. They dashed from one gathering to another. She met new people and renewed old associations. She started getting invitations again, most of which she couldn't accept because of Eugenia.

One day as Nancy was dropping Eugenia off at Three Bridges, Mrs. Kanbar said, "May I have a minute?"

"I hope there's no problem with Eugenia. She hasn't hit anyone with that sword, has she?" Nancy followed Mrs. Kanbar into her office.

"Only once, and she stopped after a time-out." Mrs. Kanbar sat at her desk and said, "Eugenia's getting along very well and her social skills are developing quite nicely. She's joined a small group and plays with them every day."

"She talks about Olivia and Pierce all the time."

"I know Eugenia's with you temporarily, but if things should change, I wanted you to know that we would be happy to have her stay. The family of the boy who left has decided to relocate."

"Oh," Nancy said. "Thank you very much, but Eugenia's mother doesn't live here. Or anywhere for long. She travels."

"I'll leave the offer open until she returns and you can talk to her about it." Mrs. Kanbar smiled sympathetically. "Now, the other matter is your boyfriend, Rick, who's become very important to Eugenia. She told me that she's anxious about him. Is he suffering from depression? Because we can give you a referral to a family therapist."

"I don't have a boyfriend named Rick. My assistant is named Derek, and he's fine."

"She said 'Rick' clearly. Her verbal skills are excellent."

"Eugenia's? Regardless of her skills, or lack thereof, she knows his name is Derek. He's perfectly well. He's delightful. I have no idea where Eugenia got the idea that he's unhappy."

Mrs. Kanbar had a skeptical "Are you sure you don't wear a bigger size of jeans?" expression and pushed a business card across the desk. "If you should ever want to talk, here's someone who's been helpful to other families."

"We're not a family," Nancy said, rising from her seat. "Thank you for your concern."

As they walked home, she said, "Eugenia, why did you tell Mrs. Kanbar that Derek is sad?"

"Not Derek. Rick is sad."

"There is no Rick. There is only Derek. He's fine."

Eugenia's look was more skeptical than Mrs. Kanbar's.

"Okay," Nancy said. "Why do you think *Rick* is sad?"

"He's sad in his eyes. He said he has to go away, and I told him no, don't go. Olivia had a birthday. When can I have a birthday?"

"I'll call your grandmother and ask her what your birthday is. If she'll answer my call."

"We can give Rick a kitten and he can bring his kitten to play with us and Blackbeard. Make him stay. Tell him we love him."

"He can't have a kitten. His boyfriend is allergic to cats. Derek is staying."

"Maybe a puppy. We can take them on our special trip to the park every day. When are we going to the park?"

"We'll go after I'm done with this party. You don't need to worry about Rick-slash-Derek. He's extraordinarily happy."

"Huh!"

Back at the apartment, after Nancy settled Eugenia down to look at picture books, she went over the latest reservations for the fund-raiser and called Mrs. Friendly to discuss the seating chart.

"You take care of it, honey. Is it important?"

"Yes, because people who aren't Mrs. Bentley Jamieson Friendly are going to feel insulted if they're at the wrong table or seated with people they hate."

"I gave up keeping track of who hates whom decades ago. If you're as smart as I think you are, you will, too, before your life is ruined trying to accommodate the whims of others."

"But Mrs. Friendly . . ."

"Bye, honey."

Nancy referred to her notes from Gigi's party, but she had to ask Derek to work with her on figuring out the tables. "This is an inexact science," she said as they stood over a sheet of poster board and moved around three-by-five cards with names and notes. "GP can have the table by the caterer's station, since it's his first year and he'll be spending his time supervising the actors."

As she moved a card across the paper, her arm brushed against Derek's. "I didn't mean that. Sorry." She felt clumsy and nervous. And then, when she glanced at his face, it was as if she was seeing someone else for just a second, someone she knew and loved more than anyone in the world.

She needed to get over him.

When Derek took Eugenia to Miss Winkles for her piano lesson and so he could change a lightbulb, Nancy called Bailey and said she'd like to go away with him. "I'll want to relax after the fund-raiser on Friday, so we can go on Saturday morning and come back early on Monday. Would you like to go to Stinson?"

"That's great, Nance. I have something important I want to ask you."

She called her mother to see if the beach house was available and if she could watch Eugenia.

"Your father won't be using it because he's in Chicago," Hester said, and Nancy heard the sound of ice tinkling against glass. "I'd love to help you, but I'm coming down with a cold."

"Mom, why don't you visit Aunt Frilly for a few weeks? You know how much you like staying with her."

"Maybe, Nanny."

"Speaking of Aunt Frilly, have you talked to her recently? I need to ask Birdie about Eugenia's preschool."

"You have her in preschool? That's nice."

"Didn't Dad tell you? There's a spot opening up and I don't know what Birdie wants to do." Nancy thought of how happy

Eugenia was at Three Bridges. Birdie would pull her out and drag her around, leaving her with slatternly hotel maids, or in hippie communes.

"I'll call Frilly later. Good luck at your party."

"Thanks, Mom. Love you."

"Love you, Nanny."

Nancy tried her cousin Sissy, who laughed and said, "I'm not taking her because then I'll be stuck with her."

"Sissy, you should be so lucky as to have Eugenia's company. She's got amazing artistic vision. I have no intention of leaving her with someone who can't appreciate that. Good day," Nancy said, and hung up and chewed at a rough edge of her fingernail.

She called Milagro, who was away on a trip, but Sloane came through with a suggestion. "The boys are having a sleepover at a friend's on Friday, but I can watch Eugenia for the rest of the weekend if Mrs. Kanbar can help you find a sitter for Friday."

"I'll do that. Thanks," Nancy said. She felt the need to confide in someone sympathetic. "I'm going away with Bailey. He keeps talking about marriage and I think he's going to ask me to make a commitment."

Nancy heard the front door open and Derek came in alone and sat at his writing table.

"A proposal?" Sloane said. "That's so sudden. Bailey always talked about not wanting to marry too soon."

Nancy had nothing to hide, except, of course, from Todd, so she said, "I think Bailey's ready now with the right person. He wants someone who shares his priorities." Somehow that didn't sound very romantic.

Sloane said, "Lloyd, stop hitting Dobler with his Elmo!

Sorry about that, Nancy. I wish you the best if you believe he's right for you."

"We're really well matched. I know my father thinks Bailey has a great future and my mother will fall in love with his renovation project, just like I did. But I'm not telling anyone anything until my divorce papers are filed."

When Nancy ended the call, she looked at Derek. His eyes were fixed on his laptop screen. "Derek, I'm going to tell Miss Winkles that she should call the building manager to help her with chores. It's part of his duties."

"I don't mind helping her, madame."

"But I need you here helping me. Since you'll be working on Friday evening, you may have Monday off."

"Thank you, Mrs. Carrington-Chambers," he said coldly.

There was a strand of cobweb in his dark hair and Nancy wanted to brush it away. "As you already overheard, I may start divorce proceedings very soon. In which case, Todd will not want to pay your salary. What is the usual procedure—do I contact your agency and have them bill me for your services, or do I deal directly with you?"

"You cannot afford me, madame."

"I'll work it out with my financial advisor," she said, peeved. She wondered exactly how much Derek was paid and knew that her father would recommend that she hire someone right out of college for less. "I'm going to pick up Eugenia and you have cobwebs in your hair."

twenty-one

construct your milieu

*F*riday morning arrived too soon. Nancy dressed in jeans and her superhero T-shirt and began going over her Froth hemp totes, making sure each contained the supplies itemized on the tags attached to the handles.

She made scrambled eggs and toast for breakfast. Sloane's suggestion had been useful and one of Eugenia's favorite teacher's aides, Eve, was going to babysit her.

"You get to stay the whole day at school and Eve will bring you home," Nancy told Eugenia. "I'm leaving the key with Miss Winkles, so show Eve her apartment. Eve said she wants to meet Blackbeard. I'll be home after you're asleep. You can sleep in my bed tonight."

"Why can't I come to the pirate party?"

"It's a grown-up party."

"I want to see the pirate ship."

"Let's ask Derek if he can arrange a visit for us some other time. Maybe we can invite Sloane, Lloyd, and Dobler."

"And Miss Wiggles and Blackbeard."

"We'll see."

When she took Eugenia to Three Bridges, Nancy stopped on the sidewalk outside the preschool and said, "Be on your best behavior tonight."

Eugenia's brows knit together. "You'll come back?"

"I'll always come back for you, Eugenia. I love you very much." Nancy put her arms around the girl and kissed her cheek

"I love you, Auntie," Eugenia said, and gave her a loud smacking kiss on her nose that made Nancy laugh.

Nancy returned to Château Winkles to meet up with Derek before they went to the warehouse. He'd loaded her totes in the Mini and was at his desk, fielding calls.

Bailey phoned midmorning and said, "Hey, Nance."

"Bailey!" She glanced at Derek, who was talking on the phone to the florist. "I'm absolutely overwhelmed with work. I'm überwhelmed, supernova-whelmed."

She expected Bailey to laugh, but he said, "I'm sure you're in control of everything. That's what I admire about you. I know I'll see you tonight, but I wanted to tell you how much I'm looking forward to this weekend. Should I bring anything?"

"Just your board shorts and sunscreen. The house is stocked, and we can pick up anything we need in town."

"You know how much I care about you, don't you?"

"I feel the same way about you." She was sure she cared for him. Oh yes, she certainly cared for Bailey.

"Bye, Nancy."

"Bye." She put down the phone and saw Derek's twilight blue eyes staring at her and she flushed hot.

"You're going away with Whiteside?"

"We're going to the beach house and I think he's going to ask me to marry him."

"Okay, that's it," Derek said, and stood up.

His voice was different and he looked different—like the man who'd made love to her.

"*What's* it?" she asked.

"I've had it with this stupid farce. Your douche husband paid an agency to place me here."

She was baffled by his American accent and his anger. "Yes, I know Todd hired you, but *what* are you talking about and *why* are you talking like that?"

"Because this is how I talk."

"Todd may be a douche—okay, he is a douche, but you shouldn't be calling him that and . . . Why don't you calm down and have a glass of water?" she said, confused. "I'll get it for you. Sparkling with lime."

"I don't need water," he snapped. "Todd hired me through an investigation agency to get proof that you're cheating on him so he could break your prenup, and now you're going off with that asshole Whiteside. What the hell are you thinking? Are you *even* thinking?"

Nancy felt as if she'd stuck her finger in a light socket. "Do you mean you've been spying on me, Derek?"

"Rick. My name's Rick."

She couldn't talk, couldn't breathe for a minute. Of course,

Todd had given in too easily to the separation. Of course, he'd volunteered too readily to hire an assistant. Of course, Derek had been too perfect. Nancy had never felt more stupid and foolish and angry and hurt in her life.

"Did you tell him that I slept with Anthony Harper?" she said. Then an even more agonizing possibility came to her. "And that's why you had sex with me, isn't it? It was a performance. You forced yourself to do it because you were paid to." She clenched her hands until her nails cut into her palms. "Oh God, oh God."

"That's how you think, isn't it? It's all about money. That's why you go from one rich jerk to another. That's why you'd never consider someone like me."

"How could I? You're gay. You and Prescott . . ."

"Eugenia's sharper than you. She figured it out. I'm not gay. I'm not English. Prescott *Bottomsley*? Are you kidding me? His name is Gregory, he's my friend, and he owns the investigation agency. He gave me the assignment because I needed the money."

Nancy was trying to absorb everything he was saying. "Then why did you . . . when we . . ."

"Because I fell for your poor-little-rich-girl act. Yeah, you made me think you were someone else for a while. You made me think I was someone else, too, which shows what an idiot I am. I even broke up with my girlfriend for you," he said. "What kind of soulless woman marries a man just to take his money?"

"I didn't marry Todd for money!"

"I don't care if you clean him out and I don't care if you clean out Whiteside, too. I don't want to have anything to do with either you or your scumbag husband," he said. "Tell

Eugenia that I love her and I wish I could have said good-bye. She's a great kid and she sure as hell deserves better than being a member of your sleazy family."

He walked to the doorway and said, "Have a *fabulous* life, Nancy Fancy."

Nancy stood where she was and watched him leave.

Everything she'd thought about him was a lie. She'd had sex with a complete stranger. She'd let him into her home and shared everything with him. Nancy Fancy. That was the name the burlesque dancer had mentioned. What was her name? Melanie. She was Derek's Mel.

Five minutes later, Froth's lines started ringing. Nancy let them ring and called her attorney. Her hand shook as she held the phone and said, "Renee, I need to speak with you as soon as possible, but not today. Tomorrow. Todd hired someone to spy on me."

Staring at the wall, the color of the water on her honeymoon, she realized that Bailey was probably part of Todd's plan to ruin her. She felt as if she was walking through a bog; everything was dark and murky and awful. If Nancy could only hold herself together through the fund-raiser, she would deal with everything tomorrow.

She went upstairs to give Miss Winkles the extra key for the babysitter.

Miss Winkles opened the door a smidgen, not enough for Nancy to see into the apartment, and scrutinized her. "Why didn't you send up Derek, Girl Carrington?"

"He's no longer in my employ. Here's the key to give Eugenia's babysitter, Eve, who'll bring her from school. Eve has my phone number if there's an emergency."

"Did you fire Derek?"

"He chose to leave."

Miss Winkles rolled her eyes. "I suppose I shouldn't have expected a man like that to want to stay with a silly thing like you, but he seemed to like you anyway."

Nancy nodded and felt tears running down her face. "Thank you for your help, Miss Winkles. Thank you for spending so much time with Eugenia."

"Girl Carrington, are you all right?"

Nancy nodded again and then said, "No, actually I'm not. Bye." Then she went down to her apartment and gathered her clothes for the evening. She was going to wear an aubergine dress that Sissy had designed for her. She saw the large purple handbag she'd taken from her mother's closet and upended the contents of her purse into it.

It was just after one when Nancy found herself sitting in her car in the parking lot of the waterfront warehouse, but she didn't remember driving. The gala started at seven and would be over at midnight. She had to get through eleven more hours and then she could fall apart.

Aldo stood in front of the coffee shack and waved at her. She waved back and remembered coming here for the first time with Derek and how it had felt to lie against his body with the cold, salty wind whipping around them.

Nancy crossed the asphalt lot and went into the warehouse. It had been transformed like the back lot of a movie studio. Windows of false storefronts were lighted from behind to give the illusion of entire buildings. Wooden walkways crossed the length of the warehouse. Signs hung from doorways announcing bars, dance halls, whorehouses, flophouses, and gambling parlors.

GP came rushing to Nancy, more excited than she'd ever

seen him before. "Come check out the music hall!" The crew was adding the final touches to a room set up as the bar, with stairs that led up to a nonexistent second floor.

"It's wonderful," Nancy told her friend.

"Wait until you see the actors. I got a coach to work with them on dialect and to do a few scenes that I scripted from old newspaper reports and diaries. Do you think it looks authentic?"

"Yes, it's perfectly authentic! You've done something amazing here."

He looked away shyly. "Thank you for trusting me."

"I always know when something is true and good . . ." she began, and she couldn't say anything else. She put her hand on GP's arm and squeezed it, then turned away so he wouldn't see her eyes.

Nancy got the managers together and distributed headsets to key personnel. She talked to the waitstaff manager and the lighting designer. She inspected the luxury mobile restroom trailers and confirmed that the pirate ship would pull up to the pier on schedule.

Sloane arrived with her team and looked at the scene with astonishment. "It's like Disneyland," Sloane said. "It's fantastic."

"Thanks to GP. He pulled out all the stops." Nancy handed Sloane a folder and said, "Derek couldn't make it, so you'll have to help with his assignments."

"Is he all right? He's not sick, is he?"

Nancy wanted to tell Sloane that his name wasn't Derek and that he was gone and that he'd tricked her and that her heart was broken. "He's fine. Would you check on the music hall and make sure they've decanted the drinks into the old bottles?"

The overhead lights were shut off and the party lighting

came on. Gas street posts flickered golden light and the taped recording of waterfront sounds melded with the real sound and smell of the bay beside them. The warehouse was so drafty that the wooden signs swung and creaked in the breeze.

No matter what else was happening in her life, Nancy was responsible for this dark wonderland. She moved away from everyone else and stood just looking at the scene. Sun Tzu had said that many calculations lead to victory. Nancy's feverish attention to detail would bring her success tonight.

She wished that Derek could see it, the Derek who'd never existed. Nancy squished down her emotions like an eiderdown packed for summer storage.

She was speaking with the catering director when the costumed actors strolled in, looking as wonderfully grimy and unsavory as GP had promised. Nancy's phone rang. She looked at the number. It was her mother. She excused herself and went outside to answer the call.

"Hi, Mom, how's everything?"

"Nancy, I wanted to wish you luck," her mother slurred.

"You already did. Thanks."

"Your father is on one of his *business* trips with the new one, Caroline. She's thirty-one. Business."

"Mom, please . . ."

"I'm sorry, honey. He works so hard to give me everything I could want. I should be more understanding."

"Go to bed, Mom, and please don't drink anymore. Don't drive, promise me, and don't call anyone else."

"Yes, Nanny."

I'll deal with it tomorrow, she told herself. She collected her clothes for the evening and went to the trailer reserved for event staff. She changed into the aubergine dress and put on makeup for the evening. She left her handbag with her work clothes. She set her phone in a case that was attached to her clipboard and tried to fluff her hair over her headset.

When Nancy returned to the warehouse, the white-jacketed waiters were carrying out food and arranging the old-fashioned saucer-shaped champagne glasses.

The slouching, rough-looking actors conveyed a sense of danger, and the women, falling out of their scandalous period dresses, screamed cheap and dirty. They also screamed, and Nancy was going to ask them to modulate their voices when the first group of guests, including Gigi Barton, arrived.

Gigi was wearing a tea-stained gathered shirt, mustard frock coat, and ruby red taffeta skirt, and she looked so spectacular that Nancy was momentarily distracted from her misery.

"Gigi, welcome!" she said, going forward to exchange air kisses with her. She gazed at her friend and said, "Is that—"

"Yes, it's from the Pirate Collection," Gigi said. "I heard this was a pirate party, so I dug this out of the vault. Let me introduce my friends."

The guests were checked in and Nancy walked them to the music hall, which was halfway down the warehouse, between the poker parlor and the hotel, where dinner would be served. A pianist and a girl, who pretended convincingly to be drunk, performed "My Darling Clementine."

The bartender plonked down glasses as soon as they walked in and sloshed brownish liquor into them. "Our finest whiskey. On the house," he said, and winked at Gigi.

"Goodness," one of her friends said. "I feel as if I'm really in the Barbary Coast."

Nancy took one of the glasses, wanting something to calm her nerves. "Down the hatch," she said, and took a swallow. It took a second for the taste of raw alcohol to scorch her throat.

"Where's Derek, Nancy?" Gigi asked. "Send him over to say hello."

"Derek couldn't make it tonight." Her voice caught as she spoke and she blinked back tears.

"Oh, that's too bad," Gigi said, and patted Nancy's hand. "You were such a darling couple, and I liked him so much more than Todd. I'm sure you can get him back."

"We weren't . . ." Nancy began. "I've got to check on things, but be sure to visit the poker parlor. All proceeds go to the museum and are tax deductible."

She was able to escape from Gigi's next question when one of the guests began coughing violently after taking too large a gulp of his drink. Nancy moved to the end of the bar and signaled the bartender. "What is that stuff?" she whispered.

"GP had it made specially from an old formula. It's grain alcohol sweetened up with cooked sugar, a kick of cayenne, and some chewing tobacco. It's the genuine thing." The bartender picked up a shot glass from the back of the bar and tossed it back. "It goes down easier if you shoot it, not sip."

"You're not supposed to be drinking on the job."

"I'm just following directions, sweetheart. If you want, I can make you a champagne flip, and we also got blackberry wine."

"I'm the boss here and I want you to stop drinking and stop serving that paint thinner. Champagne flips and wine only."

As she left the music hall, she noticed that guests were arriving quickly. More actors appeared in grimy costumes. A contingent of hookers sashayed by and a tall one said "Cute shoes" in a deep voice.

"Thanks," Nancy said automatically.

The actress said to one of her—or his—companions, "I know a couple of these rich johns. Ooh, crab legs!"

Nancy hurried down the wooden sidewalk so quickly that one heel caught between planks and she teetered into the rough-hewn boards of a hitching post. She regained her balance, but her dress snagged on a board and ripped at the seam. She tried to hold the seam together while greeting incoming guests.

She had reached the door and was going to go to the staff trailer to repair her dress when Mrs. Bentley Jamieson Friendly, in a floor-length silver and black beaded gown, entered on the arm of a silver-haired man in tails. For this special occasion, the museum's benefactress was wearing a towering wig of curls and she had new oversized glasses.

"Mrs. Friendly, welcome!"

"Hello, Nancy. I decided I should have an escort, and the ambassador stopped by, so I told him to put on his fancy duds and see how this town throws a party."

Nancy had no idea who this man was, but his jacket was so beautifully cut, she would have let him in even if he was dragging a dead body behind him. "Mr. Ambassador, so delighted that you could come. We're honored."

"This is something!" Mrs. Friendly exclaimed. She tapped at the frame of her glasses. "I had my cataract surgery and I can see swell. What happened to your dress?"

Nancy hoped that Mrs. Friendly's improved vision wouldn't spot the misery behind her smile. "I hope you'll find that the party conveys the authentic spirit of the Barbary Coast." Nancy spotted Sloane approaching and said, "One moment and I'll have a member of my staff escort you in."

She intercepted Sloane and said sotto voce, "Sloane, will

you please take Mrs. Friendly to the poker parlor and give her enough chips to keep her occupied for a little while? Her date is an ambassador, so find out his identity so we can give him a welcome during the program."

"Happy to do it."

"Oh, and make sure to give them champagne flips because the house whiskey is poisonous. Thank you!"

Guests kept pulling Nancy aside to talk. She knew she must have responded, but she couldn't recall one conversation as she moved to the next. The party grew loud as the hall filled up and more guests discovered the music hall.

When Nancy spotted GP, she waved him over and said, "I told the bartender in the music hall to stop serving that evil whiskey concoction, but I have a feeling he's still doing it."

"It's an authentic recipe."

"I appreciate your dedication to historical fact, GP, but I don't want any of our guests to get authentically poisoned."

"You're right," he said, abashed. "I'll go check on him."

Later, Nancy would remember the first crash. She was talking to the catering manager, saying, "Bring out as many hors d'oeuvres as you can because we need something that will soak up the booze," when she saw a young man dressed as a street tough shove another too enthusiastically. The second actor bumped into a waiter carrying a tray of champagne glasses.

The silver tray teetered momentarily and then fell. The huge clang and the shattering of a dozen glasses cut through the cacophony and everyone stopped talking to turn to the noise. Then one of the actors guffawed, an uninhibited, crazy laugh, another followed, and the rest of the crowd joined in.

The catering manager said to Nancy, "I'll get that cleaned

up and expedite the next rounds of canapés and what the hell is that?"

Nancy turned to see where he was looking and saw something dark and hairy with white teeth lunging through the crowd after a chicken. "A dog," she said. "What's a dog doing here? What's a chicken doing here?"

The chicken flew with a squawk onto a sign that said FRISKY AND SPORTY ENTERTAINMENT FOR FULL-GROWN PEOPLE, and the mangy dog started yelping madly and leaping at it, and another dog appeared and joined in the attempt at poultricide.

Nancy was frozen in place, unsure of whether she needed to call her doormen, but people were laughing. Then an actor, dressed as a lumberjack, shouted, "Dirty, lying, no-'count son of a bitch!" and threw a punch at an actor dressed as a dandy. The dandy retaliated with a blow, propelling the lumberjack back into a cluster of actresses dressed as ladies of the night.

Suddenly all the performers were brawling—fists hit flesh, bodies crashed against one another—but it looked much too real, and confused guests moved away from the fighting. Nancy, desperate to salvage the situation, shouted, "Wonderful performance! Bravo!"

She put her clipboard on a table and began clapping wildly, hoping others would join in, when someone put a hand on her arm. Nancy turned to see Bailey.

He was wearing a three-button notched black tuxedo jacket with a white shirt, and pleated trousers, and he was doused with a sport scent. His expression was concerned and he leaned toward her, a handsome man who was always calm because things always went his way.

"Nance, what's going on?" he said over the din as the actors tumbled against tables and guests shouted "Watch out!"

Nancy looked at the pleated pants and smelled the sports scent and thought of how she hated to be called Nance. "I was going to ask you the same thing. Are you teaming with Todd to break my prenup? Was it planned for Junie to see me at your house?"

Bailey opened his mouth, shut it, waited, and then smiled. He bent down to speak close to her ear. "I was helping out a bro in a tough situation, but it became obvious that Todd never deserved you." He stroked her arm. "We're two of a kind, Nance. We can recognize when a better opportunity comes along."

"So you're willing to shift sides?" she asked, incredulous.

"Absolutely, babe. Say the word and I'll throw Todd under the bus. No worries about Junie saying anything. She's been in the palm of my hand ever since she lived in that crappy apartment with a nylon rug."

"*You* were the one who gave her the nickname," she said.

"What nickname?" he said with a grin. He dropped to one knee and said—loudly, because the noise had gotten even louder— "Nance, will you do me the honor of becoming Mrs. Bailey Carson Whiteside the Third?"

Nancy didn't consider strategy and she didn't consider public appearance. She didn't calculate whether Bailey was still a viable option. She didn't bask in satisfaction that she had conquered one of the City's most eligible bachelors.

Instead, she emulated the lumberjack actor and cried, "Dirty, lying, no-'count son of a bitch!" as she shoved Bailey Whiteside the Third off the walkway. Someone shouted in a falsetto, "Got to be real, girlfriend."

Nancy was reveling in her act of violence when the crowd gasped. She looked around and followed gazes to the focus of the attention. A man in Western garb had pulled out a big, gleaming gun and pointed it at the ceiling. He hollered, "Yahoo!" and an earsplitting blast went off.

Guests screamed and everyone moved like a herd away from the sound.

That's when the men in black pajamas crashed through the windows, swinging in on ropes and delivering blows to all in their way. The sight of them was so astonishing that everyone stopped talking, fighting, and drinking as Mrs. Friendly's elite security force swept through the warehouse, swarmed around the heiress and the ambassador, and carried them outside and away from any threats real or amateurishly choreographed.

An actor in seaman garb beside Nancy said, "Motherfucking ninjas!" and gave her an elated, gold-toothed smile. "That's the most beautiful thing I've ever seen."

Before anyone could gossip about this incredible occurance, a woman shrieked, "Fire!"

Nancy sniffed and smelled the smoke. In a second she spied a thin gray plume rising from somewhere in the corner. It didn't look like much, but people began screaming "Fire! Fire!" and started rushing to the entrance.

Nancy yelled, "Please calm down! Calm down and exit in an orderly fashion!" No one listened.

GP was suddenly beside her. "It wasn't a real gun, Nancy! It was a prop."

"It's okay. Help people get out safely. Keep them outside until we put out the fire and we can bring them back in for dinner."

The crowd shoved her forward. She saw Sloane being jostled up ahead and then she didn't see her anymore. "Sloane!" Nancy pushed people aside and she found her friend crouched against a wall. "Are you okay?"

Sloane nodded and Nancy helped her up. Nancy looked back and saw that the room was almost empty. "Sloane, call 911 and wait for me outside!"

Nancy dashed back toward the smoke and saw flames licking up from a kerosene lantern that had fallen over, setting a tablecloth on fire.

For all the fuss, the flames weren't much worse than Todd's barbecue attempts. The actress with the deep voice had already found a fire extinguisher and was spraying foam on the flames. Nancy ran to a nearby table of appetizers. She grabbed a bin of ice and oysters and tossed them on the fire. She ran back to get a tub of ice with shrimp.

"It's going out, sugar," the actress called to her. "Don't waste those crab legs!"

That's when the firemen stormed in, jostling Nancy aside, wielding axes with unnecessary enthusiasm at the smoldering table.

"Don't use the water!" Nancy pleaded as the firefighters turned on a hose and blasted a whole row of tables.

The stench of burned seafood and smoke permeated the room and water puddled on the floor. If Nancy could find the catering manager and her staff, there was a chance she could relocate the party outside. She remembered to grab her clipboard before she ran down the wooden walkway. Her heel got caught again, so she left her shoe there and kicked off the other.

Outside, guests were milling and talking excitedly. People called her name, but she wove through the crowd, looking for one of her assistants.

"Nancy Carrington-Chambers!" an imperious voice barked, but this time the sound of her name was a rebuke.

The crowd fell silent and parted to allow Mrs. Friendly, her towering wig askew, to make her way slowly to Nancy.

Nancy smiled and said, "A lantern fell over and the fire was minimal. Crisis averted! We'll have the tables brought outside and dine al fresco!"

Mrs. Friendly's glare was especially frightening, since her recent surgery allowed her to focus her gaze like a magnifying glass focuses a beam of light on an unfortunate insect. "The ambassador has already left," Mrs. Friendly said. "You've embarrassed me and tarnished the reputation of the Barbary Coast with your sloppy execution of a simple party."

"I can explain. The gun was a prop and we were going for the authentic experience, revitalizing this event just as you asked . . ."

Nancy looked around for GP and saw him at the edge of the crowd, struggling to hold up the drunken bartender and dance hall girl.

"Save your excuses," Mrs. Friendly said. "I'll be damned if I'm paying one cent for this catastrophe and I'll see to it that you never even get near a party while I'm still alive. Now remove yourself from my sight and I'll clean up your mess."

"I can talk to the fire—"

"I said, get out now!"

As Nancy turned to leave, she saw Gigi Barton cozying up to a firefighter, and Gigi flashed an "okay" sign and a grin. How could anything be okay?

Although Nancy wanted to run away from the stares of the guests, she walked with as much dignity as she could muster to the staff trailer to get her things. She didn't make eye contact with the coat check girl, who was changing out of her costume.

Nancy's purple handbag had fallen over and when she picked it up, the empty vodka bottle rolled out. She retrieved it and said to the coat check girl, "I'll recycle it." She took her phone from her clipboard and tossed it into the bag with the empty bottle.

Nancy walked out to her car, which was parked on the far side of the lot near Aldo's coffee shack. The rear tire had a chrome yellow boot on it. Nancy had a crazy urge to laugh. Todd really had learned from Sun Tzu and planned every detail. She felt a new admiration for him.

"Nancy!" Sloane was coming through the aisle of cars. "Are you okay?"

"My car got booted."

"Mrs. Friendly sent the rest of us away and she's sending for her staff to clean up. I'll take you home."

Nancy looked toward the warehouse and saw Bailey supporting the redheaded patroness as she talked to the fire chief. "Thanks, Sloane. I'd appreciate it."

Sloane's older Volvo was nearby. She moved aside toys and drawings so Nancy could sit on the front seat. When they were in the car and on the road, Sloane said, "Mrs. Friendly's escort was the ambassador of Lithuania. What happened, Nancy?"

"Me, that's what happened." She managed a smile and said, "GP told me he was going to make the party authentic and I didn't pay any attention. Eugenia told me Derek is called Rick, and I didn't listen." She glanced at Sloane. "Derek's real name is Rick and Todd paid him to spy on me. Bailey was part of it, too."

"Why would Todd do that to you?"

"So he can use information to force me to stay with him, or break the prenup so he can get to my money. He knows that my family would want to avoid the scandal that I was cheating on him."

"But you weren't, Nancy."

"Yes, I was, Sloane."

They reached Château Winkles and Sloane parked in front.

"With Bailey?" Sloane asked.

"No, thank goodness for that. He's been trying to get me into his bed. He almost did, too," she said. "You know, Sloane, you've been one of the few people I can count on. Not that I treated you very well. I thought that you were just this *mother*."

"Maybe I didn't treat you so well, either. I should have warned you about Bailey."

"What do you mean?"

"He got Lewis into gambling. Then Bailey convinced him to invest in ventures that sounded great. Lewis lost everything, but Bailey always came out with a profit and he'd manage to lure Lewis into another scheme." Sloane shook her head. "Our credit was maxed out, my jewelry disappeared, and then Lewis took off in the minivan and left me with two toddlers and no car."

"Oh, Sloane, I didn't know it was that bad."

"When I went through Lewis's files, I found inconsistencies between his personal records of investments and financial reports. I thought these must be mistakes," Sloane said. "I still trusted Bailey then, so I went to see him—he was living with a rich divorcée—and I showed him what I had. He promised to help. Instead, he blocked my calls and e-mails and moved."

"It's awful to be betrayed," Nancy said, thinking of how she and Todd had betrayed each other.

"I couldn't believe it when I moved here and saw that Bailey had established himself with a clean slate. I hoped he'd changed. I was going to ask you to talk to him for me, since he seemed to like you, but I didn't know if you'd believe me."

"Bailey got Todd involved in a venture, too, and Todd lost every cent he put in. Now I wonder," Nancy said. "Give whatever you've got to me and I'll have my father look into it. I'll talk to you in a few days."

Nancy hugged her friend and got out of the car. All she wanted to do was crawl in bed next to Eugenia.

She took the elevator, too tired to think about toning her legs on the stairs.

Eve, the babysitter from Three Bridges, met her at the door to her apartment and said, "Are you all right? The party was on the news."

"I'd rather not talk about it. How was your evening? Did Eugenia behave?" Nancy walked into her apartment and went to her writing table. She pulled out a drawer and counted bills to pay the babysitter for the entire night.

Eve put on a puffy jacket and said, "She's a great kid. Her mom came and picked her up about an hour ago."

Fear crashed down on Nancy like an icy wave, dragging the sand from beneath her feet, chilling her to the bone. "What? You let Eugenia go?"

"Roberta, is that her name? She said you were expecting her. Mrs. Kanbar said that you were watching Eugenia temporarily, and I tried calling you about forty minutes ago, but you didn't answer."

"I didn't have my phone with me then."

"I figured you were busy when I heard about the fire," Eve said. "Eugenia was happy to see her mother, but she acted up about the kitten, so they took it with them. Her mother's boyfriend is really handsome."

"Yannis, a Greek man with a beard? Did Roberta say where they were going?"

"His name was Viktor," Eve said, looking apologetic. "I hope that was okay. I checked Eugenia's file before I came over and you'd written down that her mother, her grandparents, and her aunt were allowed to pick her up from Three Bridges."

Nancy remembered filling out the forms when she was hoping that Birdie would come fetch her daughter. "Yes, I did."

"Are you okay, Ms. Carrington-Chambers?"

Nancy tried to smile. "Thank you, Eve. Good night."

"Good night."

Nancy shut the front door and then went to the laundry room and opened her bin of earthquake supplies. She took out the Altoids tin where she kept her emergency pharmaceuticals. She picked out two Percocets, took them to the kitchen, and downed them with a glass of wine.

She went to her bedroom and turned on the light in her closet. Eugenia's nest of comforters and pillows was empty. The beautiful leather bag was gone, but books and her stuffed parrot had been left behind. Nancy picked up the red cape that Eugenia liked and held it to her face. The scent of the child clung to the fabric.

Still holding it, Nancy crawled into bed and cried in an ugly, primal way until the drugs seeped through her body, giving her a false sense of hope. Then she fell asleep.

twenty-two

the 360-degree mirror

*N*ancy awoke feeling peaceful and rested. She turned and reached for Eugenia, but the child wasn't there.

Reality bitch-slapped her awake.

Birdie had kidnapped the pirate child. Nancy's mother was an alcoholic, and her father was a control freak and serial adulterer. Bailey and Junie had used her and could give her husband enough information to break the prenup, if his spy hadn't already provided it. If Todd decided to trap her in their marriage, her parents would probably support him.

Because Nancy had approved the shenanigans at the gala, the event insurance would be voided, and she would be financially and legally responsible for the damage to the warehouse.

Beautiful, fabulous Derek had never existed, only some angry, deceitful man named Rick who'd had sex with her so that he could betray her.

The prettiness of her life had been as false a facade as the sets within the warehouse.

Nancy finally had her epiphany: she couldn't control everything around her and create a perfectly chic Fancy Nancyland.

She picked up her phone and saw that she had thirty-seven missed calls and twenty-nine messages. None were from Birdie, and she deleted all but the frantic messages from GP. The first said, "Nancy, I'm so very sorry. Call me, please." The second said, "Are you all right? I really need to talk to you about this. We can fix it." The third said, "I'm going to fix it, Nancy, I promise. I hope you're all right, but I understand if you don't want to talk to me now."

Dear, sweet GP. She'd deal with him later.

Now Nancy called Aunt Frilly. "Aunt Frilly, I've got two important things to tell you. The first is that my mother's drinking herself to death and needs help. The second is that Birdie abducted Eugenia last night."

"Nancy, you're being dramatic," her aunt said in the same voice that Hester always said "Lovely, lovely, lovely." "Your mother's always liked a tipple to calm her nerves. There's nothing wrong with that."

"She hides vodka in her closet. She passes out almost every afternoon. She's not suffering from nerves. She's suffering because my father blatantly cheats on her. That's why my sisters moved away and never come home."

Frilly was silent for so long that Nancy said, "Are you still there?"

"I'm still here. Why can't you watch your mother, Nancy?"

"Because I'm going to hunt down Birdie and save Eugenia and our cat. Do you know where they are?"

"I didn't even know Birdie was back." Aunt Frilly sighed. "Nancy, it will do Eugenia more harm than good to be tossed back and forth between you and Birdie."

"I know. That's why I'm going to try to get legal custody of my niece."

Frilly was silent for a minute and then she said, "You've always been my favorite, Nancy. Sissy's coming down tomorrow. I'll have her pick up your mother and I'll look for a rehab facility here. If you think it's that serious."

"It is. Please call me the instant you hear anything about Birdie." Nancy put the phone down and was trying to think of her next step when the intercom buzzed and a man's voice said, "Mrs. Chambers? Mrs. Chambers?"

Nancy peeked out the front curtains and saw a news van parked on the street. She didn't answer the buzzer and in a minute another car arrived. The buzzer sounded repeatedly, but she didn't answer.

Her phone rang and the ID indicated that it was her attorney, so Nancy answered.

Renee said, "Nancy, on last night's news, the reporter mentioned your name in connection with a fire at a historical landmark."

"It was only a small fire at the party I organized for the Barbary Coast fund-raiser and there's a news van parked out front, but that's the least of my worries. Todd offered to hire an assistant for my business, but the man he placed here really worked for a private investigator and was spying on me."

Renee was silent for a moment and said, "Were you discreet with this employee?"

"Actually, I told him that I'd had an affair with a squeezel named Anthony Harper," Nancy said. "Also, I had sex with the fake assistant and let's hope he didn't get hidden videos. Go ahead and run my prenup through the shredder."

"Good God," Renee said. "Let's not be precipitous. We need to talk about this and strategize."

"Todd has outstrategized me, Renee, and I can't talk right now because I have something more urgent. I need to get custody of my cousin's daughter. Can you draw up papers for Roberta Willow Carrington to release her minor daughter, Eugenia Carrington, father unknown, to my guardianship?"

"You're not in the position now to adopt—"

"I'll double your hourly fee. Triple it. Whatever you want."

Renee was quiet for a few seconds. "Your check for the retainer was returned for lack of funds."

"That can't be. I had more than enough in my personal account."

"We submitted it twice," she said. "Does Todd have access to your bank accounts?"

"Not that one. I'll find out what happened and get the money to you. But you've got to do this for me, please!"

"I'll do it, but don't tell anyone else what you just told me and don't give any interviews. Bye."

Nancy wasn't concerned about the bounced check because she knew exactly how much money she had. She went to her computer and logged in at her bank's site. She had a balance of $39.74. She stared at the screen, thinking that more zeroes would appear beside the numbers or that she'd mistaken the decimal point.

Then she looked up the last transaction that had cleared. It was an outrageous sum for the art gallery where she'd broken the antique bowl when she last saw Anthony Harper.

She called the gallery and asked to speak to the owner.

"Hello, Mrs. Carrington-Chambers, so nice to hear from you."

"Hello. I see you've cashed my check for the bowl."

"I'm sorry for the delay in billing you, but since the bowl was for exhibit only, we had to request an insurance evaluation from the owner, who's in Florence. Naturally, we included our commission in the total."

"I know I gave you a blank check, but I trusted in your integrity. The amount was surprising."

"It was a unique piece, as I recall hearing our friend Anthony Harper tell you," he said in an oily voice. "However, if you would like to purchase an additional item, I would be happy to work out a discount for you and Mr. Chambers. Perhaps he enjoys beautiful things like Mr. Harper."

Sun Tzu's advice, like a muscle memory, came to Nancy, so she feigned disorder and set out bait for her extortionist. "Oh, please, don't do that! Maybe you and I could meet and talk about my buying another objet d'art. I'll call you soon."

"I think that's best, Mrs. Carrington-Chambers. Until then."

Nancy would figure out how to deal with him later.

Someone knocked on the apartment door. Nancy crept up to it and wished she'd had one of those tacky peepholes installed. She listened and another rap came at the door.

"Girl Carrington, open up."

Nancy pulled open the door and Miss Winkles came in, looking around curiously.

Nancy became aware of the changes that had happened over the past two months. Eugenia's drawings were propped on the mantel and toys were scattered around. Her pirate books and favorite DVDs were piled on the cocktail table. There were cup rings on surfaces and grimy little fingerprints. A blue and white cape was draped over the shredded arm of the sofa. A juice box was shoved between folders on the bookshelf.

"Quite a ruckus you've caused. This is a nice apartment," Miss Winkles said. "I thought it would be frilly and pink. I saw the news last night. So Abigail Friendly is protected by ninjas. I always thought it was MI5 because of that affair she had with, you know, she was a tramp in those days . . . but we don't have time to reminisce. Eugenia can stay with me while you sort things out, or buy people off like you Carringtons usually do."

"Eugenia's gone. Birdie took her last night. I don't know where they are. My poor Pirate Girl!"

"Oh, no!" Miss Winkles put her hand to her heart. "That sweet child told me about life with that lousy excuse for a mother."

"I know. I have to get her back before Birdie ditches her again, or before anything happens to her, and then I'm going to try to get legal custody."

Miss Winkles put her hand on Nancy's arm. "Good girl. Now, how are you going to find her?"

"I don't know. Birdie could be anywhere. She's got a new boyfriend and she always carries her passport. Aunt Frilly will call me if she hears anything."

"What happened with Derek?"

"It's complicated."

"Make us a pot of tea and tell me," Miss Winkles said. "Don't look at me that way, Nancy. I know a thing or two and I might be able to help you. Otherwise, I might occupy myself by calling back the newswoman who wants to know more about my rich, irresponsible, slutty neighbor."

Over a pot of bracing Scottish Breakfast, Nancy told her story to Miss Winkles. She didn't exclude her own misdeeds, her sleazy liaison with Anthony, or her torrid affair with Derek.

"There were times when we were all together and we were so happy: the Pirate Girl, my gay English assistant-slash-lover, and myself. At least I thought we were happy. Derek-slash-Rick hates me. He was probably revolted every time he touched me."

Miss Winkles laughed and said, "It's been my experience that men don't hate sex with pretty girls no matter how ridiculous the girls are."

"That's what you think. You didn't hear the way he talked to me. I met his ex-girlfriend by accident. She's a tall, busty, raven-haired goddess, and here I am, flat and pale and puny."

"There's no accounting for taste and I saw the way Derek, or Rick, looked at you," Miss Winkles said.

"You don't seem surprised that he's not English or gay."

"His accent jumped around more than a Jack Russell and his vocabulary was a hoot. I assumed you were paying him to put on an accent and pretend to be gay."

"Why in the world would I do that?"

"It's exactly the sort of preposterous pretension that I'd expect from someone who married Todd Chambers."

"I am not pretentious. I have standards."

Miss Winkles laughed again and said, "Like dating Bailey

Whiteside when you had a gorgeous, wonderful man in your bed?"

"Derek, Rick, whoever, lied to me and spied on me and took advantage of me."

"You can't take advantage of something that is thrown right at you. Your problem, Nancy, is that you are too picky. It's the imperfections that make life interesting, and that man was a keeper. As for your cousin, you use your resources and I'll use mine. Maybe we can find the birdie that flew away."

It was only when Miss Winkles had gone upstairs to her apartment that Nancy realized that the old woman had called her by her first name. It seemed like a hopeful sign and Nancy started phoning hotels, restaurants, and salons where Birdie might go. She called Sissy, got the names of some of Birdie's friends, and called or left messages for them.

The hours passed and the room grew dark. Nancy wanted to go out and *do* something, take action, but she knew she had to stay where she was in case Birdie showed up. She wondered if Eugenia had had her afternoon snack and a decent dinner.

More calls came, but Nancy didn't answer any but Milagro's.

"Nancy Fancy-pants, I hear your party was a fiasco. Gigi said there was a wild fracas and ninjas, which is incredible. I adore a party gone awry."

"It wasn't a delightmare. It was awful. Mrs. Friendly told me I'm never going to work in this town again," Nancy said. "Many other hellacious things have occurred; however, I cannot elaborate at the moment."

"If I had twins, I think I would name them Fracas and Fiasco. Can't Derek provide comfort in your time of need?"

"That's another part of my misery, but I must get off the phone since I'm expecting an urgent call."

"I'm sorry, Nancy-pants," Milagro said. "I shall not take any more of your time, and I shall dedicate every particle of my gray matter to devising a solution."

"Thanks, Mil. I shall relate the whole wretched tale anon."

"Like Hamlet's ghost, I bid you adieu, adieu, remember me."

Because Nancy didn't want anyone on the street seeing that she was home, she crept around her living room in the dim light from her laptop screen. She went to her assistant's writing table and opened the drawer.

Besides the pens, paper clips, and Froth letterhead, she found the sketch pad that he used to take to the park. She snuck into her bedroom, went into the closet, shut the door, and turned on the light.

Derek had told her that he'd never found the right story to tell, but each page held drawings from the time they'd shared. There were sketches of her at their favorite bistro, a view upward of Nancy's legs and skirt as she held on to the warehouse ledge, a series of drawings of Nancy and Eugenia . . . There was a charming drawing of her asleep in bed. The pages were sometimes captioned with phrases from her "Theory of Style."

Nancy closed the sketchbook and held it to her chest, missing so much, feeling so alone. The painting of Birdie stared at her. She didn't want to see it ever again. She went to the back of the closet, grabbed the frame angrily, and turned it to face away. The edge of the painting pulled back one of her long coats to reveal crayon scrawls on the wall.

She crouched down and pushed away the coat. There was a drawing of three figures, ovals with stick arms and three-fingered hands. The smallest had a scribble of brown hair. The middle one had yellow hair. The biggest had short black hair. There was also a small gray blob with stripes and a tail.

Nancy curled up atop the nest of blankets and cried, choking back her sobs so she would be able to hear the phone. She stayed awake most of the night, waiting and waiting and thinking about Eugenia alone somewhere in the dark, and she thought, *I'll come get you, baby, I promise.*

Morning came and Nancy dressed in jeans and a sweater, and stared at her phone, trying to will Birdie to call. Then someone knocked on her door. She ran to it so fast that she knocked over a chair, hoping that Miss Winkles had some information. She flung the door open and saw Rick standing there.

He was dressed the way he had been in the market, jeans and a T-shirt under a flannel shirt. His dark hair was tousled and he hadn't shaved.

She hated him for still being so beautiful to her. "What do you want?" Nancy said. "Did you come here to gloat, because there's a lot to be gloaty about. My career is over, my reputation is destroyed, and I told my attorney to agree to anything Todd wants."

"I didn't come about that. Miss Winkles told me about Eugenia."

"I'm sure you think I'm an awful aunt, too, so . . ." *Don't cry,* she told herself, *don't cry.* "You've succeeded in making me see what a fool I am, what a terrible wife I've been, so don't let me keep you from your next assignment of seducing another miserable and lonely housewife and breaking— Go away."

"I wasn't hired to seduce you." Rick pulled a paper out of

his pocket and held it to her. "Birdie and Viktor are visiting his cousin and her husband."

Nancy's heart skipped and she grabbed the paper. There were two names and an address in Sea Cliff and an airline flight number and a date a week away. "She's here! Are they taking this flight out?"

"No, it's their return flight on Friday afternoon. They're in St. Maarten for the week."

Her elation was tempered by caution. "How did you find out? Why are you telling me this?"

"I found out through the Gay Mafia, of which my friend is a member. I'm telling you because Eugenia would be worse off with her mother. Take care of her, Nancy Fancy."

He turned and walked away.

"Derek! Rick! Thank you."

He stopped at the landing of the stairs and turned and looked up at her. "Nancy, I never had to force myself to touch you. All I wanted to do was touch you."

Before she could say anything, he was gone.

Her broken heart could wait. She peeked out her front door and when she saw it was clear, she ran up the stairs to Miss Winkles's. Knocking, she said, "Miss Winkles, it's me, Nancy."

Miss Winkles was dressed in her customary suit but wearing terry-cloth slippers. "Come in."

Finally, Nancy got to see the mystery penthouse. It was in a time warp, with carnation pink walls and avocado green carpeting. Miss Winkles led her to the living room, where tiers of lace and brocade frippery hid the spectacular view.

Boxes of files and photo albums sat atop the seventies mod furniture, and framed photos and advertising posters featuring the Winkles Triplets hung on the walls. "Miss Winkles, thank you for telling Der . . . Rick. He told me when Eugenia's coming back to the city."

"Excuse the mess. I've been going through all my photographs. Your boyfriend helped me take the boxes out of the closets and I finally found what I was looking for."

"He's not my boyfriend. He loathes me."

"Young people are always so melodramatic. I suppose they think it makes them exciting." Miss Winkles was sealing two manila envelopes. "This apartment is too big for me now. It was crowded when I was here with my sisters and all our admirers."

"Where are your sisters?"

"Duluth, where we're from, with their children and grandchildren."

"You didn't want to get married?"

"There was only one man for me. He wanted me to give up my career and go with him to Maui, where he was building a hotel. He did very well for himself." Miss Winkles picked up a pen and addressed the manila envelopes.

"So you lost him forever?"

"No, I acted like a grown-up and got on a plane and went after him. We had a passionate long-distance relationship until he passed away." She held out the envelopes to Nancy. "Give this to Abigail Friendly and give the other to Rick."

Nancy took the envelopes and saw that the top one was written to Rick Zivotovsky and had a Noe Valley address. "I'm not going to see him again. Mrs. Friendly ripped me apart at the gala so I'm not going to darken her door. I can mail your letters."

Miss Winkles let out an exasperated "Huh!" just like Eugenia's.

"These are much too important to be mailed. You will have to face Abigail sooner or later, so take them and deliver them."

Nancy returned to her apartment and propped the envelopes on the mantel next to one of Eugenia's drawings. Rick Zivotovsky. What kind of name was that? It was too long to write in a heart.

She had to wait until Thursday. Curiosity overcame her and she turned on the television to the local news. She watched local reports before a story about the Barbary Coast Historical Museum came on. The reporter said, "Socialite Nancy Carrington-Chambers, known for her extravagant wedding and wealthy connections, is still in hiding after a fire and melee at a historic landmark. Anonymous sources state that an empty bottle of vodka was seen among her belongings . . ."

Nancy turned the sound off and watched the images. There was footage from the party, exterior shots of Château Winkles, the photo from Rich Bitches, and photos she hadn't seen before of her at the end of the gala in a torn, grimy dress splattered with red cocktail sauce.

There were also photos from her wedding, where she had looked like a fairy princess and been surrounded by people she thought were her friends. There were photos of her horrible house and the failed development.

She was about to turn off the television when she saw a picture from Stinson Beach. She was sitting on the sand with Derek, and Eugenia was playing nearby. The family there must have taken it. Nancy went to the TV and touched the tiny figure of Eugenia until the screen was filled by the fake tan face of the overcoiffed reporter.

The next days were interminable. Nancy's phone rang many times, but the only calls she answered were from her mother, who had arrived safely at Aunt Frilly's. She deleted all text messages and e-mails without reading them.

She ate organic macaroni and cheese, graham crackers, and apple slices. She made a dozen small capes inspired by Eugenia's drawings and she tacked Rick's drawings of "The Adventures of Pirate Girl" on the walls.

She opened the composition book with her "Theory of Style," looking for wisdom, but what good was it knowing that monochromaticism isn't style, or that leopard print is a timeless classic, when one's life was in the balance?

Nancy decided to answer a call from Mrs. Kanbar. "Hello," she said, her voice cracking because she hadn't spoken to anyone all day.

"Hello, Nancy. Eve told me that Eugenia's mother is back. I wanted to know if you've had a chance to talk to her about our opening at Three Bridges."

"I'm sorry—I should have called. Eugenia's taking a vacation with her mother this week, but she'll be back on Monday and we'd like to keep her in your school."

"That's wonderful! You can pay the monthly fee then. We'll see you on Monday."

Nancy went to her laptop and calculated her personal and business expenses. Then she went to her bank's website to transfer this sum from her joint checking account. The account balance was zero. Todd had cleaned it out.

Nancy sent her father an e-mail requesting that he transfer this amount from her trust fund to her personal account immediately and then waited for her father's call, which came five minutes later.

"Nanny, do you want to explain what's going on? You haven't answered any of my calls for days. I knew you were spoiled and silly, but I didn't think you'd be so stupid as to make a public spectacle of yourself. You're destroying your marriage and you've convinced Frilly that your mother is at death's door. She also said you want to raise her granddaughter, which is ridiculous since you can't even manage your own life."

Nancy went for the indirect, immediate attack and said, "I knew it was too much to think you'd be calling to support me and tell me that you love me. Instead, you lecture me without even knowing the facts." She shifted her position. "It probably wouldn't matter since the facts are even worse than the gossip."

"Don't take that sarcastic tone with me, Nancy Edith."

"That's rich, coming from a man who ignored his children for his work, ignores his wife for his young mistresses, and would rather ignore his wife's alcoholism than do anything to help."

"How dare you!"

"How dare *you!*" she countered, coming from another angle. "If you aren't willing to transfer *my* money, then I'll be holding a very public garage sale this weekend at the House of Horrors. We'll talk when you get your affairs in order and are prepared to apologize. Adieu."

Nancy had talked back to Julian Stephens Carrington and she wondered why it had taken her so long to do it. A half an hour later, she checked her personal account and saw that the transfer had been made.

On Wednesday, she snuck downstairs to leave an envelope with a check for Sloane in the outgoing mail. Her own mailbox contained a thick pile of letters, including one from Mrs. Friendly and one from the art gallery. She opened the letter from the art gallery, which was a receipt for the vase. She threw the rest of the unopened envelopes away.

When Nancy talked to her attorney, Renee said, "I drew up your custody docs, but I strongly advise you to think this over for a month or more. Raising a child is a serious lifelong commitment."

"I know it is, and I know I'm not in the ideal situation, but I love Eugenia and I'm not going to risk her safety and happiness just so I can plop her in the perfect setting."

"All right, Nancy," Renee said, and exhaled a sigh. "Now, as for your husband, he's agreed to abide by the prenup."

"I don't understand. He cleared out our shared account, hired a spy, set up mutual friends to betray me, and had my car booted. These are hostile acts."

"That's how divorce goes, Nancy. I'd be shocked that he backed off if I hadn't gotten some info about him. Would you like to hear it now, or do you want to meet with me?"

"Tell me now."

"For the last ten months, Todd's been paying half the rent for an apartment with a June Allison Burns."

"Since last summer?"

"The wife is always the last to know," Renee said.

"I didn't want to know. I was relieved when he was gone and I didn't have to deal with him," Nancy said. She recalled how Junie had always gazed at Todd with moony moo-cow eyes. Todd liked to be admired. "How'd you find out?"

"An anonymous source, and I'd bet the same info has been sent to Todd, which is why he's being so agreeable," Renee said. "Nancy, I've got enough that we could recover everything you dumped into the house."

"I'm as responsible for the house as he is, and if he's willing to go along with the prenup, so am I. I'll come by at eight thirty on Friday to pick up the custody papers."

Nancy guessed who the anonymous source was. One person had had access to her address book and all her contacts.

She'd tried not to think about Rick and she'd tried not to miss Derek and wonder what if . . .

What if she hadn't said that stupid thing at Stinson? What if he'd confessed to her earlier, or if she had figured it all out and they'd laughed about it? What if they had just met like normal people in a market by the organic produce and gone out for a drink or to a movie?

Nancy went to his writing desk and opened the laptop that Todd had provided for her assistant. The screen saver was one of Eugenia's drawings. Nancy went through the documents, but they were all work related. She checked the files that had been moved to the recycling bin but not been deleted. There were four videos.

She opened the one labeled "Pirate Girl." It was the video of Eugenia doing her runway walk. She was grinning and brandishing her stick, her cape flapping in the wind, her eyes sparkling, and he'd set it to a song from *Muppet Treasure Island* called "A Professional Pirate."

Nancy watched it five times before opening the one labeled "Nancy Fancy." She hardly recognized herself. He'd put the video in black-and-white and set it to the theme song from *The Avengers,* the television show he'd told her about. She looked sexy and sophisticated and radiant. She looked happier than she had looked in her wedding photos.

His own video hadn't been edited. He walked down the street, a gorgeous, confident, beautifully dressed man with a secret behind his *l'heure bleue* eyes.

The last video was of all three of them sauntering, swaggering, and, in Eugenia's case, skipping. Nancy had that sense of trueness and rightness when she watched the video. She sang along to the song, "Walking on Sunshine."

Nancy rose early on Friday. Her plan was to meet Birdie at the airport. She dressed as anonymously as she could, in old jeans and a button-down blouse. She pinned on her butterfly brooch and then she packed a bag with snacks, a juice box, books, and toys.

She peeked out her front window. A suspicious car had been parked there since yesterday and she saw the shadow of a person inside.

Nancy ran upstairs and knocked on Miss Winkles's door.

When Miss Winkles answered, Nancy said, "I need to get away, but there's someone watching the building. I don't know if it's someone from a tabloid or an avenging ninja."

"Have you delivered my letters yet?"

"I haven't been outside."

"I told you they were important. If you will see that they're delivered, I could do a star turn for whoever is outside."

"Yes, yes, I'll make sure that they're delivered," Nancy said.

Miss Winkles smiled. "Just let me change into something that will look good on camera."

Ten minutes later, Miss Winkles went downstairs in a red knit suit and a small-brimmed navy blue hat with a giant red silk rose on it. Nancy, with large sunglasses and her hair tucked into a fedora, crept behind her, keeping close to the wall, where she couldn't be seen by someone at the glass front door.

Miss Winkles went out the door and walked past the parked car.

The car door opened and a man with a handheld video camera got out. Nancy saw Miss Winkles's feigned look of surprise; Miss Winkles lured the tabloid writer down the block to a sunny spot and posed for him. While he had the video camera on her, his back was to the Château.

Nancy dashed out of the building and ran down the block and around the corner. It felt good to stretch her legs after being inside for so long, so she walked downtown to her attorney's office building.

Renee wasn't in, but had left a folder for her with the custody release.

Nancy took the folder and smiled at the receptionist. "Would you do a big favor for me? I need two letters messengered today and I'm not going back to my office until late." Nancy took Miss Winkles's envelopes out of her tote.

The receptionist said, "I'm sorry, but we're not allowed to use the messenger service for anything but firm business. It's all tied into our billing." She looked regretful and said, "I can give you the number for the service we use, though, and if you arrange it with them, you can leave your packages here for pickup."

Nancy looked at the clock. She had a lot of time and she still needed to get a car so she could bring Eugenia and Blackbeard home. "Thanks, but that's okay. I'll deliver them myself."

She left the office building and walked over to the Muni station on Market Street. When a J Church streetcar came, she got on and rode to Noe Valley, where Rick Zivotovsky lived.

It was a nondescript midcentury house divided into two flats. No names were listed by the buzzers, but Nancy had seen the window treatments from the street, so she pressed on the bell for the upper unit, which had Roman shades.

When the door was opened, she saw the man she knew as Prescott Bottomsley. He was dressed in a suit she'd once seen on her assistant.

"Nancy!" Gregory said. "Nice fedora and shades. Very Catherine Deneuve in a noir."

"That's very kind. Is Rick here?"

"You don't have a gun in that bag, do you?"

"I have some books about pirates, a juice box, and graham crackers."

"Okay, come in, I guess." He led her upstairs, which was much more tasteful than the building's exterior. Masculine chic in earthy, mushroomy tones and natural materials. A gray cat curled in a chair.

"You're not allergic to cats?" she asked. "What's your name?"

"Why would you think I was allergic to them?" he said. "I'm Gregory Whalin. Whalin Investigations."

"My husband hired you to spy on me."

"Investigate, not spy. He's used us before to research start-ups. We try to keep away from domestic disputes, but Todd came to me because he wanted a gay operative." He dropped his voice and said, "Rick's a friend. That part was true. He needed the money and I hired him. His first and last job with me. Things could have gone better."

"You are a master of understatement."

"For the record, he never told me anything, even though he would have gotten bonuses for actionable information," Gregory said, smoothing his already perfect auburn hair in a move that Nancy recognized from Derek.

"Rick copied your gestures," she said.

"He's been mimicking me since grad school, when we met," Gregory said. "When I saw you two looking at each other at the market, I had a feeling something would happen."

"It was my fault. I started it."

"Women tend to do that with him," Gregory said. "You

seem like a nice enough person, Nancy, but I'd rather you run along home, if you're just looking for cheap thrills."

"Derek, I mean Rick, is not a cheap thrill to me. He's the real deal. He's like, like . . ." Nancy searched for a way to make Gregory understand the depth of her feelings. "Finding the person you want to walk down the runway of your life with in slo-mo."

"That makes no sense, but not much does lately. Rick's in the guest room down the hall."

Nancy went into the room without knocking on the door.

Rick was still in bed in the dark room, but he opened his eyes when she pulled out the desk chair and sat down.

He turned his head to look at her. "Nancy, I'm going to do you a favor and stay out of your life, so why don't you do me a favor and stay out of mine?"

"That wouldn't be a favor. I know you're happy when you're with me." She took off her hat and glasses, and placed them on the desk.

"We were playing house. It wasn't real."

"No, I played house with Todd. What you and I had was real," she said. "I thought you could never love me."

He sat up against the headboard, the sheet falling to his waist, exposing his chest. "Wasn't it obvious how I felt about you?"

"But you were *gay!*"

"I tried to tell you, but then you started going out with Whiteside. When I heard you were taking him to Stinson . . ." Rick shook his head.

"I was desperately trying to get over you." She slipped off her shoes and sat next to him on the bed. "I've been wondering how everything came to this. I tried so hard for so long to

343

do all the right things because I thought it would make my life perfect, but my life was a sham, and you know how I feel about knockoffs. I'd given up the idea that real love existed, because I'd never felt that way with anyone, and I never thought anyone would fall in love with the real me. Then I met you, and then there was Eugenia."

"I miss her."

"Me, too. On the beach that day, I wished that we would always stay that way, happy, all of us, but I thought it was impossible."

"It is impossible. You're Nancy Carrington-Chambers and I'm an unemployed journalist who's crashing at his friend's apartment."

"An unemployed journalist is significantly *less* impossible than a gay assistant," she said, and kissed his shoulder and his neck, delighting in the feel of him, the warmth of his body.

"Don't do that while I'm trying to think."

She moved closer. "Why not?"

"Because the blood is being diverted from my brain. You have that effect on me."

She slid her hand across his chest and let it rest on his heart, feeling it pulse beneath her palm. "I wish you'd seen the ninjas at the party. Oh, and the gallery where I broke the bowl billed me for it. I'm fairly sure the whole thing was set up as a form of extortion. Also, I'm responsible for the damage of a historic landmark, and who knows what that will cost."

"When I heard about the fire, I went straight to the warehouse. You'd already left by the time I got there."

"I helped put the fire out. It was the second-bravest thing I've ever done."

"What was the first?"

"Coming here to tell you that I love you, Rick Zivotovsky. I've loved you since the moment you walked into my apartment." She looked into his blue, blue eyes, hoping that he could see how much she cared for him. "Do you love me?"

"We have a few hours before Eugenia's plane arrives." Rick pulled her onto his lap and the corner of his mouth rose in a smirk. "I *told* you that you were diverting my blood," he said, and then he kissed her.

"Do you love me?" Nancy asked again.

As he unbuttoned her blouse, he said, "I had to love you after you kept flashing your fancy panties at me."

"I didn't think it was possible," Nancy said, bending over to pick up her bra on the rug.

"What?" Rick came up behind her and ran his hand over her ass.

"Rick is a better lover than Derek."

"Well, Derek is gay, so he has to be somewhat inexperienced with women."

She laughed and said, "Are you telling me that you were holding back?"

"You'll have to judge for yourself. You take a shower and I'll make coffee. Did you bring the car seat, or did Birdie take it?"

"Birdie's not that thoughtful. Also, the Mini got booted and the car seat's in there."

"We can borrow Gregory's car," he said. He pulled her to him. "I lied. I started to love you before I saw your fancy panties, but multiple viewings of your panties did confirm my feelings for you."

She laughed. "I met your ex-girlfriend."

"Melanie?"

"I thought Mel was a guy. I met her when I was out with Bailey. She told me about her ex-boyfriend, who'd left her for his employer, Nancy Fancy."

"I called you that because I fancied you," he said. "It made me crazy thinking that you were sleeping with Bailey."

"I never had sex with him. How could I, after I'd been with you?"

"We're grown-ups. It wouldn't matter if you did."

"But I didn't."

"Good."

twenty-three

good taste is not style

*N*ancy compulsively checked the arrivals board to make sure the flight was on schedule. She and Rick waited by the baggage claim, because Nancy knew that her cousin wouldn't travel without a large wardrobe.

To lower her anxiety, Nancy asked Rick questions. "Where are you from and where did you go to school, and have you ever been married, and do you have any terrible habits I should know about?"

"I grew up in Gilroy, went to school at Santa Cruz and Berkeley, haven't been married, and I have a thing for married women. Only one, actually."

"You went to a school that has a banana slug for a mascot," she said.

"Better than a mascot that's a tree."

"Touché. Criminal history?"

"I stole a cow once on a bet."

"Your brother, Peter?"

"How did you know? He's a cop in Phoenix."

Black nylon cases began emerging through the rubber flaps on the luggage carousel.

"There!" Nancy said, and pointed to the caramel leather overnight case. "That's Eugenia's bag!"

Nancy and Rick moved back and kept an eye on the arriving passengers. Then Nancy spotted them. Birdie, newly tanned, was dressed in a canary yellow sleeveless shift and flat sandals. Long strands of black Tahitian pearls hung from her slender neck.

She walked arm in arm with a short, muscular fellow wearing white linen pants and a tropical shirt. The couple beside them was also dressed in resort clothes.

"That's Birdie," Nancy said.

"I recognized her from the painting."

"Where's Eugenia?" Nancy felt her throat close, and then the group moved and she saw the small girl walking behind them, her head hanging down.

"Eugenia, stop lagging behind," Birdie said.

When Eugenia looked up, Nancy saw the shadows under her eyes and the same blank expression the child had had when her mother first brought her to Château Winkles. Why hadn't Nancy noticed Eugenia's anguish then?

Nancy uttered a small cry and Rick took her hand in his and held fast. "Be calm," he said.

Nancy nodded and they walked to her cousin.

Birdie saw her approaching and smiled. "Nanny Girl, what are you doing here?"

That's when Eugenia lifted her eyes to Nancy and Rick. Hope flickered on her face.

Nancy walked to the girl and picked her up. "Eugenia!" She kissed her cheek and then handed her back to Rick. The girl's arms wrapped tightly around his neck, and she tucked her head against his shoulder.

Nancy smiled in a way meant to disarm her cousin, because a skillful warrior can defeat an enemy without a skirmish. "I hope you had a lovely vacation, but we need to get Eugenia back to school on Monday and on her regular schedule."

"How sweet of you. Viktor, this is my cousin Nanny, who's my babysitter. Gregor, Marie, this is Nanny." Birdie's eyes went to Rick. "And is this Derek, or is it Rick? Eugenia's talked about you."

"Rick," he said. "I've heard about you, too."

Birdie gazed at him and smiled. "We can all go out tonight. After sitting for so long, I'm in the mood for dancing."

"But what about Eugenia?" Nancy asked.

Viktor said, "Marie's housekeeper can watch. The girl is no problem."

And that chilled Nancy. Because Eugenia *was* a problem. She was willful and impetuous and mischievous and very vocal and exasperating, which was exactly how she should have been. "Birdie, may I have a word?"

Birdie shrugged her elegant, bony shoulder and said to Viktor, "One moment."

Nancy pulled Birdie away. "I have a wonderful idea. Why

don't I take care of Eugenia for you? All the time. Then you would be free to come and go as you please."

Birdie laughed, and now her laugh seemed a tinny imitation of Eugenia's pure silver joy. "I know it was a little naughty of me to leave her with you, but there's no need to be a martyr and take her on." She touched Nancy's arm with a graceful, jeweled hand and all Nancy could think of was that the hand was useless and unloving. "Let's have some fun. Marie's housekeeper will babysit and we can go out."

"I don't want to leave Eugenia with a stranger, Birdie. I love her and I'd like you to sign over custody to me."

For once, it was Birdie who looked shocked. "You're talking about my baby, Nanny."

"I know our family prefers illusions, but let's be honest. You're a terrible mother. In fact, you're a terrible person. You are the most shallow, vain, selfish person I've ever met and I speak from a position of experience. Let me have her."

Birdie's green eyes narrowed. "Why should I? What do I get out of it?"

"In nontangible terms, you'll know that you've done the right thing for your daughter. In more concrete terms, you'll save yourself the cost of rearing a child, and you'll be free to roam the continents as you please," Nancy said, and thought, *Come at your enemy like a thunderbolt.* "Can you really see yourself taking a very pretty teenage girl along when you go on trips with your amoral lovers?"

Nancy ignored her cousin's scowl and took the legal documents from her bag. "Review these with an attorney. They release Eugenia into my custody so I can legally act as her guardian."

Birdie turned to look at her daughter clinging to Rick and

then she looked at attractive Viktor and her new friends. She said, "You're drearier than I thought, Nanny, already giving up your freedom."

Nancy waited, ready to change strategies, and then something incredible happened.

Her cousin flipped through the documents and signed the pages tagged with red stickers. Birdie handed them to Nancy and said, "Send copies to my parents. I don't know where I'll be."

Birdie went to Rick, who put her daughter down. The girl clutched his leg. "My angel, your auntie Nanny would like you to live with her all the time. Would you like that?"

Eugenia nodded. "And Rick and Blackbeard."

"What?"

"Her kitten. Where is he?" Rick asked Birdie.

"That thing ruined one of my dresses. Gregor left it in the garage with food and water. I'm sure it's fine."

Nancy wanted to slap her cousin. "We'll follow you back to pick it up."

"We're going out."

Gregor said, "The housekeeper will let you in. She doesn't speak English, but I'll call and tell her you're coming."

Birdie looked at her daughter and said, "Give Mama a kiss good-bye, angel."

Eugenia looked at Nancy, who nodded, and then the girl went to her mother and kissed her before running back to Rick.

"She's not a very loving child," Birdie said, and then smiled at Rick. "There's no reason for you to be stuck with her, too. Come out with us and I'll make sure you have a good time."

Nancy put her arm in his and said, "Nice try, Birdie, but I'll run you through with a cutlass if you come near him."

Birdie just laughed and went off with her companions. Nancy had one more question to ask, though, so she followed and drew her aside.

"Birdie, who is Eugenia's father?"

"You met him once, Nanny Girl."

"I don't want to play a guessing game and you've had so many 'bed-friends.' Which one?"

"Oh, darling, I'll never tell, because I've been saving Eugenia from his family. You know how families can destroy a soul. So you see I'm not such an awful person after all. Ciao."

As Birdie walked away to the next soiree, the next lover, the next adventure, Nancy stood still. She remembered that sunny day of the groundbreaking party, and Birdie arriving with the gift of perfume and Leo. Junie and Bailey had been at the party, and so had Lizette and GP.

Nancy recalled hearing about Leo's death and making the decision to leave her house and Todd.

She began to see connections and patterns, and she thought that if she could only take two steps back, all the disparate moments of her life would resolve into a picture, like a pointillist painting.

An hour later, Nancy, Rick, and Eugenia had collected Blackbeard and were driving back to Château Winkles. The suspicious car out front was finally gone.

"We're home!" Eugenia shouted, and clapped her hands.

"We're home!" Rick and Nancy said together.

It was dinnertime, and Eugenia was cranky with exhaustion, yet too excited to sleep. They ordered Chinese food and invited

Miss Winkles to have dinner with them. Nancy remembered the manila envelope and made a show of handing it to Rick in front of their guest. "As you see, Miss Winkles, I am fulfilling my obligation to deliver this. I will deliver the other envelope tomorrow."

Rick opened the envelope.

Miss Winkles looked at the little girl, who was on the floor playing with Blackbeard. "Eugenia, my apartment is too big for me, and this apartment is too small for you. What should we do?"

Eugenia pursed her lips and then said, "Trade?"

"What a good idea," Miss Winkles said. "We should trade, although I think I'll leave my piano there so I can visit and give you lessons." She looked at Rick, who was holding a photo in his hands. "What do you think?"

"Where did you get this?" he asked, stunned. Nancy took the photo. There was Rick standing beside a young redheaded woman who looked like Mrs. Bentley Jamieson Friendly. But it *wasn't* Rick.

"Striking resemblance, don't you think?" Miss Winkles said. "His name was Bill, or Tim. Maybe Tom. One of those names. My sister Ferny would know. She dated him until he caught a whiff of Abigail's fortune."

"What happened to him?" Nancy asked.

"As I recall, Abigail started getting suspiciously plump. Her father was a nasty piece of work, almost as bad as Dancing Dog Jamieson himself. Bill disappeared, and then Abby went abroad. Well, that's what girls of means did then . . . they 'went abroad' and came back several months later and were quickly married off," she said with a laugh. "Nobody was fooled. When Rick said his mother was adopted, I had my suspicions. It could be a coincidence, because I don't see much of Abigail's features in him."

Nancy said, "When Mrs. Friendly's butler saw Rick, he said, 'I thought you were dead.'"

"We all heard stories. You should talk to Abigail. She'll be thrilled to learn she has a grandson, or maybe it'll give her a heart attack. Either way it'll be entertaining."

On Friday morning, Nancy let Eugenia stay in bed with her kitten and began to deal with her problems. She called the gallery that had charged her for the bowl and asked for a certificate of value so she could have her personal insurance cover the cost. She told the manager, "If the valuation is not legitimate, you will be hearing from my attorney."

Nancy contacted the leasing agent for the waterfront warehouse to discuss the repair fees for the damage at the party.

"The new owner took care of it," he said. "That's all I know."

Now that Nancy had faced those problems, she had to face Mrs. Friendly, apologize abjectly, and try to make amends for the disaster. Miss Winkles watched Eugenia while Nancy and Rick walked to the Saloon.

As they went up the circular drive, Rick said, "I don't see any ninjas."

"The whole point of ninjas is that you don't see them."

Rick knocked on the front door and Greene eventually answered it. "You again," he said to Rick. "Go back to the bottom of the sea where you belong."

Greene tottered off and they followed him inside. "Mrs. Friendly," Nancy called. They found her in the sunroom talking to GP.

"Hello, Mrs. Friendly," Nancy said as GP jumped up and

shouted, "Princess!" He rushed across the room, hugging her tightly before she could respond.

Meanwhile, Mrs. Friendly pushed her new glasses back up her nose and said, "Holy crap!"

GP released Nancy and said, "I thought something had happened to you. You didn't answer my calls and I needed to explain . . ."

"It's okay," Nancy said. "Mrs. Friendly, I can't apologize enough . . ."

But Mrs. Friendly had walked over to Rick. She put her hand on his chin and turned his head side to side as she stared. "I couldn't tell before my eye surgery, but I sure see it now. You look exactly like someone I knew."

He handed her a copy of the photograph. "Binky Winkles gave this to me."

"That sneaky little gossip," Mrs. Friendly said, and then she looked at the photo. "That's Billy Drexler and me! Oh, I loved him! Had the face of an angel and the morals of a tomcat."

"Miss Winkles thought that perhaps you and Bill . . ." Nancy said. "You see, Rick's mother is adopted and she has no idea who her parents are."

Mrs. Friendly said to him, "I thought your name was Derek and you were English."

"Only temporarily."

"Binky was right for once," Mrs. Friendly said. "I got packed off to a private clinic and was drugged, and when I woke up, it was all over. Mr. Friendly couldn't have children, and we tried to find out what happened to the baby, but my father had the records destroyed. I never even knew if I had a boy or a girl."

The old woman looked again into Rick's face. "You're not

the first one to claim blood, so you'll excuse me for not getting sentimental just yet. We'll save that until after I've got the results of a DNA test. Now tell me about your mother."

Nancy said, "He will. But about the party, that was my fault. I stipulated that I wanted an authentic atmosphere and I want to do whatever I can to make up for that spectacle."

"I've already explained to Mrs. Friendly that it was *my* fault," GP said. "The actors weren't very experienced, and they thought that real fights would be more authentic. I kept telling them I wanted authentic, and they got into it."

"Young man, you had the right intention, but good intentions aren't enough," Mrs. Friendly said. She looked at Nancy and said, "Little miss, you're damn lucky that people thought escaping a waterfront brawl and inferno was the most exciting thing they'd done in years."

"They did?"

"Of course, the ninjas topped off their evening, and Gigi Barton has been telling anyone who will listen that it was part of a brilliant plan of yours," Mrs. Friendly said. "All the board members received handwritten notes from me saying how, hmmm . . ." Mrs. Friendly reached for a card on a small side table. "How 'thrillified' I was with the party."

"I didn't know you knew that word!" Nancy said, surprised.

"I don't," Mrs. Friendly said. "I didn't write these notes and I don't sign my name with little hearts over the *i*'s."

Nancy and Rick exchanged a look. Nancy mouthed, "Milagro."

Mrs. Friendly raised her thin, penciled eyebrows. "However, donations are rolling in and everyone wants to reserve a table for next year. I'm pretending that my anger was staged, and I suggest you do the same thing."

"I'd be happy to," Nancy said. "But I don't know how we'll top ninjas next year."

"You'll have to consult with GP," Mrs. Friendly said.

GP grinned. "We're buying the warehouse and we're going in on a Barbary Coast theme park together. We can offer permanent jobs as part of our work training program and give visitors a taste of history, too."

"Our museum society will have a gift shop," Mrs. Friendly said. "Proceeds go to the museum. Bailey Whiteside said he was interested in participating."

Rick turned to look at the view, and Nancy decided that honesty was more important than being polite. "Mrs. Friendly, you should be very careful before going into any business venture with Bailey. I wouldn't want him to take advantage of you."

Now the old redheaded woman laughed until she coughed. Nancy jumped up to pour a glass of water for her from a carafe on a table. When Mrs. Friendly caught her breath, she said, "Little miss, Dancing Dog Jamieson's blood runs through my veins, so Whiteside is the one who better keep a good grip on his wallet!"

Nancy and Rick returned to the apartment so she could find out how to get the Mini back. She'd learned that it had been towed to a long-term storage lot, but that she couldn't retrieve it since it was in Todd's name.

She went to the bedroom and closed the door and she called her husband. "Hi, Todd."

"Nance," he said carefully.

"I need to get the Mini, but the city won't release it to me since the registration is in your name. Will you please call one of your friends at City Hall and get authorization stat?" She told him the phone number of the storage lot.

"Sure," he said. "So how are you?"

"Good," she said. "Really good. How are you?"

"Good."

"So Junie . . ." Nancy said. "She's always been crazy about you."

"I feel the same way about her."

Nancy felt so melancholy suddenly. "Todd, why didn't we figure out years ago that we were wrong for each other? Why did we have to hurt each other?"

He was silent and then said, "We were damn good on paper, hon."

"Your name hyphenated beautifully with mine. I'll miss it."

"Will you miss me?" he asked.

"Who knows? Once our attorneys hash out the details, including the money you took from our shared bank account and the money you spent on your love nest, it's possible that we can be better friends than we were spouses . . . but not for a while," she said.

Todd laughed his har-har-har laugh and she realized that it wasn't a bray but an honest, good-natured laugh.

"Let's check back in a year," he said.

"It's a deal. Return the money to our account and I'll tell you something worthwhile."

"Your lawyer would get it out of me anyway, so, sure."

"Do an in-depth examination of all the records for the sports medicine venture. You might discover that Bailey hasn't been such a good friend after all."

"No shit? Huh. I'll do that. You know, Nance, since we know each other so well, we might make good allies."

"You're still a student of Sun Tzu," she said, and laughed. "So am I."

Eugenia talked and sang to Blackbeard, mewing in his cat carrier, on the winding road to Stinson. They arrived at the house as the sun was setting low in the sky. "Hurry!" Eugenia shouted, and Rick got out of the Mini and unbuckled her from the child seat. He carried the cat carrier and Nancy and the child grabbed bags and took them into the house.

Then they ran out to the beach.

"Let's race," Eugenia shouted, and she ran across the sand in her red tennis shoes.

Rick and Nancy held hands as they followed, slow enough so that the girl reached the edge of the waves first. "I win!" she said, laughing as the wind whipped her shining hair over her eyes. "Make a wish."

They faced west, watching the sun's last rays turn the ocean a shimmery gold, like vermeil.

Nancy took the girl's hand so they were all linked. "I wish we will always be as happy as we are now," she said.

"Me, too," Rick and Eugenia said together.

Rick made dinner, just spaghetti, but Eugenia and her aunt agreed it was the best spaghetti they'd ever had. Afterward, he and Nancy sat on the floor in front of the fireplace while Eugenia played with her cat, her books, and her toys. They listened to waves crashing and the wind gusting outside.

Nancy leaned back into Rick's arms and said, "I don't know how I'll feel about you if you're a tycoon."

"How will you feel about me if I'm an unemployed dude who's discovered a taste for leisurely lunches and fine clothes?"

"I'd be happy you'd have so much time to spend with me. What will you do if you are a Friendly?"

"I will try to act friendly. Also, I'd ask to see the ninjas."

"Fabulous. What next?"

"I would help my mother move to be with Peter's family. I'd like to have a family, too, and I've been thinking about marrying a fabulous divorcée with a wonderful child," he said. "Now, though, money's a problem. She's used to a lavish life, and I can't support that. We will have to survive on love and tap water."

"I can do that if you're willing to."

"I may require the occasional pizza." More seriously, he said, "I'm sorry you're losing everything."

"Who said I'm losing anything?"

He looked puzzled. "The prenup. You won't get anything from your marriage."

She burst out laughing, and he said, "What's so funny?"

"How much do you know about me and my family?"

"Besides the fact that they've got neurotic upper-class problems? Nothing."

"That's because my father pays a public relations firm to keep our names out of the paper," she said. "The prenup was to protect *my* money."

"So you have money?"

"Poodles of it. Double-latte-size poodles, not mere teacups."

"I feel dumber, but less guilty," he said. "However, I'm not going to be a gigolo, no matter how much you treat me like a mere sex object."

"We both have to work for many reasons, not the least being that I love event planning. Things will be tied up for a while with the divorce, and my father-slash-trustee is going to have a fit when he learns about you."

"I checked your voice mail and e-mails," Rick said. "You've got several requests for parties. Gigi Barton wants you to do an 'Am I Too Delicious?' intervention for her, and a parent at Three Bridges wants to know if you'd like to sell your capes in her children's boutique."

"That's all very interesting, but I couldn't do any of it without an assistant. Do you know anyone qualified?"

"I might be available, but I'd require free afternoons so I can make love to the woman I hope to marry." His *l'heure bleue* eyes looked into hers and happiness bloomed inside her.

"You seem like an ideal candidate for a permanent position."

"I'm skilled in positions other than the popular standards," he said with a smirk. "The Ride 'Em Cowboy, the Inverse Crab, the Flying Wallenda . . ."

She laughed and said, "If I hire you I have to know, can Derek come out every now and then?"

"I'm certain that we can sheh-jool visits, Miss Carrington," he said in his Derek voice. He pushed her back to the rug and kissed her.

Eugenia came to them, saying, "Me, too! Me, too!"

Nancy and Rick put their arms around the child and Nancy had another epiphany, a corollary to the first.

She had thought that if she was careful and precise, if she planned everything, she would have a perfect life—as if perfection were both possible and desirable. But true style was messy, passionate, and often impulsive.

It was letting a strange child into your life, falling in love with your assistant, using ancient military strategy, trusting a history buff. It was grimy fingerprints, feral cats, sex in the afternoon, and friends who forged letters and gossiped and babysat to help you.

It didn't happen in total isolation, but resulted when the right mix of people inspired one another in fabulous, unexpected ways. The people could be a designer, a pattern-maker, and a model muse. Or they could be an event planner, an unemployed journalist, and a pirate child.

Nancy didn't know what the future would bring, but she didn't need to try to control it anymore, because *now* was more wonderful than she ever could have planned or imagined.

Nancy's Theory of Style

INTRODUCTION

Nancy Edith Carrington-Chambers is a young socialite who appears to have it all: the perfect husband, whom she married in the perfect wedding; the perfect friends; the perfect connections; and she's building the perfect house. But appearances can be deceiving, and Nancy's perfect world comes apart when she leaves her husband to focus on her party-planning business, and doing a favor for her cousin turns into having custody of a four-year-old. Plus she finds herself falling in love with her gay assistant. Nancy has her rules about how to speak, how to act, how to dress, and how to behave. But those rules might just go out the window as she learns how to really live.

Questions and Topics for Discussion

1. "'We should always live an authentic life,' she said . . . even though Nancy believed most people should run screaming from their authentic selves." (pg. 9) This quote seems to sum up Nancy's approach to life at the beginning of the novel. How does this change as she matures?

2. Nancy plays with language, making up words like "thrillified" and "delightmare," and substituting unrelated words or expressions for the ones she means (parakeet for budget, pg. 14; parabolic trooper for catatonic stupor, pg. 43). Did you find it witty or silly? Intelligent or confusing?

3. "Although Nancy hadn't known him, Leo's death changed everything for her, like a click of the optometrist's lenses that brings everything into sharp focus." (pg. 20) Why do you think Leo's death affects Nancy so strongly? Are there other moments in the novel where one action or occurrence is more significant than it originally seems? Has this ever happened in your own life?

4. When did you begin to suspect that the people in Nancy's life (and their intentions) might not be what they seemed?

Were there clues the author planted that you caught on to before Nancy did?

5. Early in the novel, Nancy expresses the opinion that children leave their mothers "as flat and dull as a chalkboard." (pg. 83) But by the end of the novel, she's willing to fight to become a mother. What other shifts do you see in her and her point of view?

6. Nancy likes to project an image of being tough, but we discover that she actually is much kinder than she lets on: expressing disdain for children but bringing presents for Sloane's sons each time she sees them, seeming to judge GP superficially but actually helping him to fit in and make friends. Why do you think she hides behinds this façade?

7. Miss Winkles refuse to call Nancy anything except Girl Carrington. Nancy's family calls her Nanny or Nanny Girl, although she finds these nicknames childish. Even after Nancy and Derek begin their affair, he continues to call her Mrs. Carrington-Chambers. Do these nicknames signify something about how each character perceives Nancy?

8. Two themes in the novel are appearances versus reality and style versus substance. In what ways are the people and happenings in *Nancy's Theory of Style* very different from how they appear?

9. Nancy likes to think of herself as worldly, but we see that in some ways she can be quite naïve. In what other ways do we see Nancy differently than she sees herself?

10. Nancy is constantly dictating the rules she lives by, and expects others to as well. Do you think these rules help to maintain order, or do they create unnecessary barriers between her and the people in her life?

11. In *Nancy's Theory of Style,* there are various family arrangements that could be considered nontraditional. Nancy creates a family with Derek and Eugenia. Sloane is raising her boys by herself. What does this say to you about the nature of family?

12. Nancy says, "Those who don't believe I'm a slut think that I'm a priss. I don't know which is worse." Do you think it's typical for women to be faced with such stereotypes? Who tends to judge women's sexuality more harshly, men or women?

13. Miss Winkles tells Nancy, "It's the imperfections that make life interesting." (pg. 330) Do you agree with this statement?

14. "Eugenia *was* a problem. She was willful and impetuous and mischievous and very vocal and exasperating, which is exactly how she should have been." (pg. 349) "She had thought that if she was careful and precise, if she planned everything, she would have a perfect life. But true style was messy, passionate and often impulsive." (pg. 361) What do you think caused Nancy to come to embrace this unpredictability? Was there a major turning point, or was it a gradual process?

A Conversation with Grace Coopersmith

1. This novel is your first outside the Casa Dracula series, in which the main characters are vampires. Why did you decide to do something different with *Nancy's Theory of Style*?

I tend to resist categorization as a writer, because I enjoy writing everything from feature articles to satire to more somber fiction. I consider both the Casa Dracula series and *Nancy's Theory of Style* to be contemporary fiction with a strong humorous element. Much of the humor depends upon the protagonists' self-delusions and misunderstandings, and there are also those who purposely mislead the protagonists. We may guess the destination, but the fun is in the twists and turns on the journey.

2. How would you describe your own personal style?

As a general rule, I like things that are uncomplicated, and I also like vintage style. While my preference is for less froofra, I can certainly appreciate extravagance. I prefer saturated color over pastels; I like pretty, but not cute; elegant, but not ostentatious; simple, but not boring. However, I do not suffer from the burden of perfect taste.

3. What gave you the idea to incorporate two seemingly very different things: Sun Tzu's *The Art of War* and women's fiction?

I thought that Nancy's husband, Todd, would certainly be one of those MBAs who quotes Sun Tzu, as if his own privileged existence is as brutal as warfare. I began reading from *The Art of War* because I wanted quotations, and I was surprised at how relevant it still is.

When we live with someone, we learn things we wouldn't have otherwise, and Nancy would have picked up these Sun Tzu's lessons just by talking to her husband. When she finds herself in adversarial situations, she naturally goes to a master tactician for advice.

4. The novel has great details about architecture, design, fashion, and history. Can you tell us about the research you did?

My interests are eclectic, and I pick up information everywhere—whether it's visiting a beautiful building, listening to an informed friend, reading a magazine, or going to a costume exhibit at a museum. I'm as likely to a documentary about architect Maya Lin as I am about designer Karl Lagerfeld, or prostitution during California's Gold Rush.

I'd always been fascinated by tidbits of history about the Barbary Coast, and I'd bought my husband a copy of Herbert Asbury's The *Barbary Coast.* I had read chapters now and again, and I referred to it and to online essays for information about this vicious, violent part of local history.

I listen to every word that Tim Gunn says on his many design shows. I wish I was wise enough to follow all his advice.

5. What do you consider to be your own runway music?

I could never pick one favorite song. I'll say any song with "California" in the title: The Mamas and the Papas' "California Dreamin'," the Eagles' "Hotel California," Red Hot Chili Peppers' "Dani California," Dead Kennedys' "California Uber Alles," Phantom Planet's "California," the Kooks' "California" . . .

6. You live in San Francisco, where *Nancy's Theory of Style* takes place. Are there any places or notable people in the novel that were based on real life? If a reader were to visit your city, what places would you consider "musts" for them to visit?

I lived in SF for many years, but now I live across the bay. Every morning I go to the shoreline and enjoy the view across the water to the city. The locations in *Nancy's Theory of Style* are real for the most part, and any visitor to Fillmore Street in Pacific Heights would see the shops that Nancy mentions.

As for the people, one of the delightful things about San Francisco is that it is geographically small city; it's sophisticated and yet you can meet lots of people in your neighborhood or at your hang-outs. There are well-known local characters, and it's always a treat to spot them going about their everyday lives. We all have "I saw [blank] at the hardware store!" stories. Some of these people are famous for a reason, but some are just quirky, and San Francisco loves quirky.

I couldn't possibly list all my favorite things about San Francisco, but here are a few. Best views: the glass elevator at the St. Francis Hotel, the ferry boat to Sausalito, and the views from the California St. cable car.

Classic San Francisco: a second-floor window seat at Vesuvio Cafe in North Beach, buying music on Haight St., checking out the vintage and arty shops in the Mission, having a drink at one of the funky waterfront bars, taking a walk on Ocean Beach, visiting Golden Gate Park, and going to a performance, whether it's the opera or seeing a band.

7. **Birdie gave birth to Eugenia but has very little maternal instinct, while Nancy didn't intend to have children but took to mothering quickly. Do you think some women are naturally more suited to motherhood?**

Yes. Some women know absolutely that they want to have children. I was one of them and there was never any question in my mind. I admire women who realize that they don't have that mothering instinct and take care not to have children. However, I think that Nancy is more of a fabulous and wacky aunt than a mother. She's caring and loving, but has a slightly different role.

8. **There are a lot of funny moments in the novel, but it also deals with very real issues such as alcoholism, and people struggling to find their true paths. Is there a message you hope readers will take away?**

The message with this novel is fairly simple: Nancy thinks that if she can control everything, she will be happy. I think a lot of people put off enjoying the here and now because they've got an unrealistic idea of what life should be and who their spouse should be. Nancy soaks in her tub and believes that perfection is both possible and desirable.

Her need to control is the direct result of her parents' problems. Children of alcoholics often need to bring order to otherwise chaotic lives. Her own experience with negligent parents makes her especially sympathetic to her niece's situation.

9. **Who are your favorite authors? Who would you consider your inspiration?**

I know it's cliché to say Jane Austen, but she's one of my favorites. I love the sense of decency in her novels. Of course, I also love the clever banter, the well-structured plots, and the emotional depth of her characters. It's not the fashion to admire books with a moral clarity, but I find them emotionally reassuring in an unstable world.

Mark Twain has always been a favorite. I respond to his dazzling absurdity, but I also love his intelligence and the darkness and cynicism in much of his work. He was a modern thinker often confounded by a foolish world.

I've read an awful lot of Henry James and admire the complexity of his characters. No one is simply good or evil; they are motivated by emotional, financial, sexual, and social desires.

P. G. Wodehouse has been an inspiration, because I so enjoy his deliciously extravagant characters and outlandish dialogue. There's such joy in his writing.

10. **What can we expect to see from you next? Are you working on another paranormal novel? Something more like *Nancy's Theory of Style*? Or something completely different?**

The fourth in my Casa Dracula series will be released soon, and I'm also working on another contemporary novel set in San Francisco. I've also written a young adult gothic novel set in an elite all-girls academy.

Tips to Enhance Your Book Club

1. Nancy keeps a guide that defines her own personal style. Talk about your own style and its defining characteristics with your book club.

2. Nancy suggests that everyone should have his or her own runway song, "a song we can imagine when we're walking down the street and the wind is blowing back our hair because life is the ultimate runway." (pg. 241) Have each member of your club pick their own runway song and bring a recording to play for the group.

3. Nancy lists the movies she considers to be the great fashion movies. Have a book club movie night and watch one of the films. You can also look at the costumes online on a movie site such as www.IMDB.com.

4. Get a copy of *The Art of War*, and flag some of your favorite quotes to share with the group. Do you think the tenets can be applied to everyday life?